Praise for Juliana Maio's *City of the Sun*

"Juliana Maio's *City of the Sun* belongs in the '1 percent' of new novels, not only because of the way she weaves suspense to keep you turning pages, but because she has married it all to a fascinating point in World War II history with descriptions of the Middle East that will have you swearing you've been there. The kind of book that turns non-readers into obsessive ones."

—Andrew Neiderman, author of *The Devil's Advocate*

". . . A marvelous romantic spy thriller set in one of the most cosmopolitan yet exotic cities of its time—Cairo. . . [T]he novel is impeccably researched in both military matters and the details of day-to-day life, allowing us to meet as if in person characters who heretofore have appeared only in history books. A fantastic read from beginning to end—you won't be able to put it down!"

—Professor Marianne Sanua Dalin, Florida Atlantic University, Department of History

". . . A vivid novel of Cairo during the early days of the war in North Africa where café society was all but invented. This is a romantic adventure, rich with spies, Nazis, ever-changing power, and international refugees. The reckless events of the story are a distant mirror for the desperate troubles of the Middle East of today. A sexy and dangerous book."

—David Freeman, author of *One of Us*, the adventures of an Englishman in pre war Egypt

"Juliana Maio artfully brings to life a very rich and crucial period in Egyptian history. Her scenes evoke intense emotions about the fragility of love and the cruelty of war, as well as the tragedies of religious persecution. Meticulously researched, this is a beautiful novel full of life that will stay with you long after you've read it. In her first foray into writing Maio proves that she has what it takes to be a great novelist."

—Alaa al Aswany, author of the international bestseller *The Yacoubian Building*

"You feel the sweat on your forehead and smell the scents of the marketplace as you walk the colorful streets of Cairo with Juliana Maio's vividly-drawn characters . . . [Her] detailed research brings alive the ancient city and creates a vibrant setting for the twisting, racing story. This is historical fiction the way it was meant to be enjoyed—and the way it was meant to be written!"

—Kelly Durham, author of *Berlin Calling* and *The War Widow.*

"This book fuses three of my greatest passions: drama, history, and the Jewish/Arab conflict. I was tremendously excited to discover *City of the Sun*—an engrossing, first-class historical drama. It's a goldmine!"

—Richard Dreyfuss, Academy-Award winning actor and founder of the Imagining the Future Fund

"Juliana Maio's *City of the Sun* is a stunning work of historical fiction, capturing the romance, intrigue, and danger of Cairo in 1941. Against the backdrop of an increasingly threatened Jewish community in Egypt and the rise of the Muslim Brotherhood—yes, the same one that keeps coming back to haunt that country—Maio magically transforms an almost genteel love story into a heart-stopping thriller."

—Andrew Nagorski, former *Newsweek* foreign correspondent and senior editor, and author of *Hitlerland: American Eyewitnesses to the Nazi Rise to Power*

"What we don't know about Cairo during World War II makes for an enthralling novel. Egyptian-born Juliana Maio knows this territory like the palm of her hand—which is where she holds us. *City of the Sun* weaves a tangled tale of espionage, wartime romance, political intrigue, and action in a city crawling with all four. If you liked Casablanca, this story is for you."

—Nicholas Meyer, *New York Times* bestselling author and Academy Award nominee for *The Seven Percent Solution;* screenwriter, *The Human Stain*

"An ambitious work set against the backdrop of real events, Juliana Maio's *City of the Sun* provides a fascinating insight into the events that helped shape the forces at play in Egypt and the Middle East today. This book couldn't be more timely."

—Reza Aslan, international and *New York Times* bestselling author of *No god but God* and *Zealot*

"Vivid . . . a romantic thriller set during the early years of WWII . . . [a] satisfying exploration of a key time in Western and Middle Eastern relations."

—*Publishers Weekly*

City of the Sun

JULIANA MAIO

Greenleaf
Book Group Press

This book is a work of fiction. Names, characters, businesses, organizations, places, events, and incidents are either a product of the author's imagination or are used fictitiously. Any resemblance to actual persons, living or dead, events, or locales is entirely coincidental.

Published by Greenleaf Book Group Press
Austin, Texas
www.gbgpress.com

Distributed by Greenleaf Book Group LLC

For ordering information or special discounts for bulk purchases, please contact Greenleaf Book Group LLC at PO Box 91869, Austin, TX 78709, 512.891.6100.

Design and composition by Greenleaf Book Group LLC
Cover design by Greenleaf Book Group LLC

Publisher's Cataloging-In-Publication Data

Maio, Juliana.
City of the sun / Juliana Maio. -- 1st ed.
p. ; cm.
Issued also as an ebook.
ISBN: 978-1-62634-067-1 (hardcover)
ISBN: 978-1-62634-051-0 (pbk.)
1. Cairo (Egypt)—History—20th century—Fiction. 2. World War, 1939-1945—Egypt—Fiction. 3. Journalists—Egypt—Cairo—Fiction. 4. Scientists—Egypt—Cairo—Fiction. 5. Nazis—Egypt—Fiction. 6. Historical fiction. I. Title.
PS3613.A46 C58 2014
813/.6 2013950776

Part of the Tree Neutral® program, which offsets the number of trees consumed in the production and printing of this book by taking proactive steps, such as planting trees in direct proportion to the number of trees used: www.treeneutral.com

Printed in the United States of America on acid-free paper

14 15 16 17 18 19 10 9 8 7 6 5 4 3 2 1

First Edition

For Natasha
You, too, are a daughter of Egypt.

The entrance to the Shepheard's Hotel,
once the epicenter of cosmopolitan Cairo
(Courtesy Mr. Hassan Kelisli.)

"Cairo during the war was what Casablanca had been mythologized as in the eponymous Humphrey Bogart film—a romantic desert crossroads of the world, of spies and soldiers and cafés and casbahs and women with pasts and men with futures, except that Cairo threw in a king and a palatial high society gloss and grandeur that Casablanca, both on and off screen, never even tried to evoke . . ."

—William Stadiem (*Too Rich: The High Life and Tragic Death of King Farouk*)

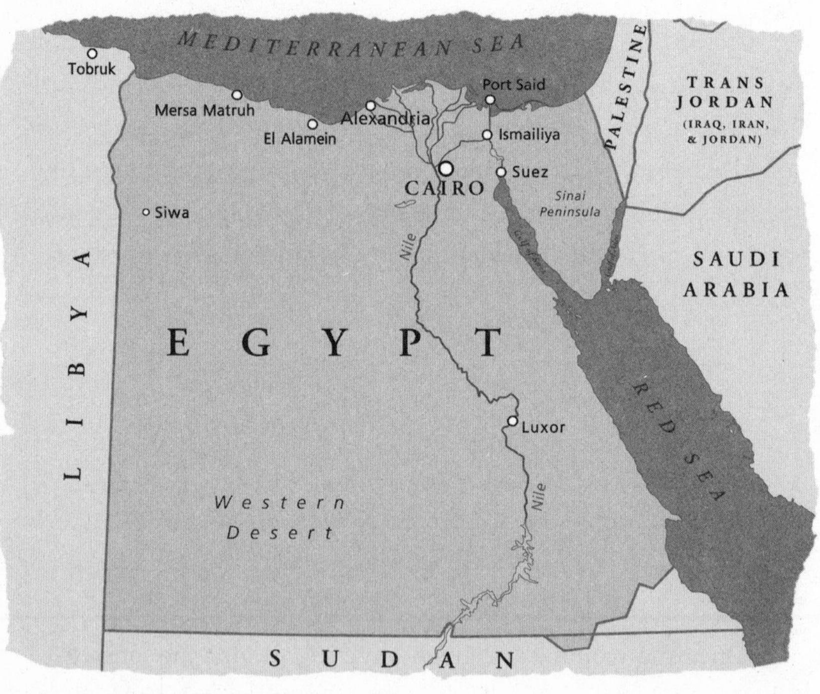
MEDITERRANEAN SEA
Tobruk
Mersa Matruh
El Alamein
Alexandria
Port Said
Ismailiya
Suez
CAIRO
Siwa
PALESTINE
TRANS JORDAN
(IRAQ, IRAN, & JORDAN)
Sinai Peninsula
Nile
SAUDI ARABIA
LIBYA
EGYPT
Luxor
RED SEA
Nile
Western Desert
SUDAN

PROLOGUE

A modern day Cleopatra without the glamour—that's me! Maya thought as she leaned against the railing of the decrepit *El Aziz* as it steamed into Alexandria's harbor on a hot and muggy morning. Like the legendary Egyptian queen who so fascinated her, she was being smuggled into the city. But while Cleopatra had designs on seducing the most powerful soldier on earth so as to assure her reign, this battered refugee from Europe could only hope to escape the never-ending persecution that came from being born a Jew and the ravages of the war on the continent. Maybe here, in this sunny Mediterranean land, she could rid herself of the nightmares that afflicted her night after night. She'd been told that Jews were safe in Egypt, but there was no escaping the war, as the gargantuan ships and submarines that dominated the horizon like ominous thunderclouds reminded her. Though she knew the fleet was British, she still shivered.

Once she would have given anything to visit the land of the pharaohs and to pull into port greeted by colorful sailboats and fishing vessels. She would have taken a barge up the Nile, one sensuously scented with the oil of lotus flowers as Egyptians had done in ancient times, and glided up the river, admiring the majestic temples along the banks. But as she gazed at the gunmetal warships, the fantasy evaporated. She was too exhausted for that. The war had robbed her of even the basic right to dream. All she wanted was a place to drop her suitcases for good.

As the boat approached the port, she saw that in addition to the British armada, hundreds of cargo ships crowded the harbor and she wondered how long it would take for the ship to dock. She had heard that it sometimes took days for boats to find a place to land. After all, this was the headquarters for the British Mediterranean navy, and who cared about a small boat full of filthy refugees? She removed the scarf from her head and pulled her long hair into a ponytail, before flipping it back and forth to fan her neck as she braced herself for a long wait.

Incredibly, only two hours later, the *El Aziz* dropped anchor. Was God finally smiling on her?

CHAPTER 1

Libyan Desert
September 1941

"He says it's true. Hitler is a Muslim, a good one. He goes to the mosque and prays five times a day," Mickey's Egyptian interpreter assured him, as he hurriedly translated the comments of the ragtag group of Bedouins who'd gathered around their Jeep. The men were tripping over each other's sentences in their eagerness to share their stories about the war with an American reporter.

"Are you kidding me, Sidi?" Mickey asked, tugging on the brim of his Detroit Tigers baseball cap.

"They say his Islamic name is Mohammed Haider and he has come here to Libya to free all Arabs everywhere from the British infidels," Sidi answered as he sheltered his eyes from the sun with his hand and squinted up at Mickey, who towered over him.

The Bedouins nodded as if they understood what Sidi had said.

"Where on earth did they get that idea?"

"They said they hear it on the radio—on the German station. They play the best music, Mister Mickey Connolly," Sidi explained.

Mickey shook his head in disbelief. He'd heard all kinds of

outrageous stories since arriving in Egypt in July, but this one took the cake. With Goebbels at the helm, Hitler's mighty propaganda machine had extended its reach into the far corners of the North African desert, and the locals were eating it up. The audacity of the Germans was galling, though he had to admit the damn Krauts were brilliant at their game.

"Don't they listen to the BBC?" he griped, batting at the flies that swarmed in front of his face.

A man with a gray headscarf and a flat nose spat out a short response after Sidi relayed the question. The Bedouins laughed heartily at the cleverness of their comrade, who puffed up his chest in pride.

"Oh, yes, they do sometimes, but it's very boring," Sidi translated, barely suppressing a smile. "They tell us how to tend to rose gardens."

Mickey cracked a smile, deciding not to argue, but he felt deflated. He hadn't driven 475 miles from Cairo and defied the British High Command by crossing the border into Libya just to listen to a bunch of nomads sing the praises of the Third Reich. He'd come here for a story. Though they were not involved, the American people needed to know about this desert war. They had to be made to understand the strategic importance of Egypt, which sat at the jugular vein of the Mediterranean and whose Suez Canal constituted the Allies' lifeline to the Orient. If Hitler won here, the world would be up for grabs.

Over the last few weeks the British Army Press attaché office had become increasingly tight-lipped, but it didn't take a genius to realize that General Erwin Rommel and his mighty Afrika Korps were racing toward the Egyptian border at a furious pace, reclaiming the Libyan territory that the British had captured from the Italians. Three weeks ago, the Germans had been two hundred miles away in Benghazi; now they were only fifty miles from the border.

"Sidi, please ask these good men who they think will win the war," he requested, resuming the interview.

The question was met with an immediate and unanimous response.

"The Germans, of course," Sidi translated.

That the Brits were getting their asses kicked was not news. Facing the Germans' new long-range artillery cannons, they were at a serious disadvantage. "I wouldn't discount the Brits quite yet," Mickey cautioned, "they didn't gain control of half the world by accident."

"If you ask me, Mister Mickey Connolly, it is because of the English that we have no money to feed our families," Sidi snorted. "They take the best jobs and then look down on us for being poor. Why are they still here, anyway?"

Mickey had heard similar complaints from the *fellahin*, the peasants he'd met on the Delta on his way to the front, who blamed the British for the country's staggering inflation. This was not their war. Neither the Germans nor the Egyptians had declared war on one another. Yet, when the conflict had started in Europe in 1939, the British had imposed martial law in Egypt, seizing control of the ports, railways, and aerodromes, and censoring the press, effectively undermining the independence that the Egyptians had fought so hard to achieve and had theoretically gained in 1936. The Brits refused to release their grip on the country.

"A storm is brewing," Sidi warned, squinting north toward the darkening horizon. "We must hurry back through the Siwa depression."

Mickey could feel a light wind pulling at his cap. He checked his watch. It was close to 8:00 AM and the temperature must have broken a hundred degrees already. It was time to wrap up. He had gotten all he could out of the Bedouins. He thanked them by distributing the packs of Lucky Strikes he'd brought as gifts. As Sidi started pouring water into the Jeep's radiator, the boy tending the camels began to shout. He was standing on a ledge and pointing frantically into the valley below.

"Tanks," Sidi yelled over the shrieks of the nomads, who were rushing toward the boy. "Oh, I hope this is no big trouble," he said fretfully.

Mickey grinned at his lucky break and patted Sidi's shoulder. Maybe he would get a story after all, a belated present to himself for his twenty-sixth birthday last week. He reached into the backseat of the Jeep for his binoculars and hurried to the ledge to join the agitated Bedouins.

He spotted a deployment of a dozen British Cruiser tanks rumbling across the sand below. Routine reconnaissance, he assumed, but quickly the *whomp* and *thump* of shells told him otherwise. The tanks were being hit. Explosions shook the earth. The Bedouins dropped to the ground, but Mickey remained standing. His heart was pounding as he feverishly studied the horizon, trying to see where the enemy fire was coming from.

There! To the left of the Cruisers, he caught sight of a detachment of six German tanks emerging from behind a small hill. An ambush. And these were not ordinary German tanks. They were Panzer IVs, monsters that were heavier, more powerful, and had greater firing range than anything the British had ever come up against. He had heard rumors about them, but they'd been dismissed by a British intelligence officer who'd told him that the Germans did not have the necessary equipment to unload such mammoth tanks at the docks.

A deafening roar shook the ground violently, making Mickey almost lose his balance, but he managed to steady himself. Huge pillars of sand and plumes of smoke enveloped the British tanks as shells flew back and forth. It was the most frightening and exciting thing he had ever experienced.

The Bedouins scattered, running away as fast as they could.

"We must leave, Mister Mickey. I don't care how much you pay me. We must go." Sidi grabbed Mickey's arm tightly and would not let go.

"Calm down, *habibi*," Mickey urged, wrestling his arm free. "We're safe here. There is nothing to fear. The action is way down below." He raised his binoculars again. Good God! The Germans had mounted their new long range 75mm guns on the Panzer IVs. The combination of range and mobility was proving deadly.

Fresh explosions created a storm of sand as the rhythm of the rounds grew faster and faster. Two Cruisers were on fire. A rush of adrenaline surged through Mickey's body as he spotted a German officer peering through his observation slit and shouting to his men. The turret of the Panzer swiveled and the tank lurched forward over the crest of a small dune, firing continuously, its armor-piercing shells plunging into a Cruiser and tearing its hull apart. In a flash, the ammunition and fuel inside ignited. Mickey bit back a cry and averted his eyes as the tank and the men inside were consumed in a fiery supernova. The Panzers were unstoppable, methodically obliterating the Cruisers one by one. The Allied shells made little impact against the Panzers' toughened turrets, bouncing off the iron armor and exploding harmlessly on the ground.

Suddenly, an ear-piercing blast erupted fifty feet away from him, throwing up a tower of sand and sending rocks and shrapnel flying in all directions. The deafening boom lifted him off his feet, and he landed on his stomach a few feet away under a massive cloud of smoke. His hands were scratched and bloody. A goddamn stray round, he thought. Stunned by the blow, he instinctively curled into a ball and wrapped his arms around his head to protect himself from the rocks and debris that rained down.

When the cascade ceased, he snapped to his feet and started to run for safety. A muffled cry stopped him. Sidi was rolling down the slope toward the battle. Mickey hesitated for a second before racing toward him as another thunderous blast shook the ground nearby. Shrapnel and rocks rained down again. He panicked. Had they been seen and targeted by the Germans? "Sidi," he yelled, looking around frantically through the smoke. He found him lying motionless at the bottom of the slope.

He had to get to him before the next round hit. Using his arms to protect his head from the flying rocks and angling his feet sideways so he wouldn't fall, he hurried to him. The Egyptian was curled into a fetal position. His eyes were closed and blood dripped from his forehead and jaw. Mickey turned him on his back. He was breathing.

"Sidi, can you hear me? Can you hear me?" he shouted, again and again.

The corner of Sidi's mouth twitched, and he struggled to formulate a response. "I hope you got your story now," he uttered in a hoarse whisper.

Mickey blinked. "Can you hold on to my neck?" he asked. There was no time to wait. He grabbed the Egyptian by his flak jacket and lifted him to his feet.

Sidi whined as his knees buckled and he fell back to the ground.

In the valley, the tanks were still firing at one another, oily smoke billowing high into the sky. Mickey knelt down and hoisted Sidi over his shoulder as best he could. They had to get out of here, out of the Germans' sight. And fast.

CHAPTER 2

"*Eins, zwei, drei . . .*" Heinrich Kesner grunted as he pulled himself up to the iron crossbar that hung from the ceiling, counting until he reached fifteen to complete his third set of chin-ups. He'd already done his sit-ups, push-ups, and weight lifting. "A sound mind in a healthy body," he told himself as he glanced out the open window and let the cool breeze from the Nile dry the sweat that had formed on his face and neck and made his undershirt stick to his skin.

From the small gym on the foredeck he could see the sun glistening over the soft waves of the river that rocked his *dahabieh,* as the Arabs called these houseboats. At eight o'clock in the morning, Cairo was peaceful, and even his neighbor, Major Blundell of the British RAF, was still sleeping off his booze.

But for Kesner the day was already in high gear. He was going to Alexandria today on urgent instructions from the SS. A Jew, a polio victim with a pronounced limp, would be arriving from Istanbul on the *El Aziz* steamship at noon. He was to keep an eye on him until he received further instructions. It was not a simple assignment, but Kesner knew he could count on the Muslim Brotherhood's assistance. The Reich had been generous to the Islamic organization, financing their ongoing guerrilla war against their common enemy, the English.

It was the first time Kesner had been contacted directly by the SS, and he felt honored to serve the Führer's elite paramilitary corps. His prior communiqués had always been with the Abwehr, the German military intelligence organization to whom he fed information regarding Allied military strength and supplies in preparation for Rommel's invasion of Egypt. His job was becoming easier because of the large number of dissident groups here. From the palace, to the military, to the religious and youth groups opposed to the British occupation, he was never short of informants.

Heinrich, you're a lucky boy. The SS has taken notice of you, he thought as he inhaled the cool air deeply. He loved being on the river, which evoked fond memories of the canoe expeditions on the Danube he had led as a rising star in the Hitler Youth organization. Who knows, maybe he'd get to live in Bavaria again if he were transferred to the SS after the war.

The Nazis had promised all SS officers that they would be given parcels of land when the war ended. He would want his near Regensburg where he was born, a charming town on the Danube. Olga, his wife, who was expecting their first child—a boy, he hoped—would enjoy raising their family there. But first things first; there was a war to be won. *Deutschland Erwache*! (Germany Awake!) was the rallying cry at Nazi Party meetings. It was time for the German people to reclaim their place in the world.

Kesner drank the freshly squeezed orange juice that his servant had left for him and stopped in front of the gilded mirror on the wall. He opened his mouth wide and inspected his teeth, pressing each with his finger for cavities—a daily ritual. Pleased, he now looked at himself. His brown eyes and black hair had won him the nickname *Schwarze Hund* (Black Dog) in his youth. Though neither blond nor blue-eyed, Kesner was proud of his rugged jaw and strong brows, which were unmistakably Aryan traits. But his swarthy coloring coupled with his fluency in Arabic did prove useful. He could pass as an Egyptian when it served his purposes, having lived here as a child. When he was eight, six months after his father died, his mother married an Egyptian man and readily agreed to move from Regensburg to Alexandria. Five years later, she buried this husband as well and they moved back to Germany where she quickly found a third husband. "Women are weak," he said contemptuously.

Before descending the wrought iron spiral staircase to his master bedroom, he passed through the living room, which, like the rest of the boat, was decorated with crystal chandeliers and ornate Louis XIV oak furnishings with gold inlay. It was too gaudy for his taste, but houseboats were hard to come by. He was lucky to have found it, and at a reasonable price. Usually the second homes of wealthy Cairenes who charged a small fortune to rent them, dahabiehs offered an escape from the smells of the city and a respite from the suffocating heat of the summer months. They were in high demand by the Allied brass who had been pouring into Cairo since Rommel swooped into Libya last February to rescue Mussolini's army.

For Kesner, the dahabieh, free of surrounding steel structures, was a perfect place from which to launch his radio transmissions to Tripoli, the Libyan capital, and conduct his clandestine activities in the seclusion he needed, notwithstanding the presence of British officers on houseboats nearby. Twice daily, at 9:15 and 4:15, the American Embassy radioed its secret bulletins to Washington. The Abwehr had long ago cracked America's code, enabling him to monitor their daily exchanges of information about Allied activities and military strength. This was one of his best sources of information. Unfortunately, today he'd have to miss the morning American communiqué as he had to leave early for Alexandria. But first he needed to send a message to his contact at the Abwehr confirming that he'd received the photo of the Jew. His radio room was in the bowels of the boat and was always impossibly hot. He would shower afterward.

He drew back a velvet curtain on the far side of the bedroom, revealing a locked, reinforced wooden door that opened to a small storage room. He kept its only key on his person at all times. Once inside the room he removed the lid of a large mahogany chest that held a phonograph and pressed a hidden catch near the turntable. The top of the device lifted up, revealing a stepladder into a claustrophobic hole.

At the bottom of the ladder was a small folding chair next to a radio transmitter. He switched on a tiny lamp and shut the lid above him, sliding the iron deadbolt as a precaution. His only means of escape would be through a hatch that opened into the river. He turned on the transmitter and tapped out his message to Tripoli over several short intervals, taking care not to stay on the air too long lest his signal be picked up. He signed off, Schwarze Hund.

Ten minutes later Kesner was showered, his wet hair parted in the middle, and was buckling the wide brown belt of a Polish officer's uniform. It was his disguise of choice whenever he left the boat, and it served him well. He'd convinced his RAF neighbor that he was a captain who, like many men of influence, was avoiding being called up. This was an easy lie to trade on—the Polish army was too disorganized to form combat units, let alone track down wayward captains. Kesner put on a black three-corner cap and fetched the photo of the Jew from his dresser. The man was in his early twenties and was smiling for his passport photo. His round nose and fat lips were dead Jewish giveaways. On the back, the words *Erik Blumenthal, Copenhagen, 1936* were written in pencil. "I'm looking forward to meeting you, *Herr* Blumenthal," Kesner said.

CHAPTER 3

Maya exhaled as she started down the street, unsteady on her legs. She could still feel the boat rocking under her feet, but at least her stomach had settled down. She needed to unwind from what was already a very long day even though it was only a little after two in the afternoon. After passing through customs in Alexandria, she and her family had unexpectedly been whisked away to the train station and sent off to Cairo along with hundreds of other refugees. German planes had been dropping heavy bombs on Alexandria and it was no longer a safe place to stay. And now, here she was in the suburb of Heliopolis, some twenty kilometers from Cairo.

She wished she could have seen more of Alexandria. She had read so much about the city's glorious past. Her brief impression of this onetime mecca for philosophers and writers was of a city in total chaos. The second she'd set foot there she was assaulted by a barrage of images glaring in the white light of the sun—British and Allied soldiers streaming by, men on the docks frantically loading and unloading endless crates of merchandise, and brazen street vendors risking their lives as they dodged between cars hawking their wares. The cacophony of wailing ambulance sirens, the honking of horns, the squealing of tram wheels, and the piercing incantations of the Muslim call to prayer still rang in her ears.

Not that she had seen much of Cairo either, but it seemed

that pandemonium ruled there as well, with perhaps fewer soldiers but more animals—camels, donkeys, sheep, and goats all over the streets and sidewalks. At least here in the suburbs, there was calm and quiet.

A siren suddenly screamed in the distance and she immediately felt agitated, but she calmed herself down.

"Everything is fine here," she reminded herself but her eyes darted about all the same. Above on a balcony, a maidservant was pinning laundry to a clothesline while a large matron in the street below balanced a basket on her head as she went about her business. Across the street, two men in European suits were talking animatedly, and a boy next to them was walking his bicycle. It all seemed so very normal. She relaxed and slowed her pace, focusing her attention on the beautiful villas that peeked out from behind the lovingly tended rose gardens that bordered the street. How long had it been since she'd strolled down a pretty street in the sunshine by herself? She stopped and sniffed the air. She detected the scent of jasmine and looked around, but she couldn't find any among the shrubbery. Just then, she heard a woman's voice calling her name.

A girl in her late teens was running toward her, trying to steady a platter and the canister she was carrying. Maya frowned, perplexed. She had just arrived here and did not know a soul. How could the girl know her name? She figured it was a mistake and resumed her walk.

"Hoohoo, Maya! *Attendez moi*, wait up!" the girl insisted.

Maya turned and waited.

"I'm Lili. Joe and Allegra's daughter," the girl said, panting and breaking into a brilliant smile as she approached. "They said you went out to stretch your legs wearing a blue scarf on your head. I must have just missed you. You're Maya, yes?"

Maya nodded as she stared at the girl. Her wavy black hair was nicely coiffed and her eyes were heavily traced with black kohl à la

Cleopatra; she was the very picture of femininity with her red dress and matching red lips and nails.

"I would hug you, but . . . " Lili indicated her full hands. So she leaned in and kissed Maya on the cheek. "I'm very glad you're here. I like your name."

Maya shrugged. "It's short for Marianna. I hope you don't mind sharing your room with me."

"Not at all," Lili laughed. "We'll have fun together. It'll be like having an older sister." She flashed another dazzling smile.

"Can I help you carry . . . " Maya looked down at the platter, unable to identify the dish.

"It's a cake in your honor," Lili quickly said. "Made with honey and almond paste. It's called *konaffa*. It's my favorite. I'm on my way to the baker. We don't have an oven at home. Why don't you come with me? I just have one other errand but it won't take long."

"Sure," Maya said, lifting the cake platter from the girl's hands. She was certainly more than appreciative of what Lili's family was doing for hers, but she was feeling so drained from her travels that she cringed at the thought of having to make conversation. And this girl seemed particularly chatty.

"How was your journey from Alexandria?" Lili asked. "It's lucky they found you a place on the train with all the evacuations." She linked her free arm around Maya's.

"We're here now. That's what matters," Maya said, taken aback by the girl's instant familiarity. "I hope we won't be taking advantage of your hospitality for too long."

Lili stopped walking and tilted her head reproachfully as she faced Maya. "Don't say that. We're here to help one another." She again linked her arm around Maya's and resumed walking, but not before adding in a low voice: "I know everything about you, you know." She put her index finger against her lips, indicating Maya's secrets were safe with her.

Maya felt uncomfortable. She did not know how to respond, and how could the girl glibly say she knew *everything* about her?

"Oh Youssef," Lili cried out as an Arab in a gray robe came out from one of the villas, his goat in tow. "The milk man. The rascal skipped our house today. I'll be just a minute," she promised before rushing toward the man.

Maya could overhear the two quibbling in Arabic, though it seemed that Lili was not fluent as now and then she needed to throw in a few words in French. After gesturing dramatically, the Arab kneeled down and began milking his goat into Lili's canister.

"Now, we just need to go to the baker's," Lili said when she was finished. "It's around the corner. There is a boy I like at the bank, next door to the baker's." She winked, then turned serious as she scrutinized Maya's face. "Do you really have to wear a scarf? It's not as dusty here as in Cairo, you know." Without much ado, she set the milk pail on the ground and removed Maya's scarf. Using her fingers, she then combed Maya's hair forward.

How presumptuous! Maya was flabbergasted that the girl had the audacity to play with her hair.

"You're so pretty!" Lili said, staring at Maya as one would study a work of art in progress. "Why are you hiding your face? And your hair . . . What color is it, exactly?"

"Brown, I guess," Maya said, trying hard to retain her composure.

"No! It's auburn. It has a lot of gold," Lili declared. "So thick and soft; you're lucky. You must squeeze some lemons into it and sit in the sun. In no time your hair will have a beautiful golden luster. I guarantee." She started adjusting Maya's hair again. "You know, I'm very good with hair and makeup."

Maya shook her head free. This girl was really going too far. "Please, I'd like my scarf back."

"Really? Scarves are for old ladies." Lili reluctantly put it back on Maya's head.

It dawned on Maya that Lili might actually be embarrassed to be seen with her. Did she really look that frumpy? Even so, how superficial this girl was! She couldn't wait to return to the apartment but realized that Lili would not be able to carry both the cake and the canister full of milk. She'd have to accompany her, at least to the baker's. As she walked, she softened—this was the least she could do.

Despite the racket of the Metro next to them, life in Heliopolis seemed to have much to recommend it. The streets were clean and exceptionally wide, and unlike Cairo, except for a few horse-drawn carriages and donkey carts, there were very few animals on the street. Here the road belonged to cars. Pedestrians had their own broad sidewalks lined with stores sporting brightly colored canopies. The signs and street names were written in French first, then in Arabic, and the buildings were tall and built in the European style, but with Islamic architectural elements, which lent them a unique charm. Lili informed her that the neighborhood boasted many restaurants and ice cream parlors, three cinemas, an amusement park, and a sporting club as good if not better than the one in Cairo. Lili was in fact an active member of the tennis team and was proud to point out that Egyptian Jews had won gold medals in fencing and canoeing at the '36 Olympics.

Maya admitted to having no interest in sports, but Lili still offered to take her to the sporting club. "They have a great swimming pool, and who doesn't like swimming? Besides, you never know who you will meet there," she said.

"The baker's is right there," Lili announced as they turned onto a large avenue framed with beautiful Moorish arcades that housed numerous stalls and stores. "My parents told me that both your father and mother were musicians? Do you play any instruments yourself?"

"Just the piano," Maya answered, "and not that well."

"You're being modest, I can tell. I'm so impressed by anyone who can read sheet music. I can't even sing." She grinned at Maya mischievously. "But I can dance! Chattanooga choo-choo!" she sang while gyrating her hips. "I'll take you dancing. It will get your mind off . . . " She didn't finish her sentence as she paused to admire a cream-colored silk nightgown with an Empire waist hanging in a store window. "I'd love that so much for my trousseau," she said wistfully. "But I imagine I need to find my groom first."

Maya was barely listening. Her attention was turned to the dozens of open burlap bags of spices at the shop next door. What colors! What smells! What an array! She didn't know what half of them were. The vendor, an Arab with a white turban and a gray galabeya, the traditional Arab robe, came out and started speaking to Maya in French.

"*Mademoiselle, je peux vous aider*?" the man asked.

"Leave her alone, Tareq," Lili warned the vendor. "She does not want anything from you."

"*Quel dommage*! A pretty girl like her! Say hello to your mother."

"*Yalla,* come," Lili told Maya, deliberately using Arabic. "Be careful of the vendors; they're big flirts."

That Lili, an educated girl like Maya, spoke French was no surprise, but Maya had not expected that the Arab, a simple and probably unschooled man, could speak any French at all. She was impressed that Napoleon's mere two years in Egypt had left such a legacy.

They passed more stalls, Maya's eyes marveling as she discovered them. Fruit and vegetables, nuts, fresh fish on ice, and those dates! Black ones, red ones, brown ones, beige ones, and yellow ones. She wished she could taste them all. There were also stalls of cotton clothing, leather sandals and belts, artisanal wares in copper, and knickknacks of every kind and shape from fans to souvenir ashtrays with Cleopatra's face inside. She found it all dizzyingly exotic. One of the store windows that caught her attention displayed Egyptian oils in tiny bottles. She was sure that one of them would contain an extract of lotus flowers, a fragrance she was dying to experience.

"Here's the baker shop," Lili said, leading her into an impossibly hot hole in the wall sporting five open wood ovens and an equal number of sweaty workers. Women were shouting their orders. Maya suddenly felt dizzy. She would wait for Lili outside.

She breathed the fresh air in slowly and deeply. She hadn't eaten since leaving Alexandria in the morning. She mustn't do that. She couldn't afford to lose one more kilo. There was a postcard display outside the bookstore next to the baker's shop, and she casually walked over to look at them. There were beautiful hand-painted representations of pharaohs and temples and depictions of life in ancient Egypt that excited her imagination. She resolved to visit the Museum of Egyptian Antiquities while here. She picked up a card she found particularly appealing. It depicted the rays of the sun shining brightly on the apex of a pyramid and said *Greetings from Heliopolis, City of the Sun*. Of course—that was the translation of the city's ancient Greek name. Maya smiled—a city dedicated to the source of all life on earth. She loved the sun and had always felt a powerful kinship with it, reveling in its warm glow and healing rays. She would drink it in, believing God was caressing her and filling her body with light. Perhaps this was so, for people often said she gave off sunlight when she smiled—at least that's what they used to say.

Lili slid up next to Maya and interlaced her arm around hers. "Should we go?"

Maya placed the postcard back in the display, and they started walking back.

CHAPTER 4

"Siwa," Sidi said, pointing to the small town just inside the Egyptian border, which shimmered in the heat like a mirage. "We've finally arrived."

Mickey shook from his head the haunting images of the decimated Cruiser tanks littering the desolate landscape like dinosaur carcasses in a prehistoric graveyard and turned toward Sidi. The poor man had been badly injured, with cuts all over his body and a broken ankle, if not more. Angry with Mickey for his recklessness, he'd sulked the whole way. The journey back had taken three times longer than expected because of the high winds they'd encountered on the way. "We'll go straight to the field hospital. They will take good care of you," Mickey said.

"I doubt it. They are British," Sidi snorted.

"I don't blame you for not liking the Brits, habibi, but I wouldn't trust this Mohammed Haider," Mickey said. "Ask the Russians. He signed a nonaggression pact with them and then he turned around and attacked them."

Sidi stared straight ahead, unhappy with this truth.

As the Jeep drew closer to town, tanks and trucks milled around in the afternoon sun. Once a sleepy plantation of dates and olives built around an oasis, Siwa was now a British military garrison. A high wire fence surrounded the encampment on the outskirts, and a British sentry emerged from the wooden hut that served as a gatehouse. He flagged them down as they approached.

"Papers 'ave ye?" the Brit demanded in a bored Cockney intonation, scrutinizing the two bloody men.

Mickey reached inside the jacket lying on the backseat for his papers, careful not to brush his wounded hands against the rough fabric.

The soldier jotted down Mickey's name from his ID and glared at the Egyptian. "Who's the camel jockey?"

"He's my interpreter," Mickey answered. "The official translator for the *Detroit Free Press* and, as you can see, we are both injured."

"Listen, mate. I don't care which press you're from. If 'e doesn't 'ave any papers 'e can't enter a bloody restricted area."

"*Maalesh*, it's okay," Sidi urged. "We go to the hotel and get my papers."

"The hell with that," Mickey retorted. "This man needs medical care and I'm taking him to the hospital." He slammed the pedal to the floor and sped off.

Sidi laughed at Mickey's brazenness as he looked back at the sentry, who was running after the car in a huff. "You are brave, habibi. I hope your paper is paying you a lot of money for all the risks you are taking."

Mickey didn't say anything, but he was not actually on the payroll. He was a stringer, writing stories and selling them to any publication that would buy them. His letter from the *Detroit Free Press* designating him as one of their official stringers was baloney, but he needed it to obtain press credentials in Egypt. Gunther Hoff, his mentor and former political science professor at the University of Michigan, had pulled strings to get it for him.

The field hospital consisted of a large compound of khaki tents. Mickey pulled up next to an ambulance where two men were unloading a bandaged soldier and putting him on a stretcher. A receiving nurse was instructing the medics where to take him after noting the serial number on the ID tag that hung from his neck.

"Just a few steps," Mickey said as he draped Sidi's right arm around his shoulder and lifted him from the Jeep.

"I'm sorry, but this is a military hospital," the nurse said as she strode briskly up to them, all business. "We don't treat civilians."

"This man needs attention," Mickey began to say.

"Is that an American accent I hear?" a woman asked.

Mickey turned to find the driver of the ambulance stepping out of her seat and coming toward them. She was all of five feet tall and in her midtwenties. She wore a red scarf around her neck, which offset the severity of her khaki uniform.

It was Mickey's first encounter with one of the infamous lady drivers of the Ambulance Corps. His college buddy, Hugh Charlesworth, who had convinced him to join him in Cairo in the first place, had waxed on about these women in his letters, assuring him that they were as bold in the bedroom as they were in the field.

"I know you!" she said to Mickey, recognition crossing her face as she reached him. "You're that American pressman. I saw your pretty face in the photo listing of foreign correspondents. There are not too many Americans." She spoke the King's English, every letter perfectly enunciated. "What is the trouble?" she asked Sidi before Mickey could reply.

"I think my foot is broken, and I have a pain here." Sidi indicated his lower abdomen.

"I'll be happy to take him in my lorry," she told Mickey. "I'm headed to Mamoun. It's only two hours away. I can drop him off at the general area hospital. I'm sure they can help him there."

Mickey brightened. He looked expectantly at Sidi, who shrugged, his lower lip still turned downward. "That would be fantastic," Mickey said.

"Brilliant. I'm Sally Harper." She gave Mickey the once-over as she offered her hand. She radiated a cool sophistication that was only slightly undercut by the dimples in her cheeks.

"Mickey Connolly," he said. "Sorry, I can't shake." He showed his banged-up hands.

"Better put some peroxide on those and bandage them up," she advised, as she delicately inspected them and blew at some of the sand that had settled into the cuts.

"That's all right," Mickey replied, pulling away. "Only a few scratches. Just take care of my buddy here."

They inched their way back to her ambulance and carefully deposited Sidi in the rear seat.

"We'll leave as soon as my friend comes out," she said before putting two fingers in her mouth and jolting everyone with a piercing whistle. She leaned against the ambulance and crossed her arms. "So, you were just taking a stroll in the desert?" She grinned impishly while tossing a lock of blond hair from her eyes.

"Something like that."

A plump redhead wearing the same uniform as Sally came out. After a brief introduction, she settled into the passenger seat.

"Maybe we'll bump into one another again," Mickey said as he opened the driver's door for Sally.

"I'm sure we will bump into one another," she said, taking a step closer and tossing a hip into Mickey's. She looked up at him with sparkling blue eyes. "We're going to Cairo soon. The city is very small. You run into the same people in the same old places all the time." She slipped into her seat.

"Then I look forward to bumping into you there," he said with a wink and leaned in to say good-bye to Sidi. The man would probably be out of work for a few weeks. Mickey unhooked his watch and handed it to him. "Here, to tide you over." He slammed the door shut over Sidi's protests and tapped twice on the vehicle as it started off.

By the time Mickey made it back to Siwa and returned the Jeep he'd rented, the sun was setting and the heat had finally begun to recede. He was beyond filthy and couldn't wait to get back to his hotel and out of his clothes. He also couldn't wait to get to his typewriter. The Brits had to be helped in spite of themselves. There was no way they could prevail in North Africa against the Germans' new Panzer IVs with their 75 mm guns. They needed better arms and a better plan. He would tell the American people what was going on—assuming he could get his article out of the country. He knew how tight-assed the guys in the Censorship Bureau could be. They'd rejected the first story he wrote after arriving, a benign account of his impressions of Cairo. He had found the metropolis alive with glamour and exuberance, not a city paralyzed with fear and suffering, as he had expected. He'd entitled the piece "The Sweet Life." It had no military implications whatsoever, but the censors feared that back home in England—where rationing had rendered an orange an extravagance and the blackouts and bombings had made socializing impossible—reading about opulent parties in chic Cairo might be offensive. He knew he would have to smuggle this new story out of the country if he wanted it published. And he knew what he would name it—"SOS"

The next morning Mickey awoke to the creaking of the slow-turning ceiling fan. He lay still for a few moments in that languid state between sleep and consciousness when the memory of yesterday's events flooded his mind. His eyes popped wide open. No, he hadn't dreamed it. His desert clothes lay torn and filthy on a chair and the ashtray next to his typewriter was brimming with cigarette butts. He let out a long, dejected sigh.

The sun outside was at its zenith. He tried to sit up and winced.

His body was as stiff as cardboard. His left arm was bandaged, but was still a little tender and his scratched hands were still smarting.

A loud knock on the door jolted him. "Telegram for you," a man's voice boomed. It was the desk clerk. "It says 'Urgent.' It came just now, sir. Right this minute."

Mickey's first thought was that something had happened to his father. What else could be urgent? A stubborn union man with a twenty-five-year career as a welder for General Motors, Patrick Connolly had so far been lucky enough to avoid having any accidents with his blowtorch, especially since he had lately developed a tremor in his hands from his drinking.

Mickey stumbled out of bed, slipped into his trousers, and opened the door just wide enough to retrieve the envelope. The telegram was short and to the point:

> Please report immediately to the American Embassy in Cairo. British authorities revoked your visa. Must leave country within seventy-two hours.

CHAPTER 5

The coffee seller had assured Mickey that making the same Turkish coffee that was served in all the Cairo cafés was very simple: boil water, add sugar and a spoonful of coffee, stir well, and turn the heat off when the first bubbles appear. But with his head throbbing from a hangover, Mickey failed to remove the copper pot from the fire in time and it boiled over in a messy spill.

He had barely slept the last four nights since returning from Cairo. The specter of having to leave the country was eating him alive. The British press office had refused to meet with him, and asking for help from the Egyptian authorities would surely be a waste of time. When he'd gone to the American Embassy, the ambassador was not available and had him meet with his secretary, who had confiscated his press badge. The English had caught him illegally crossing the border into a war zone, she'd explained, and they feared that he might have inadvertently given away the position of their tanks. She'd refused to listen to his account of how the Germans massacred the British with Panzer IVs and told him that America had to be supportive of their ally who was fighting a war on many fronts. The best she'd been able to do for him was to obtain a few days' extension of his stay here, giving him a little breathing room to figure things out.

Mickey was raging inside. He didn't like to lose. He'd come here to make his mark as a reporter and he'd barely gotten started. His friend Hugh had enticed him to come, assuring him that there was a big story opportunity here in Egypt. Indeed, newspapers in the States weren't paying attention to the war in North Africa, and the competition from American reporters would be light.

He rinsed the pot and refilled it with water, switching this time to the simpler Nescafé. While waiting for it to boil, he started to plan a note to Hugh, thanking him for the posh apartment and the contacts he'd arranged. It was woefully bad timing that Hugh had been out of town on assignment since Mickey's arrival in Cairo two months ago. Mickey couldn't imagine his unruly friend in uniform. After graduation from the University of Michigan, Hugh had returned to his native England, but quickly growing bored with the mother country, he'd moved to Cairo, where he'd been happy as a clam teaching at the American University and living a life of debauchery. Then he'd been conscripted into the army.

The phone rang.

"Howdy, you little sneak," a man's voice said. It was Carl Nelson from UPI. "How come you missed the press conference yesterday? Damn thing pissed me off so bad I'm throwing in the towel."

"What'd I miss?"

"New rules for the press. I quote. 'All contentious stories that might be detrimental to morale are prohibited. No accounts of unfavorable occurrences involving Allied troops will be allowed. Reports of air raids may not be featured in headlines. The name of Rommel is to be avoided; words like "the Axis forces" or "German Command" are to be used instead. No references to the Muslim Brotherhood or the Grand Mufti of Jerusalem will be permitted,'" Nelson concluded. "How do you like that?"

"That's ridiculous. Tell the folks in Alexandria that there are no air raids! And why can't we use the names of the Brotherhood or the Mufti?"

"'Cause they're siding with Hitler, you dolt!" Nelson answered. "You haven't heard the capper yet. Every article we write has to be approved by three separate censorship officers. I'm heading to Iraq tomorrow. I heard Syria has allowed Axis planes to fly over its territory and use it as a base. From there the Krauts are sending troops to help the insurgency in Baghdad. It's all about those Iraqi oil fields, I tell you. Want to meet tonight for a last hurrah?"

"I have a touch of the flu," Mickey lied. "I'll join you if I feel better."

"We're starting the rounds at the Scarabee Club. Ain't no fun without you."

Mickey hung up. He wanted to have his spiel together before he met his colleagues. He moved to the gas burner, where his coffee water was now boiling. He would try the press office one more time, he decided. If that failed, he still wouldn't go back to the States. That would be an admission of failure. Maybe he could string out of Lisbon. Portugal was neutral, and a lot of people were converging there. The phone rang again, catching him by surprise and making him jerk his hand, splashing boiling hot water on his wrist.

"Yes!" he howled as he picked up the receiver.

"It's Dorothy Calley, Ambassador Kirk's secretary," said the woman in a composed voice after a moment's pause. "It's a new day dawning, Mr. Connolly. The ambassador wants to see you. Pronto."

Located at No. 3 Tolombat Street in Garden City, one of Cairo's most elegant districts and home to most of the city's expensive mansions and embassies, the American Embassy was nevertheless a very friendly place. The Americans had leased the building from one of the Egyptian king's cousins, who ironically was said to have German sympathies. The rear of the beautiful villa had been made available to the tiny American community living in Cairo. It offered a mail center and carried a number of American newspapers and magazines that were otherwise unavailable. Best of all, it housed a superb PX where American goods could be bought, and cigarettes and liquor were duty free.

Mickey entered through the embassy's main reception area, where the administrative offices were located. The marine behind the reception desk confirmed that he was expected and asked him to wait. He sat down next to a well-dressed man engrossed in the sports section of the *Herald Tribune*. Though Mickey had put on his best dress shirt, he felt shabby as he looked down at his wrinkled linen trousers and jacket.

"Good to see you again, Mr. Connolly," a female voice said, startling him.

It was Dorothy Calley, the ambassador's attractive platinum-blond secretary who had phoned him. In her early forties, she was immaculately turned out in a simple black skirt and white blouse.

Mickey sprang to his feet and buttoned his jacket. "Hello, Mrs. Calley."

She laughed a throaty Bette Davis chuckle. "It's *Miss*, cowboy. There was no Mr. Calley last time I checked. Please follow me."

She led him down a corridor, her heels clacking on the black-and-white checkered tile floor. Mickey trailed behind, his eyes on her shapely derrière.

When they reached a large, solid wood door padded with red leather, she stopped and turned to him, giving him the once-over. She picked a piece of lint from his jacket and rapped loudly at the door.

"Ambassador, this is Mickey Connolly," she said formally as they entered. "Mr. Connolly, this is Ambassador Alexander Kirk."

Dressed to the nines in a light gray, three-piece silk suit with matching shirt and tie, his hair slapped down with Brylcreem, the ambassador was a dandy, and a well-perfumed one at that. The ambassador rose from a baby blue velvet armchair behind his desk, and as Mickey shook his hand, his attention veered to another middle-aged man standing in front of the window. He wore a blue suit and yellow tie, and Mickey was struck by his bold gray eyes as the man approached.

"Please, Mr. Connolly, meet Bill Donovan," Kirk hastened to say. "'Wild Bill' as we call him—lawyer, foreign affairs expert, and citizen extraordinaire."

"Stop it, Alexander, you're going to make me blush!" Donovan said as he firmly shook Mickey's hand. "Ace reporter for the *Detroit Free Press*, I'm told. Nice to meet you, Mr. Connolly."

Mickey was taken aback by the compliment given that he'd just been expelled from the country, but before he could say anything, Kirk said, "Come." He patted Donovan's shoulder affectionately and guided the group toward the office's plush sitting area, where they settled in. "If you don't mind, Miss Calley is going to join us. She's an essential member of our diplomatic team here and this was her idea in the first place."

Mickey glanced at Dorothy inquisitively but she ignored him, a cryptic smile on her lips as she pushed a chair for herself close to the sofas. Now that they were all seated, there was an awkward moment of silence. It felt staged to Mickey, and he didn't know what to expect. He quickly perused the office, which was decorated in mismatched eighteenth-century French furniture and garish modern pieces including a yellow chaise lounge with ivory feet, and shifted in his seat. He brought one leg over the other and felt even more uncomfortable when he caught Donovan studying him intensely from behind his bushy eyebrows.

"Drinks?" Kirk offered, shooting up from his seat. "I'm having a martini." When the others demurred, he continued, "I'll need a drink to face today's extravaganza—the monthly Crescent Cross luncheon affair."

"The arduous life of a civil servant!" Donovan joked, but then leaned forward, his eyes fixing on Mickey. "Mr. Connolly, Ambassador Kirk has told me about the jam you're in. That's too bad. But we might be able to calm our British friends down if you can help us with a problem."

"I'm listening," Mickey said, uncrossing his legs.

"We need your assurance that this discussion will be kept strictly confidential. Can we trust you?" Kirk asked solemnly as he walked back with his drink.

"That's your call," Mickey answered. "Your British friends think I'm reckless and untrustworthy."

"But your old professor, Gunther Hoff, has vouched for you," Donovan interjected. "He says you're a man of integrity and a true patriot, and I trust his judgment."

Mickey was jolted by the name of his old mentor. "You spoke to Gunther?"

"The editor of the *Detroit Free Press* suggested that Mr. Hoff would be in the best position to give us a reference," Kirk explained.

"By a fortunate coincidence," Donovan added, "I know Gunther very well. We fought together in the last war and I have the utmost respect for him. He told me you wrote an excellent paper for him on the rise of fascism in Spain." He formed a steeple with his hands and placed them under his chin. His voice was quiet but deliberate. "This is about our country, Mr. Connolly, and we need your word as a patriot that you will not reveal any part of this conversation. Can we have it?"

"Of course." This was getting stranger by the second.

"Bill is a close friend and longtime advisor to President Roosevelt," Kirk stated. "At Bill's urging, the president has created a new organization to gather intelligence on the war, and Bill is its director.

It's called the Office of the Coordinator of Information, or COI. He's made it independent of the other branches of government and Bill reports directly to him," Kirk explained. "Roosevelt regards Hitler as a serious threat to the world, including America, and is committed to helping the Allies. But publicly this is as far as he can go at this time."

Donovan took charge again. "Our mandate is to collect and analyze information about foreign activity that is potentially threatening to the security of the United States. So we are, in fact, an espionage organization, like the English SOE, but without its bureaucracy. I emphasize again—this is *not* public information."

"I understand," Mickey said, waiting to hear what this had to do with him.

"The president has initiated several important research programs on arms development," Kirk began. "Some of the brightest minds in these programs are German scientists, many of whom are Jewish. They wound up in the States after Hitler closed the doors of the universities to Jews in '33. We've got Albert Einstein working for us."

"Thank God for Roosevelt," Mickey said.

"There is someone else we need on our team," Donovan declared, "a Jewish scientist who landed in Alexandria recently but is probably here in Cairo now. Roosevelt wants him found and brought to the States. We want you to help us find him without anyone knowing. We think your investigative skills will serve us well, and writing for a newspaper would provide an effective cover for your activities."

Mickey was stunned. Was it a joke? "I don't know anything about espionage work," he protested.

"The truth is that none of our agents have had any experience in the spy business," Donovan responded. "Our recruits are ordinary men with guts, who are willing to give it a try. We had a man working on this case, a Jewish businessman here in Cairo, but he never made it to Alexandria. He died of a heart attack the night before the scientist arrived. We found out too late to have him replaced."

"Frankly, Connolly, you're at the top of a very short list of candidates," Kirk said.

"Then you must be pretty desperate," Mickey said with a nervous laugh.

"We know your French is pretty good, which will help you cozy up to the Jews here," Kirk added.

"I don't know anything about Jews. I didn't meet a lot of them in Detroit," Mickey remarked.

"We think you are a resourceful guy, Mr. Connolly," Dorothy cut in pointedly, crossing her arms. "This is your chance to make history, instead of writing about it. You should grab it."

The room fell silent. Mickey passed a hand through his hair. She had hit a nerve. "Miss Calley certainly gets right to the point," Kirk piped in. "And she's right. You could really make a difference here."

"We'll pay you two hundred dollars a week," Donovan added.

"What about my press credentials?" Mickey asked.

"Lay low for a little while and stay away from the press bureau," Kirk answered. "Leave the rest to us."

Mickey and Donovan stood in silence as they enjoyed the spectacular view of the city from the embassy's roof, where they continued their discussion while Kirk went to his luncheon. A bird's-eye view of winding, tree-lined streets spread out below them, where apartments and office buildings were interspersed with magnificent villas. To the northwest, the Nile forked around a small island on which was nestled the luxurious, wooded residential area of Zamalek, a British favorite. On the island's south end stood the extravagant and exclusive Gezira Sporting Club. *Fellucas* floated lazily down the river, completing a postcard-perfect vista.

"If I told the folks back home that Cairo might be the most alluring city in the world, they'd think I'd gone soft," Donovan said as he drank in the scene below. "And just listen—I bet you don't hear this many languages spoken in Detroit."

"I don't know, we've got Greeks, Italians, Germans, Chinese, Poles, Irish, Mexicans, Belgians, and who knows who else there. Seems like home to me." Mickey tried to sound light, but his mind was reeling. He'd just signed a pile of documents which, as Kirk had explained, said that any information he obtained in the course of his assignment was acquired in absolute confidentiality and that if any part of it were to be leaked and traced back to him, he was a dead man.

"Tell me about the man I'm looking for," Mickey said eagerly.

"His name is Erik Blumenthal," Donovan answered, wiping beads of sweat from his temples. "He got his PhD in physics from the Polytechnic University in Berlin in '33 at age twenty-two. After that he worked in Denmark with Niels Bohr."

"The Nobel Prize winner?" Mickey asked.

"Yes. His field is called quantum physics." Donovan shrugged at the esoteric nature of it. "He had been working in Paris when the war reached France and he was forced to flee."

"Why did he come to Egypt?" Mickey asked.

"That's a mystery. He could have relocated to England with the rest of his group, but wound up in Turkey instead. Luckily he was able to get Turkish papers. Did you know that the Turks are the only ones who refuse to let their Jewish citizens in France be rounded up and interned? They've been sending convoys of trains to retrieve them."

"Good for them. It's hard to believe that Pétain is actually handing over the non-French Jews to Hitler."

"Not only that. Last week he enacted a law confiscating the bicycles, radios, and telephones of all Jews in the country, foreign born or not. But back to the scientist, we know he boarded a ship bound for Alexandria, but there's no guarantee he'll be using his Turkish papers here. He may not even be using his real name."

Mickey's brow furrowed. "Turkey is neutral. Why didn't he just stay there and wait out the war? Crossing the Mediterranean with its mines and U-boats was very risky. Two weeks ago a Russian sub mistakenly sank a neutral ship off the Turkish coast. Eight hundred passengers, mostly Romanian Jews, were killed."

"He must have had a very good reason to leave."

"Or a strong reason to come to Egypt. Maybe he has family here. Maybe he is planning to continue his research at one of the local universities."

"Doubtful. Al-Azhar teaches only in Arabic, and the American University's science department is abysmal."

"Then he's probably going next door to Palestine. A lot of Jews have immigrated there."

Donovan shook his head. "Not anymore. The British have placed a complete halt on Jewish immigration there despite their own White Paper quotas. Pressure from the Arabs. You can't get in without a visa, and visas are next to impossible to get. If he had one, he would have gone there directly from Istanbul. Yes, you should look into Palestine, but it's a long shot."

Mickey crossed his arms. "The Jews are known for helping each other. They must have some kind of mechanism in place for resettling immigrants."

Donovan nodded in agreement and led Mickey to a bench in the shade. "We've sniffed around the immigration registries, but if we push too hard the English will want to know why."

Mickey cocked his head. "You're not working with the English on this? Finding him would be in their interest, too."

"We have reasons for not wanting them involved," Donovan said firmly. "We don't share everything about weapons research. I'm sure that in due time we'll tell them. For now, no one knows about this, not even our own naval attaché. You'll be working on this alone. However," he emphasized, "Dorothy Calley will help you as much as possible. She's already put together a dossier on the Jewish community here and she has a picture of Blumenthal my office scrambled to find. I'm sorry, but it's seven years old."

"How old is he in this picture?"

"Twenty-three. We don't have a more recent photo, but we're digging. I'll keep you posted," Donovan said. "And you'll find that Dorothy is very good. Kirk swears by her. She was with him in Berlin before they came here. He won't do a thing without her." He stood up. "Come, she's waiting for us."

"He's all yours," Donovan announced as they entered Dorothy's small office.

She looked up as she ground her cigarette into an ashtray already filled with crimson-stained butts and winked at Mickey. "Ready to play ball?"

"Fire away," Mickey replied.

"Please pass on everything you learn to Dorothy," Donovan said. "She'll communicate with me by radio. Our communiqués are encrypted and transmitted to Washington twice a day, using code names. Any preference for your own?"

Mickey scanned the room and spotted a copy of *Life* magazine on Dorothy's desk with baseball's strikeout king, Bob Feller, on the cover. "What about Fastball?" he suggested.

Donovan laughed. "Perfect." He nodded his thanks to Dorothy and shook Mickey's hand for a long moment. Many thoughts seemed to be crossing his mind, but as he retreated all he said was, "Be careful."

After Donovan left, Dorothy gave her own warning, "This city is riddled with spies, and not just the Germans. The Vichy French are watching the Free French, and the Italians don't trust the Germans. The Japanese are spying on us and everyone else in the Pacific Zone, and the Egyptians are spying on all of us. You can't trust anyone. Be on your guard all the time. We don't want anyone to catch a whiff of your activities. You and I can still meet here at the embassy. But don't come more often than you normally do."

"Why did you recommend me for this job?" Mickey asked, meeting her eyes.

"That's why," she said, picking up an envelope from her desk and tossing it to him. "I found it stuck between the newspapers you left on the chair in your haste to leave my office the other day." She indicated the chair in front of her desk.

Mickey did a double take. Inside was the SOS article he'd written in Siwa. In his distress he had not noticed it was missing.

"A detailed account of slaughter on the battlefield. It's not bad," she said with a tight grin, "but I don't know what you planned to do with it. Unless you want to be thrown out of the country, I suggest you leave it here."

"The Brits need our help. I want the American people to understand that," Mickey said, frustrated.

"All in due time, my *young* friend," she said. "Telling the folks back home about the Brits' shortcomings will only make things worse. Americans will lose confidence in them, and the English will resent you. Take a lesson from Edward R. Murrow. His broadcasts to the States lionizing Churchill have turned a grumpy grandpa into a heroic statesman. Those broadcasts got Congress to pass the Lend-Lease Act, which is saving their asses. To me, that's effective journalism."

Her expression turned serious. "I know you want to help the cause. This assignment is important, and someday you'll be grateful for it. I think you have the goods for it. I have a track record to protect, Connolly. Don't prove me wrong."

Mickey looked away, uncomfortable with the weightiness of it all as she went to fetch something from a cabinet in the corner.

"Have a seat," she continued as she returned to her desk with a large yellow folder. "This report is just for starters. I'm sure you'll have questions. I'll have more tomorrow. If you need more information, let me know."

"I could probably use some recent issues of the local Jewish newspapers. Is that possible?" he asked. "Maybe I can get some clues about what the local Jews are doing about refugees." He planted his elbows on the desk and brought the tips of his fingers to his lips. "And what if Egypt is just a stopover for Blumenthal? Can you find out about the immigration policies of other countries he might be headed for, like South Africa? In fact, we should look at Jewish newspapers from all the surrounding Mediterranean countries."

She raised an eyebrow. "My, aren't you the thorough one," she remarked as she leaned back to examine him, swinging one slender ankle back and forth.

Mickey caught sight of the edge of a lacy black slip. She was a good fifteen years his senior, but he couldn't deny her charms. Sexuality wafted from her like a lingering scent. "You'd be surprised how thorough I can be when my country calls," he said with a flirtatious grin.

"Put your flaps down, honey. It takes more than shooting a line like that at a girl if you're gonna score," she chuckled. "Besides, you're too young for me."

He laughed. Though she'd nailed him, he couldn't help liking her, tough cookie that she was.

"Back to business," she said, straightening up. She took a set of keys from her navy blue purse and unlocked one of the desk drawers. She extracted a thick envelope. "Here's a little perk that comes with the job. Cash. You'll need it. Lots of it. Now, about your cover—"

"I thought I'd tell people I'm writing an article about the Jewish refugees here," he said.

"That's good, but say that you're doing it for the *Foreign Service Journal*. We'll back you up. It will open doors and give you more legitimacy."

"I like that."

She stood up. The meeting was over. "Ready to start playing for real, Agent Fastball?"

Mickey picked up the envelope and slipped it into his jacket pocket. "You bet."

CHAPTER 6

"Guests don't lift a finger in our house," Allegra Levi would invariably say in her courteous, albeit aloof way whenever Maya offered to help with household chores. But this time, when Maya tried to give her hostess a hand with the stuffed artichokes she was preparing, Allegra just shook her head and didn't even bother to look at her. Maya didn't know what to attribute this to. She and her family had tried to be model guests. Her brother, Erik, had offered to tutor the older children in science and math, and her father was making himself inconspicuous and controlling his foul moods as best he could.

"She did it again," Maya whispered to Erik in frustration when she tiptoed out of the kitchen and found him in the hallway. "Mrs. Levi won't let me help. She just makes me feel so . . . useless—like I'm always a burden."

"Just stay out of her way," Erik advised. "For whatever reason, she likes it better this way." He limped off to the living room.

Standing still, Maya crossed her arms. Perhaps it was as simple as what her brother suggested. Maybe Allegra just didn't like having someone in the kitchen other than the maid, or maybe this was the practice of Egyptian hospitality, which, as Allegra had said, the Jews here had learned from the Arabs. "They never use half measures," she had declared. So far the only contribution Maya had been allowed to make was to help

Lili, the Levis' eldest child and only daughter, with her baker's errand on the day she had arrived.

Maya decided to forget about it. They had been in Cairo for five days and expected their new papers to arrive momentarily. Besides, she abhorred housework and had been exhausted since arriving here in spite of having caught up on a lot of sleep and eating regular meals. She had looked at herself in the mirror this morning and recoiled at the sight. Though she recognized the old Maya, the one that used to have men lining up at her desk at work in Paris to ask her to lunch or a dance, her skin had lost its luster, and her eyes their sparkle. It would take weeks if not months of rest to recover her buttery pink complexion. I'm old at twenty-two, she thought fearfully.

She followed her brother into the living room with nothing to do until Allegra called for lunch when the children returned from school and Joe, Allegra's husband, arrived home from work. She settled down on the rose brocade settee across from Erik, who picked up the magazine he'd been devouring, a special report on the Battle of Britain. His appetite for reading about bombing attacks seemed insatiable.

Except for the occasional sounds of a passing automobile or the crying of a street merchant below, the apartment was generally quiet, especially at this time of the day. It was located on the third floor of a six-story building that was nestled in a small residential street. Allegra kept a lovely home, rendering it cozy with elaborate oriental rugs spread over white marble floors, while the many crystal vases placed on hand-embroidered doilies adorning the antique furniture gave it a gracious feel. Gauzy curtains billowed in the breeze that blew in from the open balconies, letting in the delicate fragrance of the climbing jasmine in the backyard. But it was the spicy aromas that wafted in from the kitchen that captured Maya most, the reassuring smells of home cooking, even though she was not a great aficionado of these strange dishes. After their horrendous escape through Europe over the last fifteen months, she grew to appreciate the soothing feeling one gets from living within the protective walls of a family home. She folded her legs underneath her, rolled her head back, and closed her eyes. She wanted to have a home of her own one day. There would be a man there, of course, her one big love, who would cater to her every whim, and on whose shoulder she could rest her head while they talked about the future. She'd be giddy with happiness. It was an impossible dream now.

"The Luftwaffe dropped seventy-four *thousand* tons of explosives over England in less than sixty days!" Erik stated as he scribbled some notes on the magazine, breaking the silence. "How is that possible? That would mean about eighteen-thousand bombs."

Maya responded with a shrug.

He looked up and considered her for an instant before putting the magazine down. "I'm sorry," he said, "I shouldn't be talking about bombs. Are you still having nightmares about Poitier, sister?"

"Sometimes," she said, "but I'm fine." She wasn't. He was referring to the bombing that had hit the farm where they were staying after they'd fled Paris. The raid had killed the farmer's youngest boy, who had stayed in the barn with Erik, tending to the geese, refusing to go to the basement of the main house when the first air-raid siren blasted. When the boy had dashed outside seeking a safer shelter, he'd been killed right in front of Erik. They couldn't even make sense of the boy's body afterward. Maya had been haunted by it ever since.

Erik picked up the guidebook on the coffee table and flipped through the pages. "Why don't you tour the city?" he said. "I know you'd like that."

She shrugged again. This was the only response he deserved or would get from her. Though she was dying to see the pyramids, she'd be damned if she showed him any sign of wanting to visit the city. It was certainly not her idea to come to this part of the world, and he knew her feelings very well. He never took her wishes seriously. When she'd suggested that they travel by land rather than crossing the Mediterranean, he had vetoed her on the spot, not trusting that their visas would hold up under scrutiny when they reached Syria, which was controlled by Vichy France. She had secretly hoped that something bad, but not catastrophic, would happen during their voyage to prove her right. And it did. Three days of wrenching seasickness befell them, and she was its worst victim.

"You can smile, sister," Erik teased. "Remember, we're a team."

She made a tiny movement with her shoulder, her eyes still averted. Yeah, they were a team, that's what he'd been saying since they went on the run after the Nazis arrived in Paris. Erik's relationships within the scientific community had provided the contacts that enabled them to escape, while her role had been to serve as the family's link to the outside world—she was basically the courier in the family.

But she had a brain, too, a good one, and she wished he'd realize that she was no longer the same immature girl who, at thirteen, had been expelled from summer camp for sneaking into the boys' cabin in the middle of the night. She hadn't actually done anything bad—she and her friends had just sashayed around the cabin provocatively in their nightgowns during the surprise visit. The camp had promptly sent a telegram to her parents in Düsseldorf, but Erik, alone at home, had intercepted it and driven all the way to Berchtesgaden to pick her up, mercifully hiding the truth from Mutter and Vati.

Maya's relationship with her brother was complex, and she had to admit that she was partly to blame for this. Normally outspoken, she was often timid around him. It wasn't just that he was eight years older; he had been her pillar of strength and steady comfort all during her growing up years. He was the one who comforted her when she had nightmares as a child, the one who hovered over her homework after school, and the one who served her dinner, letting her babble on about her day, while Vati and Mutter were performing at one concert or another. He was even the one who gave her the talk about "the facts of life" when she turned eighteen.

Maya unfolded her legs and crossed one over the other, annoyed at having to wear trousers since her one summer dress and two skirts were dirty. Slacks were practical, but they were hot, uncomfortable, and ugly, and she couldn't understand how they had ever come into fashion. A girl with nice legs ought to be able to show them off.

"Now listen to this," Erik said as he flipped a page in the travel book:

> Cairo is often referred to as "Paris by the Nile." The Ottoman Khedive who ruled here was so dazzled by his visit to Paris that he attempted to replicate the City of Light here, and he hired European architects to do it. The boulevards are built in the grand Parisian style of Haussman, and cafés and shops in the European style abound.

"Sister, I insist that you take some time to explore this city," he said as he put the book down.

She leaned in and picked it up with a heavy sigh. She thumbed through it before settling on a quote. "Metropolis of the universe, garden of the world, and anthill of the human species," she read with theatrical flair. "So Cairo is an anthill, according to a famous fourteenth century philosopher. Now that's really arousing my interest!" She tossed the book back on the table. "It's unbearably hot and muggy in this stupid city," she said. She pulled her hair back into a ponytail and flipped it back and forth to fan her neck.

When the loud voice of the building's concierge was heard calling outside, "Monsieur, monsieur, where are you going?" she rushed over to the window.

"Vati!" Her father was aimlessly shuffling down the street, head down, carrying his dead wife's violin tightly pressed against his chest. "I can't believe he got out." She was exasperated. "We're going to have to lock the doors!"

She flew down the stairs to the lobby where the *bawab* (the doorman) pointed her to the right. Around the bend she found her father a few feet away, facing a wall with the violin at his feet, his lips moving in prayer, oblivious to the passersby around him. An intellectual and a secular man, this was very unlike him, and Maya didn't know what to make of it. She softened as she noticed how loosely his clothes draped his body. His blue eyes were pale and lifeless, and he seemed to have shrunk. What happened to the strong and ebullient Vati who played four-handed piano with her?

As if aware of her staring, he turned toward her.

"I don't know why, but I'm itching like mad," he complained loudly in German as she approached him.

"Shh," Maya whispered urgently. "Speak English, remember?" She'd reprimanded him many times about lapsing into German. An incident in France had almost cost them their lives, and even here, they did not want to risk drawing attention to themselves. She really would have to lock him up.

"I forget sometimes," he apologized. "But I'm thirsty for an orange soda," he claimed and began pulling her toward the grocer at the end of the street, a daily routine now for them. She picked up the violin and ran her nails over his back to soothe his itching.

It was rare for him to acknowledge his memory lapses. Maya was convinced that the blow to his head he'd received four years ago had permanently affected his mind. He had resisted the SS guards when they had thrown him into a garbage truck filled with other Jews and hauled them through the streets of Frankfurt. They had made him wear a sign around his neck saying, "I am garbage. I am a dirty Jew." He'd been a broken man ever since and was becoming increasingly less lucid. Just last week she'd seen him stand up, take a few graceful steps, and bow, as if to an audience.

"Maya," Vati said after a few steps. "The violin. Can I carry it myself?"

She stopped and turned to her father. All he had left to show for his sixty years of life was a violin. She suddenly regretted having become so annoyed with him for leaving the house. She pressed her fingers to the corners of her eyes, ashamed of her selfishness, and squashed any remnants of resentment.

"Of course," she answered, kissing the violin and handing it back to him.

As they approached the apartment building they saw Erik come limping out of the gate toward them. How could he have climbed down the steep, narrow staircase by himself?

Her brother had just turned twenty-four when he'd contracted polio, a cruel birthday present. From the onset he'd made it clear that he didn't want to be fussed over, quickly silencing any expressions of pity or even concern. "I'm not crippled," he'd insisted, "just inconvenienced." Though he was stoic, their escape after Hitler took Paris had been especially hard on him. They'd spent nine insufferable months hiding from Vichy police in a tiny apartment outside Bordeaux in the unoccupied south, followed by ten weeks in an attic, where the ceiling was not even high enough for him to sit up. Having his legs immobilized for so long must have caused more damage to his joints than all the walking he later endured when they trekked across the country to catch the train from Lyon to Istanbul. Through it all he never, ever complained.

How could Erik ever understand that his stoicism only exacerbated the chasm that had started to grow between the two of them when they left Germany after the schools and universities closed their doors to Jewish students? As Maya watched him struggle along, his right leg dragging painfully behind him, his face gaunt, and his cheeks sunken, she felt sorry, not just for him, but also for herself and all the dreams she had lost. Her life was over before it had even gotten started. Worse yet, Erik's heroic reaction to his polio had taken away her right to scream about the unfairness of it all.

When Erik reached them, he did not scold Vati. He did not need to. His eyes did it for him as they reproachfully met their father's. Vati acted as if he hadn't noticed and without a word started toward the apartment, leaving Erik seething behind him. Maya did not say anything either, but she caught up to her father and accompanied him, wrapping her arm around him protectively.

When she reached the apartment, Allegra was standing in the doorway, a concerned look on her face. A handsome woman by all standards, even with her six-months-pregnant belly, she had changed into a bold green dress for lunch and wore a gardenia in her chignon, which seemed at odds with her hesitant demeanor. Her gold bracelets jiggled as she put her right hand on her hip.

"Everything's fine," Maya reassured her, her arm around Vati's, Erik in tow.

"We have hot water now," Allegra said, showing them in. "I've run a bath for you."

Maya barely started to mouth the words "thank you" before Allegra disappeared. More of her aloofness, Maya thought before retiring to her room that she shared with Lili. A cot had been set up for her there, while Erik and Vati had been given one of the boys' rooms.

Once alone, Maya took in a deep breath and let it out slowly as she looked over the room. It struck her as particularly pretty today. She noticed how the soft yellow of the walls perfectly matched the trim of the white satin quilt that covered the bed. There seemed to be more face creams, lipsticks, and perfume bottles on top of the mirrored vanity than usual, and there was a new swath of sheer white fabric lying next to the Singer sewing machine in the corner.

She carefully opened the antique French armoire to retrieve her robe, tucked among Lili's dozens of brightly colored dresses, which reflected the girl's effervescent personality. Living for her tennis matches and dance contests, Lili had the world in the palm of her hand. With a father that called her endearing pet names like *mesh mesh,* meaning apricot, his favorite fruit, and *ayouni,* meaning my eyes, how could Lili not feel lucky in life? With pangs of envy, Maya quickly closed the closet.

She moved away and started to unbutton her shirt. She removed her watch and placed it inside a sock under her cot, where she kept a dozen other watches. She had worn them all strapped tightly along her arms when they'd traveled and now by reflex she passed a hand along the bare skin where invariably the bands would pinch her too tightly and leave red stripes. She had pawned her mother's fur coat for them. The watches were easier to carry and far easier to sell. She had gotten this idea from a Polish refugee in France.

As she continued undressing, she sat down on the bed.

The lovely strains of Beethoven's *Für Elise* filtered through the ceiling as a budding pianist on the floor above diligently practiced the piece. She brought her feather pillow up to her face and inhaled the scent of its freshly laundered case. In the distance, she could hear the sounds of cars and trams. People were coming home for lunch. It all felt normal, safe, like life used to be. She felt tears rush to her eyes.

"Stop it," she said, softly slapping her cheek. But her tears welled, ready to break into sobs. "Stop it," she insisted and slapped her other cheek, this time harder. Crying was not an option. "Stop it, stop it, stop it," she snapped, disgusted with herself for allowing this moment of weakness. When she heard a light knock on the door, she sat up and composed herself.

It was Allegra with a towel. "The bath is ready," she said with a perfunctory smile and quickly turned on her heels.

Maya impulsively seized her hand. "Thank you so very much for your hospitality, Mrs. Levi."

The woman averted her eyes and abruptly freed her hand. She toyed nervously with the hand pendant hanging from a gold chain around her neck, an amulet against the evil eye. "Please, don't," Allegra pleaded and quickly moved away.

CHAPTER 7

Mickey sat at the breakfast table while the radio played softly in the background and the brilliant, buttery morning light came in through the open shutters. The sounds of shopkeepers opening their stores wafted from below. He wrote down the name Simon Cattaoui. It had popped up in several of the documents in Dorothy's file. A senator as well as a wealthy landowner, Cattaoui had been serving as president of Cairo's Jewish community center for the last fifteen years.

Dorothy had opened her report by claiming that the Jews probably had more influence here than anywhere else in the world. This was no overstatement. Not only did they own most of the banks and dominate a variety of businesses, from railroads to retailing to real estate, but Egyptian Jews also held important posts in government and were advisors to the king. They were abundantly represented in journalism, medicine, and law. Mickey noticed numerous *bey* and *pasha* titles on Dorothy's list of Cairo's wealthiest Jewish citizens, but he also found many "Sirs," indicating that the English honored them as well.

Most of the Jewish population in the country, which totaled eighty thousand, was born here. A tiny fraction dated way back, but the majority traced their ancestry to the huge wave of immigration after the Suez Canal was built and the push for modernization began after 1869. They came mostly from neighboring countries—Greece, Italy, Turkey, Morocco, Tunisia, Algeria, Lebanon, and Syria.

Mickey took a last bite of his toast, which was smothered with a thick layer of his favorite pomegranate marmalade, and jotted down 22 rue Magrabi—the address of the Jewish community center, which ran a highly effective system of self-government for the community and regulated a wide range of affairs that touched on virtually every aspect of Jewish civil life. As he suspected, they also conducted an extensive web of charitable activities ranging from helping the elderly to providing dowries for less fortunate Jewish girls. He found no specific formal aid structure for refugees, but an organization this powerful and far-reaching should have a hand in assisting them. Mickey would make it the first stop in his investigation.

"Monsieur Miiickey, *s'aalam alekoum!*" the building's bawab greeted him as he came out of the elevator. The Arab was polishing one of the dozen colossal pink marble columns that decorated the foyer of the art nouveau building. He put his rag aside, wiped his hands on his light blue galabeya, and opened his arms. "You are up early. Life is good, *insha'Allah*." The Arab grinned from ear to ear, his long, curly lashes framing his sparkling dark eyes.

"Life's great, Hosni," Mickey replied. "Just great."

"Tsk, tsk," the bawab reprimanded, waving his index finger. "*Kolo Kawayes*."

"*Koulo quiece*. All is well," Mickey repeated.

"*Kolo-Ka-Wayes*," the bawab corrected his accent, a game they had played since his arrival. Mickey was eager to get going, but he repeated the phrase until he said it to the Arab's satisfaction, knowing Hosni would not relent.

"Bravo, Mr. Mickey!" he finally enthused, offering him an olive from a small dish on the desk as if rewarding a well-trained dog. Mickey popped it into his mouth. "Where are you going this glorious morning?" Hosni asked.

"The Jewish community center, and I'd better hurry," Mickey said. "It's near the Ismalia Synagogue, right?"

"Around the corner from it," Hosni said. "Please give my greetings to my Jewish brothers," he requested, bowing his head and placing a hand on his heart.

The luxurious apartment complex known as the Immobilia building where Mickey was staying was only a fifteen-minute walk from Ismail Pasha Square, the epicenter of the social and business lives of the elite. A stone's throw from the beautiful Ezbekieh Gardens, the Ismalia Synagogue stood well within this fashionable area of town. It was the largest structure on Magrabi Street and stood next to the Turf Club, one of the most exclusive social clubs in the capital. The palm tree motifs on the synagogue's façade evoked a mysterious and ancient Egyptian quality, and Mickey would not have known it was a Jewish temple were it not for the carving that framed the top of the imposing pink stone entry columns, where a large Jewish star was displayed. Perhaps the architect had wanted to remind the world that Moses had once been a prince of Egypt.

Around the corner was the Jewish community center with a line of people running more than two blocks in front. They were a sad and bedraggled group—mothers with babies, crying children, elderly men, and whole families, dragging along their piles of suitcases and knapsacks. From the babble of languages, it was clear to Mickey that they were from all over the Mediterranean basin and beyond. They all had the same resigned and weary look, knowing this would not be the end of their troubles.

So these are the "displaced," he thought, imagining the horror of fleeing one's home without knowing when you might return, if ever. It made him think of a photo he'd seen, of Polish Jews lined up at a train station waiting to be taken to the Warsaw Ghetto, a place closed to the outside world. It had been buried on page sixteen of the *New York Times*, whose owner was Jewish.

Mickey headed straight to the front of the line and squeezed inside the center. The lobby was swarming with people, their clatter reverberating off the walls. A husky, cross-eyed security man blocked his path—they were too busy to talk to a reporter, but Mickey was able to convince him that a "well-placed" article in the *Foreign Service Journal* could attract financial support from American Jewish groups. The man relented and asked him to wait.

A few minutes later, a jovial man with a receding hairline and a bulging stomach that was perfectly framed by the black suspenders he wore over his collarless shirt came out to meet him. He introduced himself as Jacques Antebie, head of the Refugees Aid Program and undersecretary of B'nai B'rith, the umbrella organization for all their charities. He said that though they usually did not like to attract publicity, he was pleased that their relief efforts were of interest to their friends in America. He took Mickey's elbow and led him away.

As they made their way through a maze of hallways to his office, the man proudly explained how they had established over a hundred relief centers in the city, not only for Jews, but for all those in need. "*Mitzvahs*. Charity is ingrained in us, monsieur," he said.

"Do you keep a record of all the refugees you house?" Mickey asked as they rounded a corner into a long corridor.

"We try to, but it's a struggle to keep it up to date."

Mickey decided to plunge ahead. "I'm trying to get in touch with a man who would be very helpful for my story. I think his ordeal will resonate with the high-powered readers of this journal. Would you be able to check the name Erik Blumenthal for me?"

"Blumenthal?" Jacques exclaimed. "That's an Ashkenazi name."

"Ashkenazi?" Mickey asked.

Jacques stopped and raised his eyebrows. "In America you've got a lot of Jews with names like Goldman, Steinberg, Rosenthal. All Europeans, mostly Russian, German, or Polish. Those are the Ashkenazi Jews and they speak Yiddish, no?"

"Yes."

"Here we have Spanish- and North African-sounding names like Messiquas, Farghalis, Salamas. Those are the Sephardim. Like me," Jacques said, the side of his thin lips curling into an indulgent smile. "Many of us still speak Ladino, the ancient language of our ancestors in Spain before we were expelled in 1492." He waved his finger and added, "Not to confuse you, but Levi and Cohen are common names in both groups." He resumed his march to his office. "And where is this Mr. Blumenthal from, exactly, if I may ask?"

"Germany," Mickey answered. "He recently arrived from Istanbul. Perhaps he wants to settle here."

"That would be very unusual," Jacques said. "German Jews generally don't like it here. We have very, very few of them in Cairo." He made a gesture with his thumb and index finger emphasizing how few. "Maybe it's our sun. I've been in charge of our refugee program for the last seven years and I don't think we've had any German refugees since a small number arrived in Port Said in '38. They were in transit to Palestine. We gave them food and clothing and some medical supplies. Anyhow, I'd be happy to check this fellow's name against our lists."

"Palestine?" Mickey repeated. "Could you help me get in touch with one of the Zionist organizations here?"

"We don't have any," Jacques said. "Why should we? Egyptian Jews are not interested in a Jewish homeland. We are very happy here. This way, please."

When they reached Jacques's office, a lanky young man was leaving, a pile of documents in his arms and the look of a deer in distress on his face. Jacques introduced him as his aide, George Zétoun, and explained the situation to him.

"Blumenthal," the man remarked. "A *Schlekht*?"

"What's a Schlekht?" Mickey asked.

"I'm sorry. It's not a very nice name for the Ashkenazim," Jacques interceded. "It means 'disgusting' in Yiddish. The Ashkenazim are very different from us, I'm afraid."

"Different good or different bad?" Mickey asked, directing his question at Zétoun.

"Well, not very good," Zétoun confessed, his ears reddening, apparently uncomfortable with his own prejudice. "They have different customs. We think they don't have much . . . how can I say? *Savoir-faire*? Manners? You should watch them eat. Even the educated ones, they will always be peasant stock. If my sister brought one home it would be as bad as marrying a gentile."

"But we should not generalize, should we?" Jacques said. "Come, can I offer you some tea?"

Mickey absentmindedly nodded yes. His mind was stuck on the words "peasant stock," which was just how Detroit's longtime Irish residents described newer immigrants.

No wonder there wasn't much of a German Jewish community here: They were not very welcome. So what was Blumenthal doing here?

Mickey spent the next few days traipsing through the refugee shelters set up by the Jewish community center on the long list Jacques Antebie had given him. He must have visited at least thirty of them. So far, nothing had panned out, and he wished he had better news to give Dorothy. He jumped out of the tram, flustered and cursing the unpredictable Cairo traffic. He was half an hour late for his meeting with Dorothy and rushed to the Shepheard's Hotel on the grand avenue of Ibrahim Pasha Street. He hoped she had waited for him. He quickly perused the patrons on the hotel's renowned white wicker terrace, but Dorothy was nowhere to be seen, so he raced up the stairs to the lobby, two at a time, pushed his way through the massive oak door, and hurried into the Moorish Hall.

Covered by an enormous colored glass dome that was supported by tall lotus pillars like those found in the ancient Egyptian temples, and adorned with imposing palm trees over white marble floors which contrasted with the rich burgundy wall panels, the Moorish hall was the heart of the hotel. Women in stylish hats conversed quietly with men in uniforms on overstuffed, quilted chairs around small octagonal wood tables. It was all so tasteful, but best of all, it was marvelously cool here. He could see why some argued that the Shepheard's rivaled the pyramids as Cairo's most famous landmark. The colonial den had accommodated some of the most famous names in history and many heads of state during its hundred years of existence.

Searching for Dorothy, Mickey walked across the hall to its very end, from which swept up a magnificent staircase, flanked by tall ebony caryatids. She wasn't there either. His gaze turned to the adjacent saloon doors of the Long Bar from which raucous laughter could be heard, but he knew the bar was off-limits to women. Straightening his rumpled bottle green blazer and smoothing his hair, he inquired at reception and was told that Miss Calley had phoned in with a message that she was running late. Perfect. He had a few minutes to collect himself and returned to the Moorish Hall.

"This is the only table available at this time, sir," offered the maître d', impeccably dressed in a black suit with a white handkerchief peeking from his vest pocket. He showed him to a banquette next to a young woman engrossed in a newspaper, her chin propped up on one hand. Without bothering to look up, she slid an inch away.

"Sorry, miss," Mickey said as he sat down next to her and asked the maître d' to have the waiter bring him a Stella beer. As he spoke, the girl turned to him and stared as if surprised to find him there. Their eyes locked for a few awkward seconds. He wasn't quite sure what color her eyes were. They could be blue, or green, or even violet, but they were light and alive, yet at the same time contemplative, almost somber. He sensed some troubling uneasiness in them.

"Is something wrong?" he asked.

The girl blushed slightly and shook her head before turning her attention back to her paper. He studied her for an instant. Though her hair was pulled back in a matronly bun with a few rebellious strands hanging loose, and she wore no trace of makeup except for the faint rose color on her full lips, she was a stunner. Especially appealing was the smoothness of her complexion and her milky pale bare arms. While some men could not see beyond breasts or legs, Mickey was a skin man.

The girl suddenly turned toward him again and gave him a cursory smile before folding the paper and fetching a book from her purse. She seemed nervous as she crossed and uncrossed her legs before opening her book.

Mickey looked away. He had business to do and felt agitated himself. He took out the community center's refugee shelters list and thumbed through it. It was as thick as a book and of course did not include the Red Cross, the Red Crescent, or dozens of other makeshift aid organizations that had mushroomed all over the city. Hotels, schools, synagogues, mosques, churches, retirement homes, hospitals, and even brothels had been turned into relief centers. And not just for the Jews; it seemed that all of Europe was flocking here. All he could do was to approach the search in a systematic way, and he started marking off the places he'd visited today, scribbling notes about each while he still remembered.

As he wrote, he noticed that the girl was sneaking sidelong glances at him. With her hands crossed over her lap and her shoulders hunched over, there was nothing in her body movements that could be construed as flirtatious. She had put down her book and was looking at the newspaper's society section. She seemed restless.

The waiter walked over and carefully placed Mickey's beer on the table. "A Stella for monsieur. And you, mademoiselle? Another *citron pressé?*"

The girl sat up straight and answered in perfectly accented French. "*Non, un verre de champagne, s'il vous plaît.*"

"It's bad luck to drink champagne alone," Mickey said. He raised his beer and took a swig directly from the bottle.

"Cheers," she said, raising her hand as if she were holding a glass.

"I'm glad to see your mood has brightened," he said. "When I first walked in and saw you reading the paper, I thought you were going to cry."

"It's the war," she said, "but since nobody around here seems to notice it, I've decided to forget about it too, at least for an hour."

There was something going on behind her pretty face. He put his pen down. "I can't figure it out," he said, turning toward her. "When I first arrived in Cairo, I wasn't sure what I was witnessing. Good God! The wolf, or let's say the Desert Fox, is practically at their door, yet they refuse to acknowledge it. They just bury their heads in the sand." He passed his fingers through his hair to push a lock away from his eyes and extended his hand. "I'm Mickey Connolly. I'm a reporter for the *Detroit Free Press*."

"I'm Maya," she said, shaking his hand. "Nice to meet you. Are you writing about the war?"

"I was," he said, "but like you, I'm taking a break from it. Censorship is making real reporting impossible. Not that I want to put a frown on your face, but the truth is that the situation is ten times worse than they're letting on. Not surprising, since the High Command wouldn't know how to fight their way out of a paper bag. But never mind, you and I are celebrating now, and everything is just dandy." He raised his beer bottle in a toast and saw a trace of a smile at the corners of her lips.

"A penny for your thoughts," he offered.

"You do look American!" she teased.

"I'm going to take that as a compliment."

"To America!" She raised the flute of champagne that the waiter had just brought.

He clicked her glass with his bottle and took a generous swig while she sipped her champagne, but he caught her grimacing at the taste.

"So . . . what's the latest scandal in Cairo's society?" He pointed to the paper.

She laughed apologetically. "It seems that husband-hunting is every girl's obsession right now."

Mickey leaned in closer and read out loud. "'Lucette Sapriel, Denise Harari, Mimi Wissa, Yvette Zarb. These ladies have now been transformed into Mrs. Makepeace, Mrs. Guysales, Mrs. Spider, and Lady Toplofty.' Wow, the most coveted prize these days appears to be a British officer. Oh, shucks," he snapped his fingers. "Guess I'm out of the running."

She smiled again, her eyes revealing a hidden glow. He noticed how perfectly her cheekbones were carved. "Do you have a cigarette, by any chance?" she asked.

Mickey patted his jacket pocket. Empty. "I'm out," he said. "Gave 'em away. Professional hazard. It seems everyone loves American cigs around here."

"I'm curious, Mr. Connolly, why would someone leave the comfort and safety of America to come here in these dangerous times?" She put her elbow on the table and held her chin in the palm of her hand, looking right at him and waiting for his answer.

"It's not really that interesting," he said, polishing off the last of his beer.

"Tell me."

"Another beer and champagne," he called to the waiter. "No, make that two champagnes."

"Tell me," she repeated, looking at him expectantly.

Their eyes locked for a long moment.

"Well, if you really want to know," he finally said, leaning a little closer to her. "Before joining the *Detroit Free Press* I worked at another paper for four years, writing obituaries and whatnot," he offered. "I realized it would take another ten years to get high enough on the ladder to be allowed to do anything meaty enough to write home about. By then I would be one of those sad men with a big belly and graying hair, wondering who stole his life. So I quit and here I am. Anything else you'd like to know, miss?"

"I'll work up a list!" she laughed. "I have to warn you, I'm a very curious girl. I even thought about becoming a journalist myself at one time, though it would have been easier had I been born a man."

"Now, that would have been a shame!" He flashed his best grin. "But there *are* women journalists, you know."

"Women here don't really work—that is, if they want to find a husband," she said, accepting the fresh glass of champagne the waiter had brought.

"Are you looking for a husband?"

"Not me! I wouldn't know what to do with one! Cheers!" She took a good sip.

"I gather you're not from around here. French?"

"Almost. I'm from Syria, a French colony. And you, if you're not writing about the war, what are you writing about?" she asked in the same breath, indicating the notebook he'd been working on.

"I'm doing a story on the Jewish community in Egypt that I think our readers back home would find interesting. We have a large Jewish population in Detroit, you know."

"No, I didn't know that," she said, lowering her eyes. "And what are you going to say about the Jews here?"

"That they have it pretty good," he casually said. "Compared to the Jews in Europe, I'd say that the North African Jews are in pretty good shape."

"I see," she challenged, "and what exactly do you know about the situation of the Jews in Algeria or Tunisia or Morocco?"

"Well, I said compared to Europe," Mickey said defensively. He thought he was just making an innocent comment. "I know from the massacre of Jews in Iraq last June that things are bad for them there, but—"

"Iraq is not part of North Africa," she cut him off. "Are you aware that the French colonies in North Africa are implementing Vichy's policies, only ten times worse? They are all Pétain's cohorts," she said with disgust. "We're not just talking about work restrictions and confiscation of property. Do you know that three hundred Algerian Jews have been placed in labor camps for opposing the establishment of a *Judenrat*, and more than five hundred have been sent to concentration camps in the south of the country?"

"What do you mean by concentration camps?"

"I mean they are being interned. Put behind barbed wire. Families broken up. Mothers crying, children lost. In Tunisia, Jews are forced to live under the same rules, and they have heavy financial penalties. In Morocco, the German army has turned synagogues into military storerooms. Why don't you write about that?"

He was taken aback by the look she gave him. "I'm really focusing on the Jews of Egypt, and—"

"But you just made a casual generalization about the Jews in North Africa that was entirely incorrect," she interrupted again. "You can't say such things in your article."

"I'm sorry. I didn't mean to sound glib, but the focus of my article is how the Jews here, in Egypt, are thriving. They've become an integral part of the infrastructure of this country. The government would never hand them over to the Germans like the other countries did."

"That's your American optimism," she said, straightening her posture. "I'd love to continue this conversation, but I've got to run. I'm sorry to have been so adamant. It's just that so little of this is covered by the press, and you in particular are in a position to . . . "

She didn't need to finish her sentence for Mickey to guess the rest of her thought. She didn't expect he'd do much to help.

She bent down to pick up her purse, but stood up abruptly, putting a hand to her head, her body swaying as if she were about to fall.

He grabbed her elbow. "Here. I have you."

"I'm just not used to drinking. I'll be fine."

"Sometimes it doesn't take much. I'll walk you out." Without giving her the chance to protest, he slipped his arm around her waist. "Where to?"

"The lift," she whispered.

As they approached the elevator in the lobby, the doors opened and a man greeted the girl as he stepped out. "Mademoiselle Levi! Your uncle is looking for you."

"Have a good evening," he said just before the doors closed.

She raised her hand and waved.

CHAPTER 8

Mickey hurried back to the Moorish Hall, feeling stupid for shooting his mouth off, but at least he knew the girl's name, Mademoiselle Maya Levi—a Jewish name. He wondered what her story was. She seemed to have liked him at first. He wished they could have talked more.

He strode into the cocktail lounge and scanned the room for Dorothy, but didn't see her. He suddenly realized he'd forgotten the refugee shelters list and rushed back to his table. Luckily, it was still there. It would have been a disaster had he lost it. He slipped the notebook into his jacket pocket and downed the rest of his champagne. As he did, he noticed a thin book peeking out from under the girl's newspaper on the banquette and picked it up. *Le Mur* (The Wall) by Jean-Paul Sartre. Hmm . . . in addition to being a knockout, she was smart. He shoved the book into his pocket, happy to have found an excuse to get in touch with her again.

Slowly, the sound of fingernails clicking persistently on glass drew his attention. It was Dorothy, sitting in a nearby alcove, nursing a martini and daintily smoking a cigarette, a bowl of pistachio shells in front of her. She waved at him, her lips pursed.

"You're late," she reprimanded as he approached her. "Even later than me. I hate waiting for a man."

"Sorry," Mickey said, letting out a sigh as he sat down. "I

was actually here early, but I had to help a young lady who wasn't feeling well."

"I bet you did," she replied, her tone friendlier. "Got a girl back home, slugger?"

Mickey pulled his chair closer to the table and shook his head. "Used to."

"You hold out for the right one. There should be a law against marriage before thirty. Take it from me," she said. Then, after looking him up and down, she exclaimed, "You look awful. Stop at Antoine's and get fitted for some new clothes. We'll pick up the tab. We can't have you running around looking like that."

He snapped his fingers to attract a passing waiter's attention and gave Dorothy a quick rundown of his last few days searching the city's shelters.

"Monsieur?" the waiter interrupted them.

"A beer please," Mickey ordered. He turned to Dorothy, checking her drink. "You're good?"

"For now." She put a refusing hand on top of her glass. "Go on."

"It ain't pretty, I have to tell you," Mickey continued. He shook his head as he thought about schools that had been converted into dormitories that reeked of urine. "But they have roofs over their heads and food for their bellies."

She downed the rest of her drink. "What are you going to do now?"

"I'll continue with the list, assuming Blumenthal is here in Cairo." He closed his eyes for an instant, feeling the fatigue of the day wash over him. His mood shifted.

"What's wrong?" Dorothy asked.

"I saw something upsetting today," he reflected. "I visited another side of the Jewish community—the old Jewish quarter, the *Hara*, as they call it. It's a far cry from the opera house. Abysmally poor and dirty, just as bad as the Arab neighborhoods of

Shubra or Bulaq. There was this kid in the street with hundreds of flies eating at the pus coming out of his eyes. He must have been blind. The mother did nothing to chase them away. Sometimes you wonder—"

"Your beer, sir," the waiter interrupted. "A fresh one for madame?"

"Why not?" Dorothy passed him her empty glass.

Mickey resumed. "I had an interesting conversation with the rabbi of the Ashkenazi synagogue over there. He said there is an international organization against anti-Semitism, known as LICA, which had once set up a branch to resettle refugees from Germany here in Cairo. It turns out that this branch in Cairo was very short-lived. "

"How come?" Dorothy asked.

"The rabbi wouldn't say. But I find it strange that they shut themselves down at the height of the Jewish exodus in '38. LICA has a branch in New York. Maybe you can find out why the Cairo branch closed, and who its members were," he said, picking out the few remaining pistachios.

"Sure thing," she said, lighting a cigarette. "Now let me update you on the immigration policies you asked about." She blew a thin stream of smoke over her shoulder. "It's very simple. Nobody wants the Jewish refugees." She looked at her notes. "Listen to this. Australia's prime minister says, and I quote: 'We don't have a Jew problem and we do not want one.' The US State Department has come up with all kinds of obstacles to prevent their admittance, saying they're communist agitators, they'll be a burden on the state, and so on. Britain claims to have no room for large-scale immigration, but that country's hardly a safe haven anyway with all the bombs falling. As for the rest of the Americas—Peru, Nicaragua, Honduras, Costa Rica, Mexico—they won't take any Jews at all. It's pretty much the same in Brazil and Argentina, where boats carrying hundreds of Jewish passengers were prohibited from landing and quarantined as if they carried the plague. They were sent back to Germany, where God knows what happened to them. We did the same thing, you know. You remember the SS *St. Louis* a few years ago when the US denied landing to a ship full of European Jews, causing a furor among American Jewish groups?"

Mickey nodded yes.

"In fact, China, is the only country with a real open-door policy for Jews," she resumed.

"What about Palestine?" Mickey asked. "Is there any way to get around the immigration restrictions in the White Papers?"

"It's tight as a drum," she said, taking a sip of her fresh drink. "To appease the Arabs, the English are enforcing the restrictions with an iron fist. They're afraid of riots like they had in '36. Just last week a ship with fifty Jewish French passengers left Istanbul for Palestine. Supposedly they all carried visas, but when they arrived they were interned by the British." She gave him a tight smile. "Apparently a group of militant Arabs promised to slaughter any Jews that stepped off the boat."

Mickey rubbed his temples. "What are they going to do with them?"

"Probably send them to Mauritius until things cool down a bit. This kind of stuff never makes the papers."

"Maybe Blumenthal could slip into Palestine illegally, through the desert?"

"You're talking about a brutal journey on the back of a camel in scorching heat. Only a Bedouin could bear it. And going by sea is out. The English blockade would grab him in a minute."

He bit his lip and shook his head. She was right—the odds of the scientist getting into Palestine were a long shot. Besides, according to the rabbi at the Ashkenazi synagogue, Jews were now leaving Palestine because of Arab violence and coming here.

"You turned up a lot of good information, *Miss* Calley."

"I just try to do my job," she said, a smirk on her lips as she crossed her legs. She blew a smoke ring in his face.

"You enjoy this, don't you?" he asked playfully, knowing better than to rise to the bait.

"Immensely," she admitted with a devilish smile.

"Is this how you got that information, by flirting?"

Dorothy's laughter echoed through the hall, drawing disapproving stares. "Hardly, darling. I only use that weapon when I have to. Actually, our COI agent in Tel Aviv gave us the scoop." She lifted a shopping bag full of papers from beside her chair and set it on her lap. "Okay, and now," she chirped, "it's reading time. Here are the newspapers you asked for—*La Tribune Juive, Israel, L'Aurore* . . . " She piled the papers, about two dozen of them, on the table one by one. "Greek, Italian, and French press—*Kathimerini, La Stampa, Ce Soir* . . . Happy reading," she said, dusting off her hands.

"You've really held up your end," Mickey said. "I hope I can do mine, but I keep feeling there's more to this puzzle. Didn't Donovan mention that Einstein was working on weapons?"

"Submarines," she corrected. "I don't know the details and even if I did, I don't think I would understand them."

"Have you contacted Blumenthal's colleagues from the Paris Group yet?"

"We can't do that. They've escaped to England, and Donovan won't risk alerting the British authorities about COI activities."

She started gathering her things, then leaned forward. "You were right, Connolly, the Germans had Panzer IVs," she said in a low conspiratorial voice. "They had been spotted being moved to the front, but High Command ignored the report." She took a deep breath. "The Brits can't afford more of these kinds of blunders or they can kiss the Suez Canal good-bye."

"And all of North Africa as well. The Germans will end up with complete control over the Mediterranean," Mickey added, his mind reeling with the consequences of losing this vital supply route.

"What a nightmare," she sighed. "Anyhow, I've got to go. The kings of Greece and Yugoslavia just arrived and the British Embassy is overflowing with dignitaries. They've asked us if we could house a few."

The sound of laughter and breaking glass spilled from the doors of the Long Bar. Dorothy rolled her eyes. "Boys will be boys," she pronounced as she snuffed out her cigarette. "I need to get home to my kitty. She's waiting for me to feed her. A pure Russian Blue, the sweetest thing you've ever seen." She got up.

Mickey gallantly rose to his feet.

She quickly assessed him top to bottom once again, saying nothing this time but shaking her head in disapproval at his choice of attire. As she walked away, she put an extra swing in her step for the soldiers exiting the Long Bar.

When Mickey returned to the Immobilia it was dark, and Hosni had gone home for the evening. The night doorman gave him a note that had been left for him.

> I'm back in Cairo on leave. Let's get together for beers, birds, and bloody fantastic lies about our sex lives.

It was from Hugh, who'd left a number where he could be reached. Hooray! Finally, he'd get to see his good buddy. It was too bad he wouldn't be able to tell him he had a gig as a spy. They would have shared a good laugh over that.

He loosened his tie as he dragged himself into his apartment. He was tired, dirty, and smelly from his day. He emptied his pockets, threw his change on the table, and opened the book that belonged to the girl from the Shepheard's. On the front page was an inscription in sprawling letters: "*Chérie, nourritures de l'esprit. On en parlera Lundi. Bisous* (Darling, food for thought. Let's talk on Monday. Kisses)." It was signed Jean-Jacques. A boyfriend, he assumed, and he wondered how serious they were. He flipped through the pages, stopping to read one of the passages she'd underlined:

> My body, I saw with its eyes, I heard with its ears, but it was no longer me: it sweated and trembled by itself and I didn't recognize it any more. I had to touch it and look at it to find out what was happening, as if it were the body of someone else.

Hmm . . . More underlinings revealed the same morbidity. He brought the book to his nose, seeking the girl's scent, but it smelled only of mildew, and he tossed it on the table. "She's definitely worth a further look," he confirmed to himself. He would ask the manager of the hotel about her. She shouldn't be too hard to find. "If you don't step up to the plate and swing, you never get any hits," he told himself.

After a vigorous shower, he felt refreshed in mind and body. He settled into the plush, oversized armchair that took up a good part of the living room, put his feet up on a pouf, and luxuriated. Splashed with cologne and wrapped in the cotton bathrobe he'd found at the Khan el-Khalili bazaar, he felt like a new man.

With the door to the balcony opened wide to the balmy night air, he started poring over the Jewish newspapers. To his surprise, most stories dealt with picnics, canoe trips, tennis matches, dance contests, and marriage announcements, amid large advertisements for local businesses—as if the plight of their brethren in Europe did not exist.

The few references to the war consisted of appeals for volunteers and contributions to the Comfort Fund for Jewish Soldiers, or the Jewish Welfare Committee for Sailors, Soldiers, and Airmen.

He did learn, however, that King Farouk, the king of Egypt, was lending his yacht to B'nai B'rith for a fund-raising ball at the end of the month. This struck Mickey as a very friendly gesture, and further evidence of a strong connection between Egypt and its Jewish community. Another article about the Chief Rabbi of Egypt, a former member of the Egyptian Senate, declaring in a speech to Parliament the unfailing loyalty of Egypt's Jews to their government, confirmed such closeness.

Nevertheless, Mickey could see that the Jews were still defining themselves as a people separate from the Egyptians. The front page of *L'Aurore* bore an inscription printed in small letters next to the newspaper's name:

> I am Jewish. I accept this designation, which for some means an insult but which I want to make a title of glory.

The publisher had signed his name beneath it.

An open letter from Simon Cattaoui, the president of the community, piqued his interest, inasmuch as it appeared in several of the papers. Cattaoui was appealing to his fellow Jews to remain calm and not to participate in the riots or to make charges of anti-Semitism against the *Banque de France* over their firing of a longtime Jewish employee. "As mature citizens of this country, we must do our share to keep Egypt stable in these uncertain times," he'd written.

Where's this guy's spine, Mickey wondered, and he was pleased to read that a lawyer was threatening to file an action against the bank for the firing.

It was close to midnight when Mickey finished reading. In his bedroom, he retrieved the photo of Erik Blumenthal from his wallet.

It was a group picture torn from a page in a science journal dated June 1934. He studied it for a long moment. Blumenthal, whose face was circled in ink, was awkward looking and had big teeth and fleshy lips. He put it on his nightstand and clicked off the light, but as he lay under the cool sheets, his mind wandered back to the photograph. He sat up and turned on the light. Why was Blumenthal the only one seated while women and elderly men were standing?

CHAPTER 9

The only decoration in Dr. Massoud's austere sitting room was the calligraphic mantra, written in gold above the entry door, *There is no God but Allah and Mohammed is his prophet*, but Kesner barely noticed it, even though his gaze was intently focused on the wooden door. It was early in the morning, before patients would arrive, and Abdoul Nukrashi was late again. How could the Arabs expect to govern themselves if they couldn't even once be on time? He was steaming. He had a pressing agenda to discuss with the king's public relations minister today, then more meetings all over the city as he sought to pick up Blumenthal's trail after missing him in Alexandria. He couldn't forgive himself for having arrived there late, after the passengers on the *El Aziz* had disembarked. Those damned roadblocks that the British had put up overnight. What would the SS think of him now? He was desperate to redeem himself. He had to calm himself down. Sooner or later he would catch the Jew.

He pressed the pleats along his gray flannel slacks tightly and adjusted his tweed jacket and the collar of his starched white shirt. With a smart-looking tarbush on his head, he was confident he conjured the perfect image of a Westernized Egyptian man of means.

It was nearly seven o'clock and Abdoul was still not here. Soon patients would be flocking in, and Kesner knew that this would make Dr. Massoud nervous. At the request of Sheik Hassan al-Banna, the leader of the Muslim Brotherhood who was currently in prison, the doctor, a devout supporter of the organization, had made his *mafraj*, the sitting room behind his office, available to Kesner for clandestine meetings and message drop-offs. "He is a foreigner, but his people will liberate us from the English infidels," the sheik had said when he'd introduced the doctor to Kesner. "I am a peaceful man," the doctor had explained as he shook Kesner's hand. "But it is time for us to return to Islam. They are making whores out of our daughters, and change will only come through the barrel of a gun."

Finally Kesner heard the clunk and thud of heavy feet climbing the stairs to the waiting room. Abdoul puffed and panted as he opened the door, conspicuous in his gaudy, silk-tasseled tarbush, pearl stickpin, and patent leather spats. With his belly protruding in front and his hunchback jutting out behind, the corpulent man was grotesque. Kesner felt a surge of disgust, which metamorphosed into pity as he watched the man traverse the waiting room. He gave Kesner a foolishly obvious nod before disappearing behind the curtain.

The Arab was pathetic. He was a nobody who'd gained his position in the palace through his friendship with King Farouk's Italian barber. But it was under Kesner's tutelage, urging him to have the king make radio addresses and otherwise reach out to his people, that Abdoul had been able to transform his insignificant post into one of the most powerful in the king's cabinet. As Farouk became hailed as a man of the people and his popularity soared, so did Abdoul's arrogance. Kesner had to suffer the vanity of this pathetic Quasimodo, but he reminded himself that Abdoul was a loyal dog for the Reich and, as Kesner's eyes and ears in the palace, one of his most crucial informants.

He picked up his black crocodile attaché case and followed

Abdoul behind the curtain and down the dark narrow corridor to the mafraj.

"S'aalam alekoum," Abdoul rasped upon seeing Kesner walk in, his words echoing off the high ceiling of the room. "*Ezayak ya akhooya*? (How are you, my brother?) Are you well?" The fat man embraced and kissed Kesner several times.

Not one for physical contact, Kesner nevertheless hugged the man back, albeit stiffly. "How is your family?" he inquired in flawless Arabic.

"Very good, very good, thanks be to God," Abdoul answered, collapsing onto one of the colorful floor cushions that lined the mafraj.

"Thanks be to God," Kesner replied, settling down across from him, a large copper tray supported by bamboo sticks separating them. "You have done good work." He pulled out yesterday's *El Misr* and *Daily Telegraph*, Egypt's most widely circulated newspapers, from his attaché case and waved them at Abdoul.

"Very good work," he reiterated. "Was it twenty thousand shoes the king distributed?" he inquired, amused at how Abdoul had followed almost to the letter his suggestion that Farouk make this kind of grand gesture to the poor.

"Twenty thousand *pairs* of new shoes," Abdoul corrected, as he pulled an ebony cigarette holder from his jacket and extracted a thin, tan cigarette. "God knows prices have doubled in the last year alone. Such a dreadful situation. Ah, but there is only so much one can do."

"Thanks be to God, the king is a kind man, but he is only as good as his most trusted advisor," Kesner flattered him. "The king is still a boy."

"Why, Herr Kesner, that is most kind of you," Abdoul bowed his head in a show of modesty. "Do you notice anything different about the king?" He pointed to the photographs of the king in the backseat of his open-topped Mercedes, a birthday gift from Hitler that graced the front pages of the two newspapers.

"He looks dashing in his white military uniform, most royal," Kesner replied, scrutinizing the photo, but not knowing where this was leading.

"Look more closely," Abdoul gushed, his face glistening with pride like a child showing a good report card to his parents. "The king is growing a beard. I thought there was no harm in having him looking more pious. The Muslim Brotherhood is growing more popular. The country is growing more religious. A ruler who wants to stay in power . . . "

" . . . is a ruler who knows how to manipulate the masses," Kesner finished the sentence. "I must say, that is quite an inspired move, something reminiscent of Goebbels himself." He had dropped the magic name.

Abdoul blushed. "Thank you, but you are too generous. Did you notice the faces of the fellahin?" He pointed at the newspaper photos again, eager for more praise. "Don't they gaze adoringly at their king?"

"Yes, they do. Perhaps the king should increase the number of his radio addresses and press conferences." Kesner paused and drew a breath before continuing. "I wish you could have known how it felt to hear our führer's voice coming from the radio, strong but calming, lifting our spirits, reminding us of our heritage and our right to reclaim it. Your people need that same hope. They need their king to take back their country and restore their pride. And you, my friend, are the man to make it happen. Because of you the king will take his rightful place in history."

Abdoul leaned against the wall, a coy smile on his lips.

"Riri Charbit," Kesner started, turning to his real agenda, now that he had Abdoul where he wanted him. "She is a very pro-English girl. I see that the king is accompanying her to a lot of tea parties for British officers. This is not good." He frowned.

Abdoul sighed deeply and shook his head as if this were a great sorrow to him. "The woman has put a spell on him. What an embarrassment to his poor wife. The king is making a fool of himself. They frolic naked in the palace pool in front of his staff!"

Kesner clicked his tongue in disapproval. "Yes, we have to get him away from this girl. Maybe a nice curvy redhead will do the trick. Our friend Madame Samina can help find one." He winked at Abdoul, who smiled an oily grin. The Lebanese-born dancer had introduced the two men to each other.

"I saw her last night . . . after hours," Abdoul whispered, his eyes sparkling with mischief. He chuckled like a randy schoolboy.

"Are you insinuating . . . " Kesner began, playing along, although he was sure the man was lying. Samina swore she never slept with her clients, but one never knew with women, especially one who liked money so much.

"Come now, I am a man of discretion," Abdoul winked. "I will do what I can to undercut the influence of this Riri."

"I am confident you will." Kesner smiled benevolently and quietly dropped the bombshell. "We must get Sheik Hassan al-Banna out of jail. Without him the Brotherhood is useless."

As expected, Abdoul's instinctive fear of sticking his neck out drained the color from his face as he shot up straight on his cushion. "That is not possible. The compound in Qena is meticulously guarded by the British army."

"We must be bold. I haven't fully thought it through yet, but we will need the cooperation of the Egyptian military police," Kesner asserted. "Any news on your side?"

Abdoul shifted in his seat, pouting, while he lit another cigarette. He took a deep drag and bravely regained his composure. "The British have taken over our radio stations in Siwa and Gazala, calling them strategic assets. Sadly, Parliament is too cowardly to do anything about it. But," he continued, "you'll be interested to know that the British ambassador is talking about evacuation plans for the wives and children of senior officers. The English finally seem to realize they are in trouble." He drew in another puff and daintily exhaled.

"The English will be thrashed, no doubt," Kesner asserted. "We have Egypt surrounded and victory is inevitable. If they are smart, the British will get out of our way, or we will chop them up like we did the Belgians." He rubbed his hands together. "Please tell the king that Rommel looks forward to meeting him when he arrives in Cairo."

"And Rommel will receive a hero's welcome when he gets here," Abdoul promised. "It will be the king's pleasure to give him a personal tour of the city."

"Excellent! Your efforts on behalf of the Reich will not go unrewarded." Kesner rose to his feet and grabbed Abdoul tightly by the elbow, effortlessly helping the fat man to his feet. He knew he was strong in a way that men respected in one another. "One last thing, though—a Jew by the name of Erik Blumenthal arrived in Alexandria on a Turkish ship about ten days ago. He has polio and walks with a limp. The Reich would be most grateful if you could uncover his whereabouts."

"Blumenthal," Abdoul repeated, memorizing the name. "Blumenthal."

Kesner rushed back to his houseboat and stepped on his foredeck. There was still time for him to catch the American morning communiqué, which he'd already missed twice this week. He entered the living room and quickly descended the spiral staircase to his bedroom, locking the door behind him. He needed to get to his radio transmitter as soon as possible; his watch read 9:12.

Ten minutes later, Kesner emerged with a transcript of the US communiqué that he'd intercepted just in time. He lit up a Corona, the most expensive Egyptian cigarette, and grabbed Daphne Du Maurier's *Rebecca,* the codebook used by the Americans. He propped himself up on his bed, ready to decipher the message.

At first, nothing dramatic was revealed—only some details about the tonnage of ships passing through the Suez Canal and descriptions of recent damage inflicted by the Luftwaffe's bombing raids on Alexandria. But then he sat up, his eyes growing wider as he made out the message.

> Crossing our fingers regarding our new recruit on the Blumenthal matter.

Kesner let his hand drop to his side as he digested this news. The Americans were looking for the Jew, too! A few seconds later he bolted from his bed and hurried back to his transmitter. The SS needed to be notified immediately of this. Black Dog was going to be back in their good graces.

CHAPTER 10

"*Sambousseks, boyos,* and *pasteles,*" Joe Levi exclaimed as he proudly pointed out some of the appetizers, or *mezzes*, as Allegra called the huge assortment she'd placed on the living room coffee table. "This one has cheese, this one spinach, and this one ground beef."

Maya wasn't very hungry, and she knew that the lunch that awaited them was a bigger meal than dinner in this household, and it would be at least three courses. Why was Allegra always overdoing it? She knew that Maya was a light eater, and it was apparent that Erik, despite his attempts to hide it, despised Middle Eastern cuisine. Only Vati indulged himself at mealtimes, particularly since Joe had reassured him that the meat in their home was kosher.

Feeling obligated, Maya tendered her blue porcelain plate to Joe, who had just arrived and was still wearing his seersucker suit jacket and his tarbush. "Just one of each," she requested.

A short man with a friendly face and twinkling, warm brown eyes, Joe had greeted them at the train station in Cairo when Maya and her family first arrived with a big "S'aalam alekoum," his arms wide open. He had indicated that he was only peripherally involved with the people who were helping them obtain their papers, but he was honored to open his home to the family. She had liked and trusted him immediately. He'd been nothing but generous and had even taken a day off from work to drive them past the pyramids.

"The children are washing their hands before sitting down," Allegra announced as she joined them. She was a good six inches taller than her husband, which made for an endearing sight when he rose on the tips of his toes to greet his wife with a kiss on the cheek.

"I saw the news in the paper," she said to no one in particular as she prepared a plate for herself and sat down next to her husband, who habitually brought the newspapers home at lunch for her to see. "Kiev has fallen. How terrible."

"Kiev?" Vati repeated, swallowing hard.

"The Russians admitted taking a heavy blow, but there are no official details," Joe said, removing his jacket and hat. "There are reports that the SS murdered twelve hundred Jewish women and children there."

Vati's face turned ashen.

"My father still has family in Kiev," Erik explained.

"But I thought you were German," Joe said.

"Vater was born in Russia. As a child he fled the pogroms with his family and took refuge in Germany," Maya offered.

"Maya," Vati said as he reached for her on the chair next to him, his hand shaking slightly. "We must go to the synagogue to light candles for the dead."

Joe stood up and kneeled in front of her father, taking his hands in his own. "We Jews are safe here in Egypt, monsieur," he said firmly, his eyes slowly sliding to Maya and Erik. He was addressing them, too.

Joe had made that point several times, and from the way he filled the house with Maurice Chevalier's happy tunes, such as *Y'a d'la Joie,* (All Is Wonderful), he must truly believe it, Maya thought.

Vati nodded slowly like an obedient child, a meek smile on his lips.

"That's better," Joe exclaimed with enthusiasm. "Now, what about trying some of these mezzes?"

Allegra sprang to her feet and took Vati's plate, filling it with a choice selection, while Joe returned to his seat.

Whether he'd suddenly forgotten about his cousins in Kiev or was just humoring his hosts, Vati took his plate and proclaimed, "This is the best food I've had in *months*."

"Monsieur Blumenthal, I know you told me you didn't like to talk about your days in Germany, and I don't mean to press you," Joe said, "but we can be better friends if we can understand a little more about you."

Maya threw a disconcerted look at her father. She knew that sooner or later they would have to divulge some information about the family's ordeal—that was the price to pay for receiving help—but she wished it wouldn't be just yet. The memories were still too raw.

"It is painful," she admitted. "But we can talk about it with you."

"When did you leave Germany?" Allegra promptly inquired as she sat down.

"Our parents left too late," Erik answered, almost by reflex, using his fork to poke at the slices of pickled lemons adorning the plate on his lap. "They waited until the fall of 1937."

"They were well connected in the community and were confident they would be protected," Maya added softly, trying to remain detached.

"I was sure it would all pass," Vati said. "And I was able to get work at the Kubu in Frankfurt as a conductor after I was fired from the Düsseldorf Opera."

"The *Kubu*?" Allegra asked, leaning forward to hear better.

"The *Kulturbund,*" Vati explained. "It was an organization of Jewish artists that was allowed by the Nazis to perform in public, but only in front of Jewish audiences."

"This was to show the world that they were not completely intolerant of Jews," Erik added.

"As if the world really cared," Maya heard herself muttering.

"They began to put all kinds of silly restrictions on the Kubu as time went on," Vati shrugged. "They policed our recitals and then ruled that only Jewish works could be performed. By the end we were not even allowed to utter the word 'blond,' because that was deemed an insult to the Aryan trait. Can you believe such nonsense?" He waved his hand dismissively, indicating that he didn't want to talk about it anymore. "When they shut the Kubu down, I knew it was time to leave."

Maya didn't contradict her father, but she knew that this had not been the final straw. That had been the garbage truck humiliation.

"You went from there to Paris?" Allegra asked.

"Yes. Erik was already there," Maya replied on behalf of her father, "and Paris was full of opportunities for musicians."

"It was good for Maya, too," Erik offered. "She had gone to a French boarding school in Geneva and speaks with a true French accent."

"And then you had to flee again," Allegra said sympathetically. "And your poor mother? That was her violin, wasn't it?"

Maya looked down at her white socks. She was not going to describe how her mother had coughed up blood for the last time on the day the Germans had entered Paris, succumbing finally to her tuberculosis. They had fled the capital that very day, but missed the ship bound for England that the British Embassy had chartered to give scientists like Erik refuge there.

"It all fell apart when Paris was invaded," Maya said. "You must have read about the chaos and hysteria that followed when people tried to leave the city." That's all she was willing to say.

"I think the radio said there were seven million people on the roads that day," Joe recalled.

Maya couldn't go down this path. Perhaps it was the hot bath that she'd taken earlier, but she felt too exhausted to withstand further questioning. She was about to excuse herself to go to the bathroom when the Levis' four young boys ran into the room, showing their clean hands to their mother. Fresh faced and energetic, they were still dressed in their school uniforms—ties and jackets.

Maya saw Vati staring at the crests on their uniforms. He'd been shocked when he'd learned that these Jewish children were attending a French Jesuit school. He had not accepted Allegra's claim that the school provided the most disciplined and best education in Cairo, nor Joe's rationalization that religion was learned in the home, and that he, too, had attended a Catholic school as a child.

"We've set Loulou's Bar Mitzvah for next May," Joe said proudly of his oldest son. "He's been studying for it all summer. Say something in Hebrew," he urged the boy.

Loulou blushed and shyly recited the first few words of the Shabbat prayer, struggling with his pronunciation.

Vati corrected him until he repeated it to his satisfaction. "You must let me help him with his Hebrew," he said to Joe. "And most importantly do not let him abandon his Jewish studies after his Bar Mitzvah as I did with my son."

To Maya's relief, Erik, who'd become an ardent atheist, did not rise to take the bait.

Lunch was served with the same panache as the appetizers, but now the endless array of dishes was brought, one at a time, by the family's longtime Egyptian house servant, Sayeda, an older woman with a large mole under her nose that distracted only slightly from her sweet smile. The meal started with a hearty soup that Maya had never tasted before and that was impossible to pronounce.

Melokhia was full of unfamiliar spices and made with dark green leaves, like gelatinous spinach, and chunks of beef. Erik wouldn't go near it, nor did he touch the chicken and peas with turmeric that followed, or the meat and vegetable dish that came after that. As always, every dish was served with rice. Even dessert included a rice pudding. Maya dutifully tried to taste everything, but was beginning to suffer from all the obligations that came with being a guest, including having to make small talk.

After discussing the price of meat in Cairo, which had skyrocketed because it could no longer be imported, and the recipe used by Vati's mother to make Erik's favorite potato latkes, Joe started to quiz the children about their schoolwork.

An accountant at Cairo's finest hotel, Joe placed a high value on education, and he insisted that his children would do even better than he had. Loulou would be a doctor, Mimi an architect, Zazi a businessman, and their six-year-old, Soussou, a lawyer. The little one, however, protested, saying that when he grew up he wanted to be a singer and play the violin like Father Thibault in their church choir. This brought a raised eyebrow from Vati. Careers for girls, on the other hand, were frowned upon, and Allegra quickly dismissed the boys' suggestion that their sister, Lili, would make a great seamstress.

"Princess Lili has arrived," Joe grumbled as the sound of keys fumbling rattled the door.

Looking voluptuous in her tennis whites, Lili sauntered into the dining room. Her hair was pulled back, accentuating her smoky eyes. She raised her racquet in triumph. "I won. Three to one. School let out early, so I stole a game at the club."

"You just missed lunch, missy," Joe reprimanded loudly.

Lili rushed to her father, smacked a loud kiss on top of his head, shutting him up, and went around the table kissing everybody on the cheek. She was a mountain of energy.

"Roommate!" Lili wrapped her arms around Maya and pulled a chair next to her. "I hope I didn't snore last night."

"No, but you walked in your sleep," Maya said. "Just kidding!"

Lili laughed and turned to her mother with an urgent question. "Mamie, did my copy of *Marie Claire* arrive yet?"

Embarrassed, Maya hastened to answer first. "Yes, and I've been flipping through it. I hope you don't mind."

"Of course not." Lili took Maya's hand in hers. "Last month I saw the most beautiful wedding dress there. Did I tell you that's where I want to get married—Paris?"

"Are you getting married?" Vati inquired, refilling his glass with the wine on the table.

"Heavens, no. I'm only eighteen, monsieur."

"You're *already* eighteen," Allegra corrected. "At your age, I was married and big with you." She gestured toward her belly.

But Lili chose not to dignify her mother's comment with a response and turned back to Maya. She pushed a strand of hair away from Maya's face. "You really should let me do your hair and makeup one day. Isn't she so pretty?" Lili gushed.

"She's beautiful," Soussou, the little one, agreed.

"You have to watch out for the boys in this country," Joe said.

"They stick like olive oil!" Allegra added.

Maya let her hair fall back over her face. She used to enjoy compliments, basking in that luscious tickle that made her feel like she owned the world. But now, they sounded patronizing to her. She knew she looked awful. It should be obvious to everyone that she was in mourning, that her fate had been sealed, and that she was destined to be the mother to both her brother and her father.

"Maya looks like our mother," Erik said, shoving a piece of pita bread into his mouth, the only thing on the table he would eat.

"That's not true," Maya protested, though she wished it were. With her flaming red hair and almond-shaped green eyes, her mother had been a legendary beauty in Düsseldorf. At least Maya had inherited her oval face and the cleft in her chin. She had to settle for much duller hair and ordinary green eyes.

"We used to say that Maya had the beauty of her mother and the charm of her father, but that was when father was more charming," Erik remarked, winking at his sister, and drawing some laughter.

What was the matter with Erik? Couldn't he see that she was squirming inside? Uncomfortable at being the center of attention, she changed the subject and said, "I see Yom Kippur will be arriving early this year."

"Yom Kippur is my favorite holiday," Lili said with conviction. "No breads, no sweets. Nothing to eat at all. The only day of the year that I'm sure to lose weight. I think God created it for us women."

Maya cringed, anticipating her father's reaction to Lili's superficial remark.

"Yom Kippur is the holiest of our holidays," Vati said solemnly, almost choking on his wine. He put the glass down and turned to Loulou. "Now I have a holiday question for the Bar Mitzvah boy. You know what Passover is about, right?"

"It's when you eat matzo?" Loulou hazarded.

Joe rushed to answer for him. "Passover is to remind the Jews of their exodus from slavery in Egypt and of their deliverance by God to the Promised Land."

"And who is the oldest character in the Bible?" Vati asked the boy, holding up his hand to prevent Joe from interceding again.

The boy's eyes went wide with panic.

"Come now, Loulou, you know this," his father encouraged.

"Jesus?" he ventured timidly.

Vati squeezed his eyes shut in frustration, and when he reopened them, he didn't look at the boy. Instead he stared glacially at Joe. He set his napkin down. "I slept badly last night. I am very tired," he said. "I need to go to my room." He stood up, holding the table for support.

Allegra rose, her cheeks blushing but her manner still polite. "Please stay. We have coffee yet to come."

"I'm sorry, I must rest," Vati said and left the room.

There was a long, awkward silence. Mortified, Maya didn't dare look up.

Breaking the tension, Erik turned to Soussou, seated next to him, and said, "What do we have here?" He leaned forward and produced a coin from behind the boy's ear.

"How did you do that?" Soussou asked, wide-eyed.

"Magic!" Erik said. "Now watch this."

While the children sat transfixed, Erik placed the coin on top of his hand and began to cover it with his handkerchief.

Maya was grateful to Erik for containing the damage Vati had done. She looked from Allegra to Joe and wiped the corner of her mouth with her napkin. She excused herself and followed her father.

When she entered his room she found him carefully smoothing his prayer shawl on the bed.

"How can you be so rude to the people who are helping us?" she demanded, biting hard on her lower lip to calm the fury she felt inside.

"The boy wants to sing in the church choir. He probably knows his catechism by heart!"

"It's none of our business how they educate their children."

"I think it is, when they have a daughter who appreciates Yom Kippur as a diet day. 'Religion is learned in the home!' Ha! And what a bourgeois the mother is."

"Bourgeois!" Maya felt the blood rushing to her head; she could barely contain herself. "She could not be more gracious. Look at the meals she's served us."

"Cooked by her servant, no doubt."

The door suddenly opened and Erik entered. "What was *that* about?" he demanded between clenched teeth. "We can't fight you and the world at the same time."

Vati did not answer and resumed smoothing his prayer shawl. His eyelids almost covered his eyes, which were small and frightened.

Maya sighed, resigned. "He drank wine and he's tired, Erik."

"We are all tired," Erik replied.

Maya picked up her father's prayer shawl and moved toward the door. "I'll iron it later."

These clashes with Vati exhausted her. She had stopped in the hallway to compose herself when she heard the hushed voices of Allegra and Joe drifting in from the kitchen. They were arguing.

"Would you help me, please?" Lili appeared at the end of the corridor, dragging an enormous cloth bag.

Maya rushed to help her, and together they emptied the brimming bag's contents onto Lili's bed—well-worn uniform pants and jackets from the Free French army. Many were missing buttons, some had broken zippers, and most had tears.

"I'll be sewing until late tonight," Lili apologized. "I hope the light doesn't bother you."

Maya didn't know what to say. She'd been so quick to judge this girl. Now she just wanted to hug her. She sat down on Lili's bed and pulled a jacket from the pile. Its collar was torn. "It will go faster if I help you," she said. "And I can tell you about Paris."

As they began to sort out the work, the door opened a crack and Joe peeked in. He was holding Maya's lost copy of *The Wall*.

"An American gave me this for you. There's an envelope inside."

CHAPTER 11

In the small foyer of the Daher orphan asylum, simply furnished with a wooden desk, two chairs, and a worn oriental rug, Mickey handed the superintendent the photo of Erik Blumenthal. The little man studied it carefully, his sad eyes rendered even sadder by his shabby gray suit. His wife, a full-breasted, dark-haired woman, pressed close against him to look.

"A German Jew," Mickey explained. "The people at the Ben Ezra Synagogue said you'd taken in some families from Western Europe."

"Not so. Who told you that? The five families we have all come from Yemen. I don't recognize him."

"In Yemen they beat Jews just for passing on the right side of a Muslim," his wife whispered to Mickey indignantly as she looped her arm around her husband's for protection.

Mickey folded the photo back into his wallet. He'd spent over two weeks searching in vain and felt enormously frustrated. But he nodded politely and thanked the couple for their time. On his way out he almost stumbled over a long line of shoes against the outside wall. Somehow he hadn't noticed them when coming in. There were about twenty pairs, most of them badly worn, and he surmised they belonged to the arrivals from Yemen. There was a poignancy about them, as if they told the whole miserable tale of the people who wore them. How many miles had they walked? It seemed fitting that these shoes had wound up at an orphanage.

The giggling of two girls in the courtyard caught his attention. They were hopping over a simple hopscotch pattern, their dark braids flying high. Wherever there is laughter, life can flourish, he thought.

As he started down the narrow street, surprisingly dark because of the clotheslines that hung between balconies, obstructing the sun, he heard someone calling after him.

"Mister, mister, wait up."

Mickey turned to see a young man in a pristine white suit running toward him.

"My uncle is the superintendent of the orphanage," he said. "He told me you are writing about the Jews here and are looking for a certain refugee from Germany."

"Yes, I am."

"My name is Bernard Agami. I work at the UK General Electric Company, and a German Jewish engineer has just joined us. His name is Hans Nissel."

A ray of hope. Mickey hastily pulled out the picture of Blumenthal.

"Not him. Sorry."

"I'm sorry too, but maybe he could be of help. How long ago did Mr. Nissel join you?"

"Three months maybe."

"Straight from Europe?"

"I don't know. He's not very talkative."

Mickey mulled this over for an instant. "I'd still like to meet him," he said, wanting to learn how Nissel got here and who might have helped him.

"The company is in the Coptic part of the city, right off Mari Girgis ferry station," the young man offered. "It's best to go by river bus.

It's easy to get lost here. I'll walk you to the station if you're ready to go now. I'm sure Mr. Nissel will want to help his fellow Ashkenazim. They're a little out of place here. Many of us tried to sponsor German families, but internal politics made that impossible."

"Are you talking about LICA?"

"Yes! How did you know?" The young man's face was animated. "My father was a volunteer for LICA here in Cairo."

"Why did they stop helping? No one seems to be able to explain this."

"It was because of the teachers' union. It was four years ago. I was just graduating from the *lycée*."

"The teachers' union?" Mickey asked incredulously.

"That's right," Bernard confirmed. "They were afraid that Jewish teachers with better education and European credentials would put them out of work. Then the other unions started worrying, too. Even the king got involved and asked the president of our community center to intervene and put a stop to the resettlement."

"Mr. Cattaoui?"

"Yes, he wanted to have good relations with the king. You already know a lot about us," Bernard said.

Now Mickey began to understand why nobody wanted to talk about this. "So Cairo's Jewish community closed its doors to its German brothers?"

"Well, yes," Bernard conceded, "but we didn't just abandon them. We raised money to send them to Palestine instead. Please be fair to us. We did our best."

"Don't worry. I think your community is holding up remarkably well in the face of current circumstances, and I will say so in my article." Mickey shook hands with him and thanked him as they arrived at the river station.

"We take a lesson from the Sufis," Bernard grinned. "'Dance, when you're broken. Dance, if you've torn the bandage off. Dance, in the middle of the fighting. Dance, when you're perfectly free.' Nice poem, no?"

Egypt's greatest treasure was the Nile, and Mickey was happy to put aside Erik Blumenthal and his investigation for thirty minutes as the ferry zigzagged back and forth across the river to pick up and deposit passengers. He drank in the sights, passing obelisks, fishing boats, yachts, social clubs, restaurants, palm groves, and finally a midriver fountain before arriving at the Mari Girgis station.

He made his way to the UK General Electric Company, located only a few blocks from the river, next to Cairo's children's hospital.

In her prim BBC voice, the woman in horn-rimmed glasses at the reception desk informed him that Mr. Nissel was on holiday, which Mickey found rather incongruous with the war on their doorstep, and he pressed her to give him the man's phone number and address. The story he was writing for the *Foreign Service Journal* was of such importance that even the American Embassy was assisting him in his research. He'd been persuasive enough for her to excuse herself for a moment to ask her superiors. However, when she reemerged, her lips were pursed and the answer clear.

"Sorry," she said. "But we cannot divulge any information regarding our employees. You know us English, we are . . . "

" . . . sticklers for rules," Mickey finished her sentence. Still, he was not ready to give up. He pulled out his notepad and ripped off a blank sheet. "I'm going to leave my number with you. If you see Mr. Nissel, or even better, should you happen to call him yourself, would you please give it to him and ask him to contact me?"

She picked up the paper hesitantly.

"No rules broken," Mickey said with a playful wink. "Just some help to your Yankee friends."

The ride back downtown was not as much fun as the ride up. The river bus was jammed to capacity this time and running late. He was hoping to go home to shower and change before his dinner at the Continental with Hugh, but he first needed to see Jacques Antebie, who had updated the refugee list. The community center was only a few blocks from the Shepheard's Hotel, and Mickey wondered whether he should stop by the office of Joseph Levi, the hotel accountant who was the uncle of the girl he'd met there. He had returned the book along with a note a few days before, but she had not yet responded.

Mickey closed his eyes. His thoughts veered back to his investigation. Looking for Blumenthal in shelters was like looking for a needle in a haystack. Hadn't Einstein said the simplest solution is usually the best? If I were a thirty-year-old physicist doing cutting edge work in my field, where would I want to go? The answer came to him immediately. I'd want to go someplace where I could continue my research. A scientist breaking new ground must be very excited about his work, eager to make his next discovery. Mickey needed to learn who else was working in Blumenthal's field of study and see if they could shed some light on what the man's next move might be. He resolved to visit the Al-Ahzar University science department's library as soon as possible to look for recently published articles on quantum physics.

He sighed, wondering how long Erik Blumenthal would elude him.

CHAPTER 12

Ataba Square, the wide-open plaza at the west end of the city, was easily Cairo's foremost commercial center, buzzing all day long with soldiers and merchants. But this evening when Mickey descended from the *arabya Hantour*, the horse-drawn buggy he'd taken to the Continental Hotel, he encountered a very different crowd. Men in linen suits and women in pearls emerged from Rolls Royces and Bentleys arriving at the hotel in battalions. Valets, dressed all in white, scurried frantically to assist this influx of Cairo's high society.

Buttoning his white evening dinner jacket, newly acquired from Antoine, the tailor Dorothy had sent him to, Mickey merged seamlessly into the glamorous throng. His hair was freshly washed and combed. There was no trace of the scruffy guy who had walked the streets only hours earlier. He caught sight of his reflection in the hotel's glass doors and struck a pose with his hand in his pocket. Not bad.

He wound his way through the crowd toward the elevator at the far end of the ornate entry hall, admiring the autographed pictures of celebrities and politicians that adorned the walls. Maurice Chevalier, Josephine Baker, Clark Gable, Winston Churchill, and Charles de Gaulle had all been photographed alongside a small Egyptian man with a broad smile—the owner, Mickey assumed. He lingered for a moment, getting a kick out of enjoying the same playground as the world's elite.

He stepped out of the elevator and stood breathless at the sight of the colonial Eden in front of him. The rooftop had been converted into a garden lush with foliage, where guests dined at immaculately set, white-linen-draped tables. The sun was setting over the many domes and minarets of the city's medieval district, illuminating Al-Azhar, the grandest mosque of them all, with a halo and bathing the terrace in an orange glow. Waiters drifted by carrying martinis and platters of hors d'oeuvres, accompanied by the soft sound of a flute being played in some unseen corner, while *suffragis* scurried to light the candles that adorned each table. As the sky darkened, hundreds of fairy lights entwined in the foliage sprang to life, provoking a chorus of "Ahhs" from the admiring guests. Mickey joined them, transported into another world—a glamorous, exotic oasis far away from the harsh reality of the war.

"Mickey!" he heard someone calling. Was that Hugh? He scanned the terrace but could not find his friend and turned toward the packed bar, which was now standing room only. The place swarmed with young men in dapper service uniforms on leave and eager to spend their back pay. They buzzed around women in chic evening dresses perched on barstools.

"Mic-key, you son of a gun!" Finally he spotted Hugh waving wildly at him and grinning just as wildly. He was sitting with two sexy girls in their early twenties.

"So damn good seeing you!" Mickey cried out joyfully.

"Finally," Hugh responded as the two men engaged in a long hug as if to ensure that this was real.

"Excuse us," said one of the girls, a redhead in a shimmering blue dress. She stood up and gathered her purse. "Our dates are here." The other followed suit and coyly signaled to two English officers making their way toward them.

"Never mind them," Hugh said, sitting down. "We'll find plenty of action later. We're going to have fun tonight." He elbowed

Mickey, his pale blue eyes glinting with mischief as he waved the bartender over.

Hugh signaled for a refill, and Mickey ordered a whiskey sour and leaned back to take a good look at his friend. Hugh's blond hair had thinned in the years since he'd seen him, but he still displayed the same happy-go-lucky air that was so endearing. The most conspicuous change was the uniform Hugh was wearing. "I see you've changed your status, but not your style," Mickey said, looking around. "This is a swell place."

Hugh laughed. "You haven't seen anything yet, my boy." He punched Mickey playfully in the arm. "Good to see you, mate. You're not looking half bad yourself."

"What about you in that uniform?" Mickey said. "What do these mean?" he asked, flicking one of Hugh's epaulettes.

"Means I'm a sapper now," Hugh said, straightening and giving a little salute.

"You're working with bombs and mines? Have you lost your mind?"

Hugh shrugged. "I couldn't stand sitting behind a desk swatting flies off my nose. I finally got a transfer." The bartender arrived with their drinks. "Defusing bombs is heady stuff, mate. It beats being cooped up in a submarine or fried to death in a tank. But what about you?" He raised an eyebrow at Mickey's smart attire. "Big time journalist, eh?"

"*Noblesse oblige*," Mickey laughed. "I want to hear it all. Last time I heard you were stationed in Suez."

"That's mainly it," Hugh said between sips of scotch. "Twenty-thousand British troops, forty overworked Sudanese prostitutes, and a puddle full of mines. We get bombed once a week, but otherwise, Suez is not bad." He downed the rest of his drink in one long gulp and banged the glass on the table. He snapped his fingers at the waiter for another. "Hell! War is one big party."

"Cleaning up minefields is not a party." Mickey frowned. "Where will they send you next time?"

"Who knows? Mersa Matruh, I think."

"That could become the front line if you guys continue . . . hmmm . . . *strategically retreating* eastward." At the last press briefing, they'd been told that the sleepy seaside town of Mersa Matruh near the Libyan border was being fortified as a fallback position. "I don't want to see you there. The Germans look too strong."

"Oh, lighten up, Connolly," Hugh said, throwing a pistachio in his direction. "You're too bloody serious, that's your problem. When was the last time you got laid?"

"Thank you for your concern. Christina turned out to be a perfect guide in more ways than one," he joked, referring to the Armenian girl Hugh had set him up with his first night in town.

"Thought you might enjoy the perk," he said with a grin. "She's very selective, you lucky bastard." He thanked the waiter for the new scotch and turned to Mickey, for the first time serious. "I still can't get over what Victoria did to you."

"Ancient history. Don't worry, I'm doing just fine. Plenty of women in my life." Mickey lifted his glass. "To the fair sex. May we get plenty of it!" The alcohol was hitting him now, and it felt good. "What about you? You ever see Barcie anymore?"

Hugh burst out laughing. "No, but I'm living in her apartment. I ran into her about a year ago at Groppi's. She'd been dating some Greek shipping magnate who was living in Cairo. He felt so guilty about breaking off their affair that he bought her a gorgeous apartment! Italian marble floors, a huge balcony, expensive antiques."

"So you moved in to help her . . . lick her wounds?" Mickey suppressed a smile.

"Let's just say I rekindled an old flame at an opportune time. She went back to Rome and left me her flat for the year."

Mickey raised his eyebrows. "Free?"

"Not entirely. I do have to write the occasional love letter."

Mickey felt the tension of the past few days melting away. He'd forgotten how much he liked being in Hugh's company.

"So tell me something the War Office is not telling us." He raised his right hand. "I swear to God, I never reveal my sources."

In a glance, Hugh surveyed the room. "I'll tell you one thing, since it won't be a secret for long. High Command has just demanded that the Egyptian army turn in their weapons. Churchill's orders. We're taking over their positions. Mersa Matruh is one, in fact."

"Wow. That's a slap in the face." Mickey felt himself sober up a bit. "It's bound to set the Egyptian people against you guys even more."

Hugh grunted. "I suppose that after catching General al-Misri trying to escape across to the German side, Churchill lost faith in the loyalty of the Egyptian army. The PM thinks the whole army is full of German sympathizers who could turn against us at any moment."

"What can they possibly do, with tens of thousands of British troops here? It would be suicide to revolt. You'd skin them alive. So much for Egyptian independence."

"I'm with you, mate. It's pretty outrageous." Hugh raised his glass in a toast. "To friendship! To hell with everything else."

"To friendship!" Mickey clicked Hugh's glass.

The big band began to play, making further conversation difficult. Mickey's eyes wandered the room, settling on a pretty brunette with a plunging décolleté sitting among some equally attractive friends. It'd be damned hard to fight temptation in this city, especially for soldiers who knew they might die soon. All around, the young singles of Cairo coupled up and took to the dance floor to jitterbug to the latest Glenn Miller tune. He loosened his tie. Hugh was right: It was party time.

The maître d' informed them that their table was ready. After Hugh slipped him a few notes, they were seated at a prime spot on the terrace with views of the city and the dance floor. Hugh scanned the menu, a gourmet's dream, while Mickey, who had learned a little about wine thanks to Victoria, chose a 1935 Château Lafite. "My treat," he insisted, but he quickly put down the wine list when he spotted a girl in a white dress leaving the dance floor with her partner. Could it be . . . ?

He rushed up to her in a heartbeat and gently tapped her on the back. "Maya?" he found himself asking hopefully. The girl, breathless and winded, turned around. Beads of sweat shone on her forehead. She was pretty, but she was not Maya.

"Sorry," he said and nodded his apologies to the girl, who wore a gold Star of David around her neck.

"Who was that?" Hugh asked.

"Mistaken identity," Mickey said, masking his disappointment, which was much greater than he'd expected. He followed the couple with his eyes as they joined their merry-making friends at a large table. He had never dated a Jewish girl. They were pretty much unapproachable and didn't often date gentiles. This might explain why Maya had not responded to him.

"Here comes Egypt's most popular singer," Hugh whispered, indicating the surprise guest, Umm Koultoum, whose appearance the emcee was announcing to the wild applause of the diners.

A large woman in a sequined black gown with a red scarf tied around her pinkie took the stage and began singing in Arabic. Her voice was deep and hoarse, and her face was contorted with anguish as she chanted a no doubt gut-wrenching love song, which drew a standing ovation. The rest of the entertainment was no less exotic, and over their lavish meal they were entertained by whirling dervishes, belly dancers, and a magician who amazed the guests with his feats.

Just as they were ready to order dessert, a waiter arrived with a silver tray carrying two glasses of champagne. He set them down and handed Mickey an envelope. "A note for you, monsieur."

Mickey tore it open.

To Anglo-American relations—Sally.

A petite blonde with curly hair was waving at him. She was at a table across the room with two other nice-looking women, all in uniform.

He finally recognized her. She was the ambulance driver from Siwa. He waved back discreetly, while Hugh flapped his hand excitedly at the girls.

"How do you manage it?" Hugh whistled. "I'm the one with all the charm. It must be your pearly white Yank teeth!"

"I told you we'd bump into one another. Cairo is very small," Sally said as she walked over and introduced herself and her friends, Linda and Dolly. "You look a whole lot better," she commented, giving him a flirtatious look. "Have you heard from your Egyptian friend?"

"As a matter of fact, I just checked on him," Mickey answered. "He seems okay. He's going back to his hometown of Tanta to teach."

The three women pulled up chairs and sat down. They were tipsy and chattered loudly back and forth, attracting attention from other tables. Sally was the liveliest. She had an easy and appealing manner. She regaled the table with outrageous stories, including a silly joke about a Scottish soldier who stood in front of the pyramids and earnestly asked, "Yes, but what are they for?" making everyone laugh to tears.

Mickey draped his hand over the back of her chair, marking his territory as he exchanged glances with Hugh. His friend seemed to like her, too, but it was clear she preferred Mickey from the way she leaned toward him whenever she laughed. It was not the first time the two men were attracted to the same girl, but rather than compete, they had an unspoken understanding that they would let the girl decide. Mickey winked at Hugh. "Sorry, pal, what about Dolly?" his smile said. Linda was wearing a wedding band.

The top buttons of Sally's jacket were open and her scarf was slightly askew. She grinned at Mickey. "Are you here for adventure as well? That's why all of us girls volunteered. Back home, we're dull as doorknobs. Linda's a copywriter, Dolly's a nurse, and I'm . . . " she giggled, "I do nothing at all, actually. But say, we could desperately use some help from our American cousins in this war. Where are you lads?" She laid her hand on his thigh.

"Right where we want to be, I'd say." He grinned, covering her hand with his.

Onstage, a black-skinned American chanteuse, glowing in the dark in a silver beaded dress, was singing Billie Holiday's "God Bless the Child" while couples danced cheek-to-cheek. The mood suddenly broke as a small army of men in beige uniforms poured onto the terrace. A murmur passed through the room and heads turned as conversations stopped.

The maître d' interrupted the singer. "Ladies and gentlemen, I'm terribly sorry to interrupt your evening." He smoothed his coat nervously. "But King Farouk will be holding a private reception here and we must ask you all to leave."

Sally snorted. "How rude. Who does he think he is? I'm not going."

"To make up for this inconvenience," the maître d' continued over noisy booing, "His Majesty has generously arranged for all of you to continue the evening at the Music Hall at his expense. Naturally, he will be picking up the tab here, too."

This prompted applause from a number of guests, but many others still protested.

"Does this happen often?" Mickey asked, shocked at the arrogance of the king.

"Yes. Pathetic, really," Sally said. "He's just throwing his weight around to make up for the fact that he has so little real power. It's his little way of telling Cairo he's still in business."

"Keep your voice down," Linda advised. "Let the poor boy have his fun. You know he was never allowed out of the palace when he was growing up?"

"Oh, please," Sally snapped. "The boy made up for that a hundred times over in England. I knew his tutor there, and I can tell you he was in bordellos more often than he was in class."

"I'm not budging," Dolly declared, crossing her arms.

"They'll have to drag us out," Sally said.

"Calm down, ladies," said Hugh, rising. "I've got a better idea."

"Come on, Sally." Mickey offered his hand to her. "The night is young."

She took his hand and sprang to her feet with a mischievous smile. "Fine. Let's."

"Everyone must leave now," one of the king's men commanded, clapping his hands together, clearing the way for Farouk's entrance as the hotel staff politely helped the diners exit.

Hugh, Mickey, and the girls made their way down to the lobby. Mickey noticed a small gathering in a side hall, tucked away from public view. He recognized the king among his entourage. Tall, thin and blue-eyed, Farouk could easily pass for a *Life* magazine cover boy in his Royal Air Force marshall's uniform. But before Mickey could get a better look, they were swept outside by the crowd.

"We can all take the ambulance. Thank God I parked just down the street," Sally shouted above the frenzy.

"Step on it, Connolly," Hugh whispered, grabbing him by the arm. "I think you're going to get lucky tonight!"

"Where to, pal?"

"The Kit Kat Club, habibi," Hugh answered in his best Arabic accent.

CHAPTER 13

The Kit Kat Club was jam packed with soldiers. From the wide array of uniforms, it seemed to Mickey that every single unit of the Eighth Army was represented here tonight—South African, Australian, Polish, Free French, Indian, New Zealander, Canadian, and Rhodesian. And of course, lots of British. They all had their hats on the tables beside ice buckets, and their cigarettes, cigars, and pipes glowed in the dark like fireflies. The slow-turning mahogany fans did nothing to dissipate the smoky haze that clung to the ceiling like a cloud and made the tops of the sweeping curtains framing the illuminated stage vanish into nothingness.

Sally snuggled up to Mickey, rubbing her body against his and roaring with laughter along with the rest of the audience as the performers, dressed in SS uniforms, bantered back and forth in the cabaret show. Hugh winked at Mickey as he draped his arm around Dolly, his hand dangerously close to her breast. God willing, they'd both get lucky tonight. Feeling like a third wheel, Linda had taken a taxi home.

A voluptuous waitress, naked to the waist except for a scanty crocheted brassiere that barely covered her nipples, served them their third round of martinis.

"You better keep your eyes on us!" Sally warned, turning Mickey's head back toward her and tapping her index finger on his nose. "There are a lot of men out there."

"It's you girls who should be concerned," Hugh laughed. "When the show is over the dancing girls are going to mingle with the crowd." He placed a kiss on Dolly's neck, who pushed him away, feigning indignation.

The act ended to rousing applause. The blue velvet curtain closed and then reopened a moment later, revealing a bare-chested man wearing a turban and carrying a wicker basket. A small band of musicians behind him began to play. He settled down at the edge of the stage, right in front of Mickey, who had managed to get seated in the front row, thanks to Hugh's influence with the club's manager.

"Ladies and gentlemen," the man began dramatically. "Let me present the king of snakes, the cobra, the ancient symbol of the Egyptian pharaoh . . . " The music soared as a low drumbeat started. He drew a flute from his pocket, lifted the lid of the basket, and began to play. The snake's head rose from the basket and began to sway.

Sally grabbed Mickey's hand. He smiled and wrapped a protective arm around her shoulder, feeling the muscles in her back relax as she drew closer.

"The cobra is also the symbol of sexuality and sensuality. As a special treat, we present to you tonight the essence of temptation herself, the one and only Queen of the Serpents—Madame Samina!"

A red curtain at the rear of the stage lifted, exposing the star of the show standing atop a flight of stairs with a large black python draped around her neck. Her curvaceous body was barely covered in a two-piece costume beneath a diaphanous veil. She glittered from head to toe with gems of every color and wore a sparkling red stone in her navel.

After wildly enthusiastic whistles and bawdy shouts from the soldiers, she pointed her toes and descended the stairs carefully, reveling in her role as their erotic fantasy, making eye contact with every man in the front row. When her dark eyes fell on Mickey, he felt a stirring.

Hugh nudged him and rubbed his hands in anticipation. "She's the real reason Rommel wants Cairo so badly."

When Samina reached the apron of the stage, she handed the python to a stagehand and exploded into an erotic blur of fluid curves, thrusting her hips and lifting her bejeweled, intertwined arms high above her head. She swirled around the stage, using her veil to tease and arouse, then crawled on the floor, gyrating her body suggestively, arms outstretched and palms open, as if begging the audience to make love to her.

Mesmerized, Mickey struggled to disguise his erection and crossed one leg over the other. But he stopped breathing altogether when the dancer got down on her knees and shimmied to the edge of the stage, stopping right in front of their table. He had barely gasped for air when Samina sprang up on pointed toes and fixed her eyes on him. He knew at this point that resisting would be in vain as she slowly lifted her leg and fondled his face with her toes, keeping her intense gaze locked on him. With her arms raised, balancing on one leg, she thrust her body back and forth as if to invite him in. Then in a flash, she was back on her feet.

The spell broke for a tiny moment when he noticed her become distracted by the sight of a Polish officer at the next table. The man raised his glass to her, but the dancer's face turned hard before she responded with a devilish smile.

She turned her eyes back to Mickey, her victim again. She planted her legs wide apart and her crotch in front of his face. The audience was roaring, but the cries sounded far away to Mickey. She thrust her hips back and forth, the music rising to a spiraling crescendo. Then, in a dramatic burst, she collapsed to the floor and the stage plunged into darkness. When the lights came up a second later, she was gone.

The men screamed for an encore, but Samina appeared to believe that audiences, like lovers, were best left wanting more.

"You *liked* that," Sally whispered as she stroked his leg.

Hugh whistled. "We should set that woman loose on the Germans."

Soldiers threw bread balls at Mickey, who felt his face turning red in embarrassment as they cried, "You lucky sod."

"Now look, you've gotten everyone jealous," Sally said, passing her fingers over Mickey's lips. "I think we should move on."

Mickey pushed his chair back. He couldn't agree more.

CHAPTER 14

Crass and shameless, Kesner thought as he opened the stiff and itchy collar of his Polish uniform. He was annoyed with himself for becoming aroused once again by Samina's blatant sexual overtures. He used to report whores like her to the Gestapo back in Germany. They corrupted the morals of the Reich's young men. But he'd heard that prostitution had now become a fact of life back home, apparently spiraling into an epidemic on the streets of Berlin.

When the crimson curtain closed to rapturous applause, Kesner rose to his feet and started toward the Kit Kat star's dressing room. The door to the diva's dressing room was ajar and he slipped in. Sitting in front of her makeup mirror in a Chinese silk robe, Samina was peeling off her false eyelashes. Her tiara lay on the dresser and her long black hair cascaded down her back.

"What the hell are you doing here?" she gasped, catching his reflection in the mirror. Her eyes, so seductive onstage, flashed with venom and cold fury. She spoke with an exotic accent, part Arabic and part French—a perfect Lebanese blend.

"I heard you had a letter for me," Kesner said.

"You are putting me in danger," she shot back angrily. "Last week the police interned two of the girls. Every cop in town is here tonight and you come barging in like you own the place."

Kesner wanted to say, "I don't own the place, but I own you, sweetheart," but he held his tongue. There was no telling what the whore might do if antagonized, and she was too important an ally to lose. Not only was she his key liaison for getting mail to and from Germany, but he'd used her several times on sensitive matters involving high-level Western officials. The extra service was costly, but invaluable. The Italians, whom she'd previously worked for, had warned him about her mercenary nature but promised she was worth it.

"Dr. Massoud's assistant said you stopped by his office twice this week. The information must be important." He approached the dressing table and played with a sparkly wig that was lying on it. Samina's robe was loosely draped around her; her erect nipples showed through the thin material. A small stream of perspiration ran between her ample breasts, making her skin glisten. He wondered if she sweated like that when she fucked.

Samina snatched the wig away and put it back on the dresser before rising and fetching a brown envelope from her purse in the closet. "Next time you wait until you hear from me. This is my life, and I'm not going to risk having you or anyone else screw it up. Understand?"

He had a powerful urge to throw her on the floor and fuck her, but he smiled, as if amused by her hysteria. He slipped the letter into the pocket of his uniform and gently stroked the side of her neck with his index finger. "You ought to show more appreciation. I've asked the Abwehr for more money for you."

"I'll do the asking myself," she said, brushing his hand away before cinching her robe tightly around her, covering her cleavage.

"You gave quite a performance tonight, Samina. Somehow I felt much of it was for my benefit, but I suppose every man must have felt that way."

"I need to fix my face," she growled and showed him the door with her chin.

Kesner blew her a kiss, and as he headed for the door, he passed a wall where a photograph of her children, a boy and a girl, was pinned. Under Lebanese law, custody had gone to the father after her divorce, and this, her weak spot, was where Kesner's leverage lay. She needed money for the lawyers.

When Kesner returned to his dahabieh he opened a bottle of Sandman sherry in celebration. *Hurra*! The SS was giving him a second chance. In their detailed letter, he was authorized to find the Jew and to use any means necessary to prevent him from falling into the hands of the Americans or the English. They noted that this matter was of the utmost importance to Hitler himself.

Kesner removed his Polish uniform jacket and lay down on the cushions in the living room, enjoying the soft breeze from the whirring corner fans. He felt a swell of pride. Finally, after months of negotiating with slimy officials and raving fanatics, he'd been called to serve the führer.

He removed the letter from his pocket and took pleasure in reading and rereading it.

He had more information now. The Jew, Erik Blumenthal, was born in Düsseldorf in 1911, the same year as himself. He was one of twenty Jewish German PhD physics students that Niels Bohr had sponsored to work with him in Denmark in 1933. He was last employed by the Collège de France in Paris. He'd failed to report when instructed to appear in front of the Vichy civic hall in Bordeaux, the last place he'd been registered. His name was subsequently picked up in Istanbul and he was put on the Gestapo's list of wanted men. He'd written a paper that was of importance to the Reich's ballistic missile program. The Jew had sent it to Bohr in Denmark, and the SS had, naturally, intercepted it. They needed to question him about his findings. Kesner's instructions were to hold him until General Rommel arrived. The letter also advised that the scientist was traveling with his sister, Marianna, and his father, Viktor. They'd included a family photo. Kesner committed the letter to memory before lighting a match to it. But he kept the photo, taking particular notice of Blumenthal's sister, finding her pretty but too skinny.

He had intercepted and decoded two more communiqués from the American Embassy regarding the Jew, both of which were sent by someone called Fastball. One of them referred to Blumenthal as "a needle in a haystack." Why were the Americans involved in this? Kesner kept wondering. Could Roosevelt be planning to enter the war even though the American people were opposed to it?

He went back to his bedroom and fetched his diary, which he kept hidden in the mahogany chest that blocked the entrance to his communication room. He opened his bottle of specially concocted ink and dipped his pen into it.

You're a good boy, Schwarze Hund, he started writing. His head was brimming with ideas of how to search for the scientist as he watched the black ink turn to brown before fading away.

CHAPTER 15

Mickey thought it was a good thing Sally's apartment wasn't far away from the Kit Kat Club and that at this late hour the streets were deserted, because Sally's wide, drunken turns could have sent them either to the hospital or to jail. They climbed the stairs to her second floor studio, one wobbly step at a time, holding each other up, not sure who was more intoxicated. He slipped his hand up her skirt as they reached the landing. She responded by sliding her tongue into his mouth and curling her leg around his. He pressed her hips closer to his body as they shared a wet kiss.

"Hold off," she said, panting and fumbling with her keys, but he kept kissing the back of her neck and fondling her breasts, his need urgent.

Once inside, she kicked the door closed and pulled off his jacket, her tongue running around his lips as she led him to the bedroom, where they collapsed on the bed. Breathless already, she unbuttoned her blouse while he unzipped her skirt and threw it on the floor. He stubbornly struggled with her brassiere as she sat at the edge of the bed removing her stockings. Equally impatient, she took over and in a snap freed her breasts and straddled him. She placed a nipple in his mouth while she unbuckled his belt and pulled his pants down. A moment later his cock was in her mouth. She was as hungry for him as he was for her. The hell with foreplay! It ended with her riding on top of him and climaxing with a victorious scream. It was delicious and delirious, and like a dam bursting, with her fingers in his mouth and his hands grabbing her butt cheeks, he released. He closed his eyes and let out a winded breath.

She collapsed next to him on the pillow, purring like a satisfied cat. She was happy and cuddled tightly up against him.

What seemed like hours later, he opened his eyes. The drapes were open to the full moon, but it was still too dark to read his watch. He reached for the bedside lamp. It was three-thirty. He'd only slept for two hours.

Sally stirred and opened an eye. She lazily rolled onto her side and reached across him to grab a pack of cigarettes from the bedside table. "Smoke?" she offered.

"No, thanks." He got up to go to the bathroom. He didn't want to spend the rest of the night with her.

He splashed his face with cold water and looked at himself in the mirror. Pretty sorry looking. He had a busy day ahead. He needed to go home for a few good hours of sleep and a change of clothes, but he didn't want to hurt her feelings. When he returned to the bedroom, however, she was getting dressed.

"I'm going to sleep at the base," she announced casually. "Tomorrow is an early day. Want a ride home, dolly?"

Surprised and relieved, Mickey kissed her on the lips. "I'll walk. Some fresh air will do me good," he said.

Outside, the night air felt crisp. Sally's ambulance was parked askew in front of the building. He noticed a soldier's helmet in the backseat, and then saw that it was only half of a helmet, badly mangled on one side. How could she deal with this day in and day out? he wondered.

It was a good twenty-minute walk to his apartment. He jammed his hands in his pockets and strode away. If he walked west, he would eventually run into Sharia Kasr el-Aini and take it all the way north to downtown.

The Abdeen district had increasingly become populated by foreigners, pushing the Arab neighborhoods ever further east to the medieval area. It had seen the sprouting of numerous bars and clubs in recent months. At this late hour, however, the streets were deserted and the bars and clubs were closed in compliance with a new ordinance. Only the Scarabee, famous for its milky Circassian girls who danced behind barbed wire, was open. Its burly bouncer was throwing out the last boisterous customer as Mickey passed by. He quickened his pace.

He made a right turn, expecting it to lead to the Maglis el Sha'ab grand avenue, but found himself on a tiny side street. Ahead of him three soldiers staggered on and off the sidewalk, slurring as they sang, "King Farouk, King Farouk, you're a dirty old crook. Queen Farida's very gay, when Farouk has got his pay." They found their improvisations hilarious as they swayed along.

A man screamed angry curses at them in Arabic from an apartment window, and another stepped onto his balcony and raised his fist in a tirade at the drunken soldiers.

"Piss off," one of the soldiers yelled before lurching forward.

No wonder the Egyptians wanted the Allies out of here, Mickey thought. War or no war, this was unacceptable. In Detroit, the police would have picked up those morons long ago and locked them up for the night.

An Arab in a white galabeya and a tarbush emerged from a side lane and walked toward the soldiers. Mickey smelled trouble.

Sure enough, when the man passed by, one of the soldiers knocked his tarbush off his head. Without a word, the man bent down to pick it up, but the soldier snatched it back and threw it to one of his buddies. The three lads began tossing it back and forth, like a volleyball.

"That's enough, guys," Mickey shouted as he neared them. None of them was a day over eighteen. He grabbed the closest one by the shoulder. "Knock it off," he ordered. "This is not a game."

The soldier's eyes were glazed over. He snorted and tried to brush Mickey's hand away, but was so drunk that he missed it.

"Give the man his tarbush," Mickey insisted. But his demand fell on deaf ears as the soldiers continued their game. "I said enough," he yelled and jumped up, intercepting the hat. "Leave him alone."

"What's it to you?" blustered the tallest of the three, and he hit Mickey with a surprise right cross that struck him just below the eye.

Mickey reeled backward. When he straightened up, he found the three squaddies circling him, ready to brawl. He didn't like to fight, but he would if he had to.

"You don't want to fight me," he warned them, looking each of them in the eye. He was a lot more sober than these stupid kids.

"Give us a try," the tall one taunted.

Feeling the adrenaline rushing through his veins, Mickey launched his attack. The tall squaddie fell to the ground with a groan. Mickey turned to the next, and it didn't take much to send this one tumbling into the gutter. He caught a glimpse of the third soldier's back as he rounded a corner at a swift clip.

Brushing the dirt off his hands, Mickey picked up the crushed hat. "Here you go, old timer," he said to the Arab, dusting it off and doing his best to restore its shape.

The old man snatched it away and stared Mickey hard in the eyes. Then he spat in his face and turned sharply on his heels and strode away.

CHAPTER 16

After three weeks at the Levis' it was clear to Maya that the household revolved around two main activities: eating and cleaning. It started at the crack of dawn when two young servants brought fresh rolls from the bakery. Their delicious aroma never failed to beckon Maya into wakefulness. Then the smell of coffee pervaded the house. Joe called it Turkish, but Allegra called it Greek. No matter its name, it was the strongest stuff Maya had ever tasted, surpassing even French double espresso, and was guaranteed to give you a mouthful of coffee grounds.

By the time she arrived in the kitchen to claim a cup, Allegra and Sayeda were already hard at work pressing prodigious quantities of orange, mango, and guava juice for the family's breakfast. Joe, an early riser, would usually have returned from the fish and meat markets with his wife's needs for the day.

Once breakfast was over and the children were off to school and Joe to work, the serious cooking and cleaning began. Allegra spent all day in the kitchen cooking and baking, making everything from scratch—from mayonnaise to yogurt. Sayeda helped, but she'd also clean and supervise the two other servant girls, whose main responsibilities were washing and ironing. It was fortunate that help was cheap in Egypt since housework seemed to be never ending. Rugs were turned over every day and pounded by hand to extract the dust. Furniture was polished, crystal cleaned, chandeliers dusted, and floors scrubbed. The house sparkled, and Maya was introduced to a whole new standard of cleanliness.

Maya knew to stay out of the way since her offers to help were always turned down, and she spent her days either on the rooftop or on one of the two balconies. Each had its own charms and provided respite from the heat at different times of the day.

The north balcony opened to Hamman Street, which was perfect in the morning when the street merchants paraded under the window with their baskets balanced atop their heads. In piercing voices, they sang the praises of the fruits and vegetables they were selling, and invariably, Allegra or Sayeda called down to them. Negotiations took place at the entrance to the building, after which the bawab carried the purchases upstairs. The rear balcony faced east and was always shaded in the afternoon. It was a good, quiet place to read or think.

After she spent the better part of the afternoon mending the last batch of uniforms Lili had brought home, Lili rewarded her with a deluxe beauty treatment, including manicure, pedicure, and haircut and set. She included, of course, the lemon treatment she had previously urged her to do. Relaxed, now Maya looked forward to a little private time on the roof where she could grab some sun. She needed time alone—a lot of it. That was the only way she could renew herself. She took deep breaths, using each one to chase away a layer of anxiety, until she could think clearly.

She cinched the belt of her robe and had started toward the spiral staircase at the back of the house that led to the roof when she saw Erik leaning on the drawing room door for support. He seemed to be in a lot of pain. The doctor in Istanbul had warned him that because of all the physical strain he'd endured, he needed to follow a tight regimen of exercise therapy or risk losing the use of his right leg altogether. The doctor had prescribed leg braces for him, but the local hospitals here wouldn't accept a foreign prescription. With his polio flaring up, Erik refused to leave the house to be seen by a local doctor and insisted he was fine hobbling around the apartment in his current state. "Erik . . . " she started to say reproachfully.

He turned, and knowing what was coming, he waved her off as he limped inside and turned on the radio.

Maya placed a hand on her hip. What a stubborn fool. If he wanted a paralyzed leg, that would not just be his problem, it would be hers, too. His stupid pride was actually pure selfishness. She felt a wave of anger starting to swell, but quickly shut it off, deciding she was not going to let this ruin her day. She needed to bring some lightness into her life. Since that drink with the American journalist, she'd realized how much she'd been denying herself even the simplest of pleasures, like flirting, or smoking a cigarette, or having a conversation about life or politics with a stranger.

"I'm going up to the roof for a smoke," she proclaimed.

"Keep it at one," Erik admonished her.

"You're not my father," she snapped, surprised at how readily she stood up to him. She bit her lower lip and headed to the stairway.

After an instant he shouted after her, "Just make sure no one sees you in those curlers. They'll get scared and call the police."

She ascended the stairs and settled into one of the rooftop chairs with the Cairo guidebook. She felt restless. They'd first expected their papers within two weeks, but now three weeks had passed, and they were told it would be a minimum of two weeks more. She'd gone off for walks around the neighborhood, but maybe she should visit Cairo after all. Her brother and father seemed to be doing fine at the Levis' and there would be no harm in going off for a few hours.

She took a deep breath, filling her lungs with the delicate fragrance of jasmine. Why was it that everything in Egypt smelled better than anywhere else? Somehow the fragrance of fruits, vegetables, flowers, coffee, and spices were magnified a thousand fold. She closed her eyes and took another deep breath, and then one more. When she exhaled, she found a sense of lightness inside her. She needed to let God into her heart again. She'd become so tight inside that no light could enter.

Mutter used to say that God revealed himself as light, and that one could see that light at the moment a person expired. In her final days, she'd asked Maya to look for this light when she died, but Maya never saw it. They learned about Mutter's passing through a call from the hospital, and circumstances dictated that they leave Paris at once. Erik arranged for her burial, but there was no time to plan a funeral. For many days and nights afterward Maya looked for some reassuring sign that Mutter had successfully made the journey to God's light, but she never found one. Nor did she see her mother in her dreams. She was just gone, leaving behind only memories. Is that what one is reduced to after death? A memory? A picture on a piano? And on whose piano would Maya's picture rest when she was gone?

I cannot let the past hold me, she told herself as a familiar, dull, aching feeling started to spread through her stomach. No! She must go forward and be grateful that she and her family were safe; grateful that they had not been one of those Jewish families that were arrested and herded into the Velodrome d'Hiver stadium to be shipped, she later learned, to internment camps all over France, in cattle cars built by the Vichy government.

Now she must focus on the good things and fill her mind with sweet thoughts. She brought back the memories of the goodnight kisses her mother would carefully place in the middle of her forehead when she returned late after a performance. They were the best of kisses—light, and tender, and perfect, and even though Maya was usually asleep, part of her was awake enough to capture them.

So with the help of God's light and the memory of her mother's kisses, Maya hoped that here in the City of the Sun, she would find the strength to no longer cry over what she had lost and even to allow herself to dream about the future.

She lit up a cigarette and wiggled her toes, happy with the fuchsia color she'd chosen for them. She spread her fingers and admired them as well. Her fingernails matched nicely with her skin color. She knew she was being shamefully shallow but couldn't deny the tickling pleasure spreading inside her, warming her like a log burning in a fireplace. Here she was, just being a normal girl.

She started flipping through the pages of the guidebook and stopped to study a picture of royal palm trees and lotus pillars sunk into tall grass. Ezbekieh Gardens, read the caption. Located in the heart of Cairo, the garden, one of many that punctuated the city, was created by the former chief gardener to the city of Paris.

Ah, Paris! She sighed, putting the book down. As much as she hated to admit it, she was still in love with the city. Despite her humdrum job as a typist at an insurance company, the three years she'd spent there were the most exciting of her life. The City of Light had awakened her senses and intellect. But now it had broken her heart. Why had so many Frenchmen turned their backs on the Jews?

Her thoughts drifted to Jean-Jacques, her ex-boyfriend, who was always clad in black, giving impassioned speeches, presenting himself as the champion of the underdogs, but who actually never did anything about the very things he talked about. The American was right—he was a poseur. She smiled and pulled Mickey's letter from her pocket to read it again.

Dear Maya,

I must have made quite an impression the other day. What kind of journalist displays that kind of ignorance about the very subject he's supposed to be writing about? The fact that I may have been distracted by the cleft in your chin is no excuse. Forgive me. I was just trying to look smart. Actually, I've just gotten started on my research, and I have lots to learn. Thank you for opening my eyes to the situation facing the Jews in the other North African countries.

I took the liberty of reading your book. Maybe it's my unflagging American optimism, but when faced with my own imminent death, I hope I won't feel as detached as Pablo does, especially from the woman I love. If your friend Jean-Jacques sees Pablo as a hero, I'd think twice about a guy like that!

Now, since you're a curious girl, and I'm the kind of guy who's always looking for answers, why don't we get together and solve some of the problems of the world over dinner? I promise I won't try to impress you. How about it? I would love to see you again.

Your uncle will not tell me how I can reach you, so please call me. Telephone: 40434

Mickey Connolly
(Ace reporter)

I shouldn't have been so tough on him, she thought, acknowledging how judgmental she could sometimes be. In fact she should have praised him for being open enough to write about the Jews in the first place. She wondered what made him choose the subject and wished she had asked him that.

His American accent had caught her by surprise when he ordered his beer. It reminded her of Sherri, her roommate from boarding school, who was from Chicago. But it was his eyes that had sucked her in. How embarrassing. She remembered them perfectly—framed with thick, dark lashes, they were vibrant green with sparkling flecks of yellow. They were the eyes of a lion, alert and electric, but at the same time, they had a softness about them. She thought him handsome with his black mane of hair, though his nose was slightly too big for his face and his lower lip sometimes turned down in an arrogant curl. As a dresser, he was horrible! He'd not only been the most casually dressed man in the room but surely the worst dressed, with his yellow tie that clashed with his blue shirt, which did not go at all with his bottle green blazer, which he never should have chosen in the first place. Nonetheless, she had to admit that she did find him appealing. Beyond the accent and the eyes, it was the ease with which he spoke and his straightforwardness that attracted her. Above all, she liked the air of freedom he exuded.

She read his note one more time. He sounded like a passionate man, which pleased her. Though initially offended that he'd invaded her privacy by reading her book and making himself privy to her personal underlinings, she was also flattered that he'd invested the time to do so.

Perhaps she should allow him to take her out, she thought, not for dinner, but for drinks or possibly lunch. With the war, secretaries were a scarce commodity, and she could probably finagle another day working for Joe at the Shepheard's. She could meet him that day. This would be her little secret, and a girl does need to have secrets, she told herself.

"My father just came home from work," she heard Lili announce as she bounded up the stairway.

Maya quickly shoved the note into her pocket and extinguished her cigarette, waving the air around her to dissipate the smoke.

"You look happy," she said to Lili, who emerged beaming, a mischievous smile on her face. It looked as if she, too, had a secret.

Lili didn't reply and kept her silly grin as she removed a curler from the top of Maya's head and ruled her hair "almost dry" before rolling it back and pulling up a chair next to her.

"So?" Maya asked.

"So . . . I met the man of my dreams," Lili said.

"In the last five minutes?"

"No, yesterday at the tennis tournament," Lili gushed breathlessly. "I didn't want to tell anyone. I was afraid to jinx it, but he just called me." She suddenly grabbed Maya's hand, squeezing it tightly in excitement. "I knew it!" she cried out. "I knew he felt the same way I did from the moment he laid eyes on me. I swear it's true!"

Maya took a deep breath. She found Lili annoyingly immature, living life's everyday ups and downs far too intensely, but her enthusiasm was undeniably contagious, making the air around her lighter and happier. "Who is he?"

"I don't know too much. His name is Fernando and he is very handsome. Dark and tall and maybe a little dangerous!" She laughed like a ten-year-old. "His family moved here last week from Zamalek. He's just joined the sporting club in Heliopolis. I'm telling you, he's the one!"

"What did he say to you?"

"He and his friends are having a mixed-doubles match tonight, and he just lost his partner. He asked if I was free. These were his exact words. I know, Maya, we barely talked," Lili protested in expectation of her skepticism, "but it's true. Love at first sight exists. We both felt it. "

"I'm not sure I believe that. It seems a bit fast to me."

"Have you ever been in love?"

"In love? That is a big word." Maya shook her head, as she reflected on how to answer. "I've had a few boyfriends, but I never said 'I love you.' None of them was *the one*." She insisted on making that clear.

"Why is it that if you can know right away if someone is not the one, you can't know right away if someone is?"

"You can't be sure at just a first impression. You have to get to know him."

"I know how I felt, and that's all I need to know," Lili stated. "I think he is my destiny."

Maya was about to respond, but what was the point?

"Come, maybe your mother will let me set the table," she said as she stood up and started down the stairs. "Can you cook as well as she does?"

Lili laughed as she followed. "Not one dish. Why should I learn? My mother-in-law will teach me how to make my husband's favorite dishes."

"Why didn't you tell us?" Maya heard Erik's voice booming from the drawing room.

It was very unlike him to speak up this way, and she scurried in, finding him leaning against a chair, face-to-face with Joe.

"There isn't much to tell," Joe told him.

"There is *nothing* to tell," Allegra shouted from the kitchen next door.

"About what?" Lili asked as she selected a grape from a silver bowl on the table.

"I heard on the radio that there has been a fire in a synagogue in Alexandria," Erik explained. "They suspect it was an act of arson by the Muslim Brotherhood. Their leader just escaped from prison."

"What's the Muslim Brotherhood?" Maya asked.

"A small group of religious fanatics," Joe tried to reassure them.

"The Nazis were once a small group of fanatics," Erik shot back.

"There have been a few incidents here and there," Joe admitted. "Some bombings of Jewish houses to show sympathy for the

Palestinian Arabs. They believe that the Jews here are working with Jews in Palestine, which is absurd."

"I've seen them distributing pamphlets at the university, Papi," Lili said. "They're saying that all Muslims must come together under one Islamic state and throw out foreigners."

"That's ridiculous," Joe said. "Imagine suggesting that all Europeans band together. Ha! Look at Germany attacking its neighbors. Let me tell you, the Egyptians look down on other Arabs, like the French on the English, the Spaniards on the Portuguese and so on. Uniting all Muslims is not possible. They are trying to make an issue out of Palestine because it's much easier to manipulate people if you have an outsider to blame for your problems."

"Is the movement big?" Maya inquired.

Allegra appeared at the doorway in her apron, holding a knife. "It's a very small group of crazies. Can we please discuss this at another time, when the children are not in the house?" she demanded. "They are already very upset with the news from Europe. There is no reason to scare them about danger here. The Muslims in Egypt will never turn against us." She moved back into the kitchen.

"She's right," Joe agreed. "It is not the Jews, it's the imperialist English, with their drinking and cavorting, who are the real enemy in the eyes of these extremists. They target us because we work closely with the British. But how can we not be friends with the English? They are protecting us from the Nazis."

Erik kept silent. Maya knew her brother wasn't so sure that the English were really such good friends of the Jews.

"I found some new war magazines for you," Joe said to Erik, opening his attaché case, happily changing the subject. "Here we are. *The Navy, Review,* and *Blighty*. Lots of fighter plane stories for you. You don't know how hard it was to find these." He handed the magazines to Erik, who began flipping through the pages immediately.

"And you, my dear," Joe turned toward Maya. "I don't know

what you do to men, but my boss keeps asking when you'll come back and help us again in the office, and he told me that the American journalist came again yesterday asking about you."

"What American journalist?" Erik asked, confronting Maya.

"Nobody!" she said. "Just some American who found a book I left at the Shepheard's Hotel." She quickly moved away lest Erik detect the flicker of excitement she felt upon hearing that the American reporter had been asking about her.

CHAPTER 17

Mickey was surprised to find liveried marines standing guard at the embassy gate, where a number of chauffeured cars sporting Union Jacks on their fenders were parked. Dorothy came out to meet him in the reception area, which was crowded with British officers.

"I wish you'd call before barging in," she said, looking frazzled. Traces of her normally perfect lipstick were caked on her lips. "I told you not to come more often than you usually do."

"It's only my second time this week," Mickey retorted, trailing behind as she strode toward her office. "Why didn't you return my calls the last two days? I think I may have a lead. I need to use the embassy phone to call Jerusalem."

Dorothy stopped in her tracks and looked away, biting her lower lip. She seemed conflicted, and Mickey could see the wheels turning in her head.

"What's going on?"

"What's going on is that I think that from now on you should be more discreet," she snapped, resuming her stride down the corridor. "There's a back door to these offices from the PX. Give me a ring when you get there and I'll unlock it for you."

"Something happened?" he asked, trotting to keep up with her.

"Nothing. Just precautionary, that's all." She turned and noticed his black eye. "What happened to you, anyway? Fell off your horse?"

"It's a long story."

They entered her office and she practically slammed the door behind them. She leaned against it and looked at him intently for a long while. "Swear on the most important person in your life."

"About what?"

"This is not the time for you to display your journalistic prowess, Connolly. Swear that I can trust you."

He slowly walked closer to her, holding her gaze, his right palm raised toward her. "I swear on my mother's grave I won't say a word to anybody."

She sighed and went to pull a cigarette from the pack in her purse. "Tobruk has fallen," she finally said, her voice cracking on the last word. Her hand shook as she lit up.

"Oh, God." Mickey sat down hard on the chair across from her desk.

"It's likely that most of the South African Second Division are dead," she added dully. "Thousands. They fought hard, but the Germans bombed the Allied troops without mercy. General Klopper eventually surrendered, after destroying all the fuel and water reserves in the town. I'm sure you understand the gravity of this news."

Mickey nodded. He understood perfectly well.

A small coastal town in Northern Libya, Tobruk had been staunchly defended by the Allies as the German advance continued east toward the Egyptian border. The town had been under siege for months, cut off by land from the rest of the Allied lines, though the Royal Navy had continued to supply it by sea, but at a terrible price. The route, known as the "Spud Run," was plagued by German *Stukas* that regularly destroyed supply ships as they unloaded. Still, High Command wanted to keep this toehold in Rommel's flank to prevent him from concentrating all his forces on Cairo, and until now it had been a thorn in his side.

"Who are all those people in the reception hall?" he asked.

"Ambassador Kirk has been in meetings with the British ambassador, Sir Miles Lampson, and members of the British military. It's been nonstop since yesterday."

"Yesterday?" Mickey's head jerked up. "I thought it just happened. How come nobody . . . the press—"

"Forget the press, Connolly," she interjected, annoyed that by now he still hadn't learned that the press was the last to know anything. "It will be announced at tomorrow's briefing. Sir Miles is making plans to evacuate the women and children from the city, and he's already made arrangements to transfer the gold reserves to Khartoum."

"Wait a second," Mickey said, getting up from his chair. "Isn't this a bit premature? Aren't there other Allied outposts between Tobruk and Cairo?"

"A few. Mersa Matruh is the next one. About three hundred miles west of here." Mickey swallowed hard and sat down again. That's where Hugh was probably headed.

"And the old Desert Fox will slice right through it," she continued under her breath.

"Don't say that," Mickey reproached her. "What are we doing about this?"

"Churchill is sending reinforcements. They're going to sound the bells in Westminster tonight, as if it were a funeral. They're calling it a catastrophe."

"It's not over yet," he assured her. "Perk up, Dorothy."

"I'm just blue today. Let's not talk about it anymore," she said as she walked over to her desk and pulled a revolver in its shoulder holster from the drawer. "I forgot to give this to you. All of our

COI agents have one." She weighed the pistol in her hand, serious. "This is a German Walther PPK, a Detective Special. It holds six rounds. Supposedly the agents of MI5 don't even bathe without it."

"So the Brits do bathe?" he asked.

"This is not the time to be funny, Connolly. You ever used one of these before?"

"Never used a PPK, but my father keeps a Browning in the house, just in case." He took the weapon and ejected the cartridge cylinder, spun it quickly, and clicked it neatly back into place.

"The trigger is stiff, and I guarantee you the recoil will be pretty snappy," she warned.

He whistled, impressed with her knowledge.

"My ex-husband collected them, along with a wide variety of women," she volunteered, closing the desk drawer and straightening her blouse. "He left me for a rail-thin brunette."

Behind that tough exterior was a broken heart, Mickey saw. He started to mumble, "I'm sorry to . . . "

"Don't fret about it. I'm better off," she stopped him.

He handed her back the gun. "Thanks, but I'm not a COI agent, and I like to take my showers unarmed. What I do need, though, is a phone line to Jerusalem. I want to talk to a professor at the Hebrew University who wrote an article about recent advances in quantum physics—'Jew science,' as the Nazis call it. I gather their physics and chemistry departments are world renowned. I bet Erik Blumenthal is—"

There was a knock and the door quickly opened wide. "Oh, Mr. Connolly. I didn't know you were here." It was Kirk. He looked worn out. "I'm glad to see you, though. Did you tell him about Niels Bohr?" he asked Dorothy.

"I didn't have a chance."

"Donovan spoke to him yesterday. Dr. Bohr has relocated to the United States, at least for now. He said Erik Blumenthal has polio."

Mickey looked at Dorothy with an "I told you so" smile. He'd guessed from the photo there was something wrong with his legs. He turned to Kirk, encouraged.

"What else did he say?"

Kirk exchanged wary looks with Dorothy before answering. "In the last letter Blumenthal wrote to him, he promised to send Bohr the paper he'd been working on, but he never did." Kirk started to leave. "Dorothy, when you're done, I'd like to talk to you. Ambassador Lampson has gone." He was about to close the door behind him when Mickey called out.

"About the fighting in the desert, sir," he glanced hesitantly at Dorothy, who glared back—he'd better hold his tongue. "Is everything all right?"

"It will be." Kirk winked and exited.

"Sorry that with all the excitement we haven't had a chance to talk about Blumenthal," she said as she sat behind her desk. "Interesting news. Erik is traveling with an older man and a young woman. His father and wife, we presume. We're looking further into this."

"Interesting," Mickey said, but before he had time to muse on this, she continued.

"I did hear from the LICA folks in New York. They're sending me a list of all the past members of their Cairo branch." She picked up a note. "I've also received a message from the UK General Electric that Mr. Nissel is not interested in talking to anyone from the press."

"Maybe I can change his mind," he shrugged. "I'll get his address from the Jewish community center." He knew that most Jews were registered there.

Later in the day, Mickey headed home, feeling tired and discouraged. He had phoned the Hebrew University in Jerusalem, but the professor he was looking for was now teaching at Princeton, and no one there had heard of Erik Blumenthal. They had suggested he try the Daniel Sieff Research Institute in Rehovot, a new advanced research facility established by Chaim Weizmann, who was the Hebrew University's founder and was also the president of the World Zionist Organization. Mickey had left the embassy curious to learn more about Weizmann, and Dorothy was going to get the COI agent in Tel Aviv to poke around the Rehovot institute for him. She was taking his new lead seriously.

When he arrived at his building, Hosni, his bawab, took a good look at his purple and swollen eye and prescribed: "Vitamin E oil, mixed with two or three drops of the milk of the jenny, the female donkey, and a bit of honey. Three times a day." He also gave him a note from Hugh inviting him to join in an evening promising women and alcohol galore. Mickey smiled, but he was too despondent to do anything tonight. As he neared his apartment door, he heard the phone ring. He raced to open the door, but the key got stuck in the lock. When he finally freed it and was able to unlock the door, he rushed to the phone, but the line went dead just as he picked up the receiver. Damn it.

He didn't have to wait long before the phone rang again.

"Pronto," he found himself saying.

"Pronto? Don't you say 'hello' in America?" a voice teased.

A grin spread over his face. "Maya!" he said.

CHAPTER 18

> With al-Banna free, more acts of terrorism can be expected against Jews. In a joint statement yesterday, Rabbi Haim Nahum Effendi, the Chief Rabbi of Cairo, and Simon Cattaoui, the president of the Jewish community, urged Jewish shopkeepers to close their businesses next month on the anniversary of the Balfour Declaration, as a precautionary measure.

Erik read aloud from today's newspaper, his feet propped up by pillows as he lay reclining on his bed. He finally glanced up at Maya, who was standing at the doorway, shaking her head, while Vati, his back turned, was bowing silently in prayer, facing the window.

Of course Maya was interested in learning about the extremist group, but this was not the time. She had just stopped by to say good-bye to her brother and father on her way out to her secret rendezvous with the American journalist, and she was impatient to extricate herself. She'd planned the whole outing carefully. She was to meet him at Groppi's, a coffee house in the center of town, and had carved out the whole afternoon on the pretext that she was visiting the Museum of Egyptian Antiquities. What she didn't bargain for was that the entire family would be home today because of a school holiday. She had to get out of the house before some crisis or another made her escape impossible.

"This is horrible," Maya said, crossing her arms and discreetly peeking at her watch. "Why is it that wherever we go we find bad news for the Jews?"

Erik stared at her, stone-faced for a moment before continuing, "Last year's bombing of two synagogues, killing three and seriously injuring fifteen, and the looting of Jewish stores on Kasr el-Nil—"

"Joe never told us about that," Maya interrupted. "He just said a few bombs had been placed in Jewish homes."

"Egyptian police and British infantry troops have committed to placing additional security at the gates of Haret el Yahud, the Jewish quarter, to guard against a repeat of last year's violence by youths demonstrating against Jewish immigration to Palestine," Erik went on.

He was reading excruciatingly slowly, and Maya grabbed the paper from him. She didn't have all day. "Let me see this." She scanned the rest of the article, which went on to explain how the 1917 Balfour Declaration was a sore point for both the Jews and the Arabs. The Jews felt that the British had gone back on their promise of allowing a Jewish homeland in Palestine, and the Arabs had immediately denounced it as invalid.

"Read out loud," Vati suddenly demanded, turning around.

Maya froze at the sight of her father. It wasn't just the prayer *tallis* that he wore over his shoulders, but now, like the orthodox Jews, he'd wrapped the long leather straps of a *tephilim* around his arm and head and positioned its little black box on his forehead. Only loosely observant, he must be feeling so desperate now to dive into religion this way.

"Go on," Vati grumbled.

Maya pressed her lips together, trying to smile, camouflaging her shock, and with a soft voice started to read:

> The Brotherhood, which was begun in 1928 by Hassan al-Banna, then a young teacher, has developed into a political force with five hundred branches in Egypt and a growing network in neighboring Arab countries. Its membership is estimated at half a million, with an equal number of sympathizers.

She looked up. With the wave of his hand, Vati urged her to go on. "Their popularity is not only due to Egyptian nationalism, but to the medical clinics and the social and educational programs they run."

"A small group of fanatics!" Erik snorted, recalling Joe's dismissal of the group. He sat up and started to rise.

"Not so fast," she warned, rushing toward him. But it was too late. Erik had already twisted his foot, his leg too weak to withstand the pressure of his weight. Thankfully, he fell back on the bed before anything worse happened.

"Will you stop being so stubborn and use the crutches Joe gave you?" Maya reprimanded. "And keep them close to your bed." She walked to the corner and handed him an old set Joe had once used when he broke his foot. Erik shrugged.

"I want to know why Mr. Levi played down the truth about these extremists," Vati stated.

"And why it's taking so damned long to get our papers," Erik added.

Maya looked at Erik. He had aged five years in the last five weeks. The uncertainty and delay were taking their toll on him. "Just think how much you will miss Allegra's cooking!" Maya said lightly, trying to cheer him up.

"Aren't you supposed to go to the city today?" Vati asked Maya.

"And it's getting late," Maya said.

"Go, go," Erik said. "Enjoy."

She blew Erik a kiss and wrapped her arms around her father. "I'll bring you back some chocolate truffles."

She hurried down the corridor and locked herself in the bathroom. She hastily applied some of her new red lipstick, but in her rush to add mascara to her lashes, she poked herself in the eye. Now it was tearing up, and her black eyeliner was running. Calm down, Maya. Get a grip on yourself. She cleaned her face and straightened the black sleeveless turtleneck she wore over her gray skirt, hoping that the American wouldn't notice she'd worn this same outfit when she'd first met him, though today she'd added a belt for panache. As Mutter used to say, "A well-chosen scarf, belt, or brooch turns drab into dazzling." It was all in the accessories. She thought about adding Mutter's hairpin, the only talisman she still retained, but dismissed it since this would mean returning to the bedroom and being questioned by Lili about why she was wearing makeup.

She examined herself one more time in the mirror, surprised that she cared so much, and was about to exit when she heard Allegra softly singing as she passed by. Allegra's repertoire consisted mainly of Ladino songs whose lyrics were recipes for Sephardic dishes. This was how recipes were passed down from generation to generation. Maya had been taken by surprise once when what she had assumed to be a love song turned out to be a recipe for eggplants.

All was quiet now, and Maya stuck her head into the hallway. No one. She tiptoed toward the front door and heard Joe's voice coming from the living room. She froze. She didn't want to risk facing him either. What if he offered to drive her to the museum?

She liked Joe and he'd been nothing but hospitable, but he had not expected to shelter her family for so long, and Erik and Vati were not the easiest of guests. His four boys were crammed into one bedroom and were always quarreling. The Levis must be getting weary of them, especially with Allegra's pregnancy, and probably feeling resentful about not being able to invite friends and family over to the house. Joe seemed very concerned about attracting unwanted attention. He'd coached Maya ad nauseam about the ways of life in Syria in the event a nosy neighbor questioned her. As for Allegra, she was usually aloof and as tightly wound as a coiled spring. But there were occasional bursts of kindness, like this morning when she'd surprised Erik at breakfast with blintzes.

Maya took a deep breath and didn't let it out until she reached the landing, carefully closing the front door behind her. Freedom! She raced down the stairwell, but had barely reached the ground floor when she heard Lili calling after her.

"Maaaaya, wait up!"

Maya squeezed her eyes shut. Now what?

"My dress is ready," Lili exclaimed, breathless when she caught up to her after flying down the stairs. "You must come with me to pick it up at the tailor's. My parents won't let me go downtown alone, and they're both busy."

"I'm on my way to the museum," Maya said firmly, peeved at Lili's demanding tone. "We have to do it another time," she added.

Lili was stunned that her request was being denied. Her face metamorphosed into that of a spoiled child, her lower lip turned down. "Please, pleeease," she begged. "It can't wait. I must find a shawl for my dress." And then, eyes lowered, she confessed in a whisper: "I just found out that Fernando will be at the B'nai B'rith ball. I have to look perfect. What if I can't find a wrap I like?"

Maya was nonplussed. Lili was such a child. There were still another ten days before the big fund-raiser soirée on King Farouk's yacht, plenty of time to find the "perfect" shawl for Lili's "perfect" dress. The girl had to learn to accept "no." Maya looked her squarely in the eyes and said, "I'm sorry, Lili, but not today."

Lili didn't say anything and cracked her knuckles. Then slowly opening her mouth, she pronounced in all innocence, "This time you should wear a *fichu*. The wind will mess up your hairdo."

Maya's resolve began to melt. She was unable to suppress a smile. These Egyptian Jews had the most quaintly endearing way of speaking. Though their French was impeccable, they used so many archaic words that she sometimes hardly understood them. "Around our neck and on our head we wear not a fichu, but a *foulard* (a scarf)," she corrected Lili once again.

"I know," Lili replied with a sad smile. "And I shouldn't keep pronouncing my Hs. I keep forgetting H is silent in French. It's very difficult remembering it all."

Here she was trilling her Rs, like the locals did in their flowery, singsong accent! Maya's resolve continued to melt. Lili could be so annoying, but she was certainly well meaning. Maybe there was time to both go shopping and meet with the American.

"Can you keep a secret?" she asked.

It turned out to be a good thing that Lili was accompanying her on her foray into the city. The metro to the Ghamra station was a forty-minute ride, after which they had to take a tram, changing twice before arriving at Midan Soliman Pasha, the heart of the shopping district. Maya would never have found it by herself. After leaving Heliopolis, camels and donkeys had gradually given way to fancy cars, and cotton galabeyas had yielded to linen suits as they passed through the last of the Arab neighborhoods and arrived in the center of town.

"The museum is just ten minutes away, off Midan Ismail Pasha, the largest square in Cairo," Lili said as she fought her way through the mostly western crowd.

Except for the *épicerie* and the flower shop in Heliopolis that had closed up in the aftermath of Tobruk, it seemed that people had taken again to the streets in droves. Lili, eager to prove her gratitude, pointed out various landmarks on their way, taking seriously her role as guide. She showed off the colossal stone statue "The Reawakening of Egypt," which the Egyptian people were very proud of, and which Maya had noticed outside the train station when she first arrived. Lili then gushed about the Ezbekieh Gardens, behind the Shepheard's Hotel, where every year she and her brothers celebrated the Jewish holiday of Purim in masks and costumes. The opera house came next, and she explained that it was modeled on La Scala and built by an Italian architect, like many of the buildings here. Finally, the tour wound up in Ataba Square, Cairo's main commercial venue, which was home to the city's central food market, post office, and fire station, as well as the Sednaoui department store. Lili said that she personally preferred to shop at Shemla or Cicurel, where they were headed next. Maya drank it all in.

Maya had never studied architecture, but she knew the difference between the Italian Renaissance buildings with their arches, domes and classical columns, and the French Baroque style with wrought iron balconies, richly sculpted surfaces and strong curves. And then there were the unmistakable art deco buildings, with their flat rooftops and etched glass windows and doors. Added to this eclectic mélange were structures with strong Islamic elements. But one thing they all had in common was an abundance of ornamentation, whether it was Egyptian motifs such as lotus flowers, palm leaves and scarabs, or European ones, like medallions, angels, and garlands. There wasn't a single door, window, or façade that didn't have one form of embellishment or another.

Maya turned and smiled at Lili. She liked it here. "I can't believe

I'm just seeing this now," she said, eyeing the arcaded boutiques along the streets, which reminded her of the Rue de Rivoli in Paris. And what of the open-air terraced café across the avenue? With its small round tables and green wicker chairs, it reminded her so much of the bistro where Jean-Jacques had kissed her for the first time. She still reddened at the thought of their brazen public kiss. A far cry from her first kiss at sixteen, when she'd insisted her boyfriend put a handkerchief between their lips.

"Groppi's is across the square," Lili said, linking her arm with Maya's. "Come, my tailor is on the other side, just down the avenue."

Made of shiny black satin with a thick, mustard yellow beaded trim that followed the plunging V of the décolleté, Lili's dress for the B'nai B'rith ball was truly beautiful, and she looked ravishing in it. However, since finding a matching yellow wrap proved impossible and Lili rejected every black shawl they saw as boring, she settled on a red bolero, which she would wear with a red flower in her hair. At the time of payment, she surprised Maya with a gift—a magnificent, shimmering aqua scarf of sublime softness that she'd seen Maya admire. She'd insisted on underlining Maya's eyes with black kohl. This way her eyes were alive like never before, attracting everyone's attention because their hue took on every one of the shawl's blue and green shades, depending on the light.

"Wait," Maya said as they approached Groppi's red-and-green awning as the clock tower across the plaza rang three o'clock. She had tried wearing her new scarf around her neck, but her outfit was so dull that she decided instead to tie it around her waist as a belt, letting it drape over her hips. "What do you think?" she asked, suddenly feeling very nervous. "I need a new skirt."

"No offense, but you need new everything," Lili said. Then, untying the scarf, she wrapped it back around Maya's neck. "Show off your eyes, will you!"

On the glass double doors of the eatery was a notice warning customers that the shop would be closed on November 2, the anniversary of the Balfour Declaration. Maya felt a chill run down her spine as she read it. Maybe this was a sign she shouldn't be meeting with the American. What was she thinking? But, sensing Maya's hesitancy, Lili took her arm firmly and dragged her inside.

The place was abuzz with soldiers and civilians, their jolly voices bouncing off the high-domed establishment. Some waited to be seated, while others ordered French pastries that were displayed behind the immaculate glass étagères. Maya felt mildly scandalized by the insouciance of the patrons. Hadn't the Eighth Army just lost an important stronghold? She broke free of Lili and started marching out.

"*Mon Dieu,* you really *are* impossible." Lili grabbed her and pinched her arm.

"What are you going to do while I have coffee with him?" Maya asked.

"Hide in the bathroom." Lili kissed her on the cheek and then, taunting her, singsonged, "Destiny!"

CHAPTER 19

"Can't talk. I've got something to do for Kirk," Dorothy said hurriedly as she grabbed Mickey's hand and pulled him in from the back door to the ambassador's office. "We just received the Daniel Sieff Institute's curriculum via diplomatic pouch from Tel Aviv." She handed him the booklet and started striding toward her office.

When she reached her office door she paused and, with her hand on the doorknob, began to quickly brief him. "Donovan is tracking down the other scientists in Blumenthal's field who left Germany. I've checked up on Bose, the Indian. He's working for the engineering department of the East India Railway and is no longer teaching, so it's doubtful that Blumenthal is headed to India. I've contacted the Anglo American Hospital here, but no one treats polio. However, I did find someone at the Israelite Hospital named Dr. Ben Simon, who specializes in the disease, but I can't pin him down for an appointment. You'll have to wear some nice cologne and be charming to his secretary. That's it for now." She squinted for a second and studied his face. "Your eye is looking better, Connolly. You're almost pretty again."

"I've been putting some kind of magical Arab concoction on it," he said. "Can we go inside and talk instead of doing this on the fly? I've got some news of my own."

She cocked her head and sighed. "Spit it out, Connolly, I'm a busy girl," she said as she opened the door a crack.

"Erik Blumenthal is here in Cairo," he announced. "I found out through the Israelite Hospital; Dr. Ben Simon's office, no less." He tried to sound casual, but he couldn't control the self-congratulatory grin that spread across his face. "Some gentleman tried to obtain leg braces for a friend of his with a prescription for custom fitting from Istanbul. The friend's name was Erik with an Ashkenazi last name. The nurse remembered the Erik part because she'd never seen Erik spelled with a K. Anyhow, it's policy not to honor a foreign prescription. Fingers crossed, the real Erik will eventually show up. She knows how to contact me." Mickey was pretty pleased with himself to have dug this one up.

"Why didn't you say so sooner?" She opened the door to her office wide and shoved him inside.

Mickey was still rubbing off the lipstick from the kiss that Dorothy had planted on his cheek when he floated into Groppi's at three-thirty, right on time for his date with Maya. He had confirmed that Blumenthal was in Cairo, but he hadn't actually gotten any closer to finding the man. With forty thousand new refugees having fled here from Alexandria since the fall of Tobruk, and with emergency trains running round the clock, the task had grown even more daunting. Life had been much simpler when he was just a reporter, even though reporting on the war had become more and more like taking dictation from the British PR team.

He found Groppi's much too crowded for his liking, and his ears throbbed from the shrill cacophony of laughter mixed with the sharp clinking of teacups, forks, and knives. How would they ever be able to make conversation amid this din? He had tried to suggest a more intimate setting for their rendezvous, but Maya had insisted they choose a place that was easy to find, casual, and very public, though for some reason she'd nixed the Shepheard's flat-out.

Frustrated at being unable to find the hostess, Mickey started wandering around the main room haunted by a nagging feeling that the girl was not going to show up. She had called him three times to push back the date and was never able to commit to an exact meeting time. Her calls had come at the ungodly hour of seven in the morning, and she could never talk for more than a minute. But her voice had a lovely, velvety quality to it and it lingered in his mind. She'd teased him for being asleep while she'd been up for hours, making loaves of bread and cakes for her family, which she was going to take to the neighborhood baker's oven for baking. She'd promised to bring him a sample. She sounded pressed, and though her tone was light, he felt the lightness was somewhat forced. The girl intrigued him, and he'd been looking forward to seeing her all week. Should he have tried sending flowers or chocolate via her uncle? Just as he was giving up hope the girl would show up, he reached the garden patio in the back—and there she was.

Hunched over a newspaper, her elbow on the table, holding her chin in the palm of one hand while twirling a lock of hair with the other, she was even more beautiful than he'd remembered, despite the fact that she was frowning. She sat with one leg entwined around her ankle, her foot shaking as if beating to some unheard music. An empty cup and plate sat on the round, white cast iron table in front of her, along with a tall glass of water. Behind her, goblets were neatly lined up on mirrored shelves next to a fountain. She looked like . . . a flower was the first word that came to his mind. This would make a beautiful picture, he thought, and he raised his hands to his eyes as if he were holding a camera and made a clicking sound.

She looked up and smiled.

An unruly curl fell across her forehead, and he felt his knees buckle. Forget Rita Hayworth. The most beautiful girl he'd ever seen was right here in Cairo.

He moved closer, hands in his pockets, terribly self-conscious about walking like a gentleman in his new beige linen suit. He wracked his mind for a clever greeting line and came up with "Hi."

"Hello," she replied, seeming pleased to see him. "I've been here since three. I wasn't sure what time I'd said."

"What's in the news?" he asked, taking a seat across from her and indicating her paper. "More fancy weddings?"

"The Germans are laying siege to Leningrad," she said. "They've taken both Peter the Great's and Catherine's palaces."

"I know. It seems there's no stopping the Hun," he said, staring into her eyes as he took the paper from her hands. "Can we forget the news for now? I'm glad to see you."

Unlike the first time he met her, her eyes today were heavily circled in black and appeared to be dancing in her face. Her lips were drenched in an alluring red, and once again her bare arms grabbed his attention. Bits of glistening skin revealed themselves as her shawl hung down off her shoulder, exciting his imagination.

"Nice suit," she commented. "I had given up on you as a dresser."

"I'm a man of many layers and surprises," he grinned. "So . . . you've let on that you're a baker. Are you any good?"

She laughed. "Very good! I was going to make a cake with figs and walnuts today, but one of my little sisters beat me to it. It wasn't ready or I would have brought you a piece." She shrugged and flipped her hair back. "What happened to your eye?"

"Oh, some stupid fight I got into, trying to salvage a bit of dignity for an ungrateful Arab. It was four or five o'clock in the morning. I wasn't thinking straight."

She raised an eyebrow. "What happened?" she pressed.

He told her about the incident with the drunken Tommies and how he'd been spat on by the Arab after recovering his hat. "I guess all Westerners are the same to them."

"What were you doing out at that time in that part of town?"

"I was on my way home."

"From where?"

"Aren't we curious?" He shifted in his seat.

"I told you I am." She leaned over the table and smiled expectantly. "Tell me."

"A party, if you must know."

"A party with a girl?" she grinned devilishly. "Why would you have been so disoriented otherwise?"

"You really *are* curious." He was feeling hot, and he loosened his tie.

"You said you like that about me." She batted her eyes, enjoying having him cornered. "So, was it with a girl? It doesn't matter to me, but I think it'd give your story a poetic dimension. Feeling all soft and cozy from his night with a girl, the ace reporter bravely faced the unknown to battle for justice!" she said theatrically.

"Please!" He laughed nervously, feeling himself reddening.

"Tell me," she said again.

"I was with a friend."

"A friend who is a girl?"

"Yeah, but not a girlfriend."

Her smile disappeared and she sat up straight in her chair. She'd trapped him.

"I knew it!" she declared, summoning a brave smile. "You *were* with a girl."

"It was nothing. I barely knew her. Don't be upset."

"Who says I'm upset? You don't owe me any explanation. You're a free agent. I'm just disappointed. I don't like a man flirting with me when he's already involved with someone else. I don't have time for games."

"I told you it was nothing."

He could see the wheels in her head turning as she studied him for a while.

"I'm sorry. I shouldn't have come," she finally said, her face crumbling, pained and vulnerable. "My family doesn't even know where I am. Thank you for returning my book. I was very angry with myself when I thought I had lost it." She started to rise, but he reached for her forearm.

"Please," he said, "just stay for coffee. I don't like games either. Honestly, I am not involved with anyone." She remained still, just staring at him. "I know you think I like to play the field, but I don't. I had a steady girlfriend for three years until six months ago."

"What happened?" she asked, a flicker of uncertainty in her eyes, but still not budging.

"She dumped me," he admitted and shrugged.

"I'm sorry," she finally said, shaking her head. "I've developed the reflex to run at the first sign of trouble. I have to learn to control that." She relaxed back into her seat. "What did you think of the book?"

"I enjoyed it, though 'enjoyed' may not be the right word," he said.

"You did not like the character of Pablo?"

"I thought he was smug, and he was pretty nasty to his cell-mates. You like him?"

"I'm ambivalent, though I admire his bravery in the face of death."

"I'm sure Jean-Jacques has a very highbrow opinion on this," he scoffed, greatly exaggerating the French pronunciation of the name with the intonation of a jealous lover, which made her smile. "You know, it's a classic ploy for a man to give a girl a philosophy book to win her affection. I hope you didn't fall for that."

"And what if I did?"

"Did you? No games now!"

She smiled. Touché! "It's in the past. I was young and impressionable. I'm seeing things very differently now."

"Well in my case, I was a fool and not that young. But I really don't give a damn about her now." He immediately bit his lip, realizing how bitter he must sound.

"Breaking up hurts, even if it's the right thing to do," she said, looking him in the eye, expectantly.

He did not look away. What the hell! We said no games, he reminded himself.

"She ran off with her ex-boyfriend," he blurted out, "a month before our wedding." There it was. He felt naked and foolish for exposing himself that way.

"Monsieur-dame," the waiter interrupted, "what can I bring you?"

She ordered a *millefeuille,* but he wasn't in the mood for dessert. All he wanted at this point was to get out of there, having embarrassed himself and ruined his chances with the girl. "I don't know . . ."

"A millefeuille also for monsieur," she told the waiter. "It's a napoleon. They're my favorite." She reached for his hand and squeezed it, smiling warmly. "So tell me about America."

"Well . . . it's big. It's protected by two oceans . . . " he started to joke.

"C'mon," she said, taking her hand away and letting her shawl slide down her arms. "Let's start over . . . I was really looking forward to seeing you."

"Me too" he said. "I thought about you all week. Tell me more about yourself, besides your talent as a baker."

"And cook," she added with a little smile.

"Syrian dishes?"

"Yes," she nodded. "It's easy. We just smother everything in apricots—*mesh mesh*."

"And you're a refugee here?"

She lowered her eyes and nodded.

"I'm sorry about my ignorance the other day. I've been studying up. Apparently, a couple months ago fourteen hundred Syrian Jews were escorted to the Palestine border, only to be turned away by the British. Many of them were killed in the conflict." He shook his head. "Unbelievable . . . having to flee their homeland like that. I can't imagine what they'd even take with them."

"Very little," she said. "Important papers, a few photos, a small suitcase, some food, and lots of prayers. Embroidered linens and the family china become very insignificant."

"I don't doubt that. What about you? Are you planning to settle here in Egypt?"

"I'm not sure what my family is going to do at this point."

"Of course. It's all so uncertain, for everybody. Are you staying with your uncle in Heliopolis?"

"No," she protested. "And how do you know he lives in Heliopolis?"

"Ace reporter!" He thumbed toward himself. "I'm guilty of curiosity."

"Please, don't bother my uncle again," she said. "We're staying with some cousins. And I really don't like to discuss my situation here in Egypt. I was hoping that this would be . . . " She shrugged. "How is your article coming?"

"Promising," he said, respecting her wish to change the subject. "But I'm still not sure what the best angle is. I'm finding that Egyptian Jews are extremely generous people, and they seem comfortably assimilated, but below the surface there is a lot of fear, and not just about the Germans invading. They're very careful not to rock the boat and jeopardize their position here."

She leaned in closer. "What do you know about the Muslim Brotherhood? Do you think they represent a real threat to the Jews here?"

"Under the present climate? Absolutely. But their problem with the Jews is really a political one, nothing like in Europe."

"My uncle says that the Brotherhood hates the English."

"True, and they're a thorn in the Brits' side. Their guerrilla tactics are very hard to defend against, but the organization is extremely dependent on its leader and the British are pulling out all the stops to make sure that he is recaptured."

She sat back and frowned, ruminating for a moment before asking, "Who actually runs this place, the Egyptians or the British?"

"Officially, the English have nothing to do with the government, but in reality they run the country," he said, noting the intensity of her gaze as she listened carefully. "There is a parliament and a king, but they fight all the time, and the Egyptian Constitution doesn't have checks and balances, so the English are the arbitrators."

"I guess better the British than these Nazi puppets, the Vichy French, who run Syria," she said, accepting Mickey's offer of a cigarette. "My brother hates to see me smoke." She grimaced. "What kind of name is Connolly, anyway?"

"Irish. My family is from the south of Ireland."

"Catholic, then?"

"Is that a problem?" He looked into her eyes.

"Why should it be?" Her gaze veered away.

"I don't know . . . In America the Jews don't mix much with—"

"Gentiles?" It was she who sought his eyes this time. "I didn't know gentiles wanted to mix with Jews."

"That all depends." He made light of it. "When I was a kid I carefully avoided some of the tough Jewish neighborhoods! Ever heard of the Purple Gang?"

She shook her head and puffed on her cigarette, and he realized she wasn't inhaling. "I only heard about the Chicago gangs from my roommate who was from there. I went to boarding school in Switzerland," she told him. "Chic*aaa*go, as she would say." She laughed.

The sight of her face lighting up made him smile.

"Do you really think Americans in Detroit will care about the Jews in your article?" she asked. "I've read about Father Coughlin and his anti-Semitic radio broadcasts."

"The world is full of bigots, but I believe a good story will sell, even one about Jews. But back to you for a moment. How come you went to boarding school? In America only the very rich can afford that. Do many girls in Syria do that?"

"I love my parents, but they are real snobs." She looked away and seemed to be reflecting on what she'd said.

He took the opportunity to stare at her shamelessly, drinking in every feature, from the small scar on her temple to the fine blond fuzz gracing her cheeks. He watched her nostrils delicately flare as she breathed. Yes, a flower, that's what she was. He wished he could kiss her.

"Maya," he said, wanting to reach for her hand, but afraid that would scare her away. "It's a very pretty name. Did you know it means 'illusion' in Hindi?"

"And it also means 'water' in Arabic," she said. "My parents just liked the name. They picked funny names for all of us."

"You have a large family?"

"Twelve brothers and sisters."

"Oh, my goodness!" He whistled. "I must come from the only Irish Catholic family in the world with just one kid. I wish I had siblings. I want to have a whole bunch of children one day."

"Is your mother worried about your being here?"

"She died a long time ago," he said. "Of course, she would have worried. But she would have loved it here herself. Like you, she was a very curious lady." He winked. "Though she'd never been there and couldn't speak the language, she adored everything French. She named her bakery La Parisienne and sang 'Frère Jacques' to me every night. She had a bottle of French perfume, Joy, which was absolutely sacred to her. She dabbed it on her neck every Sunday before church."

"That's very sweet," Maya said.

"I just wish I had helped out more around the bakery. I had no idea that my time with her was running out. She died my junior year in high school. She had me promise to go to college. She always believed I would make something of myself."

"And you did, Mister Ace Reporter! And a nicely groomed one at that!"

He smiled sheepishly, enjoying the compliment. He'd tried hard this morning.

She placed her elbow on the table, her chin in her palm. "I have to tell you," she said. "I also had a boyfriend who cheated on me. He was the first one I really cared about. I was seventeen. He was much older. I think loyalty is the most important quality, for a lover or a friend, don't you?" Suddenly she looked behind him and motioned to someone to go away.

Mickey turned and saw a girl anxiously tapping her watch at Maya.

"I have to go," she said, uneasy, and leaned to pick up her purse from the floor.

"Please," he insisted. "We haven't even celebrated yet." He looked around for the waiter. "I doubt this joint has any champagne, but let's not let that stop us. Mademoiselle, your glass, please." He mimicked holding a bottle with one hand and pouring into an imaginary glass in the other. He then offered to pour her some.

"Come on! Your glass! I can't do this by myself."

She obliged, humoring him, and pretended to hold a glass. "I must go, really, and what are we celebrating, anyway?"

"Shh, shh." He tilted his hand as if pouring and then clicked his imaginary glass against hers. "To our first date."

CHAPTER 20

The Jew has vanished,

Kesner wrote, dipping his pen into the bottle of disappearing ink that sat on the wrought iron table under the white parasol on the foredeck of his boat. He'd woken up in a foul mood and more than ever he felt the need to write in his diary.

> Despite his contacts, Abdoul was unable to trace him after he got off the boat in Alex. The Jewish community center here in Cairo is inundated with refugees and even with that silly little Jewish cap on my head I couldn't extract any useful information. It's clear the Jew must be getting help from somewhere. Given his importance, I bet it's coming from powerful Jews. I must send Samina to that big Jewish soirée on the king's yacht. No doubt the American spy will be there. With her smarts and instincts she'll help pick out this Fastball.
>
> I snooped around the American Embassy the other day, but without any contacts, I had no success. Who would have thought I would have to worry about the Yanks? The American community here is small and dispersed, and they don't have a restaurant or club where they gather, but Abdoul,

> bless his fat heart, is getting me a list of all registered Americans. Maybe he can even find out which Americans will be invited to the party on the royal yacht.
>
> I did discover that representatives of an American consortium are here to investigate oil prospects in the Middle East. The Americans are catching up.

Kesner put his pen down and took a tentative sip of the black Egyptian Arousa tea that he drank for breakfast with honey and walnut rolls. It was still piping hot. He checked his watch: 6:50. He'd better get going. He had an important meeting this morning with Anwar Sadat, the cofounder of the Revolutionary Committee, as the rebels within the Egyptian army called themselves. Kesner was hoping to introduce the young lieutenant to Hassan al-Banna and convince him to arm the Brotherhood. With the two subversive groups joining forces, Rommel, whose Afrika Korps had already entered Egypt in several places, would sail through the country easily. Rumor had it that they had taken Mersa Matruh, leaving only El Alamein as the last Allied stronghold before Cairo, a mere sixty miles beyond. Feeling chipper that Rommel would be here in no time, he grabbed the Biro ballpoint from his shirt pocket and jotted down in big letters:

> Kairo
> Wednesday, October 10, 1941
> Max. 29° C Min. 19° C

Sometimes he provided more details, like wind and other trivial facts, masking his journal as a weather log, but today these would be the only notations he'd make. He shut the diary and read the quote from Sun Tzu's *The Art of War* he'd inscribed in large printed letters on the cover of the journal: *Invincibility is in oneself. Vulnerability is in the opponent*. He read it every day for strength and inspiration.

"*Haz saeed* (Good luck)," the taxi driver said as Kesner stepped out of the cab. The driver wouldn't take him deeper into the City of the Dead, or Araafa, as the cemetery was referred to. Even for thick-skinned Egyptians, the poverty here among the tombstones and catacombs was too wretched to face. Kesner knew that it was against Islamic teachings to dwell among the dead, yet fellahin from poor villages and impoverished city dwellers had formed shantytown communities here. Tea stands and fruit markets had sprung up between the graves all through the enormous cemetery where Egyptians of all social standings had been burying their dead for centuries.

"A city within a city," Kesner thought as he negotiated his way inside the cemetery's walls. Row after row of tombstones formed a labyrinth of alleys that stretched as far as the eye could see. He searched for the obelisk he'd been assured he'd find near the south gate entrance, where he was to meet Sadat and Sheik al-Banna. Kesner could easily understand why the sheik, like many other wanted men, had adopted this area as his hideout. He could sleep and strategize with his cohorts in different sepulchers for months on end, and, in an emergency, he could disappear through one of the innumerable exits, either into the city or into the desert. But this kind of emergency was unlikely, since both the Egyptian and British police shied away from this place as if it housed the plague.

Kesner breathed easier when he spotted a rose-colored marble obelisk next to a tomb covered with dry flowers and desiccated food offerings. It must be a saint's vault, he surmised. He could see a soldier's cap partially visible behind the obelisk.

"Good morning, Herr Sadat," Kesner called.

Sadat came around. His Egyptian army uniform was immaculate, hardly what he expected from a revolutionary leader. Kesner hadn't seen the young officer since he'd been sent off to Mersa

Matruh three months ago. With his new, well-trimmed mustache, he looked older than his twenty-two years, but his beady, youthful eyes were as fiery as ever.

"Good morning, Herr Kesner," Sadat answered, standing erect. "I almost did not recognize you in your galabeya."

"It is I, it is I," Kesner said, adjusting the gray cap he'd chosen to wear today instead of a tarbush, which would have attracted more attention in this neighborhood. "You're looking fairly well, Herr Sadat, although I know it must pain you to wear a uniform after that terrible insult of having your weapons taken from you by the British." He placed his hand on his chest. "My heart went out to you when I heard about it."

Sadat did not flinch. "I must tell you right away that we do not intend to arm the Brotherhood," he declared. "My colleagues assisted you in getting Sheik al-Banna out of prison, but that is as far as we will go."

"Nobody's talking about arming anybody," Kesner responded, annoyed with the youngster's naïve idealism. "I just ask that you meet with him. You may have more in common than you realize."

Sadat looked away. When he looked back, his face wore a pained expression. He gestured at the laundry that hung between tombstones to dry. "This is what the British have done for Egypt. They've reduced us to animals." He suddenly pointed behind Kesner. "There he is, I think."

"That's him, all right," Kesner confirmed as he turned toward the slight silhouette of Hassan al-Banna. The sheik wore his distinctive red *abaya* with the hood pulled low over his face, his long beard sticking out. He was carrying a heavy wooden staff and stood on top of a large stone. Kesner waved to him.

Al-Banna did not wave back but raised his stick over his head—*follow me*—and began to jump from stone to stone over the broken ground like a mountain goat. Although he was wearing sandals, he was spry and moved quickly as he led them deeper into the cemetery. He finally came to a halt in an uninhabited section and crouched down behind a rock.

Two men appeared out of nowhere, rifles on their shoulders.

"He is swift for an old man," Sadat whispered, panting.

"Old man? He's only in his midthirties," Kesner replied, wiping sweat from his forehead with his sleeve. He looked around, feeling claustrophobic amid the closely packed tombstones and cenotaphs. Except for the occasional buzzing of a fly, the cemetery was a strange and creepy oasis of calm.

The sheik sprang to his feet as they approached and pulled back his hood, revealing deep-set, sad eyes and leathery skin. He reminded Kesner of a lizard. There wasn't a single bead of sweat on his face. Al-Banna and Sadat sized one another up.

"Unusual place to set up shop, eh?" Kesner joked in Arabic, trying to break the awkwardness of the moment. He shook hands with the sheik and tapped his back, but the sheik was still eyeing Sadat.

"Peace be with you." Al-Banna spoke first, addressing Sadat with a toothy smile and offering his hand.

Sadat took it. "And also with you." He embraced him before continuing. "Sheik Hassan al-Banna, you may not know that we have met once before—some years ago, when I was only a boy. I came to hear you speak outside a mosque near the Bab El Khalq."

"That must have been a long time ago. I have not spoken publicly in Cairo for many years," the sheik replied.

"How are you enjoying your freedom?" Kesner asked him.

"As long as the British are in Egypt none of us are truly free. But I don't wish to seem ungrateful." Al-Banna took Kesner's hand into his own two hands. "Thank you, my friend, for releasing me from jail. I did not understand at first why I was being transferred to a higher security jail, but then, when I was taken to the car and heard the crickets in the reeds along the banks of the Nile and smelled the sweet scent of the river, I knew I was being set free. Thanks be to God." He raised his eyes piously to heaven.

"Thanks be to God," Kesner agreed heartily. "Without the Almighty the operation would never have been successful." From the corner of his eye, he noticed Sadat giving him a dirty look, impatient with this religious pronouncement.

"We will go somewhere we can talk," the sheik announced, turning on his heel and leading them to a doorway. Stairs inside would lead down to catacombs, no doubt. Above it was a cenotaph still richly carved with Arabic markings even though the white glare of the sun had bleached the color from the weather-beaten stone.

The burial chambers below had been transformed into tidy rooms furnished with cots and tables and chairs where men could gather in groups. The sheik showed Kesner and Sadat to a private room furnished with large pillows.

"We thank Allah, the Merciful and Compassionate, for giving us the strength to lead the struggle against the infidel," the sheik began when they'd settled. "Lieutenant Sadat, I understand you, too, are involved in the *mujahida*." His voice was soft, and the light from the torch illuminating the chamber cast long shadows on his face.

"You could say that," Sadat replied, folding his legs Indian style. "I am an officer in the Egyptian army, but I am a member of the Revolutionary Committee."

"And they are striving in the path of Allah?"

"We are striving for the people of Egypt." Sadat spoke solemnly. "We are seeking to throw the colonialist invaders out of our country and overturn the feudalism that persists."

The sheik smiled, pleased. "And this will mark a return to Islam."

"The aim of the Revolutionary Committee is to establish a people's republic in Egypt. We are not interested in going back to the

Middle Ages or becoming a theocracy," Sadat stated flatly, staring defiantly into the sheik's eyes.

Kesner bit his lip. "But as you said," he quickly reminded Sadat, "you both are dedicated to getting rid of the occupier." The young officer was being impetuous. Kesner thought that as a leader of his group he should show more diplomacy.

"Anwar, why do you seek a path that turns away from the light of Allah and emulates foreign systems of government that we know do not work?" the sheik asked, looking pained. "Why overthrow something, only to replace it with its copy? The Holy Qur'an contains all the laws you need." He counted on his fingers: "Human rights; equality; brotherhood; right to freedom of speech; right to life, to property, to dignity and to justice. All this is in the sayings of the prophet."

"Yes, and they are also the principles of the French Revolution," Kesner interjected, knowing this would strike a chord with the young officer. "*Liberté, égalité, fraternité.*"

"The Qur'an is a great and wonderful book, Sheik Hassan," Sadat replied, ignoring Kesner, "but it is just a guide. It is not government in practice."

"There you are wrong, my young friend!" the sheik cried out, his voice rising for the first time. "The four caliphs governed only by the Holy Book, and for centuries we had a golden era for Islam."

"The caliphs ruled in another time," Sadat argued.

"The caliphs were entrusted with their power from God. Sovereignty belongs to Allah alone. Man is merely a temporary custodian. Even the king is not empowered by God."

"That's right, he owes his throne to the British," Sadat responded.

"The true representative of Allah's power here on earth must be pious and unfailingly dedicated to His word."

"Who do you think Allah has in mind for the job?" Sadat asked sardonically.

Kesner was dying inside. Sadat was going too far.

But the sheik did not flinch. He just looked to heaven and opened his hands, gesturing that he didn't know—or, perhaps, that it would be him.

"The ruler must be chosen by the people," Sadat continued.

"The ruler is chosen by God," the sheik corrected.

Kesner had to stop this conversation before it spiraled into an argument. "First things first. Why don't we wait and see what comes after the British have been removed?" he suggested. "They have brought such shame and misery to your country that you must unite to overthrow them and settle your differences afterward." He looked from Sadat to al-Banna.

After a short silence, the sheik waved his hand and said,"Herr Kesner is right. We must be brothers now. Our country is suffocating."

But Sadat looked wary.

Kesner nodded to the sheik and got to his feet. "Come." He held out his hand to Sadat on the floor. "Let's you and I talk in private."

He led him to the room next door where three men scurried away when they entered.

"Lieutenant, you must understand," Kesner whispered. "The Brotherhood can bring about the collapse of British rule. They are brave guerrilla fighters, loyal to the sheik's every word. They have been very successful at sabotaging communications lines, as you know."

"You want me to arm them," Sadat replied loudly, confronting Kesner.

"The sooner they are armed, the sooner you will have your revolution," Kesner conceded, whispering hoarsely and gesturing with his hand for Sadat to lower his voice. "Only God knows what will happen afterward."

"Understand me," Sadat replied in a softer voice. "I am a Muslim, and I believe that our people should be taught the prophet's teachings about humility and charity and goodness. But I cannot arm civilians and send them hopelessly against the might of the English. That is the job of the army. I am sorry." On these words, he strode out of the chamber toward the exit.

As Kesner started after Sadat, he noticed in the adjacent room, lit by a feeble candle, the silhouette of a young man sitting at a table, one hand placed on the Qur'an, the other on a revolver. He was repeating the oath of initiation into the Brotherhood that an officiate was administering: "Dying in the way of Allah is our highest hope. The messenger is our leader. The Qur'an is our law. And Jihad is our way." He pledged with such passionate religious fervor that it gave Kesner goose bumps and he stopped in his tracks. He'd catch Sadat another time.

When he returned to the chamber, he found the sheik crouched on the floor, cleaning his nails with a large curved knife that he'd produced from the folds of his robe.

"He will come around," Kesner assured him. "But I need a favor from you. I'm looking for a Jew. His name is Erik Blumenthal."

CHAPTER 21

"Pssst . . . Lili," Maya whispered, "are you awake?"

But no response came back from the girl, who, along with the entire household, had gone to bed right after the enormous meal Allegra had served following the Yom Kippur service. She found the Levis' custom of breaking the fast with coffee and sweets to be rather strange, and she wondered how the family could still have an appetite after that. But they'd gorged themselves at the dinner table nevertheless, except for Maya, who was furious with Erik for having gotten into a fight with Vati. Since returning from schul, Vati had been complaining about how lax the rabbi's service had been and criticizing the Sephardim for their materialism and lack of spirituality. Erik, the atheist, had finally exploded, expressing his contempt for all forms of organized religion, including his own family's Ashkenazi brand of Judaism. He called his father weak-minded. The two men did not talk to one another all evening.

Mutter would have been horrified by this rift, Maya thought, too agitated to fall asleep. She tossed and turned, trying to find a good position. But sleep still did not come. Her mind was restlessly replaying the events of the day and churning with the innumerable other anxieties that haunted her relentlessly.

Finally, she sat up and looked at her watch. It wasn't quite midnight. She wondered if Mickey was awake. It had taken some doing, but she'd managed to talk to him a few times since their first date. She would cheerfully offer to do errands, such as taking Allegra's unbaked cakes and breads to the baker's oven, fetching the mail at the post office, and picking up the children from school. These ventures provided her with the opportunity to place a call to him, and the excitement of sneaking into telephone booths in strange places was becoming intoxicating. He was a breath of fresh air in her life—her secret. His quiet strength and gentle sense of humor never failed to calm her down. And why not indulge in some momentary pleasure? She would be leaving Cairo soon. There had been some kind of complication with their papers, but everything was back on track now, and the tension in the house had eased somewhat.

Maya quietly slipped out of bed and went into the living room, where the telephone was located. She dialed Mickey's number and smiled when he answered.

"Hi, it's me," she whispered, biting her finger. "I hope I'm not waking you up?" She couldn't believe she'd had the nerve to call Mickey while everybody in the house was asleep—at least she hoped they were.

"No, not at all," he said in a groggy voice. "I was just thinking about some of the people I interviewed today. Pretty boring stuff. What about you? Did you go to synagogue today?"

"Yes, I went. It's our holiest day, the Day of Atonement. It's the only time I go. It was boring, too. Everything was in Hebrew and I don't understand a word of it. I just like it at the very end when they blow the shofar."

"What's the shofar?"

"It's a ram's horn. They blow it at the end of the service in long, powerful bursts. It always gives me goose bumps."

"How come?"

She shrugged. "It's a strange, shrill sound. It's very plaintive. It makes me cry. It's hard to explain. It goes straight into my heart."

"In many parts of the world sound is considered to be the primal vibration. People who meditate also use it in chanting to tune up their nervous systems."

"How come you know so much about Eastern religion? You're Catholic."

"Many layers!"

She laughed out loud, then immediately covered her mouth with her hand. "Don't make me laugh," she whispered. "I'm going to wake up the whole house." She sat on the arm of the sofa, the phone very close to her ear. "Mickey, I read in the paper that the Germans have crossed into Egypt."

He sighed. "They got in awhile back. It only just made the papers now."

"What's really going on? Do you know? I hear the Allied Eighth Army is very overstretched. Please tell me."

"Rommel's troops are even more overstretched, and they're undersupplied."

"So . . . what else?"

"I don't know . . . Just rumors."

"Like what? Wait . . . sshh!" She suddenly turned around, thinking she'd heard a sound. But all was still. "Tell me."

"A lot of men are deserting from the Allied Eighth Army. They're losing faith in their High Command. I don't blame them. But I think that the Allies can stop the Germans at El Alamein. There's an impassable sand depression there, Rommel won't be able to outflank them. Don't lose hope. The Germans are starting to make some bad decisions. But let's talk about what's really important. When can I see you again?"

She sighed. "I don't know. My parents are scared; they're

making plans to go to the Sudan. A cousin of theirs is already there. I don't want to go, but I have to."

He did not say anything for a long while. "Mickey, are you there?"

"I'm here . . . I just wasn't expecting this. Is there anything I can do for you? You know, I have excellent contacts with the American Embassy here."

"There is nothing you can do really. But let's not talk about that now. Tell me one fun thing that you did today before I hang up."

"I rode a donkey for the first time. He farted loudly when I mounted him."

She laughed. Her eyes quickly surveyed the room, making sure no one could hear her. "Did that make you happy?"

"It made me embarrassed. But if you want to know what made me happy, it's hearing your voice. That makes me happy."

She felt herself blushing. "Goodnight," she said.

She remained motionless for a minute as if to seal the sound of his voice inside herself, before tiptoeing back to her room and slipping under the covers.

"I heard everything," Lili said, turning over and covering her head with her sheet.

CHAPTER 22

"I'm Mr. Connolly from the *Foreign Service Journal*. I'd like to speak with Mr. Nissel, please," Mickey said, taking his hat off when the engineer's servant opened the door of the imposing two-story Victorian house. "The American Embassy has sent me on a special inquiry."

"*Etfadal, men hena*. Please, this way." The soft-spoken Egyptian led him into the living room.

Except for a large Persian rug and two upholstered armchairs, the room was devoid of furniture. It was littered with cardboard boxes and stacks of books. A dozen or so oil paintings leaned against the walls—mostly of palm groves along the Nile and other typical Egyptian subjects. The community center's files had indicated that Nissel had moved twice in the last three months, and Mickey wasn't surprised that the man had not settled in yet. He paced the room while he waited, holding the gray fedora that he now wore whenever he wanted to present a more polished appearance, and stopped to examine a handsome book about famous bridges that sat on top of one of the stacks. As he flipped through the pictures he found a bookmark at a page displaying a sprawling red suspension bridge. *Tblisi, Georgia. 1928. Hans Nissel* was credited as the engineer. Mickey heard hushed voices coming from the other side of the door and closed the book.

"Dr. Hans Nissel," a middle-aged man with sunken brown eyes and eyebrows that spread like butterfly wings introduced himself. He was followed by a junior version of himself, his teenage son, Mickey assumed. "What can I do for you, Herr Connolly?" Nissel asked curtly in his heavy German accent, without offering Mickey a seat.

Mickey apologized for showing up without an appointment, but the matter was important. "This is sensitive information, sir," he started, "but the American Embassy has asked me to locate a German Jewish scientist and his family, who, like you, have escaped the Nazis. They have just been approved for an American visa," he said. He went on to explain that because of his own research for an article on Jewish refugees, the embassy had engaged him in this inquiry.

"It's my understanding, sir, that you have recently arrived in this country," he continued, aware of Nissel's growing stiffness, "and the circumstances of your own arrival might be of great help to us in finding the family we're looking for. This is a humanitarian—"

Nissel cut him off sharply. "Considering America's policy toward Jewish immigration, I'm surprised the matter is so important to your embassy."

Mickey realized it would take some doing to reach this man, and as much as he hated it, he had to expand the lie. "Sir, my understanding is that President Roosevelt is personally sponsoring the resettlement of a number of Jewish refugees despite the State Department's policies. We are offering assistance to a family in need, and you, sir, can be of great help by providing us with some details from your own experience."

"I can't imagine I can help you," the engineer declared. "Every person's escape is different."

At this point the son began to speak to his father in German, and a spat ensued. Nissel silenced the boy and with a glacial glare, turned to Mickey and declared: "My papers are in order. I do not want any problems. I wish you good luck with your search."

This was one tough cookie. Mickey softened his approach. "If you could be so kind . . . "

"The war has taught me not to be so kind," Nissel interrupted. "Please, I wish to be left in peace. I think I have made it clear that I do not wish to speak about my affairs to anybody. " He extended his arm, showing Mickey to the door.

The son argued again with his father, but in vain, and stormed out of the room. It was clear that Mickey was not going to be able to shame this man into helping him. He apologized for the intrusion and bid him good-bye.

Frustrated, he stopped in front of the house to light a cigarette, wondering how Nissel could be so callous about the fate of his fellow refugees. So much for the reputation Jews had for banding together. He took a long drag on his cigarette. As he started walking away from the house, he spotted Nissel's son across the street, polishing his bicycle. He stomped out his cigarette on the ground and started toward him.

"Nice bike," Mickey said. "I love Fongers. I used to have a cruiser myself."

"It's an old one, but it races good," the youngster said without looking up.

"I hope I didn't offend your father. I don't blame him for not trusting strangers. Escaping from Germany must have been a nightmare."

"He's suffered a lot. Even here in Egypt. Shortly after the war started he was interned by the British because he was German."

"But you're Jewish." Mickey frowned.

"They interned all Germans, without distinguishing between Jews and Nazis," said the youth, who stopped buffing the bike for a moment. "Still, my father should be helping you."

Mickey folded his arms. The boy was eager to talk. "When did you and your family arrive in Egypt?"

"In the spring of '39. By boat to Alexandria from Trieste, Italy."

Mickey was surprised the Nissels had been here for two years. "Why did you choose Egypt?" he pursued.

The boy glanced up toward the house to ensure that no one was watching and continued, "My father was an executive with the Berlin power company, an engineer, and he had many international contacts. We were on our way to Haifa in Palestine, but a business acquaintance in Alexandria warned him not to go there, because of the problems with the Arabs, and convinced him he could make a better life here. He found a good job very fast with the Egyptian public works ministry. Then, after six months came the war, the internment, the bombing of Alexandria. We arrived in Cairo four months ago. He was lucky to get a job with the UK General Electric."

"Yes, indeed. The city is full of refugees without work." Mickey said. The boy was talking and Mickey decided to take his shot. "When you arrived in Egypt, did you turn to anyone for help?"

"Yes, of course. He-Haluts, a Zionist group in Alex."

"But I was told there were no Zionist organizations in Egypt," Mickey said.

"Well, there were then," the youth said. "They no longer exist. It's because of the Islamic extremists who have been attacking Jews. Everybody's scared, and last year the president of the community thought it best to shut down all Zionist activities. Now, if you don't mind, I need to finish what I'm doing."

Mickey thanked the boy and started looking for a taxi. He wasn't very familiar with Maadi, a new suburb that was popular with the city's well-to-do expatriates, and he followed his nose to the center of town. Why had Jacques Antebie misled him about the Zionists? Was he trying to protect Simon Cattaoui? Were they embarrassed that their desire to avoid confrontation might seem cowardly? Maybe the Zionist organizations were gone, but that did not mean there were no Zionists left here. They must have gone underground, he thought. In any event, if the Blumenthals were heading to Palestine, they would need both entry and exit visas from Egypt. Help from the Turks would not have been enough, and Zionists within and outside of Egypt would have had to be involved. He needed to talk to Donovan.

The center of town was very crowded because of a street fair and it was nothing short of a miracle that Mickey found a taxi. A very pretty avenue lined with bushy trees linked Maadi to Cairo, but Mickey barely paid attention as his thoughts were on Maya the entire ride back. He wondered if her parents were bitter like Nissel. Would they oppose her dating a non-Jew? It did not seem to bother her. She had told him during a phone call that none of her boyfriends had been Jewish. Being away at school since age fourteen had allowed her to develop values that differed from those of her family, causing no small friction. He understood what she meant, having himself developed a very different view of the world from that of his father, who believed that college was a waste and that writing for a newspaper was for sissies. His only constant advice to Mickey had been to get a job with a good pension.

The cab arrived at the American Embassy in no time, interrupting Mickey's reveries. Mickey got out and reached for his wallet but could not find it. He patted all his pockets. No wallet. How could that be? He had used it last to pay for the taxi to Nissel's house. Mentally he retraced his steps, and it dawned on him that he had been pickpocketed on the crowded streets of Maadi.

"I'm sorry. I can borrow money from a friend inside. I'll be back in a flash," he told the driver while standing outside his rolled-down window.

"You have American chewing gum?"

"I don't, habibi. Lucky Strikes?" Mickey offered as he reached for his cigarettes.

The driver shook his head. "Next time. My gift to the American people!" He touched his heart and sped away.

Suddenly Mickey panicked—*Blumenthal's picture*! It was in his wallet.

"Congratulations, Connolly! You were right all along." Kirk said, stepping out of the embassy car that had just arrived. He patted Mickey on the back. "Erik Blumenthal is going to Palestine," he announced in a low voice. "He'll be joining the staff of the Sieff Institute."

Mickey walked with Kirk through the front reception hall, enjoying the fuss that came with the greeting of an ambassador. He was feeling pretty important himself, now that he'd cracked a big piece of the puzzle.

As they entered Dorothy's office, Mickey was feeling as if he'd grown half a foot taller.

"Oh, God, here you are," Dorothy gushed. She clicked the cradle of the phone back and forth hurriedly, trying to salvage a connection. "Hello? Hello? Mr. Donovan? Hello?" It was too late. She hung up. "Shucks! I had Donovan on the line. You just missed him, sir," she said to Kirk, while giving Mickey a thumbs-up and grinning like a proud mother. "Donovan was very pleased with your breakthrough."

"It made sense," Mickey said, shrugging off the compliment.

Kirk patted him on the back again.

"Donovan was a little surprised, frankly," Dorothy continued. "But obviously Erik Blumenthal could be important enough to the building of a Jewish state that top-level Zionists would want to find a way to get him there. Our COI guy back there has no leads yet."

Mickey took a seat on the rattan chair across from Dorothy's desk. "I've learned something interesting about Chaim Weizmann," he started. "Of course he's well known as a champion of Zionism, but did you know that he is also a scientist? In fact, he studied at the Polytechnic in Berlin, the very same university Erik Blumenthal attended."

"Weizmann could never get involved in this," Dorothy objected. "He's a statesman, and it would be political suicide for him to risk alienating the English. They hold the key to his dream of a Jewish homeland in Palestine, and he would never risk losing their goodwill over one man, no matter how important."

"I agree," Kirk added. "But other highly placed people could be involved. David Ben Gurion has openly challenged the White Papers."

Mickey was only half listening as a sheet of paper on Dorothy's desk caught his attention. He pulled it toward him when he saw the word LICA in bold capital letters.

"Is this the list of the LICA board members?" he asked.

There were a dozen names on it, including those of publishers, doctors, lawyers, and other professionals in Cairo and Alexandria. "Yvette Cattaoui?" He frowned upon finding that name. "Is she related to Simon Cattaoui?"

"She's his sister, and she's the number-one lady-in-waiting to Queen Nazli, Farouk's mother," Dorothy answered.

"Wow! The queen's closest confidante is a Zionist activist!" Mickey crossed his arms. "I wonder how she felt when her brother forced her out of business."

The shrill ring of the telephone made everyone jump.

Dorothy grabbed it. "Yes, it's Miss Calley." She did not say anything except a few "rights" and "uh-huhs" for a long while.

"He's here. I'll tell him. I'll tell him. Jacques Antebie," she mouthed at Mickey. "Just checking if we need anything," she said, her hand covering the mouthpiece.

Mickey waved urgently for her to hand him the receiver. She hesitated, but he snatched it from her.

"*Bonjour*, Jacques. Mickey Connolly. Yes, I got a hold of Hans Nissel, thank you. But I'm a little confused. Why didn't you tell me there had been Zionist organizations here in Cairo until recently?" he asked sharply.

"Ancient history. And they were never very significant," Jacques protested, his voice booming over the telephone. "We were talking about the present situation."

"Tell me, was there a connection between the Egyptian Zionists and LICA?"

"No," Jacques replied. "The Zionists fight to help Jewish immigration to Palestine in order to create a Jewish state, while LICA fights against anti-Semitism everywhere and helps Jews resettle all over the world, not necessarily in Palestine." He cleared his throat and added, "Some members of LICA were Zionists, but most strongly opposed it. This created a lot of friction within the group, but again, this was a while ago."

"I see," Mickey said. "What about Yvette Cattaoui? Was she a Zionist?"

"Very much so."

Bingo. Mickey thanked him hurriedly and hung up. "I have to speak to Yvette Cattaoui," he demanded. "If anyone would know how to get false papers, it would be her. She might have a personal axe to grind, a score to settle with her brother."

"Slow down, kiddo," Dorothy said. "We appreciate what you've done, but this is Donovan's worry now."

"Connolly," Kirk said, visibly flustered. "You've carried the ball up to this point . . . "

"It sounds like you're showing me the door," Mickey interrupted, the smile on his lips quickly fading as he realized they were serious.

Dorothy lit a cigarette and looked away from him.

He was shocked that she wasn't taking his side. "What's going on, Dorothy? I thought we were pals."

She lowered her eyes and shook her head, her face showing her forty or so years of age as she frowned. "I am being your pal," she said softly.

"Ambassador?" Mickey sought a response from Kirk, who continued to avoid his eyes as well. "Hey, I may not be an expert, but I know my way around the Jewish community here better than any new COI guy you'd bring in."

"We don't know how Donovan wants to go about this," Kirk said hesitantly.

"Donovan is taking over," Dorothy said. "He'll be in Cairo in two weeks."

"Two weeks!" Mickey was appalled. "Blumenthal is a moving target. Things can't stand still for two weeks, you know that," he said angrily.

"Sorry. You're off the case, Mickey," she insisted, her face flushing. "The stakes are way too high to include anyone who isn't a pro."

"Well, I'm sorry, too, but I'm not done yet," Mickey declared. "You did too good a job recruiting me." He crossed his arms.

Kirk and Dorothy exchanged glances.

"Maybe we ought to think this over," Kirk said. "Let me talk to Donovan."

"I don't think we can put him in touch with Madame Cattaoui without compromising ourselves," Dorothy said to Kirk, sensing defeat.

"What about that big B'nai B'rith affair that the king is throwing on his yacht?" Mickey said. "I can't imagine Madame Cattaoui not being there." He turned to Dorothy with a big grin. "I'll bet my bankroll you can find me a ticket, sweetheart."

CHAPTER 23

> Photo of scientist can be found in Copenhagen University Science Journal, Spring 1936 issue. Check library at Fuad University.

Kesner let out a victory cry as he deciphered Washington's radio communiqué in response to Fastball's inquiry. Sitting in his claustrophobic communication room, swallowing dozens of Benzedrine pills, and pissing into a bottle the liters of water he'd drunk to fight off sleep, he'd been waiting for this for the past thirty-six hours. Although the American Embassy in Cairo sent its transmissions out at fixed hours, Washington was unpredictable, and Kesner couldn't afford to be away from his radio lest he miss this one. This was his chance to catch the American spy, who would undoubtedly be going to the library to retrieve the photo. Kesner would follow him and eliminate his rival.

He furiously radioed Tripoli, which had reiterated that this assignment was top priority.

> Am on the trail of the American spy. Schwarze Hund.

Forgetting his aches and pains and general exhaustion, he climbed back upstairs to his bedroom, his heart beating rapidly from the rush of adrenaline. What a story this will be to tell his son one day! It was 6:30 AM. He pulled out a guidebook and found that the library would open at 7:30. He had time for a quick shower before going down there to study the terrain and wait for Fastball's arrival.

As he anticipated, there was very little traffic on the road, with the Arabs just stirring from their Sabbath prayers, and it took no time to reach Fuad University. To his puzzlement, when he got there at 7:15, the doors to the main library were already open. He went straight to the mezzanine, where the scientific journals were shelved, and had no problem finding the journal in question.

He anxiously flipped through it, only to discover that the page he wanted was missing, a fresh, clear tear along the side. Furious, he threw the journal on the table. "Someone has torn a page from this journal," he complained bitterly to the librarian in charge.

"Ay! It must have been that woman from the American Embassy," the man said as he inspected the damage. "She'd called before and asked as a favor to the embassy if we could open the library early."

"When did she come?"

"Shortly before 7:00. She showed me her card. I could not deny this courtesy to the secretary of the American ambassador," the librarian explained in a plaintive tone. "But I will call the embassy and insist she bring the page back."

"You remember her name?"

The librarian shook his head. "They all sound the same to me."

Kesner started out, but his nose twitched from the faint smell of tobacco. On one of the nearby desks, he found an ashtray with two lipstick-stained Viceroy cigarette butts. Fastball?

All Kesner had to do to transform himself back into a Westerner was to exchange the tarbush he had been wearing with his suit for a fedora he'd bought at Cicurel. He stuffed a handkerchief into his chest pocket for added panache. *Et voilà*! Just another European dandy. He'd also bought at the department store a women's purse, which he'd filled with basic feminine paraphernalia—face powder, lipstick, a mirror, and a comb.

An hour later, he walked into the American Embassy with a relaxed gait.

"She forgot it on the banquette at Groppi's," he said, laying the purse in front of the marine manning the reception desk. "She mentioned she worked with the ambassador."

"Must be Miss Calley, Ambassador Kirk's secretary," the young marine replied, his crisp white-brimmed hat shadowing his eyes. "Let me buzz her. I'm sure she'll want to thank you in person."

"That's quite all right. I'm in a hurry. Just tell her to be more careful next time." As he spoke, his hands started to twitch and his scalp itched as if it were crawling with bugs. The damned Benzedrine! He quickly turned on his heels and pretended to head for the exit, but instead slipped into the visitor's telephone booth, where he could observe the front desk. He removed his hat and gave his scalp a good scratching.

A few minutes later, a strawberry blond in a tight black skirt and a white ruffled blouse strutted in. She examined the purse and shrugged. After looking around, she returned it to the marine.

"Oh, my darling, aren't you a lovely one," Kesner muttered under his breath as he exited the embassy and walked to a bench a little way down the street. He checked that his Mauser pistol was securely tucked into his belt and leaned his head back. The sky was blue and cloudless. Another beautiful day. Like the banks, most embassies were open only half a day on Saturday. It wouldn't be long before Blondie came out.

Shortly after one, the American girl, wearing white cotton gloves, descended the steps and strolled down the street.

"Excuse me, madame. May I bum a cigarette?" Kesner asked her.

"Sure thing," she said in a raspy voice. "I hope you like filters." She dug out a pack of Viceroys from her bag. "Here, finish the pack. I have another."

Kesner smiled. He had found his prey.

He could hear her humming along to the strains of "Lili Marlene" on the radio as she shuffled around in her bungalow, calling out, "Fiji, come here, kitty." Gun in hand, Kesner stood motionless behind the entry door, which had been left ajar for the cat, his heart and mind racing. He'd never considered that Fastball could be a woman. He hadn't killed a woman before. He did not like killing. He had even thrown up the first time. "You can't think about it; you just have to do it and forget it," he had been told on his first day of training. "This is war." He felt nauseous, but he had to press forward. Suddenly he felt a warm body brushing against his feet. It was her damned cat, and it refused to go away. Kesner kicked it, sending the cat scurrying away, meowing loudly.

"Fiji!" the woman called, coming to the door in response to the cat's cry, and was startled as Kesner shoved her back inside and smashed the side of her head with the butt of his gun. She flew backward and fell to the floor, her hair curlers scattering everywhere. He slammed the door shut and locked it. When he turned around, the bitch was back on her feet, her claws out as she jumped on him, making him drop his gun. She scratched his neck and kicked him in the leg, trying to scream for help as he covered her mouth. He wrestled her to the floor and pinned her. But she fought back with everything she had—a tigress—kicking, punching, and scratching his face. Finally, he had to slam her head against the floor until she passed out.

He had to restrain the bitch before she regained consciousness. He dragged her to a chair, and using the window curtain ties as ropes, he bound her hands and feet to it. He used his own tie to gag her. Breathless, he paced, looking around. He saw his gun on the floor and picked it up. He wished he had brought a silencer. At the first shot, the whole neighborhood would be here. He turned up the volume of the radio and found his way to the kitchen, where he opened drawers. He took pliers and matches and returned to the living room. The bitch was now moaning and he heard the cat at the door meowing. He raised the volume of the radio some more, then went upstairs, to her bedroom. Clothes were neatly laid out on the bed. On a chair he found her purse and emptied it. Nothing of interest. But on top of the dresser was a small evening clutch. He opened it. There was an invitation in the name of Dorothy Calley to tonight's ball on the king's yacht, and neatly tucked in the corner he found the page of the scientific journal she'd torn out. In the middle of the page was a photograph of the Jew. The woman knew everything.

"I don't know anything about a Fastball, or a Blumenthal," she repeated over and over when he removed her gag.

She took him for an idiot. He showed her the picture. She shook her head. She did not know who he was. When he brought the photo very close to her face, she spat on him. That's when it all became a blur—her tears, her explanations, her pleading, his ferocious yelling at her. It was a whirlwind as he brought the matches to her fingertips, then the pliers to her nails, pulling out her pinkie nail from the skin. But that was not enough. She still claimed to know nothing. She was just a secretary. That could well be true, but he no longer heard her, or the radio, or the traffic outside. Just the sound of waves crashing in his head as he clutched her head and deftly snapped her neck.

CHAPTER 24

El Emir Farouk, Mickey read the green letters painted on the side of the king's gleaming white yacht, which was moored two hundred feet away from the Khedive Ismail Bridge. The three-deck vessel was the largest private boat on the Nile, and with its upper platform fluttering with streamers, it stood ready to receive the hundreds of guests that were expected for one of the year's biggest social affairs, the B'nai B'rith fundraiser for the British war effort. This was his chance to meet Madame Yvette Cattaoui and dig up some information about the local Zionists. He'd been allowed to stay on the case until Donovan's arrival.

"Get ready to meet the beating heart of the Peach Tin," Dorothy had said when she informed him that she'd gotten him into the event.

Peach Tin—he wondered how the Brits came up with that name for Cairo's smart set of royalty, aristocrats, businessmen, military officers, and artists. It couldn't get any swankier than this, he thought as he reached the dock, admiring the women in ball gowns and men in uniforms and tuxedos as they stepped out of their chauffeured Bentleys, Daimlers, and Rolls Royces.

Mickey thought that for once he looked as spiffy as any of the dandies here, in his tailored tuxedo and with his hair slicked back with a dollop of pomade. If only his new black patent leather shoes were not killing him.

"*Bienvenue,* monsieur. Welcome," a young volunteer greeter chirped, as the last rays of the sun caught her gold chandelier earrings. "The reception is on the middle deck in the Lounge of the Pharaohs."

Straightening his bow tie, Mickey made his way past a small group of loud partygoers, drinks in hand, and ascended the intricately carved wooden staircase. The evening was balmy and there was a soft breeze. He could hear the gentle slapping sounds of the waves against the ship. It was a perfect evening for a cruise.

It would be nice to take Maya on the water for their next date. He'd proposed horseback riding at sunset at the pyramids, but she'd said that would be too long an excursion for her. Yes, he would rent a felucca right here on the Nile and surprise her next Wednesday.

It had not been easy nailing her down for a date. As the oldest sibling, it was difficult for her to get away, but they had talked several times since their last encounter. She was always the one initiating the calls, as she wouldn't let him phone her at her cousin's and refused to give him any information about her whereabouts. He never knew when these calls would come, making them all the more exciting. For God's sake, he hadn't dated a girl who had to hide him from her parents since junior high. Her family must really be old-fashioned. Had they promised her as a bride to another man? Mickey quickly dismissed that idea—she would not have allowed that. He would just have to accept the fact that Maya was elusive and that he'd have to jump through a hoop or two to see her. She was worth it. She was beautiful and delicate, and there was depth to her. She had an inner life that she kept very private, and whenever she let her guard down, he felt privileged.

Welcomed by the warm sound of a jazz piano wafting out of the lounge on the deck, Mickey squeezed past a large crowd milling around the entrance and found himself inside a room that felt like a royal tomb. The ceiling and walls were covered with frescoes depicting scenes of pharaonic life, while torches on long brass poles created dancing shadows with their flames. The air was filled with a luscious scent emanating from enormous arrangements of orange blossoms and roses on tall pedestals positioned throughout the room. It was fantastic.

"*Entrez, monsieur. Ne soyez pas timide* (Come on in, don't be shy)," said a pretty volunteer in a flowing pink gown, offering mezzes from a silver platter. He counted a dozen or so such lovely young women floating from group to group, while flutes of champagne were served by suffragis clad in white with large gold headdresses in the traditional Egyptian style. As he made his way through the packed room, he was struck by the jewelry adorning the women. He was ready to bet that every jewelry store and safety deposit box in the city had been emptied.

He noticed Robert Stahl, the American naval military attaché, approaching him, a drink in each hand.

"Connolly, right? I'm Robert Stahl. We met at a cocktail reception at the French Embassy last month," he said.

"Yes, of course, I remember. How are you, sir?"

"I liked your piece on General Catroux," Stahl said, referring to the story Mickey had filed about the five-star French general who'd come to Cairo to help De Gaulle raise an army of Free French, only to run up against a wall of obstacles created by the pro-Vichy French Embassy here. "It kills me that the Brits are permitting an enemy embassy to remain here," Stahl continued.

"They have no choice," Mickey said. "Egypt is a sovereign state and King Farouk won't close it down. There are a thousand Egyptian citizens living in Paris, and he fears reprisals by the Vichy government."

"I think there's more to it," Stahl said. "Maybe he just wants to ruffle the British ambassador's feathers. Well, if you'd excuse me, I have to deliver a lady's drink. Nice cummerbund," he added, gesturing to Mickey's purple waistband before moving away.

Mickey grinned. Dorothy's doing. When he'd spoken to her this morning, she had told him the color purple brought good luck and he must wear it. Where was she, anyway? She had gone to Fuad University and picked up a picture of Erik Blumenthal to replace the one he'd lost. She was going to bring it tonight. He scanned the room for her, but not seeing her, he decided to get a drink.

He made his way to the bar, behind which five pretty volunteers were magically lit by the warm glow of hundreds of small candles. He asked one of them, a brunette who reminded him of Ava Gardner, for a scotch, straight up.

"Have you got a lottery ticket, sir?" the girl asked as she poured the drink. "Winners get a dance with Madame Samina," she said flirtatiously, handing him his scotch. "It's for a good cause."

"Count me in," he said. "I'm always good for a good cause." The exotic dancer from the Kit Kat Club was apparently more of a star than he'd thought. Mickey obliged the girl by filling out a card before he walked away.

Always the reporter, he made it a point to catch snatches of conversations as he meandered around the room on his way to the library. According to one British officer, the tide of the war would change, especially now that reinforcements were on their way. A man with a goatee was describing Hassan al-Banna's escape from prison in broad daylight. His matronly wife seemed more worried about the shortage of rubber and its impact on ladies' undergarments. He heard snippets about the looming railway strike and how this would not have happened had the government not nationalized the trains, as well as speculation about how big a crowd would attend Nahas's rally. The speeches of the leader of the widely popular Wafd nationalist party were invariably anti-British. But the biggest concern seemed to be the news that the Eighth Army had retreated all the way to El Alamein.

He strolled out onto the deck and into the library, where the atmosphere seemed more relaxed, with people gathering around oversized armchairs. The air here, too, was perfumed by extravagant floral arrangements.

Mickey spotted Kirk easily in his bright yellow bow tie and matching cummerbund. He was holding court with no less than King George of Greece and King Peter of Yugoslavia. But kings or not, they both looked miserable. King George was drawn and sallow, and the wild-eyed, mustachioed King Peter looked more like a guerrilla leader than a monarch, despite his tuxedo.

When Kirk saw Mickey, he turned and nodded, giving Mickey a discreet thumbs-up, meaning all was in place and that Mickey would be sitting next to Madame Cattaoui at dinner.

Good old Dorothy. She did it again, Mickey thought and smiled. But where the hell was she?

"Hello, stranger!" Someone grabbed his arm.

It was Sally, looking resplendent and every inch a woman in her low-cut, long black dress, a far cry from her ambulance driver's uniform. He hadn't seen her since their sexy tumble after the Kit Kat Club, and he felt awkward about not having called her.

"Didn't I tell you Cairo was a small world?" She winked.

From the way she smiled at him, it was clear that she wasn't holding any grudges.

He kissed her on both cheeks, happy to see her, like bumping into an old friend. "It's nice to see you again. You look lovely."

She linked her arm through his and introduced him to her friends as an intrepid American reporter. "You know Linda, of course, and this tall, gawky lad is Randolph Churchill," she said of a husky man in uniform next to her. "He's one of the devils in the Special Air Service."

"A commando? Risky job, I hear," Mickey said. "Any relation to—"

"Winston's his uncle," Linda interjected, "and mine, too. Randolph, I'm sorry to say, is my cousin."

"You're lucky to have me in the family! I bring us personality," Randolph teased, impishly tousling Linda's hair and dislodging some of her impeccably rolled curls.

She slapped him on the wrist and patted her hair back into place.

Mickey shook hands, pleased to be in such company. "What does your uncle think about your work here?" he asked Randolph.

"Not much," Randolph replied, a line of irritation on his forehead. "I suspect our relationship has precluded my being selected for the most exciting missions. Top brass is always fearful that I might be captured and spill some top secret," he said, making everyone laugh.

"So finish your story about the Japanese ambassador," Linda demanded of Randolph.

"Yes," Sally said. She turned to Mickey. "He was telling us about the run-in our own Ambassador Lampson had with him two days ago."

Mickey nodded. Yesterday's headlines said that the Japanese ambassador, had been passing secrets about the Suez Canal to Berlin.

"Well," Randolph started, "today, even after his betrayal was revealed, the Nip ambassador had the gall to ask Lampson if he could travel overland to the Suez and connect with his ship in the Persian Gulf. The route would have taken him and his entourage through some of our most sensitive installations and military defenses."

There were murmurs of outrage from the group.

"Naturally, Lampson refused," Sally said.

"Speak of the devil," Linda said as she grabbed the hand of an impossibly tall and imposing man who was passing nearby with his very pregnant wife, who was a good twenty years his junior.

Mickey did a double take as he recognized the British ambassador, Sir Miles Lampson, himself. With his impressive build, full mane of hair, and red-spotted bow tie, the man had quite a bit of flair for an old fart.

"Are you only just now arriving?" Linda asked after introducing Mickey, the only "stranger" in the group, and calling the ambassador's wife "Jac."

"*Mea culpa,* as usual," Jac hastened to explain. "Miles accuses me of shaving one day off his life every time I'm late. Now isn't that the saddest thing to say to your wife?" She intertwined her fingers with the ambassador's and nestled against him, looking minuscule by comparison.

"I have a nephew who just returned from studying in America, Mr. Connolly," Jac said. "All he talks about are Rita Hayworth and baseball."

"Then he's halfway to becoming a citizen," Mickey replied.

"I fear you won't find many baseballers here in Egypt," Jac commented.

"I'm afraid not. It seems that everyone here prefers cricket," Mickey agreed.

"A gentleman's game, Mr. Connolly," Lampson remarked.

"Well, in that case, I should probably steer clear of it," Mickey countered, provoking laughter from the group, though the ambassador remained poker-faced.

"Is the king here?" Lampson asked as he picked up a fizzing flute brimming with champagne while Jac helped herself to a canapé from a passing tray.

"I'm afraid not," Linda replied. "Madame Mosseri is up in arms. We're supposed to weigh anchor in fifteen minutes."

"Pshaw!" Lampson muttered, nodding to a well-wisher nearby. "I'm sure the boy is racing his cars around the palace grounds, killing time so he can make a grand entrance. Teach him a lesson and get started without him."

"Of course, he does not mean that," Jac quickly added, laughing. A woman with a large, beaded black hat passed by and Jac whispered to Sally, "That's Delsyia."

"I understand she will be singing in French and English," Sally said. "And I saw Madame Samina earlier." She elbowed Mickey.

"No dancing tonight," Lampson firmly warned Jac, placing a gentle hand on her stomach.

"Oh, Miles!" Jac protested. "I'm just pregnant, for God's sake; I'm not ill!"

"Everybody is eager to hear your speech tonight, Ambassador," Mickey said. "Will you be talking about the situation at El Alamein?"

"There is no need to worry," Lampson answered casually, before offering his hand to a short, corpulent man who looked as if he had been shoehorned into his tuxedo.

"Ah, Sally, good to see you," he exclaimed. "This must be your beautiful daughter."

Mickey recognized the Egyptian prime minister, who warily shook Lampson's hand. Lampson leaned toward the man to say something when a British officer urgently pulled him away and whispered something in his ear. Lampson turned red. "That little tyke," he said through gritted teeth.

"What is it, dear?" Jac asked.

"The boy has arrived in his red Mercedes, that's what. I've half a mind to put the little blighter across my knee and wallop some sense into him."

"Miles!" Jac exclaimed. "You're talking about the king of Egypt!"

"He's an ungrateful little sod!" Lampson exclaimed as he stormed off.

"Miles, please," Jac pleaded after her husband in vain. She exhaled loudly, at her wit's end. "King Farouk has arrived in a car that was a gift from Hitler. He'd promised to return it." She shook her head. "These two with their cat and mouse game. Excuse me." She rushed out, cupping her belly with both hands.

"Gossip has it that MI5 caught a note the king wrote to the führer welcoming him into Egypt," Sally commented.

"That's bollocks," Randolph said. "The king is for the king and no one else."

"Whatever the case, the king would be crazy if he really thought the Germans would make better partners than the British," Mickey declared.

"I think it's lovely of him to lend his yacht for this affair," Linda said. "That speaks volumes about his loyalty."

"I don't like to sound cynical," Sally said, "but we all know we owe the use of his boat to Riri Charbit alone. She orchestrated the whole thing."

"Who's she?" Mickey asked.

"The king's mistress," Linda responded. "Like his father, he seems to have a weakness for Jewish girls."

"Should we go to the deck and see what's happening?" Sally suggested, but just as she started, a delicate tinkling sound was heard.

"The king has arrived, the king has arrived," announced a woman jingling a small bell, parting clusters of guests as she walked through the room. She was wearing a superb long scarlet dress with ruffles at the shoulders and too much makeup.

"That's Madame Mosseri," Sally whispered into Mickey's ear, "the organizer of the ball."

The ship's horn blasted loudly, provoking shrieks of delight from the guests, and Mickey felt the yacht slowly begin to move. The piano player led the band in a lively rendition of "When the Saints Go Marching In," and balloons descended from the ceiling.

The ball had officially begun.

"Shall we?" Sally asked, offering Mickey her arm, but he thought he recognized a familiar silhouette turning the corner. "Go ahead without me," he apologized and rushed away.

"You're Maya's cousin, Lili," Mickey said as he walked up to the girl, recognizing her.

"She's here," Lili whispered.

CHAPTER 25

With only two hours of sleep out of the last twenty-four, Maya was surprised she wasn't exhausted. In fact, she was feeling oddly energized as she inscribed the name *David Caro* on what must have been the six hundredth seating card she'd written this evening. Her calligraphy, which had won her the job of writing Cousin Henri's Bar Mitzvah invitations, was a saving grace for Lili today, who had volunteered her father to have the menus printed for the fund-raiser on the king's yacht. But Joe, usually as reliable as a Swiss watch, had somehow forgotten to get the task done, and with the printers closed on Saturdays and less than twenty-four hours before the big event, Maya had stepped in and offered her services. The organizers of the ball had liked the beautifully scripted menus so much that they had asked Lili if she could bring her cousin to the ball to help with the dinner seating cards as well, since last-minute seating changes were to be expected.

Maya happily agreed. Even though she would have to work for the first part of the evening, she would later have the rare opportunity to mingle with pashas and beys and sirs, and to be in the company of not one but three kings. Besides, she was feeling suffocated by her family, trying to make peace between her father and brother.

She grabbed every chance to get out of the house and had come up with an elaborate alibi that would allow her to spend a whole afternoon with Mickey next Wednesday. She was surprised how often she caught herself thinking about him and how much time she spent plotting how to make her next call to him. She loved their talks, even though he always teased her about all the drama and secrecy she brought to them.

He was handsome for sure, and funny, and he was also a man of substance—steady and real. An anchor in her tumultuous world. He was a wealth of information about what was really going on in the war as well as what was going on in Cairo. He liked history and movies and claimed to be as big a Charlie Chaplin fan as she was, though that would be impossible. At the end of their talks, she could almost fool herself into thinking that life was bright and promising.

She hated all the lies she had been telling him, yet it was probably a good thing that she was not more available because frankly, she was starting to fall for him, and it frightened her—what was she thinking? Soon she'd have to say good-bye. She cringed at the thought, but the timing was all wrong.

Maya put her quill down and, bringing the card close to her lips, blew on it gently to dry the ink. There were still over a dozen to write. The organizers of the ball had miscalculated the number of tables, and the seating cards for all three hundred guests had to be rewritten. Hearing the hoopla emanating from the rooms on the upper deck, she was jealous of Lili, who must be waltzing from guest to guest offering appetizers while she was confined to the dining room with an aching hand.

"Lights off, please," a woman's voice commanded.

The room went black, but a few seconds later a soft green light emerged from the overhead spots. Its effect on the shimmering gold silk fabric that draped the ceiling and covered the walls and tables dazzled Maya. With the chairs upholstered in green satin with large green ribbons affixed to their backs, it was like being inside a secret glade. It was magical.

"Green is the king's favorite color," a matronly woman in a sparkling caftan pronounced as she approached Maya and nodded approvingly when she saw that only a few cards remained. "You're looking lovely in white."

Maya smiled brightly at the compliment as she watched her leave the room. Having had no time to make or buy a dress, she made do with one of Lili's old ones. Cut low in a V, it tied around the neck, and with handkerchiefs stuffed inside of her brassiere and a few tacks along the seams, it molded to her figure sensuously, showing off her best feature—her long, thin waist. But what made the dress stand out was the gold belt she'd cinched just below her breasts. Accessories again! With gold shoes, gold bangles and, of course, Mutter's hairpin, et voilà! She was no Cinderella, but she was more than passable. And with her eyes heavily lined with black kohl, her face powdered with a light bronze color, and her lips glistening in lavish red, she knew she looked good.

"No, you look sensational," Lili had told her. "You will make many heads turn," Erik had added. The whole household had trickled into the room to admire her, each with a superlative more flattering than the last. But it was Sayeda, the maid, who had trumped them all when she declared, "You're coming home with a husband!"

"The guests will be coming any minute," a woman's voice announced, drawing Maya out of her reverie.

She turned and saw Madame Mosseri, the chief organizer of the ball, storming into the room, the trailing end of her scarlet dress catching momentarily on the door. The woman studied the magnificent dessert buffet behind Maya and questioned the staff about the whereabouts of a seven-foot-tall mountain of custard balls before she addressed Maya.

"I'm sorry, dear," she said, "but the girls forgot to arrange for a lemonade stand for the king and his Muslim cohorts who don't drink alcohol. We're rushing to set one up right now. Would you be a darling and manage it?" She indicated an alcove tucked away in the back of the room.

Siberia, Maya thought, trying to smile as she nodded. So much for her plans to mingle with the crowd.

"And we have one more change," the woman had the audacity to say, her lips pressed forward in the shape of a heart. "Please seat this gentleman at Madame Cattaoui's table, number twelve." She handed Maya a piece of paper.

Mickey Connolly.

Maya's stomach dropped.

"Ladies and gentlemen, please take your seats," a volunteer shouted to the crowd as they entered the dining room to the sound of "Alexander's Ragtime Band" and gasped at the magical décor. "The king will not enter until everyone is seated."

After placing Mickey's seating card in front of his wine goblet, Maya quickly leaned over to smell the pink lotus flowers that had been arranged in a crystal bowl with Egyptian irises at the center of the table. Almost by reflex, she stroked the back of his chair, still digesting the news that he would be here. And thank goodness that he was here alone. She was happy, nervous, and excited to see him, but was baffled by the fact that he was being seated between a countess and the chief lady-in-waiting for the king's mother, Queen Nazli. And the other guests at his table were no less impressive. Except for a brigadier general and an Indian prince, they were all Egyptian royalty. What was an American journalist doing at this table?

She took her station at the lemonade bar, but couldn't just stand there and miss Mickey's arrival. She slipped away and stopped close to one of the large columns in the back. While her eyes searched the room for him, she couldn't help gawking at the fabulous dresses the women were wearing. The influence of Hollywood was undeniable. There were Empire-waisted gowns with ties in the back or trains, low and dramatic necklines edged with wide scallops or ruffles, and butterfly sleeves. Accents such as bows and fabric flowers abounded. Maya spotted a woman wearing a carbon copy of the dress worn by Joan Crawford in *Letty Lynton*, a dress so striking that Maya had never forgotten it, though she was only fourteen when she saw the movie. Her own dress seemed embarrassingly modest compared to these.

These people have never known a day of suffering, she thought. Perhaps Vati was right: The Sephardim only care about material things and good times, while the Ashkenazim are the deep thinkers and intellectuals. "Name one important Sephardic composer or mathematician," Vati had challenged her. She could only think of Moses Maimonides, the great philosopher from the Middle Ages. But now, as she spotted Lili welcoming the guests and pointing them to their tables with the warmest of smiles on her lips, Maya had a revelation. They have grace and laughter and generosity, she would now answer, and they don't *kvetch*! Maybe that's what brought us Ashkenazim our troubles. Better do as the Sephardim say: "Smile to life so that life smiles back to you."

"Please remain seated, sir," she heard a volunteer gently reprimand an elderly gentleman as he started to rise. "The king will enter soon. Then we will all rise at the same time."

Where was Mickey? Maya wondered, her stomach a ball of nerves. Most people were now in their seats, and just a few latecomers were trickling in. Could there be another man named Mickey Connolly? What were the chances of that? She kept her eyes on his table, where his seat remained empty. But so was Madame Cattaoui's. Perhaps the two were upstairs chatting?

Suddenly a pair of hands folded over her eyes from behind, startling her.

"Guess who?" the voice asked.

She twirled around, a surge of joy sweeping through her. It was him. He looked so dapper in his tuxedo that she barely recognized him. She instinctively moved forward to greet him with a kiss as she would a friend, but stopped. There was more than friendship there; a kiss even on the cheek would be loaded with sensations as their skin brushed. They both shifted awkwardly on their feet, grinning. He made the first move, taking one of her hands as he stepped away to better admire her. He shook his head.

"You're a flower," he finally said. "Your cousin told me you wrote the menus for the dinner."

"And the seating cards," she added.

He let go of her hand and crossed his arms, frowning. "Then I should be angry with you," he said. "You knew all this time I was here, and you didn't even try to find me. How come?"

She felt her cheeks reddening. "I didn't know until a few moments ago," she mumbled. "They only just gave me your name for a seating card." Recovering her wits, she put a hand on her hip and added pointedly, "Sitting with royalty now?"

"I've got friends in high places," he said, flashing his best smile. "The US Embassy is behind this. They really want to see my article published in the *Foreign Service Journal*, and one of the guests at the table could be a mother lode of information."

She wasn't familiar with the journal, but it sounded impressive, and she nodded appreciatively.

"I can't tell you how happy I am that you're here," he said, looking her straight in the eye, his sincerity completely disarming her.

"This is the third time our paths are crossing," she said, feeling her heart beating fast.

"And three is the charm. It looks like the winds of fate are blowing in our favor."

She shrugged. "Or the winds of coincidence," she said.

"Whichever, you're mine tonight."

She didn't know what to say and felt increasingly ill at ease with his intensity. She craned her neck. Everyone was seated now. She said, "You should . . . "

"I know. Sit down. I will. After I'm done with my business at the table, I will find you."

"Won't be hard. I'm stuck here all night." She indicated the bar behind her.

"No, you're not," he said. He kissed the tips of his fingers and pressed them against her lips before rushing to his seat.

She was light-headed. She was flummoxed. Had he actually stolen a kiss from her? She realized that the band had stopped playing and that Madame Mosseri had taken the microphone on the podium.

"Ladies and gentlemen," the woman announced, "the king!"

A herald trumpeted the king's arrival, and the guests rose, all attention riveted on the double doors at the end of the room. They swung open, and the king entered, cutting a dashing figure in his naval officer's double-breasted blue coat, which was adorned with an array of gold braids and medals. Maya thought him quite handsome, but younger looking than his twenty years. A striking blond who looked like Jean Harlow and wore a sequined and feathered green dress was on his arm. Maya presumed her to be his infamous mistress, who was rumored to be paid by the English to be with him. Gossip about the couple's sex life, or lack thereof, abounded, though the king had a reputation for being a skirt chaser, believing it was his absolute right to demand that any girl sleep with him, whether she was married or not.

Maya watched with fascination as he and his small entourage settled in at the head table with King George of Greece, King Peter of Yugoslavia, the British ambassador, the Egyptian prime minister, and several high-ranking Allied generals.

Once everybody sat down again, Madame Mosseri acknowledged the presence of the two European kings, thanked King Farouk for his generosity in allowing B'nai B'rith to hold this event on his yacht, and praised him for maintaining the strong relationship his father, King Fuad, had forged between the royal family and Egypt's Jewish community. Her remarks were often drowned out by applause, but the most thunderous ovations came when she spoke about the Jews' love for Egypt and her people, concluding, "May our tradition of friendship with our Arab brothers continue forever." On their feet, the crowd joined her for a toast to Egypt with such verve that Maya felt a lump in her throat as she was reminded that she herself belonged nowhere. Madame Mosseri then dedicated a toast to England, thanking their British friends for their consistent generosity and fearless protection in this hour of need, before introducing Ambassador Lampson.

Maya glanced toward Mickey's table. She could only see his back, but he was clapping and whispering something into the ear of his neighbor, Madame Cattaoui, a petite woman in a simple black gown, who must have just slipped into her seat. As if sensing her eyes on him, he turned and caught her staring, which made her blush. He picked up his glass and toasted her. She raised her palm to acknowledge him and returned her attention to the stage, where the courtly Lampson was kissing the hand of the hostess with much grace.

"Once again, Madame Mosseri has shown us that war is no impediment to throwing a good party," the British ambassador said, prompting laughter from the audience and cries of "Good show." Then, one hand in his pocket, oozing confidence, he continued, "The commander of British troops in Egypt, General Wilson, and the Allied commander for the Middle East, General Auchinleck, couldn't be here this evening, but they have given me the task of relaying this message to you." He wrapped the microphone with his two hands and cried, "*This is it*. I'm sure you have all heard the news that the line has held at a place called El Alamein. We want you all to know that this will be the turning point. We are going to stop the Nazis here and chase them right back into Libya."

The crowd cheered and applauded wildly.

"I can't believe they are sticking you in a corner for the night," Lili whispered, sidling up to Maya.

"I know."

"You had to see the smile on his face when I told him you were here."

Maya hid her delight at hearing this. She knew it must have been true.

CHAPTER 26

"He's truly revolting," whispered Countess Sunderland, loud enough for Mickey to hear though his head was momentarily turned to the back of the room as he searched for Maya, who was no longer standing by the column.

"Who is?" he asked, turning his attention to the countess, assuming she was referring to Lampson, who had been thanking the Jews for their contributions to the war effort and the enrichment of life in Egypt.

"The king!" the countess said. "That's who! He's having a bread ball fight with his friends."

Mickey followed her gaze to Farouk's table. He didn't see any food flying, but the king did seem to be up to no good as he clowned with his cronies, oblivious to the ambassador's remarks.

"His Majesty seems to be a prankster," he said in a low voice.

"Indeed." The countess frowned. She cupped her mouth with her hand and whispered, "Did you know that when he met Churchill, he pickpocketed his watch?"

"That must have created an interesting first impression," Mickey offered, smiling at Madame Cattaoui when he noticed her watching him from the corner of her eye. She had dressed modestly, with only a pair of diamond earrings as adornment to her evening gown, and had seemed sensible and pleasant enough when he'd introduced himself.

"Good God, the ambassador did not thank the king!" exclaimed Prince Fawzi, sitting to the right of Madame Cattaoui, when Lampson stepped down from the stage.

"Tsk, tsk. A terrible faux pas," Mickey hastened to agree. "I agree with you . . . " he began fumbling for the proper term of address when he felt Madame Cattaoui kick his foot under the table.

"Royal Highness," she mouthed to his rescue.

" . . . Your Royal Highness," Mickey finished quickly. "Perhaps the ambassador was a bit nervous on stage." He nodded thanks to the lady-in-waiting.

"I doubt that," the prince said. "He's a seasoned speaker."

The microphone creaked as Madame Mosseri, the hostess, came back to the podium. "And, of course, we thank you again, Your Majesty, for your generosity," she said in an attempt to rectify Lampson's glaring error. "Dance and be merry! The king has a wonderful surprise for us later this evening."

"Thank you for coming to my rescue," Mickey said in a low voice to Madame Cattaoui as the band struck up a soft tune. "I'm afraid we don't learn how to address royalty in America."

"Perhaps that's what gives you Americans your charm," she responded.

He was about to ask her if she'd ever visited the United States, but he felt the countess pull at this sleeve.

"I don't understand what all the fuss is about this Madame Samina," she whispered, her gossipy eye now targeted on the Egyptian dancer, who was sitting at a nearby table, her forehead decorated with a gold pendant. "She's utterly vulgar as far as I am concerned. What do men see in her?"

Mickey shrugged and wisely avoided responding to that question, but when he turned toward Madame Cattaoui again, Prince Fawzi and his wife had captured her attention. He reached for the menu in the center of the table and smiled as he admired Maya's exquisite calligraphy. He turned again to look for her. Suddenly he saw her face peeking out from behind the column. He wiggled his fingers hello, and her full face appeared, bearing a huge grin, before disappearing again entirely. A suffragi arrived to serve the dinner's first course—*truffles à la sauce de champagne,* thinly sliced mushrooms under a delicate white sauce.

Seated to the left of the countess was US Air Force Brigadier General John Meyer, who was dominating the conversation as he bragged about the capabilities of the latest American aircraft, the B-24 Liberator. He punctuated his speech with gestures and sound effects, dramatizing a town being wiped off the map by these new stratospheric bombers. He was boring everybody, even the British RAF colonel next to him, Thomas White, who only nodded politely.

Mickey leaned toward Madame Cattaoui. "Are you still sure that we Americans are so charming?" he asked softly.

"Perhaps not all of you," she chuckled.

"King George looks gloomy," the countess interrupted, tugging on Mickey's sleeve again. The Greek monarch was being pulled aside by a guest who was undoubtedly offering his condolences for the travails of the king's country. "And with good reason," she added. "His country is being ravaged and he just narrowly avoided death. You've heard the story, I suppose? He escaped on a donkey, like Jesus Christ. Eventually the Royal Navy rescued him, just after German paratroopers landed only three hundred yards away. A terribly close shave."

"Terribly!" Mickey said. He returned his attention to Madame Cattaoui, but she was busy soothing the prince, who had been scandalized by the lurid paintings he'd seen in the yacht's Royal Chamber. Mickey sopped up the succulent sauce of the mushroom appetizer with a piece of bread, his mind drawn back to Maya. He wanted to turn his head again and look for her, but he restrained himself so as not to be impolite to his tablemates. How incredible that she was here tonight. Maybe his lucky purple cummerbund was doing its job. Speaking of which, where the hell was Dorothy?

"I didn't have a chance to tell you how sorry I was, Countess, to hear that your husband had been captured," Colonel White told her, jumping at the first chance to break away from the overbearing American general.

"Thank you," the countess replied. "General Auchinleck assured me that prisoners of war are being taken overland to Tripoli and from there to Italy. My husband is probably sunning himself in Brindisi, for all I know."

"You should be grateful that the war is over for him," Colonel White said. "You're going back to Blighty, aren't you?"

"I am going to Palestine, actually," the countess replied.

Mickey's ears perked up.

"Without my husband, there isn't much for me to do here in Cairo. I've decided I might as well make myself useful, so I'm leaving for Jerusalem next week to help in the administration. They are desperately short of secretaries and support staff."

"The Arabs and the Jews are at each others' throats there," White said. "There is nothing but trouble in Palestine. If your husband were here, I'm sure he'd warn you to be careful."

"You needn't worry on my account. Nothing will happen to me." The countess daintily dabbed the corners of her mouth with her napkin.

"Palestine is a lot quieter now than it was before the war," General Meyer commented.

"Probably because Churchill has mollified the Arabs with the latest White Paper restrictions," Mickey said, thrilled that the conversation had turned this way.

"I'm afraid restrictions is no longer an appropriate term,"

Madame Cattaoui corrected him. "There is now a complete ban on immigration."

What do you know! The lady-in-waiting had been eavesdropping on their conversation, and from the flush of her cheeks, he saw that the subject was an emotional one for her.

"It's a temporary expediency," White said. "The loyalty of the Arabs has to be gained at any price, or we risk their forming an alliance with the Nazis."

"I'm afraid that alliance has already been forged," Mickey said. "Isn't the Mufti of Jerusalem in Germany with Hitler as we speak?"

"Exactly," Madame Cattaoui nodded in agreement, resting a soft hand on his arm.

"If we don't put a freeze on Jewish immigration right now, we risk a full-scale Arab revolt, and where would that leave us?" White asked.

"But where does this leave the Jews?" Mickey retorted. "Nobody wants them."

"Including your own president," the British officer fired back.

"Now in all fairness, President Roosevelt—" Meyer started to say.

"In all fairness," the countess interrupted, "it is not right that exceptions are being made for members of the British staff here to be transferred to Palestine, while they won't allow even the Jews who work closely with them on high security matters to emigrate there. If the Germans arrive here, they would undoubtedly be the first ones to suffer."

"How can this be?" Mickey asked, turning to Madame Cattaoui for an explanation. "The Jews here are major contributors to the war effort," he gestured around the room. "Surely the British ambassador—"

"There is nothing Ambassador Lampson can do," Madame

Cattaoui interrupted. "The Palestine administration categorically refuses to relax its rules under any circumstances."

"The king will protect the Jewish people in the unthinkable event that Rommel takes Egypt," the prince said.

"But how long will he be able to do that?" Mickey asked. "I know Jews can count many Arabs as friends, but in the mosque Hassan al-Banna of the Muslim Brotherhood is winning over the hearts of more and more Egyptian people every day."

"That will be the day, when the Egyptians turn against us!" Madame Cattaoui answered. "It will never happen. They are our greatest allies."

"Absolutely," said the prince. "Did you hear about the Egyptians who risked their lives by saving thirteen German Jews and smuggling them into Palestine?"

"No. When did that happen?" Mickey asked, trying to sound casual.

"Just before the war broke out," Madame Cattaoui responded. "This is off the record, of course. An Egyptian policeman told his surgeon at the Jewish Hospital in Alexandria that there were thirteen Jews being held hostage offshore aboard a German freighter. I don't remember all the details, but between the surgeon and the policeman and his fellow friends on the force, they created a ruse to get the refugees off the ship and arrested by the port authorities. The refugees were then transferred to the prison in Port Said, and from there they were put on board a police patrol boat and taken to a fishing vessel that carried them outside of Egyptian waters and on to Haifa."

"What an exciting story!" the countess exclaimed.

"I should point out," the prince added, "that many Egyptian policemen and their families are treated by Jewish doctors at the Jewish Hospital in Alexandria. There is a lot of goodwill there."

"When the authorities found out, the Egyptians received only a slap on the wrist. Everyone closed their eyes. Even the British authorities in Palestine did not pursue the incident," Madame Cattaoui went on. "That would not be the case today."

"But Jews today must be finding ways to get in," said the countess.

"You tell me how," Madame Cattaoui responded. "Bribes don't work anymore."

"Can they buy visas on the black market?" Mickey asked.

"Oh, you journalists!" the countess said, giving him an affectionate tap on his head. "You look for intrigue everywhere."

Mickey forced a smile, but registered Madame Cattaoui's body tensing slightly. As an intimate of the queen, she had to be wary of reporters. He wanted to strangle the countess.

"Let's talk of brighter subjects," Madame Cattaoui said, turning to the prince.

"One more question, if you don't mind my asking, madame?" Mickey said, alarmed that he was losing his chance to pursue this line with the lady-in-waiting and deciding to take a gamble.

"As you know, madame, I'm writing about the Jews of Egypt," he started. "And I'm interested in the role of Zionists in Egypt today."

Madame Cattaoui looked into his eyes. She crossed her arms, guarded.

"I know that the Zionist organizations were disbanded, essentially by the Jewish community itself, in the face of intimidation by Arab zealots. But I'm sure that the Zionist dream of a Jewish homeland still exists and that people are still working for the cause," he pressed on. "Can you give me some guidance about how I might find such people who are still active? The world needs to be informed about the tremendous pressure being felt by the Jews here and in other parts of the Arab world as a result of British policy in Palestine."

She hesitated for a moment. "I'm sorry, but I can't help you, and you shouldn't be so quick to judge us," she finally responded. "I would like to point out that the well-to-do German Jews in your own country lobbied the State Department to restrict Jewish immigration to America, and they didn't face the pressures that my brethren here do. No one is bombing Jewish homes in New York, as far as I know." She turned to the prince.

The game was over. He would get no more from her.

As the yacht glided through the darkness and the suffragis began serving coffee and tea, Mickey could see faint firelights on the banks of the river through the dining room windows. Madame Mosseri had invited everyone to the dessert table, and some diners were already lighting cigars, reclining in their chairs, satiated and happy. Others were table-hopping, greeting friends, or dancing. At Mickey's table half of the guests had left, including Madame Cattaoui. It was safe now for Mickey to go find Maya without being rude.

"I think the king's men are up to no good. All three are Italians, his best friends, you know," the countess whispered as he prepared to excuse himself. "Really, what kind of king has an electrician, a barber, and the keeper of the royal kennels as his best friends!"

Mickey watched one of the king's Italian cronies put a green goblet in front of the king and bring his fingers to his mouth, kissing the tips of them as if to say, "Delicious." The king laughed in response. The behavior seemed juvenile but harmless.

"For the past half hour his friends have taken turns bringing these goblets to the king. I don't trust them. Who knows what could be in that drink?"

Indeed, there were a great many goblets in front of the king, but Mickey couldn't care less. From the corner of his eye he spotted Lili passing by. She smiled at him and with a jerk of her head indicated the back wall. Mickey didn't need to be told twice. He placed his napkin on the table and pushed back his chair.

"Pardon me," he said, bowing to the countess. "I have to say hello to a friend." He fastened his jacket and straightened up as he navigated the crowded tables. He picked up a dessert plate from a suffragi along the way and nodded to Randolph Churchill, who was dying of embarrassment as the large woman seated next to him, undoubtedly soused, hung around his neck. "You save a dance for me, good looking," Sally shouted. Kirk was seated at the last table at the end of the room. He stood up and motioned Mickey to a corner.

"How's it going?" Kirk asked.

"Blood is thicker than water," Mickey said. "Yvette Cattaoui is not going to talk about her brother, but I did learn a few things."

"Good. I can't wait to hear the details." Kirk lowered his voice. "Mickey, I'm worried about Dorothy. She is not here. This is very unlike her."

"Maybe she got a better offer," Mickey said, sure that Dorothy would have some amusing explanation for her absence.

Kirk pursed his lips and nodded, but it was clear he wasn't convinced. Mickey patted him on the shoulder and moved on. He rounded the corner to the lemonade stand, and there she was . . . with the king casually leaning on her counter. Two men in dark suits stood nearby, the king's bodyguards, he assumed. Maya was nervously pouring from a pitcher into the king's goblet, her eyes lowered, her face tense. Suddenly all the shenanigans at the king's table made sense: The king's pals had discovered a pretty girl for the king. Now he had come to check her out for himself. Not so fast, you son of a bitch, Mickey thought.

"Brought you some dessert, darling," he told Maya, who looked up at him with relief. "You must be starving, working so hard. Mickey Connolly, US press, Your Majesty," he said, turning to the king and extending his hand. The king did not take it, but with the palm of his hand stopped the bodyguards who were already stepping forward.

"I was thrilled to see you on the front cover of *Time* magazine not long ago," Mickey continued. "They did a splendid report on your wedding. I think you'll find that you have a lot of fans in America."

An irritated expression passed over the king's face. "Really? I thought Americans were not too fond of kings. Except for King Kong," he joked, looking at Maya to see if she laughed.

She didn't.

"Oh, no, Your Majesty. We all thought you looked quite dashing," Mickey said.

"The king was very kind to invite me to his private gathering tomorrow night, darling," she said, her voice thin. "But isn't your friend arriving from London?"

"Precisely. But very kind of you, sir."

Farouk did not respond and picked up the glass Maya had poured him. He took a sip. "I must compliment my friends on their excellent taste," he declared.

"Here you are!"

Riri Charbit, the king's mistress appeared. She grabbed him by the arm. "Madame Mosseri is just about to announce your surprise." She nodded apologetically to Mickey and Maya before tearing Farouk away and parting the small crowd of curious onlookers that had suddenly formed.

"Saved by the bell," Mickey said.

"I don't believe what just happened!" Maya exclaimed, covering her cheeks with her hands, flustered. "He was making me terribly uncomfortable. All I could think about was how some of the girls described his bedroom downstairs. There's a mirror above his bed, and explicit paintings of men and women . . . you know . . . "

"I've heard. Let's go look," he said with a grin.

"No!" she said, elbowing him. "And don't get any ideas."

"Who said I don't already have some?" he said with a twinkle in his eyes.

She looked at him, arms crossed.

"Just teasing, just teasing. Whenever I think of you, you're always fully clothed! Swear to God."

"I'm sure," she said, shaking her head in mock disapproval.

Madame Mosseri's voice came over the loudspeaker announcing gaily, "You are all invited to the upper deck for fireworks, courtesy of His Majesty. *Et la fête continue*."

The news was greeted with cheers, and a brouhaha ensued as the guests began to migrate toward the upper deck.

Maya saw Lili emerge out of the crowd with a young man in tow. He had chubby cheeks and his dark, shiny hair was combed into a wavy pompadour.

"Maya, this is Fernando Lagnado. *Mon amoureux*, my sweetheart," Lili proudly announced.

"And you are the famous cousin from Damascus!" he said with a gallant bow. "Lili told me you'll be chaperoning us next Wednesday."

"Next Wednesday?" Mickey said, looking expectantly at Maya.

"I was going to tell you," she rushed to explain.

"We'll be double dating," Lili said with a wink.

"In that case we might as well start getting to know each other. I'm Mickey Connolly," he said, extending his hand to Fernando. "Let's go find a good spot to watch the fireworks."

"I'll need to find my aunts first," Fernando said.

Mickey frowned. "Don't bring them along. We'll have more fun just the four of us."

Lili gave Mickey a grateful smile and linked her arm around Fernando's.

"I just want to let them know where I will be," Fernando said. "So they won't worry. It won't take long. I'll join you upstairs."

Lili's face fell, but she nonetheless left with her amoureux.

"What's with him and his aunts?"

"His parents died when he was very young," Maya explained. "He was raised by his mother's five spinster sisters. I should really ask permission before leaving the booth."

"Come on! This room will be completely empty in sixty seconds."

Maya was about to protest, but he put his finger on her lips. "Shh," he whispered.

CHAPTER 27

Maya shrieked as a thunderous explosion boomed across the water and the night sky lit up with color. The loudspeakers sounded "The Grand March" from Verdi's *Aida,* the perfect choice, she thought. She was glad Mickey had insisted she come with him. But the deck was mobbed and they found themselves at the back of the crowd.

Mickey handed her a bottle of champagne he had "borrowed" from a suffragi on his way out of the dining room and jumped up and down to see what everyone was looking at.

"There's a light show over the pyramids," he reported. "But we'll never see anything from here." He scanned the area and pointed excitedly. "The poop deck!"

"It's off-limits," Maya said. "See the ropes?"

"To a reporter, that's an invitation. Come. We'll have a great view."

He took her hand and dragged her away from the crowd.

"I think it's this way," she indicated toward the right, her excitement winning out over her concerns. "There must be a stairway."

Tracing a path along the side of the yacht, they found a narrow passageway chained off with a red sign that read *Crew Only*.

"You're a volunteer. That means you're crew today," he

stated and stepped over the chain. He turned back to give her a hand, but she refused it, preferring to manage herself.

Lifting her dress slightly, she tried to raise a leg over, but found she'd have to hoist it way above the knee to climb over. Changing tactics, she crouched down to crawl under the chain, but the stairs blocked her way. Hmm? Before she could decide, Mickey picked her up and lifted her over the chain in one swift move, putting her down on the other side. He continued on, climbing two steps at a time, while she stood for an instant, feeling a little unsettled. His hands had come awfully close to her breasts as he lifted her, before they slid down to her waist again.

"Are you coming?" he asked, already at the top of the stairway. "You're a snail!"

She hurried up and as she reached the top, a rocket exploded in the sky, sending thousands of red and green sparkles down the front and sides of the Sphinx. She gasped, as did the crowd below. It was as if the lion had come alive, roaring after thousands of years of sleep. She turned to share her excitement with Mickey. He was taking off his jacket.

"Don't put it on the deck," she said. "It's brand new."

He looked at her quizzically.

"The pocket seams are still sewn up," she said. "You forgot to pull the thread."

Embarrassed, he examined the pockets and grinned. Suddenly he cried, "Look!"

She turned to see that the yacht had shifted position and a cascade of orange lights was falling like raindrops over the Great Pyramid of Khafre behind the Sphinx.

Mickey spread his jacket on the deck with a gallant flourish, and they sat with their backs against a wall as a long series of explosions lit up Egypt's most wondrous marvels, creating a virtual orgy for the eyes. Her mind, usually an endless train of obsessive thoughts, was now light and filled with delight. She smiled as if there would be no end to the bountiful offerings. Time was suspended.

"I can't think of anybody I'd rather see this with," Mickey said.

She tore her eyes away from the sky and glanced at him. He was looking at her so intensely that it made her look away.

"Stop it!" she purred. But as she pushed his chin away, she gasped in surprise. A rocket exploded in the sky right above their heads, its red and green sparks coming down so close that she thought they would land on them. Mickey laughed with glee and slid down onto his back, his head tilted up toward the sky as a new series of explosions began. She followed suit and lay next to him, joining in his laughter as each explosion reverberated inside their bodies, the burning embers coming dangerously close to their faces. She raised her arm to protect herself, while he bravely faced the sparks, his excitement growing.

"Green!" he shouted. And a green explosion ignited the sky.

"Red!" she wagered. And a red one followed.

"Red and pink," he predicted, but it came up red and dark blue.

"Yellow," she shouted. But her winning streak had ended, too. A violet and green one with specks of orange lit up the sky. But the next one was yellow.

"I think I know what the color of the grand finale will be," he said as she buried her face against him for protection from the ashes. "And if I'm right, I get a kiss," he declared, but she was too busy letting out shrieks of excitement to agree, as the following explosions, each one louder than the last, led her to burrow deeper into his chest. "We're going to see all the colors of the rainbow at the same time," he bet.

The explosions that followed filled the entire sky and were so loud that they shook the boat. The finale finally came, illuminating the heavens in red, orange, yellow, green, blue, indigo, and violet.

Indeed the crescendo was a spectacular multicolor rainbow, leaving them in awe. And when everybody thought the show was over, one last rocket exploded, casting a green glow on Mickey's face, illuminating his eyes, which had turned calm and tender.

"That one was for the king," she said, veering her eyes away, uncomfortable again with his gaze. "Green is his favorite color."

"Do I get my kiss?" he murmured.

"Nope," she said with a grin. "I didn't take the bet."

"What about one for bringing you here?"

"Nope."

"Okay, what about one for saving you from the king? He was targeting you for his next conquest."

"Nothing would have happened! What kind of girl do you think I am?"

"The kind of girl who gives me a hard time."

"Fine." She relented. She rose on her elbow and leaned over, giving him a small peck on the lips before lying back down again, straight as a soldier.

"That's it?"

She let out a defeatist sigh. "Okay! But only because I'm a good-hearted person." She leaned in again and pressed her lips against his for a brief kiss. He didn't move his lips, not even slightly, and his eyes remained closed as he savored the kiss. She bent over and kissed him again, this time a bit longer, but he still didn't respond. Then he opened his eyes and looked right into hers. He was systematically disarming her, and there was no escaping him this time. She let herself stare back in spite of the conflicting emotions inside her. She couldn't possibly allow herself to fall for him. Having some fun was one thing, but those longing looks between them were quite another.

As if reading her mind, he smiled gently and with the back of his hand caressed her cheek. She returned his smile, just a little, but enough to encourage him. He slowly sat up, and, taking her in his arms, cushioned her head with his forearm as he laid her down. Barely breathing, she lay immobile, knowing what was coming next as his face drew close to hers. She felt her spine stiffen, and he must have sensed it, too, because he urged her to relax. But how could she? Her life had been nothing but chaos for so long that she didn't remember how to relax anymore. Any happy thoughts would inevitably be interrupted by images of Erik and Vati, and her mind was constantly churning. No, not this time, Maya, she told herself, taking a lungful of air and commanding herself to release her tension. She let her breath mingle with his as he leaned patiently suspended above her, waiting for a sign. She gave it to him by closing her eyes, and before she knew it she felt the tip of his tongue parting her lips. The moisture of it jarred her. They were intimate now. She wet her lips with her tongue as if to awaken her appetite and sighed. The sound of it echoed deep inside her, arousing her. She was ready to kiss him freely. She threw her arms around his neck and let her lips and tongue tell him how much she loved being with him tonight.

They couldn't stop kissing, and when they had to stop for air, they both smiled, embarrassed at their inability to let go of one another. When their mouths weren't joined together, it was an eye or an ear or a cheek that had to be kissed. Time had disappeared again, and they forgot who they were and where they were. Slow kisses, hurried kisses, long ones, short ones—they tried them all, and each had its own luscious flavor, making them even hungrier for more.

"This is crazy," she finally said between breaths, rolling her head back.

"It's only crazy that we waited so long," he said, shushing her with kisses on her throat. She felt his hand gliding up the side of her dress, starting at her thigh, going up to her waist, and pausing on her breast. She held her breath for an instant, wondering what he might do next, excited by his boldness. She tightened her grip around his neck as he pressed her breast gently while his tongue traced the length of her neck. She sighed, wanting him never to stop. But he did, letting go of her breast and coming up to meet her mouth again as he caressed her hair.

"My pin!" she said, breaking the moment, remembering she was wearing her mother's hairpin. She sat up and found that it had already slid to the end of her curl. "My mother's," she explained, finding herself suddenly jittery.

The guests on the deck had gone back to the party now, and sounds of dance music filtered up from the dining room. They were completely alone. Mickey rolled over and lay on his back, his hands behind his head as the boat rocked gently. There was only a crescent moon in the sky, but it was enough to illuminate the silhouettes of the pyramids and the palm trees and reeds on the shore. The setting couldn't have been more lovely, but her mind was already gnawing at her.

"I have to get back to my lemonade bar," she said.

"No, you don't," he said. "It's an open bar. People can serve themselves."

He was right. Besides, what could they do to her for not being there?

"Tell me more about yourself," he said.

The simple question caused her to panic. She began to rattle on, making up stories about how she had to take care of her infant brother, who was sick. She complained about how she always had to be the peacemaker between her younger sisters and brothers, who fought all the time, and how exhausted she was from having to play so many roles. She talked so fast that she didn't allow Mickey to ask any questions, and when she was finished, she felt disgusted with herself. "I have to go," she said and started to rise.

"Come over here," he said calmly, pulling her toward him.

She resisted only slightly, allowing herself to lie down again.

"What's going on?" he asked, stroking her hair.

"What do you mean?" she protested.

"In here." He tapped her head. "Your mind, I can always hear it buzzing."

"You won't understand."

"Try me."

She wouldn't know where to begin even if she were to tell him the truth. "There is so much on my mind that I can hardly sleep," she said. "I wake up in the morning and I don't know what to expect. My life is so full of uncertainty. As you can see, I can never plan anything."

He placed a kiss on top of her head and put an arm around her. "Uncertainty is very difficult. Are you worried about where you'll be living?" he probed.

"Yes, of course. I can't imagine living in the Sudan," she said, unable to reveal that it was really Palestine she was thinking of. Why would a city girl like her want to live in a barren desert like Palestine, where immigrating lawyers and doctors were stripped of their professions and reduced to milking cows and working on farms?

"I'm sure the Sudan will just be a temporary solution until things calm down," he said. "When are you planning to leave?"

"My parents don't tell me much, only that it will be soon."

"It might not be all that soon. There may be a transportation strike. First it was the bus and tram unions, now the railway workers are threatening to strike, too."

She shrugged and sat up. "We'll get there by car if we have to."

"I have an idea," he said dreamily. "I'm going to show you around the city and make you fall in love with it so that you won't go to the Sudan. You have the right to make your own choices, you know," he argued. "My father thought I was a complete loony for coming here, but I came!"

She looked away. He did not understand. How could he?

He must have picked up on her change of mood because he pulled her back down toward him and said softly, "Maya, I don't want you out of my sight. I'm just plain selfish, forgive me. Let's not talk about this anymore. Tonight is our night, right?"

She thought for a moment and smiled. "Yes, it is. Tonight is our night." As she said the words, she could feel a lightness replacing the wave of anxiety that had passed through her a moment earlier. She inched closer, basking in the intimacy. He kissed the tip of her nose, and then their lips met for another long, slow kiss. When they stopped, he brushed a lock of hair from her eyes and caressed her face.

"You're the most beautiful girl I've ever seen," he murmured.

"Liar!"

"Nope. It's true," he asserted. "And you know you're beautiful."

She accepted the compliment with a little smile. She thought of herself as pretty, not beautiful, and vividly remembered the day she'd studied her face in a mirror for a very long time, and, deep in her eyes, she'd seen her soul reflected in them. She'd only been thirteen at the time, but she'd known then there was beauty in her. She put her head on his chest and listened to the sound of his heartbeat. What a luxury it was to kiss and talk with this man all night. "You're a good kisser, you know?" she said.

"Is this coming from an expert?"

"Maybe," she teased.

"Better than Jean-Jacques?" He pronounced the name with mock disdain again.

"Maybe." She raised her head and traced his lips with a finger. "Tell me about your ex-girlfriend. Did you love her?"

He straightened up and looked at the sky as he pondered the question. "I don't know . . . I thought I loved her, but I think I talked myself into it. We had been going steady for two and a half years and she wanted to get married. I thought it was the right thing to do," he said, shaking his head. "All I can tell you is that a month before the wedding we had dinner with her parents to go over the plans—you know, she came from a wealthy family from the South, so she wanted a big wedding—and there was another couple dining next to us. The girl was very sweet, and I remember thinking the other guy lucky. That night my own fiancée ran off with her college sweetheart. I must have been blind!"

"Ouch! I guess they had unfinished business, huh?"

"I guess so. And he was from a purer bloodline. A true Southern aristocrat! Didn't really have to work. Not exactly the kind of guy I admire," he said. "At the time it was rough on me, very humiliating, but looking back, it was only my pride that got hurt." He turned toward her. "Truth is, I ought to thank her for saving me from what undoubtedly would have been a miserable marriage."

She cozied up close to him again. "So where are you taking me on Wednesday?"

"I'm planning a nice surprise and I really don't want to go on that double date!" he said, almost panicked. "I want to be alone with you."

"Ay, ay, ay! I promised my cousin's parents I would chaperone," she said.

"How important is this guy to her?"

"Serious enough," she answered, sitting up. "She's ready to ask him about his intentions."

"Then we have to give them some time alone," he said, sitting up and settling in behind her. He encircled her with his arms. "I'm only thinking of them, no selfish motives here, really!"

"I'll work on it," she said, knowing it wouldn't be easy. Joe was reluctant to allow Lili to even take the metro into the city alone.

He placed a gentle kiss on her shoulder.

The boat had turned around and was now lazily heading back toward the city.

Cairo stretched before them like a beaded quilt of lights against the black desert.

"Am I dreaming?" she asked. "Is there really a war going on?"

"Yes, and yes."

"Nothing seems real tonight. Not even me. I don't recognize myself."

"You're real," he said. "I see you."

She let his words percolate and smiled—she did feel that he saw inside of her. She snuggled a little closer. "Do you think the Germans would dare bomb the pyramids?"

"If it helped win the war, I don't think Hitler would think twice about a pile of old stones." Suddenly he raised his index finger. "Listen . . . " He strained to hear.

The voice of a singer floated up from the ballroom.

"Parlez moi d'amour, redites-moi des choses tendres. La la la la la," he started to sing along. "This was my mom's favorite song." He was silent for a moment. "She was very special. I think you would have liked her—and she you."

She could feel the warmth of his breath tickling her neck, and she shivered. She was so completely happy. "Who do you look like more? Your mother or your father?"

"My mother, for sure. I have her long limbs. My father is stocky and . . . ignorant about a lot of things, I'm afraid."

"He's your father nevertheless."

He hugged her tighter. "I like this city," he declared dreamily. "Where else in the world today can you dine and dance under a beautiful moon with a small gathering of a couple of hundred close friends?"

"I didn't know we were dancing!"

She smiled, wishing time would slow to a crawl this evening.

She grabbed his wrist and read his watch. "We've been here for two hours! We're going to be docking any minute." She stood up and straightened her dress. Her hair was a mess, and she pulled it back with her pin. He stood up, too, and slipped into his jacket.

"You didn't even shake it," she reprimanded and started brushing it off with her hands. Then she adjusted his bow tie. "That's better."

He wrapped his arms around her and pressed his forehead against hers. "I don't think I can last until Wednesday," he said.

"You'll have to," she whispered.

"We're only just beginning, Maya," he said, stroking the back of her hair.

"The timing couldn't be worse, Mickey," she said, although she was melting from his touch.

He raised her chin so she'd look at him. "It's too late to worry about that," he said. "The cat is out of the bag."

"Say sex," the photographer cried out when they entered the dining room, using the more risqué French equivalent of America's "cheese," before blinding them with the flash of his camera.

"Monsieur Connolly! They've been calling your name," a man shouted, a few yards away by the bar.

"It's General Catroux," Mickey explained to Maya as he waved to a gaunt man standing next to Ambassador Lampson. "He's De Gaulle's right-hand man. I want to introduce you. He's been spending a lot of time in Damascus trying to persuade the army there to join the Free French. He could be of help to your family."

She flinched, alarmed now that Mickey was going to poke into her affairs. "That won't be necessary. I told you we'll be fine," she said.

A woman's voice came over the loudspeaker calling Mickey's name to the dance floor where a voluptuous woman in an elaborate gold dress was shaking a piece of paper that she'd drawn from a hat.

"*Vous êtes chanceux ce soir* (You are lucky tonight)," the French general shouted to Mickey. "You've won the dance with Madame Samina."

"I have to go. The boat has docked," Maya said, moving away.

A man next to Mickey pushed him toward the dance floor. "Go on!"

"Don't leave yet," Mickey cried after Maya.

The lights dimmed and the orchestra started playing a slow tune. Maya turned and watched the woman in the gold dress swishing her long black ponytail left and right as she snaked toward Mickey and pulled him to the center of the floor. He resisted but she insisted, and wrapped her arms around his neck, demanding his full attention. They started a slow dance. Maya felt a pang of jealousy as she joined the stream of guests who were leaving, finding it unsettling that her magical evening was ending on this note.

CHAPTER 28

"All I can tell you is that your fellow did not attend the last four embassy press briefings," Abdoul stated as he leaned forward to give a picture to Kesner. "His accreditation with the *Detroit Free Press* has been suspended." Abdoul reclined in the chair behind Dr. Massoud's desk, as if he enjoyed the position of authority.

"Suspended?" Kesner said, annoyed with Abdoul's posturing and taking a quick look at the picture of the American reporter.

"That's what the record shows. The last story he filed was seven weeks ago," Abdoul said as he puffed on his cigar.

Kesner rose and paced the doctor's office, where they had gone because the mafraj was occupied. "He told Samina he was writing a story about the Jews of Egypt, but that's nonsense. It's a cover, and a pretty good one. The American Embassy is behind this," he asserted. "Out of the four Americans on the invitation list you obtained for us, Samina picked him out to be the spy. He's the only fresh face among the four. The others have been around forever. While they danced, she pressed him about the story he was writing. He fumbled and then tried very hard to sound enthusiastic. No one can read men like she does, and she says he's a liar. It all adds up. He must be the one looking for Blumenthal."

"Whether he's writing about the Jews or looking for

Blumenthal, he was in the right place with the right people at the ball, and he's making some very good connections," Abdoul said. "He was seen talking with Sir Miles Lampson, Ambassador Kirk, and General Catroux. And at dinner he sat next to Madame Cattaoui, which was no small honor. He seems to be mixing well with the Jewish crowd."

"I see that," Kesner agreed, his mind racing as it dawned on him that the American, by enlisting the cooperation of the Jews and the British, was in a far better position to find the scientist than he was. "What else do you know?"

"The waiter overheard him engaged in a lively discussion about British policy in Palestine."

Kesner rubbed his hands. Palestine. That was just where Hassan al-Banna had suspected that the scientist would be going. The sheik and his men were on the trail of a group of lawyers who had gotten two Belgian Jewish physicians into Palestine with false papers. It all made sense. If Connolly were any good, he would look into this too. He turned to Abdoul, his mind made up. He would not kill Connolly just yet. The American would prove more useful alive for now. "I need to have the American followed day and night," he said. "I can assure you the Reich will be most generous in its appreciation for what you are doing."

"It is my honor to serve," Abdoul responded. Then, playing another one of his aces, he announced, "You'll be interested to hear that yesterday Ambassador Lampson requested an immediate audience with King Farouk. On a Sunday! When the king did not respond, the ambassador marched right in, uninvited."

"Who does he think he is?" Kesner said.

Abdoul went on to recount the British ambassador's bold visit, where he'd presented the king with a list of demands, including the return of Hitler's red Mercedes, the severing of relations with Vichy France and the closing of their embassy here, and the expulsion of the king's Italian friends. Finally, in an egregious breach of protocol, he'd demanded that the king force an emergency decree through Parliament to prevent any potential transportation strike.

"What nerve!" Kesner said. "What did the king say to all of that?"

"The king was trembling like a girl," Abdoul said. "But I reminded the ambassador that 'the king is the king.'"

"Well said, my friend."

"To which Lampson insolently responded that the king is the king because they made his father king, and that just as they could make kings, they could unmake kings."

Kesner shook his head. Lampson was dangerous. Kesner had to renew his efforts to spread the message that the transportation unions had to strike. And the Brotherhood had to step up publishing its anti-British propaganda pamphlets. He returned to his seat and looked at Abdoul gravely. "Thanks be to God, the king has you by his side. But I must warn you, if the king intervenes with the strike, he will be seen as blatantly pro-Ally, and there will be a risk that your beautiful city here will be flattened by the Luftwaffe. I'll have no control over that."

Abdoul extinguished his cigar and shifted in his seat.

"Do you want to be remembered as the man who destroyed the pyramids, because everybody knows you are the power behind the king?"

"They would never destroy the pyramids. Would they?"

Kesner just shrugged.

Abdoul looked away. After an uneasy moment, he declared, "The king will not interfere with the strike. I'll make sure of that."

"I know we can count on you, my friend. Did you know that the First Panzer Army took Rostov yesterday?" Kesner said proudly. "The road to Moscow is wide open now and the city is less than 250 miles away. The Soviets will capitulate quickly. We only need to kick in the door and their whole rotten structure will come crashing down."

"Very good," Abdoul said.

Kesner thought of mentioning his displeasure about the king's mistress Riri Charbit's involvement in Saturday night's Jewish event on the royal yacht, but decided to wait. Abdoul had all he could handle. He might have to take care of Miss Charbit himself. "Well . . . " he said as he started to get up.

Picking up on the cue, Abdoul also rose. "I'll put some men on this American reporter's trail immediately."

"Excellent."

CHAPTER 29

On Monday morning, Mickey bounded up the stairs to the embassy gate, whistling and feeling light as a feather. He was still basking in the afterglow of that most beautiful night. Now, however, he needed to push aside his ever-present daydreams about Maya and ready himself for that "little chat" Dorothy had wanted to have. It was too bad she'd missed the spectacular evening on the yacht. When he'd rung her office at nine, she hadn't arrived yet. Was she ill? This was not like her, dedicated bird that she was.

He decided to swing by the mail room on his way to her office. It would only take a second. The clerk had rung him this morning; there was a postcard with a view of Lake Saint Claire waiting for him. Must be from his father, who loved going there to fish. Dad wouldn't be too pleased to learn that he'd found a Jewish girlfriend. "They think they're too good for the rest of us," his old man would say, and not only when he was drunk. Mickey could never get him to understand the inconsistency of his thinking. On the one hand he accused the Jews of being Communists, on the other, he vilified them as money lovers. Which is it, Dad?

Mickey was ashamed of his father's bigotry, which included not only Jews but also every segment of the population that differed from him—basically the entire world. But Maya was right: Bigot or not, his father was his father.

He softened for a moment, reminding himself that deep down his father was a decent human being, just a fearful and ignorant one, and Mickey promised himself to be more patient with him.

As he looked at the picture of the lake on the postcard, a man raced into the mail room, shouting, "Dorothy Calley has been murdered!"

As Mickey's taxi raced toward Dorothy's bungalow in Zamalek, he wondered why anyone would want to kill her. He took in deep gulps of air, his chest heaving. He was flattened by this news. When he arrived, an ambulance and police van were pulling away from the house, leaving only one Egyptian police car, a Jeep with an American flag on its fender, and Kirk's black embassy Packard.

Kirk's chauffeur recognized him as he got out of the taxi. "The ambassador is inside," he said in a solemn voice.

The front door was wide open and Mickey raced in.

Egyptian police were swarming around Kirk, who sat on the sofa, his face in his hands. Two US marines also stood near Kirk and hurried to block Mickey's rushed approach.

"Ambassador!" Mickey cried out, pushing away the marines, who stepped aside when Kirk rose and opened his arms to Mickey.

"God bless you, you're here, Mickey," Kirk cried. His pale eyes were bloodshot and swollen, and his face looked like a rag that had been washed too many times.

"I'm so sorry," Mickey said. "I know how close you were."

Kirk quivered. "They broke her neck." He started to cry, but quickly got ahold of himself. "I apologize. I'm still very shaken. She was my anchor. I don't know what I'll do without her."

"What happened?" Mickey asked.

Kirk shook his head, unable to speak. "No robbery. No sexual assault," he finally said. "Her purse had been emptied, but her wallet had plenty of cash." He pointed to a spot on the floor where the bag's contents had been dumped. "Her jewelry was still in a silk pouch in her bedroom, behind her dozens of nail polish bottles. You know how important her nails were to her . . . "

"Then why?" Mickey asked.

"I don't know," Kirk answered plaintively. "I've gone through this with the police. She didn't have any enemies or jealous lovers that I'm aware of. We never talked much about personal things, you know, but I think she would have told me if she had a fellow. She seemed pretty content with her cat. When I came by this morning, I knew right away something was very wrong when I found the cat howling outside the door. The neighbor said he's had to feed her for the last two days."

Mickey took him by the arm and sat him down. He kept quiet, waiting for Kirk to find the strength to go on.

"She was getting ready for Saturday night's ball. She'd laid out her clothes for the evening," Kirk explained. "They found curlers scattered everywhere . . . " He swallowed hard and resumed. "I tried to reach her yesterday morning. She hadn't called, and I was worried she might be sick, but I had to leave for Alexandria on a hospital tour and didn't return until very late. I should have tried again last night." His voice was riddled with guilt.

Mickey put a hand on Kirk's shoulder. "It wouldn't have done any good. She was already dead."

"I told her she should live in a building with a doorman, but she liked this place's charm. And the oak tree out front," Kirk sighed. "The back door was unlocked. The killer must have opened it with a blade, that's easy enough to do, and caught her by surprise . . . " His voice cracked and he fought to compose himself. "I found her tied to that chair." He pointed to a chair tucked against the small dining room table in an alcove. "Her ankles were bound and her arms were tied behind her. Her neck was broken," he choked.

Mickey winced, but his throat was too constricted for any words to come out.

Except for the sounds of the police photographer's camera and some movement upstairs, the room had now fallen silent. Mickey stood up and walked around aimlessly as the reality of Dorothy's murder fully sank in. His chest ached from the pain. He stroked the back of the chair she had sat on, trying to feel her one last time. His eye caught her gold watch on the dining table. He picked it up and recoiled—it was still ticking.

"She was tortured," Kirk said, his voice shaky. "My poor little girl was tortured. The tips of her fingers were burned and her nails were scorched. Her face was covered with blood and bruises. She was hit hard."

Tortured? Mickey held his head in his hands as he tried to fully digest the word in his brain. He kneeled in front of Kirk.

"What kind of information could someone have expected to get out of her?"

Kirk shook his head, more and more rapidly, his face pained as he wrestled with his thoughts. "She was privy to all kinds of top-secret information," he muttered. He passed a heavy hand through his hair and winced as some new realization came to light. He turned to the marines. "Would you please wait outside?" he asked them.

Mickey frowned, his heart beating. He sensed that Kirk was about to reveal something important.

When the marines were gone and the Egyptian police were out of earshot, Kirk spoke softly. "Blumenthal's new photo. You know she went to fetch it at the library. Did she give it to you?"

"No, she told me she would be bringing it to the ball," Mickey responded, scratching his head. "Why?"

Kirk just kept looking at Mickey, his expression inscrutable, but Mickey understood that Blumenthal's photo might have something to do with Dorothy's death. Mickey jumped to his feet and rushed to the spot on the floor where the contents of Dorothy's purse had been dumped. He furiously sifted through them. No photo there. He sprinted upstairs. As Kirk had said, her clothes were all laid out on her bed—dress, girdle, stockings. She'd even put aside a black lacy brassiere. Mickey surveyed the bedroom. There, on the dresser, was a beaded, golden clutch.

"*La-eh.* No," one of the policemen stepped in front of him, wagging a finger in his face. "No touching, sir."

Mickey ignored him and opened the purse anyway. There wasn't room for much. A lipstick, a miniature comb, a perfume vial, a handkerchief, and the invitation to the ball. It was obviously the bag she had intended to take to the ball.

"Ambassador," he shouted as he charged down the stairs. "I found her evening bag. No photo."

Kirk's eyes widened.

"Sir, I need the truth," Mickey demanded. "Just who is Erik Blumenthal?"

They waited while the police wrapped up their search of the house. Mickey could barely contain himself. He needed answers *now*. He was pacing the room, his hands in his pockets, his mind racing a mile a minute. They had not told him the whole story about the scientist. Why had Dorothy pressed him so forcefully to get off the case? And why did she want him to carry a gun?

"We'll be back tomorrow," the police captain told Kirk in a quiet, respectful tone.

"I'll lock the place up when I leave," Kirk said. "Please tell the marines to go."

Kirk listened to the sounds of the police car and Jeep driving off before turning to Mickey. "I'll try to answer your questions as best I can. But first things first. I need a drink."

As he headed to the bar, Mickey spun one of the dining room chairs around and straddled the seat, waiting. The ambassador poured himself a generous glass of scotch and downed it. He refilled his glass and headed for the sofa.

"Dorothy wanted to warn you that someone else had come looking for Erik Blumenthal," he began. "She received a call a week ago from a fellow you met at the Jewish community center, Jacques Antebie. Apparently a Westerner with an indistinct accent was also looking for our man. Dorothy went down to the community center to check for herself and learned that the man was in his early thirties and was wearing a tweed suit. He left no name or address."

"Why didn't she tell me?" Mickey asked.

"Ambassador Lampson alerted us that there is a master German spy operating in Cairo," Kirk responded. "She thought this might be the guy and she wanted to take you off the case and out of harm's way."

"Why would the Germans want Blumenthal? I thought the Nazis rejected 'Jew science' and expelled their Jewish scientists from their country."

"Perhaps what Blumenthal knows now has become of interest to them."

"Like what?"

Kirk crossed one leg over the other and downed his drink. His eyes revealed his inner conflict about saying more.

"Please," Mickey asked. "I'm up to my neck in this, too. I deserve to know the truth."

"Erik Blumenthal's research with Niels Bohr had something to do with atomic energy," Kirk finally admitted. "In France, he had been actively working with the French team on using nuclear fission to produce a weapon, an atomic bomb of unimaginable power, equal to thousands of tons of TNT."

"Is that really possible?" Mickey asked.

"We believe it is, and Roosevelt has given the project a green light. Enrico Fermi, our lead scientist, is going full throttle, in complete secrecy, of course. Even the English don't know. That's why we can't get them involved, although this will soon change."

"The Germans must be working on an atomic bomb, too," Mickey deduced.

"Yes. Einstein warned Roosevelt about their potential to build such a bomb two years ago, but we didn't know the status of their program."

"And now you do?"

"A week ago we learned that Hitler bought all of Norway's heavy water, one of the key components."

The information was spinning around in Mickey's head like a tornado. Whoever got the bomb first was going to win the war. "How far away are we?"

"Nobody knows. A year? Five years? We're well into it."

"Why is Blumenthal so important?"

"He wrote a paper on a new approach to nuclear fission. The paper interested Fermi, a lot. The president wants Blumenthal on our team."

"Can another scientist from his French team continue his work?"

"Not really. None of them have Blumenthal's expertise in this new area and would need a lot of time to catch up. Nothing has progressed since they arrived in England. The British, who are taking a different approach to starting a chain reaction, have not been funding their research."

"I see," Mickey said. "So the British would have no interest in Blumenthal?"

Kirk shook his head. "They don't believe in the heavy water

approach. They think that fast, unmoderated neutrons would work best." He sighed. "I've already told you more than I should. Dorothy is dead. Your life may already be in danger. Perhaps you should be leaving town."

"I'll take responsibility for my own life." Mickey stood up and paced. "I'd like to talk to Donovan."

"He won't be available for ten days."

"Ten days! I'd think this would be a top priority for him."

"I've told you all I can, Mickey. We're going to take it from here."

"Well, I work for Donovan, and until he fires me, I'm not quitting," Mickey said flatly. "Dorothy died because I lost that picture, and I'm going to find the son of a bitch who killed her."

"I sent her to get the photo, so we can share the blame," Kirk said, biting his lower lip.

"What I want to know is how in the world that bastard knew that Dorothy had Blumenthal's picture." He walked back to Kirk. "I need a gun, a Jeep, and more cash. And I want my press badge back."

"Be careful, Mickey. Who knows what Dorothy might have revealed under duress," he choked out before resuming in a more even tone. "You should assume that the spy already knows about you and is on your trail. And it may not just be your own life you're putting in danger, but possibly those around you as well. You've seen how he operates."

A chilling thought immediately occurred to Mickey: Would he be endangering Maya by seeing her again?

CHAPTER 30

It must have been the tenth outfit she'd tried on in the last two days in preparation for her date with Mickey on Wednesday. All that he had said was that it was a surprise and to meet him at the entrance to the Museum of Antiquities, next to the Khedive Ismail Bridge. She had no idea where he would be taking her and she was going crazy trying to be ready for anything. Lili had been an angel, coming up with all kinds of makeshift outfits from her own wardrobe and sewing up a storm. Maya finally settled on a blue skirt with polka dots and a white blouse, which she would wear with a white belt and high-heeled shoes if they were going to a nice restaurant, or without a belt and flats if they were going on a picnic. She'd take a large bag to carry the extra choices. In both cases she would wear the scarf she'd worn on their first date, which had been a big hit with him.

She and Lili had hatched their cover story, telling Allegra that they were going on an outing with the Judeo-Spanish club here in Heliopolis. They'd planned to go to downtown Cairo together and then split up. Lili would join Fernando at the cinema while Maya went off with Mickey.

She sat on Lili's bed, trying to collect herself. In a few minutes they would be out of the house. Her mind had been continuously buzzing since that magical night on the yacht, savoring and replaying every word, touch, kiss, look, and declaration they'd exchanged. It was rare for a man to openly discuss his feelings, and she was glad that he trusted her enough to talk about his ex-girlfriend. He had dared to let her glimpse the man inside, and she saw behind those lion eyes, the eyes of a child, curious and vulnerable. And playful, too. She loved the way he teased her. Here she was telling Lili not to trust love at first sight and that relationships took time to develop, yet she thought she was already in love herself.

But where was all this going? Where could it go? The timing couldn't be worse. In a few weeks, she and her family would be in Palestine. And then what? She thought of all those romantic poets she'd read, from Goethe to Baudelaire, who glorified the pain of impossible love. Was that going to be her fate too? Once she would have reveled in the twisted pleasure of being a tortured soul, but she'd known suffering, and now she just wanted plain, simple happiness. But was it in the cards for her? She cracked her knuckles. She was nervous. Call her pessimistic, but she'd had a premonition all day that bad things might be in the offing.

It had started in the morning when she awoke to an unfamiliar, pungent odor and was greeted with thick, foul-smelling smoke in the hallway. She'd followed the fumes toward the living room, where she found Allegra and Sayeda swinging braziers of burning coal as they circled the furniture, chanting in Arabic. They looked like witches.

"That's the *bokour,*" Lili had explained later. "It's used to cast the evil eye out of the house." What evil had befallen the house, Maya wondered. Is it us? She could not get any further explanation from Lili, but later Allegra locked herself in her room for the rest of the morning, complaining of a splitting headache. She had rudely declined Maya's offer to bring her a cup of tea. Perhaps Allegra was still angry with Vati for reprimanding Soussou so sharply the day before when he'd found the boy playing with Mutter's violin. He had nearly brought the child to tears, but Vati later apologized and helped him with his clarinet. Nevertheless, it was clear that something was going on when Joe, who had left the house hurriedly after an agitated phone call early in the morning, had not returned home for lunch as he always did. All the while, the hot desert winds of the *khamseen* were blowing hard, which was unusual for this time of year.

If this weren't unsettling enough, Maya had only been able to reach Mickey once in three days, and they'd only spoken briefly as she'd caught him dashing out the door.

Enough, enough, enough! Maya had to control this nonstop worrying mind of hers. All was well, she assured herself. To make herself cheerful, she started humming the French song Mickey had sung on the yacht. She went to the dresser and was putting some perfume on when the door opened and Lili appeared, frazzled and wild-eyed.

"You'd better go to the living room," she said. "Your brother and my father are having a big fight."

"Your father? He's here?" Maya repeated, her heart sinking. This could spoil her plans for the afternoon. "What are they fighting about?" she asked.

"Palestine," Lili said in a hushed voice. "They kicked me out of the room."

Maya's heart sank. The subject seemed to be a taboo in this house, with Joe and Allegra always avoiding it. She feared that Erik had exhausted his patience and was going to confront their hosts about what was going on with their papers. She shared his frustration, but did not want to rock the boat. It had been such a long ordeal getting here, and she felt very vulnerable. They were stateless, with only temporary visitors' papers, and were very frightened by the rapid German advance toward Cairo. Making matters worse, there seemed to be no place in the world that would accept

Jewish refugees. Perhaps Erik's colleagues in England could help them again as they had with Turkey, but the visa process would take months with no assurance as to the outcome. The Jewish Agency in Istanbul had tried to get them visas for Palestine, but they were told there would be no exceptions to the British freeze on immigration.

But while their efforts at the Jewish Agency had failed to win a visa, they had won them an ally. A woman who worked there had taken notice of them and, impressed with Erik's credentials, had clandestinely sought them out. "How badly do you want to go to Palestine?" she'd asked. Erik, who had been voraciously reading Zionist literature, answered without hesitation—very badly. He was convinced that assimilation would not succeed anywhere in the world, and that a Jewish homeland in Palestine was the only solution. The woman had been pleased with his response. She could make no guarantees but said that she was connected to a "highly reliable and effective" network of Zionists in Egypt. There would be risks involved, and they would surely be interned by the British if caught, but Erik had wanted to take the gamble. He did not feel secure at all in so-called neutral Turkey, because of its uncomfortable amount of "friendly" communication with Germany. He had feared a Vichy-type regime would emerge there too. Yes, their best hope would be illegal immigration to Palestine—*Aliyah Bet*. But now they were faced with this inexplicable delay.

Maya wiped off some of her lipstick with a handkerchief and headed for the living room.

Joe, who usually spoke with great equanimity, could be heard through the closed doors, and when she entered, he was visibly emotional. "Are the Jews a tribe? A people? Yes. Do they need a homeland? Probably yes. But does it have to be in Palestine? No."

"Palestine is the homeland of many—the Christians, the Muslims, the Jews . . . " Allegra said, holding her belly. "It does not really belong to any one people—it belongs to everyone."

"The English made a promise to us," Erik replied, "and they were the rightful governors of the land." He was sitting on the edge of the settee, Vati next to him.

"Yes, the Balfour Declaration, but they made that very same promise to the Arabs!" Joe countered.

"Forget the English. It has always been our land," Vati shouted, the veins in his temples throbbing.

"That was long ago," Joe retorted. "Let's talk about the realities of today. We've had nothing but trouble with the Arabs there. How much more blood must be spilled?"

Just then, the laughter of the children was heard in the hallway as they returned from school with Sayeda.

"Shh," Allegra hissed. "Quiet, please. I don't want the children to hear this."

"Why not?" Vati exclaimed. "Your children should know where they come from and they should learn to be proud of it," Vati continued, his voice less strident. "Why not, when German children are taught about their Aryan superiority in kindergarten? Perhaps none of this is what you want to hear, but where will your family go when the Germans invade Egypt?"

Allegra's face flushed. "The Germans are not going to invade Egypt, monsieur. The English will stop them. We understand you, but Egypt is our home and we will never leave. We have no problems with the Egyptians."

"What about the looting of your stores and the burning of your synagogues, madame?" Erik interjected. "I see how you ignore it, like my parents did when it happened in my country." His words cut the tension in the room like a knife.

Joe lowered his eyes, while Allegra looked away and stroked her belly.

"What you see now is only the beginning, I promise you," Vati warned. "For two thousand years we have tried to gain acceptance in other countries, only to be met with contempt and violence."

"I am not religious," Erik proclaimed, "but as long as there will be anti-Semitism, I will be a Jew. Please understand, we are one-hundred percent committed to emigrating to Palestine, but this delay is agonizing to us. I do not wish to offend you, but we need to know what's holding things up. Please be honest with us. This is our lives."

Joe and Allegra exchanged nervous looks as a heavy silence fell over the room.

Maya walked to a chair next to the settee and sat down. "What happened this morning?" she asked bluntly. "Something happened."

Joe exchanged another weary look with his wife, who nodded her acquiescence. He bent forward and interlaced his fingers before speaking. "After Hassan al-Banna's escape from jail, they found a list of fifteen names in the home of one of the members of the Muslim Brotherhood. Most belong to the underground Zionist network we are in touch with. The police thought it was a list of targets for assassination. They were right. Three weeks ago one of them was murdered. Today, another was found dead." He swallowed hard and continued, "The man helping you is also on that list."

Maya felt sick. She realized that by helping them, their hosts were now also in jeopardy. Of course Joe and Allegra were scared. "We won't put you in danger one more night," she said. "We'll pack and leave this evening."

"Nonsense. You're not going anywhere," Joe immediately objected. "You will stay with us until your papers are finalized. We will be fine. We have no overt connection to Zionist activities, and very few people know about us. Those who do can be trusted. As for the man on the list who is helping you, he is not one who can be intimidated."

He stood behind his wife and placed his hands on her shoulders.

"Being Jewish is complicated for my wife and me," he continued. "Our religion is Judaism, but our citizenship is French, and our homeland is Egypt. My family does not share your politics, but we want to bring you to safety. If you wish to go to Palestine, you can count on our help." He looked at each of the Blumenthals with an unwavering gaze.

"You are welcome to stay here," Allegra added firmly.

There was no doubt that she meant it. Maya had clearly underestimated her.

"Can you tell us who the man on the list is?" Erik asked.

"He's my brother," Allegra answered flatly.

Her head gently bobbing against the window of the metro as it rattled toward Cairo, Maya kept her eyes shut, still shaken by what she had just learned, while Lili, oblivious to the danger descending on her family, rambled on about Fernando. The girl had been sulking since the ball because Fernando had neglected her and chosen to watch the fireworks with his aunts. But he'd recaptured her good graces when he called last night, whispering sweet nothings. Maya couldn't take Lili seriously. Here she was, babbling as if she were ready to get married, yet she continued to sunbathe on the balcony in her scanty suits, enjoying the stares of the young men below. The girl was a paradox. At times she seemed superficial and frivolous, but then she would surprise Maya with her keen interest in things as esoteric as Turkish pottery and, of course, her staunch commitment to do her share for the war effort. In truth, deep down, Maya saw her as a kindred spirit who shared the same longing to be free and who had now become her partner in crime.

However, at this moment, while Lili could barely sit still from the excitement of having won her freedom for the next few hours,

Maya was despondent. She was torn as to what to do about Mickey. Any attention to her family, especially from a journalist writing about Jews, could potentially place the Levis and their other benefactors in danger if the Muslim Brotherhood caught wind of it. She wasn't exactly sure who Mickey was talking to as he investigated his story. She sighed deeply. Should she take a chance and tell Mickey the truth? She trusted him. He would never do anything that could possibly hurt her, and if anything, he might be able to help. But what did she want from him, anyway? In two or three weeks, she and her family would be in Palestine. And then what? She shook her head, realizing how ridiculous she was to be looking so far ahead. They'd really only known one another for a few weeks, and their romance was in its infancy. Still, she was not sixteen anymore, and she knew that the feelings she had were all too rare and special to ignore. Though there was very little time, she wanted to give this a chance. She resolved to push away her worries about her circumstances and meet Mickey with as open a heart and mind as she could.

"Are you listening to me?" Lili asked, snapping her fingers in front of Maya's face "I was asking, how far have you ever gone with a boy? Nothing below the waist, I hope," she said with a straight face.

"Liliiii," Maya reprimanded, embarrassed but grateful that Lili had shown enough discretion to ask her question in a low voice.

"Sorry, I was just curious."

Maya averted her eyes. It was true that she'd never gone below the waist with any of her boyfriends, even with Jean-Jacques, who had tried a few times to bring her to his *garçonière*. But she had locked away the secret memory of that fateful night outside of Poitier when British bombers had killed the farmer's youngest boy. The older son, a doctor in the medical corps, happened to be home after being wounded on the Eastern Front. Maya had heard him sobbing in his room and went to comfort him. Torrents of her own tears poured out of her, for him and for the cruel tragedy that her own life had become. She hadn't even been able to grieve for her own mother. She had held him tightly, trying to ease his pain and desperately needing to be held herself. Before she knew it, they were making love on the floor. The urgency with which their bodies had sought one another was primal and liberating, a defiant affirmation of life while the world around them crumbled. It was not the way Maya had fantasized her first sexual encounter, but she'd never regretted it.

"We're almost there," Lili declared, nudging Maya's knee.

Maya looked up and saw the iconic statue, "The Reawakening of Egypt," in front of the Ramses train station as the metro came to a stop. From here they would take a tram downtown. Outside, they were met by the blowing gusts of the khamseen and a wall of sand gummed up their eyes and chafed their skin. They valiantly pressed forward, fighting to hold their dresses down in the fierce wind, and boarded the tram, each with her own agenda. Lili jumped off first. Maya rode on a few stations farther toward Midan Ismail Pasha, Cairo's largest square, but the conductor announced that they would have to disembark one station before that because Mustafa Nahas Pasha was giving a speech and the square was closed to traffic.

Maya didn't know who Nahas Pasha was but realized he had to be important when she saw the size of the crowd. Close to a thousand people, mostly in traditional Arab dress, had gathered around a man in a three-piece suit who was standing on a platform in the center of the enormous square. He was too far away for her to make out his face, but he was a forceful orator, wailing passionately into a megaphone to the wild cheers of his banner-waving fans. Most of the signs people carried were in Arabic, though some were in English: "Egypt for the Egyptians." Local police as well as soldiers on horseback were monitoring the crowd, which included many women and children.

She nervously crossed to the other side of the esplanade and headed toward the pink stone Museum of Antiquities, relieved to be moving away from the expanding throng, which had begun to spill onto the bridge. Mobs invariably made her tense; they reminded her of the first anti-Jewish demonstration she had witnessed back in Düsseldorf. She knew they could turn violent in an instant. When she reached the museum, the gates were closed and Mickey was not there.

A gunshot rang out and she whirled. Police were wading into the crowd. She had no idea who had fired the shot. Some men shouted angry slogans at the speaker, shaking their fists. She climbed onto the rim of one of the tall flowerpots framing the museum's gate to get a better view and watched the struggle going on in front of the speaker's platform. More people were now involved, shouting and jostling each other to see what was happening. Suddenly, the Pasha stopped speaking and disappeared into the crowd. Another shot sounded and the mob began to panic. Troops on horseback entered the melée, firing their pistols into the air, screaming for calm. But it was too late.

Pandemonium ensued.

The mob started to disperse, but in the hysteria, women and children were knocked down and trampled. Maya watched in horror as two men pulled out knives and moved toward one of the soldiers, dragging him down from his horse. He was engulfed by the furious crowd. She heard glass breaking and saw men smashing the windows of the shops surrounding the square. The air smelled of gunpowder and she knew it was time to run. But her feet wouldn't move. As she began to scream in fear, someone grabbed her hand and pulled her away. It was Mickey.

"Run!" he shouted.

CHAPTER 31

Mickey flashed his press badge and the security guards let them cross through the museum's vast courtyard to the riverbank. With the smell of gunpowder in the air they raced to the corniche, but they found the road closed to traffic. A crowded British military checkpoint permitted only resident pedestrians to pass through to their homes. Mickey's press papers got them through once again, but the MP warned him that he wouldn't be able to move his car. The entire area had been cordoned off so that the agitators who had disrupted Nahas's speech could be contained and arrested.

"I couldn't tell who started firing first. Maybe it was the Egyptian soldiers," Maya rasped, struggling for breath as Mickey held her elbow and quickly ushered her to the quieter side of the street along the river, while stranded drivers honked in frustration.

"I doubt they would do something that stupid," Mickey said, catching his breath. "Nahas is a hero to the Egyptian people, their voice of independence. If anyone had an axe to grind against him, it would be the Brits."

"You don't really think the British were behind this?" she asked, slowing her pace now that they were out of harm's way.

"I can think of a hundred reasons why they'd want the speech stopped, but I'm sure that their priority is to keep things stable right now." He stopped and pointed north. "My car is near the American University, but we might as well wait here until this blows over. At least we'll be safe."

"Hi," she said gently, pulling his arm and making him stop. She faced him, expectantly, so drawn to him that she felt her legs buckling under her. Her attraction to him was visceral, but she noticed stubble on his chin and that his eyes were bloodshot.

"Hi," he said, making only fleeting eye contact. "It's nice to see you." He gave her a peck on her lips and resumed their stroll.

What? She was confused. Not that she expected him to take her in his arms and kiss her passionately in the middle of the street, but he could certainly have been more affectionate. She tried to mask her disappointment and continued cheerfully, "Is this what you were planning for my surprise? A riot?"

He smiled a little. "I'm sorry. I wanted to change our meeting place but I did not know how to reach you."

"No, this is fine. I like walking."

He glanced at her and then away, his face expressionless.

"So, how long did you end up dancing with Madame Samina?" she asked after a moment, seeing that he was not volunteering to tell her where he'd planned to take her. "She is beautiful. Don't you think?"

"She's attractive." He then turned and looked at her tenderly. "But she's not even in the same league as you."

She smiled as their eyes locked in a sweet moment, making her heart skip a beat. But again, his gaze veered away. He seemed lost in thought.

They passed under the bridge close to the square, the site of the demonstration. Gunshots and screams could still be heard, but they couldn't see anything from down below.

He sneezed. "That damned wind."

She tugged on one of his earlobes and then the other, and before he had a chance to ask why, she explained, "It's to guard against the evil eye." She chuckled. "Haven't you learned how superstitious Egyptian Jews are? *Hamsa*!" she teased, flashing the palm of her hand in front of his face. "Another charm against evil."

"Is that what those hands on chains around women's necks mean?"

"Yes," she said. "And you must never leave a shoe upside down. That will bring bad luck as well. See all the valuable things you learn from me!"

He cracked a smile.

"How are you doing with your story? It's been awhile, no?"

He shrugged. "It's going. Those stories can take on a life of their own. Do you know this part of town?"

She shook her head.

"It's a beautiful residential area called Garden City. It's the palace district. One royal palace after the other, *Kasr* this and *Kasr* that. Each one has its own garden on the Nile. Most of the embassies are here. It used to be known as the European quarter."

"I wish I could assemble a book of photographs of just the windows and doors here," she said, admiring the buildings. "I love the interesting mix of ornamentation."

They passed an intricate black iron gate with the Queen's emblem protecting a large white Victorian house. Stone lions stood guard on either side.

"That's the British Residency," he said.

She peeked in. "Beautiful lawn."

"It stretches down to the Nile. I was at a party here once."

They walked in silence. He did not try to kiss her, nor did he compliment her on her outfit. He didn't ask about the status of her family's plans to leave. And worst of all, he did not say one word about what had passed between them Saturday night. He was just making small talk and cursing the sandy wind. And now that she looked at him more closely, she realized that it was not just stubble that he had under his chin, but rather sizeable patches of beard. That was one poor job of shaving for a guy who was planning to see a girl he was supposedly crazy about. Something was wrong, very wrong.

They were back on the corniche and passed a small group of people who were sitting cross-legged on a patch of grass devouring thick slices of watermelon with white cheese and green pimentos. "Beer and watermelon taste better in Egypt than anywhere else," he pronounced, breaking another silence between them.

"What's wrong, Mickey?" she finally asked.

He stopped and deliberated. After a moment's hesitation, he said, "How about I tell you over a cool drink?" He waved at a drink seller who was making his way between the exposed roots of the giant banyan trees that dotted the riverfront. A harness rested on his shoulders, where a jug with a long spout was fastened.

"What do you have here? *Maak eh henna*?" Mickey asked, venturing his Arabic as they approached him.

"*Assab*," the Egyptian responded. "*Taig*," He pointed to a lump of ice strapped to the harness.

"Do you like cold sugar cane juice?" Mickey asked. "It's the best thing in the world for quenching thirst."

The seller served the drinks in cardboard cups that he had wedged behind his belt. They found an unoccupied bench next to a banyan tree and went to sit there. A few sailboats were still valiantly crisscrossing the river, but with the thick layer of dust brought in by the wind, the view had lost its romantic luster.

"I had planned a picnic for us on a felucca like one of those," he said without batting an eye and pointing to one of the sailboats. "Champagne and caviar. There is a very private and beautiful embankment I discovered just past the old Cairo station that I thought you might like . . . " He finally looked her straight in the eyes, and she saw anguish there.

"What's wrong?" she asked softly, her hand reaching for his.

He squeezed his eyes shut and reopened them. Then took her hand and kissed it. "A close friend of mine was murdered," he said numbly.

Maya's hand flew to her mouth to smother a cry. She expected anything, but not that. "Murdered?" she repeated. Until today the word had never been in her vocabulary. She was familiar with death and war, but murder?

"That's why I'm such lousy company today." He smiled miserably.

"Oh, Mickey. I'm sorry. I don't know what to say. Why didn't you tell me sooner?" She stroked his face and arm. "Who was he?"

"She was the American ambassador's secretary. She was helping me research my article. No one knows what happened. I'm still in shock."

Maya shook her head, at a loss for words.

"She was one hell of woman," he continued, "though she'd probably refer to herself as a broad! Someone followed her home after work and broke her neck." He snapped his fingers. "*Bam*! Just like that. Alive one minute, dead the next. I keep wondering what went through her head during that split second."

She threw her arms around him and hugged him tight, but he remained stiff, just placing a light hand on her shoulder.

"I'm so sorry," she said disengaging. "What can I do?"

He blew out a long breath as if to exorcise his pain and said, "I'll be okay. It's just still very unreal to me. I left Detroit four months ago on what I thought was going to be a grand journalistic adventure, but now I'm finding myself a little too much in the story. I feel like I'm caught up in a sandstorm. I can't see what's going on. I just need to get my equilibrium back."

"Is there anything I can do?" she said, trying to meet his eyes, but he still avoided them.

He cleared his voice and said, "I'm afraid I won't be able to see you for a while, Maya."

"What do you mean?" she asked, feeling like she'd been hit by a brick.

"The embassy has warned those of us who worked closely with Dorothy to be very careful. She had access to some highly sensitive information and it's possible that we may become targets ourselves. When it's safe, I'll come find you. I swear it. I'm sorry." He started to stroke her shoulder, but this time it was she who pulled away.

"Did the killer try to force some information out of her?" she asked, biting her nail.

Mickey hesitated before answering. "She was tortured, if that's what you're asking."

"Are you in danger yourself?" she asked, carefully looking at his reaction.

He shrugged, then added, "Maybe. And it may not be safe for you to be near me."

A torrent of thoughts started swirling in her mind as she started to realize that Mickey was not the person he had said he was. Here he was, writing an article about the Jews, yet he hardly ever talked about it. He was much more interested in keeping up with the developments regarding the war. Surely the ambassador's secretary was in contact with many people on a variety of matters. Were they all in danger? This did not completely add up. What kind of sensitive information could the woman have possessed about the Jews here? And how did a young reporter manage to get so chummy with ambassadors, generals, and royalty in just four months? It was clear Mickey was involved in something beyond the story he had given her. Was he mixed up in spying? At least one thing he'd said she believed to be true—being around him might not be safe and could endanger the people she cared about. She turned to face him.

"Who are you, Mickey?" she demanded. "I think you've been lying to me all along."

"And what about you?" he shot back. "I should be the one asking who *you* are. You're intimate with me, but won't tell me where you live or let me call you. You're a refugee, but you won't consider accepting help even though you know I have valuable connections. You forbid me to talk to your uncle. What is it? Are you ashamed of me? Is there another man?"

"You have to trust me," she said softly.

"And you have to trust me," he replied, looking her straight in the eyes.

She held his stare for a long while, reading darkness and fear as well as vulnerability and pain in his eyes, and she was sure that hers read the same way. She began to feel overwhelmed by a sense of helplessness as if she were a pawn in a game that was bigger than the two of them. This was crazy. She was caught in a crossfire of murders and state secrets. Any future with this man would be impossible. Her whole world was crumbling, and from a place deep inside of her, she felt tears surging. She immediately hid her face with her hands, ashamed to let him see them.

"Maya," he said softly. "You will write to me and I'll come to you after the war, I promise." He placed a gentle hand on her shoulder, but she pushed it away. "Please, Maya, don't do that. This is killing me. Don't you know I'm in love with you?"

"Don't say that!" she shot back, only to turn and see his face raw and naked with emotion, his eyes telling her he was speaking the truth here. She couldn't veer away, nor could she mask her urge to throw herself in his arms and tell him she loved him too and didn't want him to get hurt. For a moment they remained in anguish, lost in one another. She suddenly felt a surge of tears rising again, but soon her inner voice came loudly—she had to assert control and cut things off with Mickey at once. After all Erik and Vati had endured, she could not risk endangering them and those helping them by bringing a man into her life who told her lies. She dried her tears with the back of her hand and took a sip of her juice as she built up her protective wall.

"Whatever you're involved in, please be careful." She took a deep breath and said, "We'll be leaving for Khartoum in a few days. Our entry visas came yesterday and we're expecting our exit papers any day now."

"The war won't last forever. I'll come to you wherever you are."

Summoning all her strength, she faced him. "I'm not going to write to you, Mickey. What happened on the boat Saturday night was beautiful, but it isn't what you think. I've been going through a very difficult period. I was lonely. I needed a good ear," she said, astonished that she could put on such a collected front.

"What are you saying?" His eyes penetrated her like a bullet.

"The setting was so extraordinarily romantic, and it was wonderful to be with you, but I think we just got carried away."

Mickey pulled away, incredulous. "What do you mean we just got carried away?"

"Please don't be angry with me. I—"

"Save it," he snapped. "You're talking nonsense. I know what happened on that boat. And you do too. It was real."

He stared at her so intensely that she had to lower her eyes. "Maybe it was different for you, but whatever it was that I felt then, I don't feel that way now. I'm sorry," she said.

He looked away, his jaw clenched. Though his face was unreadable, she knew that she had hurt him deeply, and she hated herself for it. She felt the old aching in her stomach, gnawing at her like a poisonous snake. Why didn't he say anything? Why didn't he get angry again? His silence was torture for her. She felt tears rising again, but she fought them back. Don't you dare! Don't you dare cry! she demanded of herself. She was desperate to leave.

The sound of engines was heard and the cars in the street started to move.

She stood up. "It's better this way."

"One more lie gets added to the bucket," he responded. "But, okay. I won't hold you back. We'll play it your way."

She strode off and crossed the street quickly, threading in between cars, trying mightily to keep her composure until she was out of his sight. She was starting to feel sick, and as soon as she reached an alley, she bent over and vomited.

CHAPTER 32

Mickey bristled with energy as he hopped out of his Jeep to meet with Kirk at the embassy. He'd just returned from early morning target practice in the desert, a routine he'd adhered to religiously since Dorothy's death ten days earlier. Blasting away with the Walther PPK pistol the ambassador had given him was cathartic; it made him feel as if he were doing something in response to her murder. Unfortunately, there had been little progress in finding her killer. The best the local police had dug up was that on the day of the murder a smart-looking European man had come to the embassy to drop off a purse that Dorothy had supposedly left behind at Groppi's, but when Dorothy saw it later, she'd said the purse wasn't hers. Other than that, the police had come up empty, but that was to be expected since Kirk insisted on keeping the most important clue secret: the disappearance of Blumenthal's picture.

This did not prevent Mickey from doing some digging on his own, and he discovered that a smartly dressed Egyptian man in his late twenties, wearing a suit and tarbush, had visited the Fuad University library right after Dorothy, asking for the very same journal. The man had flown into a tirade when he'd discovered that the page with Blumenthal's picture was missing and had pressed the librarian for information. The librarian indicated that a woman who worked for the American ambassador must have been the culprit.

Were the man who'd come to the embassy and the one from the library connected? They were probably working for the German spy who was certainly on top of his game. He'd known exactly which scientific journal contained Blumenthal's picture. Mickey found it too much of a coincidence that Dorothy and the mystery man from the library had been seeking the same journal at the same time, information that had been radioed from Donovan. The spy either had an informant at the embassy or had been listening in on the airwaves and had cracked the American code.

"Coincidences are the stuff of everyday life! There is no spy working out of our embassy!" Kirk cried out, banging his fist on his desk.

Mickey was disappointed that the ambassador so adamantly rejected his theory. They'd spoken on the phone, but this was the first time he had seen Kirk in person since Dorothy's death, and he was uncharacteristically irritable and uncooperative.

"Who decodes the embassy's messages, sir?" Mickey asked calmly.

"A fellow by the name of John Wayman. I'd stake my life on his loyalty," Kirk insisted.

"Then someone who has broken our radio code is listening," Mickey said as he leaned back in his chair across from Kirk's desk and crossed his arms.

"You understand the implications of what you're saying?" Kirk asked.

Mickey nodded—the ambassador had been sending daily reports about the war to Washington. "We can run a test. The stakes are too high not to."

His brow furrowed, Kirk thought for a while. "Very well. I'll transmit some false information and see what happens." He pushed his chair back and got up. His face was contorted. "Good God, I hope you're wrong, Connolly! It would be an unmitigated disaster, and the Brits will never trust us again."

"But at least we'll know it and prevent further damage," Mickey said. "Now, on another front, did you ask your COI agent in Tel Aviv to poke around the Sieff Institute to see who's responsible for bringing Blumenthal there?"

Kirk slowly shook his head. "Let it be, Connolly. I'm sure Donovan has his own ideas about how to go about pursuing this. He'll be in Cairo by the end of next week."

"It's just that I got a request from General Catroux to interview a powerful lawyer who handles anti-Semitic cases this afternoon. I'm sure the general is more concerned about filing a grievance against the Vichy Embassy here than about fighting anti-Semitism, but I agreed to do it. Maybe I'll learn something. You never know."

Kirk slumped back into his chair, looking drained. "I'm glad to see you still have it in you to fight, Connolly. I've been unable to function since we lost Dorothy. Every time I pass by her office, I . . ." He shook his head.

"I know. I was dreading coming here myself," Mickey said. In fact, he found the atmosphere of the entire embassy heavy with the weight of her death.

"Here, I almost forgot to give you this." He handed Mickey a large, shiny photograph along with its brown envelope.

Mickey felt a sharp pang in his stomach. It was a photo of himself and Maya with their arms linked. It had been taken by the photographer on the king's yacht.

"Who is the belle on your arm?" Kirk asked. "Dorothy suspected you might be falling for someone."

"I wonder what made her say that," Mickey said, slipping the photo back inside the envelope.

"She just knew," Kirk said.

"Let me know what you decide to do about transmitting false intelligence," Mickey said, avoiding the subject of Maya. He got up to leave.

"Be careful Mickey," Kirk said.

Mickey opened his jacket and revealed the gun tucked in his belt.

Sitting comfortably in one of the luxurious quilted chairs in the Moorish Hall at the Shepheard's, Mickey looked longingly at the photo of him with Maya. He'd been drinking himself to sleep every night to forget about her, but it wasn't working very well, because the girl was always on his mind when he woke up, despite the hangover. He suddenly turned over the picture and slammed it on the table. He was angry with her for not giving things a chance. He knew how she felt about him. He'd felt it on the boat, and he'd seen it again in her eyes, even at the very moment she'd denied it. Whatever was going on in her life, together they could work things out.

He thought it was funny to be getting her picture now; he had decided just this morning to try to reach her. There was always a backlog for exit visas, and there was a chance she might still be here. He was not going to give up so easily. He slipped the photo back in its envelope and pulled out the card he'd just bought. He began to write.

> Dear Maya,
>
> I'm sorry I had to withhold some things from you, but I promise that at some point I will explain it all. I know this is a very stressful time for you and your family, and embarking on an affair of the heart right now might be frightening for you, but please don't deny the truth of what happened between us. Do you want to be haunted

for the rest of your life wondering about what we lost? I don't, and I'm not going to give up on us. Please call me or write to me. We can, and we must, figure this out.

Mickey

He planned to give the note together with the perfume he'd bought to her uncle in the accounting department on the second floor of the hotel. He glanced around the lobby, wondering if he might have been followed here. He found the prospect of being tailed nerve-wracking. He ordered a beer and nonchalantly got up, leaving his newspaper on the table. "I'm just going to the john," he said to the customer next to him, "if you don't mind keeping my seat."

He headed to the back of the room and into the hallway where the bathrooms were located, then made a sharp right to a staircase that led to the mezzanine. He waited in a corridor for a moment to make sure that no one was following and from there took the elevator to the second floor.

Upon entering the double doors of the accounting department, Mickey found himself face-to-face with Joseph Levi, who was just leaving, which made for an awkward moment, especially since the accountant did not seem happy to see him. They stood in the hallway.

Mickey pulled out the letter and the gift-wrapped perfume. "Would you be kind enough to give—"

"My niece is no longer in Cairo. She has left the country," Mr. Levi said, jiggling the coins in his pocket.

"I . . . see," Mickey fumbled, feeling somewhat intimidated by the man although he towered over him by at least a foot. "If I could have her new address, I'd like to send this to her."

"I will forward it to her myself," the man said. He took the letter and the package and inserted them in his attaché case. "If you don't mind, I'm expected for lunch." He tipped his hat and walked away, leaving Mickey feeling like a fool.

Sitting on a leather banquette in the waiting room outside Léon Guibli's office, Mickey waited for his interview with the lawyer. General Catroux wanted to file an action against the local Banque de France branch for shooting at Free French protesters, and he wanted Mickey to write about it. The protesters had come to demonstrate in support of the Jewish community against the unwarranted dismissal of one of the bank's long-standing Jewish employees. Three of Catroux's men had been seriously wounded, but the pro-Vichy Embassy here had taken no action against the bank. To Mickey it was just another spat between the French.

He leaned forward, his hat in his hand. He was bitterly disappointed at having learned that Maya had left Cairo and doubted that Joseph Levi would ever forward his letter and package to her. He checked his watch. He'd been there for forty-five minutes. Maybe Guibli was a bigwig, but that was no excuse for keeping people waiting like this. He stood up and knocked on the office door of the secretary, who curtly explained that her boss was still on the same important call.

Annoyed, Mickey paced the room and stopped in front of the lawyer's expansive bookshelf. In addition to law books and reviews, it housed a sizeable collection of American authors, including Hemingway's recent book about the Spanish Civil War, *For Whom the Bell Tolls*. A book with a bright yellow cover caught his eye. It was the same book he'd seen at Hans Nissel's house, documenting the famous bridges of the world. He picked it up and opened the cover. Inside he found an inscription, *To Léon, with much gratitude. Hans Nissel, Cairo, August 1941*. Small world!

"Maître Guibli is free to see you now," the secretary, a slight woman with rosy cheeks, informed him.

Mickey placed the book back on the shelf and followed her into Guibli's office.

"I've learned to avoid the press since I've never been quoted accurately, but General Catroux is a friend and he insisted I meet with you." Guibli extended his hand. He was a lanky man in his late forties with an intense blue-eyed gaze. Though he wore neither tie nor jacket and worked with his shirtsleeves rolled up, his presence was commanding.

Mickey shook his hand firmly. "I'll do my best to be the first to quote you faithfully," he said. The office, like the reception room, was lined with mahogany paneling and had rich wooden floors. A huge banner bearing a quote from Goethe dominated the wall behind his desk: "Anti-Semitism is a shame. It is condemned by all civilized nations."

After a brief discussion about the impending transportation strike, which the lawyer was negotiating on behalf of the government, the focus returned to the purpose of the interview. Guibli explained his understanding of the circumstances surrounding the French bank's firing of the Jewish employee and described his own efforts to call for a boycott of the bank, which, ironically, was located on the ground floor of that very building. He had received death threats because of his involvement in the matter.

"But that never deters me," the lawyer asserted. "I will speak up whenever I find anti-Semitism. And as you can see, there are no bodyguards in my office."

With such a commitment against anti-Semitism, Mickey wondered why Guibli had not belonged to LICA and put the question to him.

"I very much sympathize with LICA's mission, just like I sympathized with the concerns of our Zionist groups when they were operating here, but despite the best intentions, most organizations end up compromising their ideals and becoming corrupt," Guibli declared. "The only organization I belong to is the Wafd. This is a legitimate political party one can vote for, and it stands for an independent Egypt."

Mickey was surprised that the lawyer had mentioned the taboo subject of Zionism, and he jumped at the opportunity to question him about it.

"As a Jew living in the Middle East, you must have an opinion about Zionism," he probed. "Do you believe that Zionist activities present a danger to Jews in the Arab world?"

Guibli didn't seem to mind the question, but he didn't answer it directly. He commented instead on the sorry state of the movement, using it to support his point about ideals becoming compromised. "There are so many factions," he lamented. "The Revisionists, the Bundists, the Socialists, the radical Zionists . . . Oh mon Dieu, so many! They have been so divided, my friend, arguing endlessly about what form the Jewish state should take, that they failed to mobilize European Jews quickly enough, and now . . . " he shook his head and continued, his face pained. "A colleague of mine in France is hearing about mass deportations of Jews out of Germany into concentration camps. They are said to have dumped fifty thousand of them into internment camps in the south of France. Who knows where the rest were sent? And where are the Zionists, I ask you?"

Mickey listened carefully. Although Guibli criticized the Zionists for being ineffective and disorganized, he didn't condemn their dream of a Jewish state. "Do you believe that Eretz Israel is no fairy tale?" Mickey asked, eliciting a smile from Guibli, who recognized the quote from Theodor Herzl, the founder of the Zionist movement.

"It is not reasonable to expect that a Jewish state could be founded under the current restrictions imposed by the British," he said, "but this is a long conversation for which I'm afraid I don't have time right now."

"One last question," Mickey asked, knowing he was stretching his welcome. "Putting aside the temporary freeze, who normally decides who gets a visa to Palestine and on what basis?"

"Under the latest White Papers, the British authorities will leave that decision to the Jewish Agency and the General Federation of Jewish Labor. After the freeze is lifted, who gets in will depend on which Zionist faction yells the loudest. Sometimes preference is given to those who can bring capital, and sometimes it goes to those who can milk cows, shovel dung, and do strenuous labor. It's all about building a country."

Erik Blumenthal had something all the Zionist factions would want, Mickey thought—unique expertise in a new frontier of science.

"If you're interested in the matter, I'd be happy to refer you to some colleagues of mine who are much more knowledgeable about this than I am," the lawyer offered.

"That would be very helpful," Mickey said.

"Now, if you will . . . " Guibli had pushed his chair back, indicating the meeting was over, when a knock on the door interrupted them and the secretary tiptoed in, handing the lawyer a note.

"Outrageous!" Guibli exclaimed upon reading it, his face flushed with anger. "Sir Miles Lampson is trying to suspend unilaterally the Egyptian Parliament! This is what you should be writing about, my friend," he ranted. "British imperialism!"

CHAPTER 33

Located on a limestone spur, with massive walls and protruding towers, the fortress of the Citadel was one of the world's great monuments to medieval warfare. It was only fitting that this was where Kesner would plot with Sadat against the English.

Kesner arrived early at the appointed place inside the Citadel and looked around as he adjusted the Polish uniform cap on his head. A soft breeze brushed his face and he took a seat on a ledge overlooking the city while he waited for Sadat. Situated at a high altitude, the Citadel was said to have the freshest air in Cairo. Legend had it that Salah al-Din, the warlord who built it, chose the site after hanging pieces of meat all over the city. While everywhere else the meat spoiled after a day or two, in the Citadel area it remained fresh for almost a week.

Peering down the thirty-foot walls, Kesner surveyed the chaos that was Cairo. Why could it not be more orderly and clean? He cringed. With Churchill having panicked and sacked all of his top military men, Rommel might get here in a few weeks. The PM was making a big mistake by making both the army and the RAF of the Eighth Division report directly to his new commander in chief for the Middle East, Admiral Sir Cunningham. The eyes of the world were now on El Alamein, and what a splash Rommel would make when he took the British stronghold and marched toward Cairo. Kesner hoped dearly to get his hands on Blumenthal before then. Following the American spy had yielded nothing so far. Either he suspected he was being tailed or Abdoul's men were incompetent. Kesner needed to search the American's apartment, but he had to find a way to get past that impossible bawab.

A bell sounded inside the barracks, and Kesner spotted Sadat rounding the corner, clutching a large envelope. He stood up and stretched out his hand to greet the lieutenant. "Good morning, Herr Sadat."

Sadat shook hands briefly and took a quick look around before opening the manila envelope. Getting right down to business, he withdrew a file and handed it to Kesner.

"These are the plans of the Kasr el-Nil barracks next to the Museum of Antiquities and some photos I took from the bridge," Sadat said, his voice calm and firm. "The British have been unloading crates from the river, and if you look closely you can see the markings. I've enclosed a guide telling you which markings relate to what: tanks, shells, aircraft ammunition, food, and so on. They've been stocking up."

"How long have they been unloading?"

"A week."

Kesner flipped through the file. Sadat had done an impressive job organizing the material. He lingered for a moment on another photograph.

"That one was taken inside the barracks," Sadat explained. "It's quite small compared to the military garrison here at the Citadel. I've drawn up a rough list of the regiments at Kasr el-Nil, but it may be incomplete."

"You've done a magnificent job, Herr Sadat. Cigarette?" Kesner offered, pulling his cigarette box from his pocket.

Sadat shook his head and cast a nervous eye over his shoulder. "Our men are ready to move into action at a moment's notice. We will do whatever we can to support Rommel's advance and disrupt

Allied resistance. We are preparing transport and storing away weapons and explosives in private houses. We're still working out our plans for capturing strategic locations, but we know the radio tower will be our first target."

Kesner studied Sadat for a moment. Passion burned in the young man's eyes, yet he never lost his professional demeanor.

"You know that your life is at stake should you be caught?" Kesner finally asked.

"My men know the stakes. If we win, we will be statesmen. If we lose, we will be hanged as criminals. Allah will decide. All I know for certain is that there is more explosive power in our ideas and beliefs, Herr Kesner, than in all of your bombs."

"I'm glad you are on our side," Kesner said.

"You can count on our full cooperation," Sadat continued, "but we will need something in return."

Kesner cocked his head. Could this idealist be looking for a bribe?

Sadat pulled another document from the envelope. "This is a declaration of Egyptian independence. We want the führer to sign it. Hitler, and only Hitler, will do."

"Don't you trust us, Herr Sadat?"

"We need a guarantee of independence in exchange for our help," Sadat declared, his face impassive. "The Egyptian people have suffered too often from British half-truths and unfulfilled promises. We won't take the risk of that happening again."

"But how in the world will I get the document to Hitler?"

"I'm sure you will find a way," Sadat replied, thrusting the paper into his hands. "I think two weeks will give you enough time to get it to Berlin and back."

Kesner almost threw the letter back in Sadat's face. Who was this cocky, dark-skinned little weasel to make demands of the führer? But he kept his cool. "Come, come now. Let's be reasonable.

Germany is a dangerous journey away. What about Rommel? It would surely be easier—"

"Hitler," Sadat replied without blinking. "If you want our help, it must be his signature."

Kesner swallowed hard and slipped the document inside his green jacket. Payback will come later. "I'll see to it immediately," he said with a tight smile and took Sadat's arm, leading him away. "But as I am going to extraordinary lengths for you, I hope you are willing to reconsider our request that you help arm the Brotherhood."

"Hassan al-Banna is an autocrat who wants an Islamic state. There is a fundamental incompatibility between us. Arming him would be sowing dragon's teeth."

Kesner stopped walking and faced Sadat. "You are mistaken, my friend, and you are being pigheaded. You must put your differences aside for the sake of Egypt and become allies in fighting the common enemy."

"Why should I ally myself with a man who uses violence against his own people?" Sadat spat, his face red as he lost his composure for the first time. "We had reliable witnesses at the rally for Nahas Pasha. They saw with their own eyes men from the Brotherhood deliberately start the rioting, not the English. This strategy will only result in greater repression against all Egyptians."

"Please, I understand your distress, but I beg of you. Right now nothing matters more than the liberation of Egypt from the British."

Sadat shifted his gaze, his eyes revealing inner turmoil. For a moment, Kesner thought he was reconsidering. "Get our declaration signed first, and then we'll talk. Until then, I will not consider any alliances. Good day, Herr Kesner," Sadat said over his shoulder as he strode away.

The insolence of this man! The audacity! Kesner wanted to wring his neck but forced himself to take a deep breath. Very well. He would have to humor Sadat now, but he would not forget this affront. Although he was beginning to dislike dealing with Samina, he would entrust the document to her. She was well acquainted with the Swiss undersecretary who was leaving for Berlin this weekend. For the money that he was paying her, she had better not give him any trouble.

CHAPTER 34

Maya woke up with a start, sweating and whimpering, her ears ringing from the sound of airplanes droning overhead and the high-pitched whistling of falling bombs. She'd been dreaming of the time she'd come home one summer to find her mother crying in the dark because the neighbors did not want her "Jew car" in the street anymore, but in her dream, her mother was hit by a falling bomb and shredded into a million pieces just as she'd reached her. Maya sat up, disoriented until she heard Lili snoring softly next to her, and slowly slipped back between the sheets, her heart still racing.

After two consecutive nights of air-raid alarms in Heliopolis, it was no wonder that her nightmares about Poitier had returned. But why was she now dreaming about her mother's agony over the escalation of anti-Semitism? Could it have been because of the Jewish newspaper Joe had brought home? The headline screamed *30,000 Jews Killed in Kiev*, and on the front page there was a photograph of German soldiers pointing their rifles at the heads of a Jewish family kneeling before an open pit. In his eyewitness account, the reporter had described how, before the execution, the grandmother was tickling a cooing baby in her arms, and the father was stroking the head of his ten-year-old son while the mother looked on with tears in her eyes. He'd written about how the other family members had kissed each other and said their farewells as an SS man stood near the pit with a riding crop in his hand. There was no weeping or screaming, no complaints, no pleas for mercy. Rifle shots were fired in quick succession and the bodies fell into the hole like dominos. A few weeks earlier, similar executions had occurred in Kovno, Lithuania, with no opposition from the locals.

They are killing the Jews, Maya agonized as tears rolled down the sides of her face and dripped onto her neck. She didn't wipe them away. She needed to let them flow. She was crying for the Jews, for Vati and Erik, and for everything that was wrong with the world and with her life. She cried for Mickey and their aborted romance. They hadn't even had a month to savor each other. She cried because she knew he was in love with her, and he was right to say she would forever wonder what they had lost. Yes, it was love that had burst forth that night on the boat. She did not know how else to describe it.

She had called the press office at the American Embassy, which confirmed that Mickey was affiliated with the *Detroit Free Press*. That much was true, but she wondered what kind of secret he was involved with and hoped that he was safe. The Levis had assured the family that their new passports were on their way. It couldn't be soon enough for her, because she couldn't endure much longer being in the same city as Mickey without seeing him.

"Lili," Maya whispered. "Are you awake?"

She didn't answer.

Poor Lili, she had fallen off her bicycle two weeks ago. She'd suffered a broken foot, rib, and wrist, and had been stuck at home ever since. Even that couldn't dampen her spirits. She was still the same effervescent girl she'd always been and actually seemed to enjoy being read to, manicured, spoon fed, dressed, and bathed by Maya, who became her primary caretaker, as well as her go-between with Fernando, passing on the love letters they secretly exchanged.

"Lili!" Maya called again, louder this time.

"Leave me alone," Lili grumbled and turned over.

Maya sat up. She would get a glass of milk to help her get back to sleep. Unfortunately, she couldn't turn on the light because blackouts had been imposed on Heliopolis due to its proximity to the airport. She fumbled around the nightstand looking for the lighter she'd put there, almost knocking over the pretty hand-painted glass vial of lotus flower essence that Mickey had entrusted to Joe as a gift for her. Ay, ay! There was no escape from this man. How did he guess that she loved this scent? She cautiously opened the bottle and inhaled the sweet fragrance of the dark yellow oil before dabbing a few drops on her neck. What was she doing wearing his perfume? Did she want to plunge further into melancholy? Disgusted with herself, she put the bottle down and fumbled again for the lighter.

She found it and tried not to step on the army uniforms scattered all over the floor. They'd just received a new batch, and with Lili unable to sew now, they were her responsibility. She tiptoed into the corridor, where an oil lamp had been placed, and saw that the door to Erik and Vati's room was open. That was odd. They both liked their privacy. She peered in and flicked on her lighter. Erik was in bed, but her father's bed was empty.

Worried, she searched the apartment, room after room, even the balconies. "Vati? Vati?" she whispered anxiously. Could he have gone to the roof? Sometimes Sayeda slept there on hot nights. She ascended to the rooftop, but there was no sign of him and she went back downstairs.

"Erik, Erik." Maya shook her brother awake. "Vati is gone," she cried out. "Gone!"

"The Lord is my shepherd; I shall not want. He maketh me to lie down in green pastures; he leadeth me beside still waters. He restoreth my soul," Erik read aloud from Vati's bible from the backseat as they drove though the deserted streets of Heliopolis in Joe's car, searching for him in the dark. Joe's headlights weren't much help because they had been painted blue due to the blackout.

"He was reciting this psalm over and over last night before he went to sleep," Erik said.

"Are you looking for some hidden message?" Maya snapped. If Erik and Vati had been on better terms maybe this wouldn't have happened. "Where can he be?" she agonized as she tried to peer into the darkness.

"Vati! Vati!" she called out of the rolled-down window.

"Why would he have taken his violin?" Joe asked.

"I don't know." Maya bit her lip.

"He's been sleeping with it," Erik admitted.

"And you're telling me that now?" Maya said.

"I told you I was concerned."

"He left his watch in his shoe the other day, and Sayeda found his shoe in the shower," Joe said.

Maya sighed, upset she hadn't been told these things and worried that she had been too involved in her own problems to notice her father's unusual behavior. "He's losing his mind," she concluded, crestfallen.

"Allegra couldn't understand what he was talking about this morning," Joe added, scraping a curb he had not seen in the darkness.

"Do you think we should go to the police?" Maya implored.

"Let's think about this rationally first," Erik said.

"I am!" Maya snapped back again, biting her index finger.

"The bawab said he heard some noise around midnight," Erik said. "How far could he get in two hours? He must still be here in Heliopolis. He will be safe."

"Unless he walked into the desert," Joe corrected.

"Oh, God," Maya lamented, imagining the worst. "If he's lying unconscious and there's a wind, he'll be buried alive."

"This is not what I call rational thinking," Erik remarked. "There is no wind."

"Now, now," Joe said, brushing the curb again.

"Shh," Maya admonished, at the edge of her seat. "I think I heard something. Listen. Stop the car, please."

Joe turned off the ignition and they sat silently. They heard nothing but the intermittent chirping of crickets.

"What are we going to do?" Maya cried. She closed her eyes and made a promise to God that if they found Vati, she would never again complain about him or her brother.

"Wait," Erik commanded, just as Joe was about to start the car again. They could hear the faint strains of a violin in the distance. "It's Chaconne in D minor!"

"Vati!" Maya exclaimed, jumping from the car and running toward the music.

She found her father standing on a bench in a lovely park of palm groves, next to the Americana Theater, with the moon and the stars as his audience. He didn't stop playing when he saw her. In fact, he didn't even acknowledge her. She stood in front of him, tears running down her cheeks, waiting for him to finish. Waves of emotion swelled inside her.

"Bravo," she cheered when he stopped, drying her tears with the sleeves of her shirt. "That was beautiful."

"Have you seen my wife, Hanna?" Vati asked, still standing.

"Come down, Vati," Maya offered her hand.

"Perhaps Berta will find her. You know how much she and Hanna like one another. They love to sing together."

Berta was Vati's younger sister. She'd died long ago. "Maybe they are together now," Maya said, pulling on her father's leg and realizing he was wearing two pairs of trousers. "Come now."

"You're so sweet," Vati said, but he still wouldn't climb down from the bench. "I bet your parents are proud of you, miss."

"They are," Maya said, choking back her tears. "I'm your daughter."

"That's nice."

"*Vater*!" Limping, Erik arrived along with Joe. "We've looked everywhere for you. Why did you do this?"

Maya took her brother's hand, filled with tender feelings toward him, and gestured to her father to come down. "He's your child, too," she said. "His name is—"

"Erik, would you help me get down, please," Vati implored, reaching out to him.

"Let's go home," Joe said, giving his hand to Vati.

"Erik!" Maya scolded. "Help your father."

Erik complied and raised both arms to help Vati down.

"You're a good son," Vati said as he climbed down and rested on the bench, exhausted from the effort.

CHAPTER 35

By the time Mickey arrived at the embassy, Kirk and Donovan were waiting for him on the roof of the building, watching the sun as it rose over the Nile.

"You've done a tremendous job," Donovan said as he embraced Mickey like a long-lost friend. "I am terribly sorry about the death of Miss Calley." He looked tired and seemed to have gained some weight. The button on his suit jacket was ready to pop.

Kirk, on the other hand, had shed a few pounds, which made his cheekbones more prominent. He looked solemn. Mickey guessed that he had news and it was not good.

"I transmitted a false message about an ammunition depot at a location outside of Alexandria. It was bombed," Kirk said, pursing his lips.

"You were right, my friend," Donovan said, tapping him on the shoulder. "The Nazis have deciphered our code." He sat on a bench.

"The Brits took it rather stoically when I broke the news to them. Lampson did not even bat an eye, but these people are trained to show impossible sangfroid in the face of the worst circumstances." Kirk settled on a black iron chair opposite the bench.

Mickey shook his head as he took a seat next to Donovan.

"Frankly, even though MI5 is closer to catching the German spy . . ." Donovan started to say.

"They've identified a doctor's office he's been using for meetings," Kirk clarified. "Two Italian spies blew his cover. He is a chameleon, a master of disguise, who speaks fluent Arabic. He sometimes goes by the name of Nader Barudi."

"That explains a lot," Mickey said, realizing that the man at the library and the man who'd returned Dorothy's purse must have been the same man.

"But the fact that the Nazis broke our code is a blessing in disguise," Donovan said. "It now gives MI5 a real shot at getting him. They've set up a trap for him tomorrow."

"They're sure not wasting any time," Mickey said.

"They made it clear they don't want any of us involved," Kirk added. "They've even dictated the wording of the radio transmission I've had to send to ensnare him, as if I were a moron, claiming that they had more experience in these matters."

"Don't take it personally, Alexander," Donovan said. "You are not to blame here."

Kirk shrugged and handed Mickey a piece of paper. "The communiqué I sent. MI5 felt that only bare-bones information should be fed, just enough for the spy to make sense of it, or he'd see through the ploy."

> Finally located the scientist and keeping him secure at the embassy until Friday. Please inform our agents in Lisbon to meet his flight departing 7:05 and arriving at 9:05 AM and make arrangements for immediate transport to New York.

Mickey read the note and then turned, incredulous, to Kirk. "You told the Brits about Blumenthal?" he asked.

"Had to," Donovan answered. "MI5 will be coordinating with

us and the State Department in investigating the possible involvement of major Zionist figures in Palestine, but they insist that we leave everything else about the Blumenthal case to them."

"Fine," Mickey said.

"You'll never guess where Wild Bill has just come from," Kirk said, rubbing his hands, his eyes lighting up, eager to share the news, but he gestured to Donovan, inviting him to speak.

"I was in the middle of the North Atlantic, in Placentia Bay, off Newfoundland, with President Roosevelt," Donovan responded.

"You must have heard rumors about the president's disappearance over the last ten days?" Kirk added.

"The *New York Times* wrote that his polio was acting up and he'd flown to his vacation cottage near the hot springs of Pine Mountain."

"Not true," Donovan said. "The president was meeting with Winston Churchill on board the battleship HMS *Prince of Wales*. With the dangers posed by U-boats, this had to be done in complete secrecy."

Kirk checked his watch. "In a few hours the news will be reported to the world."

"They shook hands over a joint vision of the world after the war," Donovan resumed. "I'll be flying back to London to work on the language. We expect most governments to go along with it. Basically the charter will call for an end to colonialism as we know it. It will affirm a nation's right to self-determination. All very important precepts to Roosevelt, as you know."

"Churchill agreed to it?" Mickey asked, surprised.

"He didn't have a choice. He knows that without America the empire won't stand," Donovan said. "I was there when the prime minister conceded that the mantle of leadership was slipping from Britain's shoulders to America's. It almost moved me to tears. America is dictating the terms of peace. We are the new leaders of the world."

Mickey mulled over what was being said. "Does this mean we're entering the war?" he ventured, barely breathing. "Forming a military alliance with the Brits?"

"Not quite, but you can bet your bottom dollar that we will be supporting their efforts in a very big way. Roosevelt has promised to send them 150 of our newest Grant tanks equipped with 75 mm guns immediately."

Mickey shook his head, overwhelmed by what he was hearing.

Donovan leaned back to get a better view of Mickey and exchanged quick looks with Kirk. "Do you ever wonder what happened to the article you tried to smuggle out of the country?"

"Well, yes, sure."

"I think you should know that it was not written in vain," Kirk said.

"Miss Calley sent it via diplomatic pouch to someone she knew—a member of Roosevelt's cabinet. The president had your article in his dossier when he met with Churchill," Donovan said.

His words hung in the air while Mickey tried to grasp the enormity of what Donovan had told him. A wave of emotion welled up inside him. Embarrassed, he leaned forward, his hand blocking his face as he fought mightily to hold back his tears.

"She thought you were right on the money," Donovan said, putting a fatherly arm around him.

"She was very fond of you," Kirk added. "Though she did think that your sense of color coordination was beyond redemption."

Mickey shook his head and laughed. "Hey! I thought I was doing great!" He stood up and showed off his suit. "Even got the handkerchief right."

"You look very debonair to me," Donovan approved. "Cairo suits you well."

"It's been quite a journey since our first meeting on this very roof, sir," Mickey said as he sat back down.

"We really appreciate all you've done, but at this point you're officially relieved of your duties. We don't want you to be in danger any longer. I've talked about you to a friend of mine, the editor-in-chief of the *Washington Post*, and he's very interested in meeting you."

Mickey slowly nodded. Somehow he felt deflated. The adventure, the sense of urgency and responsibility, were now over for him, but funnily enough, he did not feel relieved. "I just hope they catch the spy. At least Dorothy will not have died for nothing."

With Maya gone and MI5 taking over the Blumenthal case, there wasn't any point in staying in Cairo, Mickey thought as he drove to the Gezira Sporting Club to have lunch with Hugh. He had asked his friend to find out through his black market sources how one would go about obtaining papers for Palestine, knowing everything could be gotten for a price in Cairo. But now it was moot—the Brits were in charge. Maybe they had more experience in intelligence matters, but Mickey had every intention of secretly watching tomorrow's ambush. He'd been too deeply involved to miss it, and he couldn't return to the States without getting a shot at blowing the spy's head off if things went that way.

He checked his rearview mirror to see if he was being followed and made a series of sharp turns just in case. With the change in military command, the continuous air-raid threats to Heliopolis, the mass exodus of refugees out of Alexandria and Cairo, and no good news coming out of El Alamein, people's nerves were frayed. It seemed that pedestrians walked faster and drivers never stopped honking and cutting one another off in their cars. Even donkeys, laden with the belongings of fellahin fleeing for calmer surroundings, seemed to be jittery. The flow of refugees had put a heavy burden on buses, and traffic was abominable. Mickey turned on the radio to get his mind off the chaos of the city and smiled when President Roosevelt's voice came over the airwaves to announce his pact with Churchill.

The Gezira Sporting Club, the quintessential symbol of British imperialism, was the most exclusive sports club in Cairo, and it required its members to sign in any guests who would be joining them at the Lido, the club's dining room. Mickey was therefore surprised that a golf caddy was waiting for him at the entrance instead of Hugh. Wearing a blue galabeya, a white hat, and a red belt, the young, slender Egyptian explained in perfect English that Hugh had gotten drafted into a polo match and asked that Mickey be brought up to the field. They traversed the club, which with its many gardens, polo fields, golf course, racetrack, cricket pitches, croquet lawns, and tennis and squash courts, must have been among the most lavish sporting grounds anywhere in the world.

When they reached the polo field, a game was on, and they stood on the sidelines behind a white wooden fence surrounded by an enthusiastic crowd. "There's Mr. Charlesworth," the boy said, pointing to Hugh, the number three player on the red team.

Mickey proudly watched Hugh's horse roughly bump a member of the opposing team. "That's my guy!" But his attention quickly turned to another member of the red team, number seven, who came racing down the pitch in full gallop, the ground shaking under the thunderous hooves of his magnificent thoroughbred. In one swift move, he stole the ball from the blue team and started pushing it toward the goal.

"Cover him!" yelled a spectator next to them, tensely holding his binoculars.

Too late. The player had smashed the ball into the goal. The crowd in the stands went wild. The red team whooped in triumph, but not their victorious teammate, who trotted away alone.

"Who is number seven?" Mickey asked.

The caddie shrugged. He didn't know.

"It's Ali Rashad. Who else?" the man with binoculars barked.

"Ali! I should have known," the boy exclaimed and clapped his hands above his head. "He is the best player in the club. He has eyes in the back of his head."

"I thought only players from British regiments were allowed to play here," Mickey said.

"Except when their fathers own half the horses in the stables," the caddie responded. "Ali is a captain in the Egyptian cavalry. I have to get back, sir. The game is almost over."

Mickey reached into his pocket to tip the boy.

"That's quite all right, sir," the caddie stopped him. "Mr. Charlesworth takes very good care of me." He pulled a round red box from the pocket of his robe. It was British shoe polish, which was very difficult to find.

Mickey watched him go and leaned against the fence as the arbiter yelled the score: 9–8 Blue. When play resumed, number seven immediately charged, galloping with ferocious determination. In a whirlwind of energy, he beat every trick thrown at him by the Blues, scoring two more points and leading his team to victory. The crowd stood on its feet and cheered. Polo was a rich man's sport, so Mickey didn't know much about it, but he could tell a good player when he saw one, and Ali was superb. But he was also reserved, shaking hands formally with the other players when the grooms took his horse away. Hugh was the only one he embraced warmly. The two were clearly good friends.

Mickey whistled to catch Hugh's attention.

"Hey!" Hugh brightened when he spotted him, and with his arm around Ali's shoulder, he strolled toward Mickey.

"That was one hell of a game. Well done." Mickey patted Hugh's back in congratulations. "And you, sir, were terrific," he told Ali, who was removing his helmet. The dark-skinned Egyptian was tall and well proportioned, and like most cavalry officers he boasted a thick mustache. Mickey thought he cut a dashing figure.

"This is my Yankee friend, Mickey Connolly," Hugh said by way of introduction, wiping his sweaty, dust-caked forehead. "I've told you about Ali Rashad. We trained together at Sandhurst. He's the reason I'm in Egypt in the first place."

"Yes, of course. Hugh told me how wonderful you and your family have been to him." Mickey recalled Hugh's stories about Ali's father, one of the wealthiest cotton magnates in the country, who was such an Anglophile that he demanded that his children speak English at home and hung a picture of Queen Victoria in his study.

"Hugh has told me about you as well," Ali replied, shaking Mickey's hand firmly. "You're the journalist from America."

"I told him what a bore you were," Hugh interjected. "Always babbling about politics, censorship, and the unfairness of the world."

"Better a bore than a drunk!" Mickey joked.

"How about we all have lunch together?" Hugh suggested.

"I don't have much time," Ali apologized.

"Rubbish!" Hugh said. "We'll join you at the Lido after we shower. Get us a table with a good view of the girls at the pool." He winked at Mickey and grabbed Ali's elbow, steering him away.

The Lido terrace was flanked by two wings jutting out of the white and red clubhouse, the hub of the sporting facilities. Mickey was lucky to be seated at a prime table with a bird's-eye view of the swimsuit-clad women who lazily flicked through magazines while lounging on deckchairs below. Hugh would be happy. Nearby children frolicked while their governesses watched and gossiped. On the terrace, except for a few well-to-do Westernized Egyptian families, the clientele was mostly British, military as well as well-dressed expats. Alone at a table sat a Scottish officer wearing a kilt, with a bagpipe by his side. What on earth did the locals make of these men?

Mickey ordered lemonade and picked up the menu.

"Don't despair, I'm here!" Hugh sidled up next to him, a martini already in his hand. "You know, you don't look good—at all. Lost weight or what?"

Mickey shrugged it off. "Just not sleeping so well these days. Where's Ali?"

"Still in the changing room," Hugh replied as he grabbed the menu away from Mickey. "He's listening to some new announcement on the radio." He waved to a lovely girl in a strapless bathing suit, who blew back a kiss.

"Who's that?"

"Ali's sister. If it weren't for my friendship with Ali, I'd go full steam for her." Hugh elbowed Mickey conspiratorially. "Come to think of it, I could use a little hanky-panky, as you say in America. But business first. Regarding your inquiry, I didn't forget about you, mate, but they sent me to Suez for a week to clean up mines that had been dropped all over the canal. Anyhow, my Greek fence can get you anything you want: perfect invoices, checks, receipts, tax returns, you name it. He can get you papers for anywhere on earth—but not Palestine."

"Why not?"

"Apparently visas to Palestine are printed on special paper. Forgeries have to be made from valid, existing passports purchased from immigrants who have entered the country legally, and these have become impossible to come by. Why are you so interested?"

"It's important for my article."

"Hmmm . . . still working on that story." Hugh took a generous sip of his martini, but from his look he didn't seem too convinced.

The waiter arrived with his note pad, ready to take their order.

"Give us a minute," Hugh asked. "We're expecting one more." He turned to Mickey and said, "If he ever shows up."

"Why, what's wrong?"

"He's been brooding for weeks over his army's humiliation at having their weapons taken away from them at Mersa Matruh. He's ashamed of himself for having handed over his pistol. You have to understand, this lad lives and breathes his love of Egypt. It's not for prestige that he went into the military."

"He had no choice. The order came from General Neguib."

"I'm surprised that for a newspaper man you're that naïve," Ali said as he arrived and sat down. "The order came from London."

"I'm sorry about what happened," Mickey said. "I know it's a terrible insult."

Ali shook his head and put his white cloth napkin on his lap. "They treated us like dogs. After months of breaking our backs, cutting trenches into what turned out to be solid rock under two feet of sand, we're told to pack up and hand over our weapons within the hour. And now we've been reduced to filling sandbags in the desert. You should write about this!"

"Good Lord, Ali, you should be relieved to be away from the front. I don't know why you're in such a damn hurry to get your legs blown off," Hugh interjected.

"Don't tell me how I should feel," Ali lashed out. "This is my career, and every day I have to look my men in the face and pretend that it's all right to be pissed on."

"Don't be angry with me. I'm with you, mate," Hugh said, patting Ali on the back to assuage him. "You've always defended the English, and now they've betrayed you. But hey, don't turn your head," he whispered in the same breath, throwing sidelong glances at a nearby table. "I think that blonde bombshell is looking at you!"

"Bloody women! Is that all you think about?" Ali grumbled.

"Be patient," Mickey said. "When the war is over, Egypt will have its day. Sooner or later you will get your independence."

"But when?" Ali shot back. "Just like in America, it will take a revolution. Thousands of men will die."

"Maybe not," Mickey said.

Ali locked eyes with Mickey, evaluating him for an instant. "Have you heard about your president's Atlantic Charter with Churchill?" he asked.

"Sure did," Mickey responded.

"What do you think about it? Is it just words?" Ali asked.

"Just words?" Mickey said. "Remember, you're talking to a newspaper man."

Ali laughed. "I like your friend," he announced. "What should we order for lunch?" He reached for the menu as a young man in tennis attire appeared at the table. He looked familiar to Mickey.

"I'm Fernando Lagnado." He extended his hand to Mickey. "We met on the king's yacht. I'm a friend of Maya's cousin Lili."

Mickey's throat tightened at the mention of Maya's name. "Sure, I remember."

"Are you coming to the premiere of *Gone with the Wind* tomorrow night? Maya will be chaperoning us."

CHAPTER 36

Kesner radioed Tripoli.

> All plans have been made for the capture of Erik Blumenthal. Will hold him in safe house until further advised. Schwarze Hund.

He signed off feeling satisfied with himself. In spite of losing his convenient meeting place at Dr. Massoud's, he was doing very well. The Americans were about to deliver the scientist right into his hands.

As he splashed cold water on his face in preparation for his day, he heard the five o'clock call of the muezzin and checked his wristwatch. Right on time. He saluted himself in the mirror. The telephone rang upstairs, jolting him.

"Abdoul, my friend, calm down," Kesner sighed into the receiver.

"They arrested Samina last night." The poor man was beside himself. "They grabbed her backstage after her performance. They're going to make her talk. She knows I'm working with you. I'm finished."

"This is not good news, I agree, but get ahold of yourself. She can say anything she wants, but she doesn't have any evidence against you."

"I'm finished," Abdoul wailed again. "With the Italians arrested and Samina under interrogation, I am in grave danger."

"What do you plan to do? Disappear?" Kesner sneered. "You must stand your ground. The king will not allow—"

"I will not meet you at Café Riche later. It's too dangerous." The Egyptian hung up the phone before Kesner could respond, infuriating him.

He should never have given the fool his number, but at least Abdoul didn't know where he lived. He picked up an ashtray and threw it against the wall. "May Samina rot in hell!" He summoned up the teachings of Sun Tzu, reminding himself to keep a cool head. He would deal with Abdoul later. Today he had an important mission, perhaps the most important of his life.

Parked behind a huge ficus benjamina three houses down from the American Embassy, Kesner waited for the car carrying the Blumenthals to emerge from the garage and take them to the Heliopolis airport for their seven o'clock flight to Lisbon. Kesner had the ambush all figured out. Hassan al-Banna had generously made his best men available for the mission, and they were already in place, ready to pounce. The only complication was that there were two routes to the airport, and Kesner had no way of knowing which one the American car would take until it reached Sharia Kasr el-Aini, near the Semiramis Hotel. So he would have to follow the car up to that point and telephone his fellow conspirators, advising them of the route chosen. Men had been placed on both routes to cover either eventuality.

Sitting in the back of a taxi driven by Rafat, one of the sheik's most trusted lieutenants, whose fourteen-year-old son sat at his side, Kesner tapped his front teeth with his fingernails, his eyes locked on the garage, his stomach in a knot. He was wearing a brown galabeya, which he kept twisting.

"There it is!" Rafat's son suddenly warned.

An official black car with the American flag on its fender, its curtains drawn, drove out of the garage.

Kesner checked his watch: 6:10. "That must be him. Perfect. No escort, just as I suspected." His eyes were transfixed. "*Yalla*! Let's go," he ordered, feeling euphoric.

"With the help of Allah, we will be successful today," Rafat said softly as he made a U-turn and started to tail the American sedan.

With Friday morning prayers marking the beginning of the Egyptian weekend, most Arabs were still asleep and there was little traffic. They crossed Garden City and arrived downtown in no time. The city was just waking up as European café owners opened their doors and laid out tables on the sidewalks. They were now on Sharia Kasr el-Aini, and Kesner waited on pins and needles to see which turn the American car would make. It made a left turn just before reaching the Semiramis Hotel, and Kesner let out an excited cry.

"They're taking the Salah al-Din route!" Kesner said.

Rafat jerked the car to a halt. He took his boy's head between his hands and kissed it. "Dying in the way of Allah is our highest hope, my son."

The boy thrust the door open and shot from the car like a bullet, vanishing around the corner to alert the Brothers of the route the embassy car was taking.

The Salah al-Din route was by far the most desirable. The embassy car would be going through a large intersection in front of the Citadel with arms that reached out like an octopus, feeding many of the city's main arteries. That was where Kesner had planned to ambush the car after blocking it with the Brotherhood's vehicles that would converge on it from all directions. They would pull Blumenthal out and drag him to Kesner, who would be waiting in his taxi between two monumental mosques that stood side by side across from the Citadel. Blumenthal's father and sister would also be taken, but only if the task proved easy. Should anything go wrong, there were many escape routes into the city or out into the desert behind the Citadel.

A soldier of Allah, Rafat pushed down on the gas pedal, his eyes fixed, his ears closed to unwanted distractions, and took a shortcut through the City of the Dead, which he knew well. The roof of the taxi had been painted white so it would be easily recognized from above, and as they reached the back of the Citadel, Kesner and Rafat looked up and saw a man waving a small red flag at them.

"It's all good by the grace of God," Rafat said.

They had men posted on the roofs and minarets of the Citadel as well as the two mosques across from it, which made for easy signaling.

The street was empty except for two large camel trucks heading toward them, both of which turned into the back entrance of the Citadel before passing the taxi.

"The camel market is open on the Sabbath?" Kesner asked, finding it odd that the trucks would go inside the Citadel.

"Every day. The market starts very early in the morning," Rafat replied, then with his eyes on his rearview mirror, he calmly said, "Police behind us."

Kesner twisted around and saw the green and white Egyptian police car. "Let it pass," he suggested, barely breathing.

They drove around the Citadel and crossed the intersection, but as Rafat began to turn into the passageway between the two mosques, he had to brake suddenly to allow two farmers and their herd of sheep to pass.

"Where did that imbecile come from?" Kesner fumed.

Rafat didn't say a word, his eyes darting in all directions, then relaxing, he stretched his arm around the back of the passenger seat and waited patiently for the animals to pass. But after the sheep came another farmer with a pack of goats.

"Is this a joke?"

Rafat didn't budge.

Kesner took a deep breath. Patience.

Finally, the way was clear and Rafat drove into the alley between the two mosques. He turned the car around so that it faced the intersection, ready to pounce like a tiger once the ambush was under way.

Kesner's attention turned to the two camel lorries, which were exiting from the front entrance of the Citadel. Camels were brought to Cairo from the Sudan after a long trek through the desert, and Kesner found the lorries surprisingly clean. He also found it odd that the driver was not the usual black Nubian, but an Arab.

Something was not right.

He jumped out of the taxi and slammed the door over Rafat's protests. He scanned the premises. Nothing unusual. There was nothing unusual either in front of the mosques, just a handful of faithful scattered about. Very few. Too few. He walked to the entrance of one of the mosques, where two men collected the shoes of worshipers in exchange for a small *baksheesh*.

"*Samaa Allah leman hamad* (God listens to what one says)," Kesner greeted them.

"*Sobhan rabina el A' la* (God is high)," one of them responded, putting down the Qur'an he had been reading behind his pulpit.

"Why so few faithful?"

"Only the students of the *madrasa* next door are allowed in the morning. The rest not until the midday prayers."

Kesner glanced into the dark, quiet recessed entrance. Nothing unusual. "*Allah akbar* (God is great)," he bid good-bye and strode away.

He quickened his pace back to the taxi, his eyes darting right and left before resting on a street sweeper, whose broom barely touched the pavement as he stared at one of the mosque's arched windows. Following his gaze Kesner could see the silhouette of a man in a khaki uniform. A soldier? The Brotherhood men were civilians. The street sweeper was awfully young and robust for a job normally held by stooped, old men. Kesner tried to quiet his suspicions, attributing them to his general edginess, but as he approached the taxi, he saw that the street behind the mosque complex was now clogged with camels, several of them just sitting in the road. He squinted. Then he saw it—a man in a white galabeya plunging a syringe into the hindquarters of one of the standing beasts. The animal's leg buckled immediately and it collapsed to the ground.

This was a trap. The plan had to be called off.

His chest pounding, he continued toward the taxi, careful not to run and draw attention to himself. Anyone around him could be part of this trap. Then all hell broke loose as the embassy car reached the intersection and the Brotherhood's cars converged on it, only to find themselves surrounded by police vehicles, which appeared out of nowhere. Kesner let out a cry when he saw the doors of the American sedan burst open, yielding not the Blumenthals but half a dozen heavily armed commandos. It was total chaos as cars screeched and gunfire echoed everywhere. Allied soldiers, many disguised in galabeyas, rushed out of the surrounding buildings, brandishing their weapons and shouting war cries.

"*Yalla*! Come!" Rafat yelled.

Frantic, Kesner glanced back at the square. Allied soldiers were streaming out of the camel trucks and rushing toward the trapped Brotherhood cars. Behind him, camels, goats, and sheep were blocking the back streets. They were surrounded. He pulled up his galabeya and started to sprint for his life.

"There's another bloke. Get him!" a soldier yelled in a Kiwi accent, chasing after him and alerting a small contingent of fellow soldiers, who followed suit.

Racing toward one of the arched gateways, Kesner was near panic. Gunshots rang past him. He approached the gate, praying to God he would find it unguarded, when a man came out of a wooden shack behind the mosque, running toward him and cutting him off. Kesner swerved left, away from the gate.

"I'll get him," the man yelled as he raced behind Kesner.

Kesner climbed up a stairway as fast as he could and vaulted over a small wall onto a terrace. He stumbled over the planted shrubbery and flowerbed and ran toward a small mound of rubble. He couldn't tell what was on the other side. In a desperate dash, he ascended the debris and leaped over, sliding on the other side and creating a small avalanche as he fought to retain his balance. Reaching the bottom, he found himself in a small open patch enclosed by a wooden fence. Below him, he could see merchants setting up their food stalls for the morning market. How far was the drop to the street below? Six feet? Eight feet? Sweating and gasping for air, he raced toward the fence, the sound of his shoes on the gravel resounding in his head as a spray of bullets exploded near him. He reached the edge and grimaced when he saw that the fence was a good ten feet from the ground. He looked back. *Shit*. His pursuer was none other than Mickey Connolly, the American spy with a gun in his hand, twenty feet away, with a pack of soldiers close behind him. The decision was obvious: Better to break an ankle than be dead. He jumped, landing hard on his feet, scaring the pigeons away. He wobbled for a moment, then hurled himself down the street without looking back.

He heard a torrent of angry voices and curses echoing behind him, but clearly not aimed at him: "You idiot! He was heading right into our hands and you made us lose him!"

CHAPTER 37

Kesner sat in his communication room, his head slumped over his radio, waiting for his appointed airwaves rendezvous with the Abwehr agent in Tripoli. He felt nauseous, the bitter taste of defeat in his mouth, humiliated at having to admit that he'd failed at his mission. The Americans had tricked him. They obviously knew that the Germans had broken their code. He shut his eyes tight, swallowing hard to wash away the shame that stuck in his throat. The fantasy of his dream house on the Danube was crumbling. He felt alone and vulnerable. Many of his accomplices had been arrested, and even the pathetic Abdoul would not return his calls. For God's sake, he had almost been caught himself. He had underestimated the American. Oh, the pleasure he would get out of snapping his neck! His watch said 5:00 PM. It was time. He'd prepared the text in advance and started to tap:

> It is with abject mortification that I must report that the mission was a failure. I was fed misinformation by the Americans, who must have known that I was listening and that we had broken their code. I narrowly eluded capture, and our entire operation is now in jeopardy. I swear that I will strive to my last breath to complete my assignment. I already have some thoughts. I remain faithfully committed to the Reich, and . . .

Kesner suddenly stopped, realizing he'd been transmitting for too long a stretch, creating a risk by staying on the air for so long. He could not allow himself to get sloppy. Short bursts only. He sat back and waited a few minutes before resuming, but as he leaned forward again, he felt his boat rock slightly. He jerked upright. A passing vessel? All ears, he waited. Nothing. But then came the sound of muffled footsteps overhead, echoing off the water. It couldn't be his servant; he'd gone home already. His neighbor? But the man always whistled when he wanted to see him. He started up the ladder and felt the boat sway again as the sounds of footsteps got louder. There was more than one man up there.

"Open up," a voice ordered. "Police. We know you're in there."

Kesner bolted back down. He was trapped. It was impossible for the radio scanners to have picked up his transmissions and tracked him down so quickly . . . unless they had already been on the quay. His mind raced. *Stay calm,* he told himself, his legs shaking as he reached the bottom. He had prepared for this eventuality and started to count silently in an effort to keep his wits about him. *Eins, zwei, drei.*

The men above were shouting, pounding on the door.

Shoes first, Kesner reminded himself, trying his mightiest to control the trembling of his hands as he removed them. He had a full set of dry clothing in the watertight bag he kept along with his diving gear inside his escape chamber in the cramped communication room. He opened the chamber, which was the size of a phone booth, and pulled out the rubber suit. He put it on over his trousers and shirt and zipped it up to his neck. It was too tight. He removed his belt. He put on his fins. It all seemed unreal. Stay calm. *Eins, zwei, drei.* He heard a shot, then a loud kick—the door upstairs burst open. The police threatened to shoot on sight if he did not surrender.

Eins, zwei, drei. It had all been carefully worked out. The booby trap he'd made was in place. The stairway was wired with a fishing line connected to the gas burner in the kitchen, which was right above the communication room. All he had to do was pull the trip wire to activate the trap and then flip on the incendiary line. The gas burner would ignite when the police tripped the stairway wire and the blast would destroy the radio and create a fire that would sink the boat in minutes. He hoped the cash he'd put in the dry bag along with passports and other important papers would be adequate.

He heard another door smash open. *Eins, zwei, drei.* He put on the rebreather diving unit, the vest first, making sure its valves were tightly connected to the hoses in the mask. Then, after taking one last deep breath, he pulled on the mask and adjusted the straps around his head. There were more shouts upstairs as the boat rocked violently. He had to hurry. Within seconds they would be coming down the stairs. He stepped inside the chamber and closed the door. He activated the wire trip, then with one hand on the incendiary line switch, and the other on the hatch, he opened the hatch ever so slowly so that water would not come rushing in and pulled the switch. He grabbed the dry bag and crawled out.

Seconds later a massive explosion shook the boat, but Kesner was already safely on his way.

He could stay under water for thirty to forty minutes, but with all the attention on the quay being paid to the boat in flames, Kesner didn't need much time before resurfacing. He reemerged ten minutes later in a marshy area, hoping it was under the Zamalek Bridge. His calculations turned out to be fairly accurate, but when he removed his mask and looked up, he saw red lights blinking and police lorries parked on the bridge above. He quickly dove back under and swam downstream, where he reemerged on a secluded bank covered with reeds. He hastened to get rid of his diving gear, shoveling it all into his dry bag. He loaded the bag with rocks and threw the damn thing into the water, where it dropped to the bottom. He was now close to Dokki, and he walked across the English Bridge to Gezira Island, where he grabbed a taxi to Café Riche. He stored his clothing disguises there, and, since the loss of Dr. Massoud's office, he had been using the café as a message drop as well.

Ironically, Café Riche, a haven for Egyptian intellectuals, was located in the heart of the foreign-dominated downtown. Kesner felt like hugging the owner when he got there. A friend of Sadat's, he was a patron of Egyptian arts and a committed nationalist. He had made the bar in the basement available to the Revolutionary Committee as a meeting place, and though he would not allow Kesner to conduct his operations from the café, it was a perfect place for the spy to regroup.

Arriving in his shirtsleeves and sagging trousers, Kesner needed to wash up and change. He also needed a cup of coffee, some cigarettes, a telephone, and a pen and pad of paper. He had to formulate a new plan of action. If he could find Blumenthal, he could redeem himself in one stroke. If he couldn't deliver him to Rommel alive, he would kill him to prevent him from falling into the hands of the Americans and Brits.

"It's good to be among friends," Kesner said to the owner as the Egyptian ushered him down the stairs into the main room, which was thick with cigarette smoke.

In a corner under the filtered light of a brass lampshade, Kesner rolled up his sleeves and began to write:

Things to do:

Number one: A place to stay.

The Windsor Hotel would do for a night or two, but he needed to borrow a private, furnished apartment with a telephone and basic amenities in a discreet building. He would have to force Abdoul back in line to find him such a place.

Number two: Must have radio.

It was vital for him to stay in touch with Tripoli, and Sadat, being a signals officer, would be his best bet. But he knew he would first have to address Sadat's inquiries about whether Hitler had signed the letter promising Egyptian independence. He pulled out another piece of paper and began to write: *Happy to confirm that the document is safely in Germany and has been signed by Hitler. Expect it back shortly.* A lie of expedience. He would leave the note with the owner.

Number three: Men.

If he was to revive his mission, he would need help. The American spy needed to be followed. He had to put his personal feelings aside. As much as he would love to kill him, the spy could still lead him to Blumenthal. Here he would have to rely on Abdoul. He braced himself and called the fat idiot at his home.

"Hello? Hello? It's me!" Kesner shouted into the mouthpiece, sure he'd recognized Abdoul's voice before the line cut off abruptly.

Annoyed, he rang again, but this time a servant answered.

"Mr. Nukrashi is not here," the fellow lied.

"But I just talked to him!"

"Sorry, sir. He's gone out."

"Fine," Kesner barked. "I'll call back in a couple of hours."

"He's not coming back until very late, sir."

"It is urgent I reach him tonight. How late is late?"

"I don't know, sir," the servant said nervously. "He was

dressed in his tuxedo for the cinema event tonight. Who can I tell him is calling?"

"Never mind." Kesner hung up. If the mountain would not come to Mohammed, Mohammed would go to the mountain. The weasel was not going to get away so easily.

CHAPTER 38

Mickey banged on the door. "Open up!" he demanded. "You have no right to detain me. I am an American citizen," he shouted, giving the door a solid kick. He'd been locked up at GHQ, the British Army General Headquarters, after being interrogated all morning about his interference with the ambush. His requests to talk to Kirk or Donovan had fallen on deaf ears. Making matters worse, they'd refused to let him know the outcome of the entrapment operation. Given the way he'd been treated, he had to presume that the German spy was still at large.

He passed his hand through his hair, dejected. The chief of police had been livid, saying that he ought to be shot for interfering with a military operation. Men with rifles had been stationed behind the gateways of the compound, and thanks to Mickey's amateurish and disastrous interference, the man they were chasing had changed course, escaping into the market below instead of running into their waiting arms at the guarded gateways. Mortified, Mickey felt like the foolish amateur that he was.

He understood he'd messed up, but still, he was a friend, not an enemy. He paced his five-by-ten, windowless cell restlessly. The premiere of *Gone with the Wind* would be starting in two hours, and he did not want to miss the opportunity to see

Maya there. He needed to confront her and find out why she had her uncle lie about her leaving the country.

"Let me out," he yelled, hammering at the door again.

Miraculously, it opened this time.

"Stay back," warned the gruff sergeant posted by the doorway. "This way, Ambassador."

In his white dinner jacket, Kirk was the picture of elegance. Mickey leaped toward him, never having been more glad to see him.

"This man is no criminal. You can leave us alone, and please close the door." Kirk dismissed the sergeant. Once alone, he turned to Mickey. "Mickey, Mickey, *Mickey*!" he reprimanded forcefully, his lips tight, his expression severe. "What have you done? Why on earth did you go there when you were specifically told not to?" He enunciated each word with great severity and crossed his arms.

"I wanted to see the son of a bitch get caught," Mickey admitted sheepishly. "I owed it to Dorothy."

"You owed it to Dorothy? Messing up the capture of her killer? Making all of us at the embassy look like imbeciles?"

"I'm sorry. I guess I haven't been thinking too clearly these days."

"That's right, you haven't. I don't know what's going on with you, but that was plain stupid," Kirk cried out. "The man you were chasing *was* the German spy."

Mickey was speechless. He slammed his palm against the wall in frustration, wishing he could undo his egregious mistake.

"It's not all bad, though," Kirk sighed. "They've arrested a number of people connected to the Muslim Brotherhood. One of them was the spy's driver, Mohammed Rafat, who is Hassan al-Banna's number-two man. MI5 put pressure on his son, who admitted to participating in their kidnap attempt and said he saw the spy crossing the Zamalek Bridge. The field police believe he must be living on the other side of Gezira Island. They sent a truck with radio-detecting equipment into the Agouza area, and guess what?" Kirk asked, the trace of a smile beginning to peek out.

"I wouldn't know," Mickey answered as he took a seat.

"The fellow was operating out of a houseboat. He even had the audacity to put a small antenna on the roof. I don't know how they didn't notice it sooner. Anyway, he blew up the boat and vanished just as they were closing in on him."

Mickey shook his head. "I can't believe that the one guy I chased turned out to be the spy."

"They'll get him sooner or later," Kirk said. "The net is closing around him. They've arrested a lot of people who they think are in cahoots with him, including that dancer, Samina."

"Samina?" Mickey said as it dawned on him that he'd been played. "Shit, I bet my winning the lottery for the dance with her was rigged. She pretended to be so interested in me," he said as he shook his head. He jumped to his feet. A sparkle of light. Here was a chance to redeem himself. "I can help nail her."

"Whatever you can tell MI5 will be useful, but I have to warn you, Mickey, they want you out of the country. This time there is nothing I can do about it."

A silence fell over them. Rather than argue, Mickey let it slide. With the spy at large and Maya still in town, he had a lot to do. "Fine. I'll leave," he said. He rested a hand on Kirk's shoulder. "But now, I need you to get me out of this cell, Ambassador. Right away."

CHAPTER 39

"We can't let you in unless you hold a ticket, sir, and we can't deliver your note until intermission," insisted the American marine at the entrance to the Museum of Antiquities, where the American Embassy was holding the Egyptian premiere of the smash hit film *Gone with the Wind*. The grass plaza in front of the museum had been converted into an outdoor cinema, and through the railing Kesner could see row after row of chairs, holding perhaps as many as a thousand people.

"This letter is urgent," he explained, pressing the envelope into the marine's hand. "I know Mr. Nukrashi would want to learn of this situation immediately. What is your name?" he threatened, pulling a note pad from the inside pocket of the Polish uniform he now wore.

"I'm not even sure where Mr. Nukrashi is seated," the marine said, giving ground quickly.

"He is only the king's public relations minister," Kesner said. "Where do you think he would be seated?"

The marine took the envelope and signaled to a colleague to watch the entrance as he disappeared inside the gates, making his way down the red carpet, which was lined on both sides with lighted votive candles.

Kesner strolled around the outside of the compound, waiting for the marine to come back. Though he was at a distance, he could still see the screen.

"I couldn't find him," the soldier announced with a long face when he returned.

Kesner resigned himself to waiting—he wouldn't budge until he confronted that weasel, Abdoul. He positioned himself to watch the film from behind the railing. Even though it was at a far distance and at an odd angle, he became fully captivated by it, right up until the last image of part one, Scarlett O'Hara's silhouette against the dawn light, her fist clenched toward the heavens. When the lights came up, rousing him and the rest of the audience from their hypnotic state, he inquired again at the entrance, only to find the marines besieged by latecomers who'd been refused admission until the intermission. Kesner was preparing to wade into the fray and protest when he caught the shimmer of a white satin blouse behind the barred gate. He had to look carefully to be sure, but the girl looked a lot like Marianna Blumenthal, the scientist's sister. She was shaking the hand of a tall man in a dark business suit and a grey tarbush.

Praise be to Allah . . . It was the lawyer, Léon Guibli.

CHAPTER 40

After a quick shower and a change of clothes, Mickey made it to the museum during intermission. He snaked his way through the boisterous premiere crowd. "Pardon me," he repeated as he hurriedly danced between lines of people holding plates loaded with hush puppies, corn bread, fried oysters, and shrimp. He had no time to waste. Intermission was only forty-five minutes long, and the first thirty minutes were already gone.

"Not so fast." Mickey felt a hand tugging on his jacket.

It was Sally, surrounded by friends, including Randolph Churchill. She flashed him a big grin and grabbed his hand, intertwining her fingers with his and pulling him toward her crowd.

Mickey tried to free his hand, but Sally held it tight. "You haven't even called me!" she pouted.

"Sally, why don't you tell everybody about the king's Italian entourage," a blonde in a khaki uniform sputtered with laughter.

Sally laughed. "Oh, you have to hear this one," she said to the group as Mickey squirmed, eager to move on, but Sally wouldn't let go of his hand. "As you all know, Ambassador Lampson loathes the king's Italian friends, and he's been trying for months to oust them as enemy nationals. Of course, Farouk won't hear of it. These fellows are practically his family. So he came up with the solution of having them convert to Islam and making them Egyptian citizens." She began to laugh uncontrollably.

"The poor lads had their circumcisions today!" the blond finished for her, sending the group into paroxysms of laughter, except for Mickey, whose eyes kept searching the crowd.

"Give her my regards." Sally blew him a kiss, finally setting him free.

He ran into a dozen people he knew, including Léon Guibli, the lawyer, who was accompanied by a flaming redhead half his age. Each greeting was an unwelcome impediment as he searched for Maya. Kirk was mercifully brief, not wanting to appear too friendly, since the chief of field police was attending the premiere as well.

Red and white lights started to flash, signaling the audience to return to their seats. Frantic to find her, he almost knocked over the life-sized cardboard cutouts of Vivien Leigh and Clark Gable that flanked the museum entrance as he dashed inside and jumped over the red rope that blocked the stairs. He ascended them two at a time to the upper floor, oblivious to the Tutankhamen treasures housed in the room. From the balcony he had a bird's-eye view of the front lawn. The lights were dimmed but the moon was full, and he could vaguely make out the faces of the guests. He was determined to find her, even if it took him the entire remaining hour and a half of the movie to comb through every single row, and search every nook and niche of the garden.

Biting her nails, Maya stared at the screen, though she couldn't pay attention to the movie. She'd seen Mickey in the crowd exchanging words with none other than Allegra's brother, Léon Guibli. Alarmed at the danger this could bring, she'd ducked away. He hadn't noticed her, and she hoped that she could avoid him by hiding in the crowd. But now she spotted him again, standing on the balcony looking down at the guests. She started to panic—there was a good chance he would see her this time. She leaned forward, cupping her chin in her hand, her elbow propped up on her crossed knee, blocking her face.

She had to be honest with herself. Though she'd jumped at the opportunity to accompany Lili and Fernando to the premiere to meet and thank their benefactor, who had at last obtained all of the family's papers for Palestine, part of her had been secretly hoping to run into Mickey at this very American affair. She longed to see him, even if she'd have to come up with more lies. What did it matter? She was leaving in two days and had to be gone before the imminent transportation strike could thwart their plans. But right now Mickey had to be regarded as a danger. How on earth did he know Allegra's brother?

She squirmed in her seat, trying to devise an escape plan, while Lili, next to her, irritated her by noisily cracking pumpkin seeds with her teeth in the tradition of Egyptian cinemagoers. Maya snapped to attention when she heard her name whispered. She didn't need to turn her head; she knew who it was.

"Psst," Mickey hissed a couple of times despite the growls of nearby spectators.

She ignored him. She had nothing to say to him. She owed him no explanation.

"Psst, Maya," he called again, louder this time.

"Shh," the guests protested.

My God, he was making a scene, and she couldn't ignore him. She felt Lili's elbow in her ribs and straightened in her seat. Her heart pounding, she slid her eyes sideways to the aisle. Mickey's white jacket glistened in the dark.

"It's your American friend," Fernando whispered. "I ran into him yesterday." He waved at Mickey.

Maya reluctantly turned to face Mickey. It was too dark to see his expression, but she could make out the gesture he was making with his index finger—*Come over here*.

"Later," she mouthed, waving him off.

"Maya," he insisted louder, disregarding the increasing rumbling around him. "I must have a word with you."

Maya saw a marine guard heading their way. She exchanged a nervous look with Lili, and rose to her feet. She squeezed through the row of seats, flushed with embarrassment.

"We need to talk," he said when she joined him in the aisle.

"Can't it wait until the end of the movie?"

"No, it can't," he responded, looking sternly at her while the guests escalated their protests.

Maya looked toward Lili. She and Fernando were craning their necks. Mickey signaled for her to proceed down the aisle in front of him, which she did, feeling like Marie Antoinette on her way to the guillotine. She tried to think of Erik and Vati and how they needed her, but when Mickey took her elbow to direct her away, she melted instantly from his touch. She was so glad he was all right. She'd worried a great deal about the things he was mixed up with.

He stopped when they reached one of the luxurious palms that were interspersed among the mango trees and ancient statues in the vast courtyard.

"I can tell you the ending," he said. "She loses the guy because she's stubborn and stupid."

"Her life changed her," Maya retorted. "It made her hard and defiant."

"That's too bad, because underneath she loved him all along."

"What do you want from me?"

"Just the truth," he said, pinning her to the palm tree. "If you're capable of that." He looked daggers into her eyes. "I see you're wearing the perfume I bought you."

She shrugged.

"You put too much on," he said matter of factly. "A lady should be more subtle."

"I don't like what you are insinuating." She pushed him away hard and took a step back, but he grabbed her.

"I'm sorry," he said. "I just don't want to be toyed with. I thought we laid out the ground rules on our first date."

She looked away.

"Why did you have your uncle tell me you had left Cairo?"

She wished she could say, "Because you talk too much. You know too many people. I saw you talking to the very man who is helping us get our papers tonight. You're dangerous to my safety and to those I love." But she swallowed the impulse and instead just murmured, "You wouldn't understand."

"That's not good enough," he shot back. "The fact that you needed to lie is baffling to me. Did you think I was going to disregard your wishes?"

"You *are* disregarding my wishes," she fired back, but then sighed deeply. "Mickey, I'll be leaving Cairo in less than forty-eight hours, and I've already explained to you that I don't want to see you anymore." She met his eyes straight on. It was a mistake. They were disconcertingly intense and vulnerable, and she couldn't resist being drawn into them. The light from the projector danced across the frown on his forehead. She had a powerful urge to smooth it by pressing her lips against it but closed her eyes instead. She opened them again. "I'm not Scarlett O'Hara," she declared calmly, "and you're not Rhett Butler."

He shook his head and gave her a terse smile. "Well, I tried." He turned and walked away, leaving her confused and distraught.

While a band on the lawn played the film score, marines in red, white, and blue top hats directed the guests to the museum entry hall where the party was being held and dancing was the order of the night. The line was long and the American ambassador stood by the door, pumping hands eagerly and accepting congratulations as if he had produced the movie himself. The crowd was bubbling with praise for the film and its stars and gossiping about its budget while stealing sidelong glances at the buffet table. Maya wished she could enjoy herself with such delights, but all she could think about was Mickey. She wondered if he was still here and didn't know whether she wanted to run into him again or escape this place as soon as possible. She had the nagging feeling that she had made a terrible mistake.

She looked around for Lili and Fernando. The two had not seen one another since Lili's bicycle accident three weeks ago and seemed blissfully happy to finally be together. The night was perfect for lovers. There was a full moon and the delicate scent of ripening mangoes filled the air. She imagined Lili kissing Fernando passionately behind one of the courtyard statues, and she searched for them on the terraced lawn. She couldn't allow "an accident" to happen. A girl's virginity was crucial in this community—perhaps not as extreme as among the Arabs, but still of enormous importance. She had been horrified to learn that the Arabs held off festivities on the wedding night until the bride's mother-in-law waved a red-stained handkerchief in front of the guests, confirming that the bride, whose hymen had just been punctured, had been a virgin.

Even beyond her responsibility as chaperone this evening, Maya was not too sure about Fernando. Whenever she delivered Lili's letters to him at the Heliopolis sporting club his aunts had always been there, hovering over him, bringing him juice, and mopping his brow between tennis matches. He would be a demanding husband. Lili should think long and hard before tying the knot.

After searching the outdoor area for them, she walked back inside and made her way toward the atrium where most of the festivities were taking place. The spectacle of people dancing to a calypso beat while surrounded by ancient stone sculptures was an incongruity that she thought would have horrified the pharaohs. She stood on the side, batting one of the countless red, white, and blue balloons that festooned the pillars lining the ground floor as she watched the dancers.

"*Rum and Coca-Cola*!" Lili cried, waving at Maya. With one foot still in a cast, the other firmly planted on the ground, she gyrated her hips wildly to the music, while Fernando held her by the arm.

Maya waved back, ashamed to have envisioned this girl giving her virginity away behind a statue. Maybe that was her own naughty fantasy.

"We should get going," Maya shouted. "We don't want to make your father wait."

"Don't be such a spoilsport," Lili shouted back. "We still have time. Come join us."

Maya shook her head. She didn't have the heart for dancing. She stared up at the moon through the large skylight in the roof, which, like all windows and most display cases, was crisscrossed with adhesive tape to protect against shattering in the event of an air raid. "I'll meet you out front in ten minutes," she shouted to Lili and wandered away toward the ancient stones and lingered there, studying some ivory figures in a glass case.

She eavesdropped on a small group of men nearby. They were talking about the assault on King Farouk's mistress. A man had jumped out of a car and smashed her nose with a pistol, breaking it and knocking out a few teeth before speeding off. The news had made the headlines in today's papers, and one of the men was complaining that it overshadowed the really significant news that the military and consular offices in Alexandria had been burning their files.

Suddenly, a terrifying shrieking noise pierced the air and grew louder and shriller every second.

"Stuka bomber!" one of the men yelled.

A split second later an explosion shook the room, shattering windows and sending glasses, bottles, plates, trays, and food flying. The glass case Maya had been studying broke, despite its protective tape. A glass shard struck her foot, and she gasped as she saw blood oozing from her ankle. An orange and green fireball lit up the sky and the electricity flickered on and off.

"The British barracks must have been hit," a man bawled.

"Rita!" someone yelled over the roar of the room.

Maya watched in horror as an elderly woman held her neck, a stream of blood leaking through her fingers, while everyone around her ran for their lives. Maya started to run toward her, but then the shrieking noise filled the air again—the unmistakable sound of an airplane diving—then another explosion. This one threw her backward as more glass broke amid the frenzied cries of frightened people. Sirens wailed. She instinctively covered her head with her arms and curled up into a ball.

Her ears told her the full story of the chaos around her: the trampling feet, the desperate calling of names, the shouts, gasps, moans, the prayers, sobbing, and agonizing cries repeated over and over again. Death had come, no doubt. At the thwack-thwack of antiaircraft batteries, Maya began to hyperventilate. She was back in Poitier, experiencing her first air raid. She'd hidden in the farmer's shelter, a wooden construction with a corrugated iron roof dug deep into the earth that reeked of dank and mildew. She could smell that awful stench again and fought off a wave of nausea. She began to sob as she remembered the farmer's wife, who'd sat across from her, crying, "Philippe, Philippe," certain that something had happened to her youngest son—a mother's intuition.

Maya snapped back to the present when she heard an authoritative American voice shouting, "Everybody to the basement! To the mummy room! To the stairs! This way." She looked up and saw a marine, arms outstretched to prevent people from going past him as they rushed toward the exit. Through the window she could see a tree ablaze in the courtyard. People were blindly running toward certain disaster. She felt a rush of adrenaline surge through her. No, it is not going to happen again. There will be no more deaths. In a flash she was on her feet, racing to the side of the marine to help him.

"To the basement! To the mummy room!" she yelled, echoing his words. "Where are the stairs?" she asked.

"To your right, but get out of the way, miss."

Oblivious to her wounded foot and the orders of the marine, she shouted at people, blocking their way and forcing them toward the stairway. A wild-eyed woman with blood on her shirt became hysterical and fought her, but Maya shook her and slapped her face hard. "Down the stairs," she shouted and shoved her.

Then she heard a cry, "Maya!" It was Mickey as he raced toward her. But another explosion sounded. The chandelier crashed down, leaving the room illuminated only by the dim lights of the sconces on the walls and sending people into even greater panic. Out the window, she saw the dotted red lines of antiaircraft shells bursting across the sky while a fire raged in the courtyard.

"Maya!" Mickey screamed again. As he got close the shrieking sound of another diving Stuka came right toward them, and he hurled himself at her.

Boom! Another explosion shattered the air. Water gushed and the ground shook. Maya feared the pillars would collapse. Mickey had been knocked to the floor, but didn't seem hurt. "To the mummy room," she screamed, her voice hoarse by now.

"You have to get out of here," Mickey shouted, rising to his feet.

"Take her to the basement," the exhausted marine yelled at him.

But Maya wouldn't move and kept directing people toward the stairs as if in a trance. *No more deaths. No more deaths.*

Mickey grabbed her by the shoulders, but she shook herself free. When she saw him again, he was ushering a heavyset man toward the staircase. Then side by side, their arms outstretched, Maya, Mickey, and the marine formed a blockade, forcing people toward safety. After a while Maya saw that there were more marines in the room than civilians, and she let Mickey lead her to the stairway.

They flew down the stairs. It was safer here. She didn't want to think about what had happened to those who had fled into the open, nor did she want to think about the people around her, moaning and crying, each in their own private hell. Mickey and Maya crouched between two sarcophagi, and she focused her attention on the mummies, with their thick heads of false braided hair and painted white shells for eyes. But even that was too much. She shut her eyes tight and put her hands over her ears to block out the sounds.

Eventually, the shelling subsided and the antiaircraft guns were quiet.

"It's over," Mickey murmured as he gently removed her hands.

She started to shake uncontrollably and felt his arms envelop her. She let him cradle her, rocking her back and forth. "It will be all right," he promised. "It will be all right."

She didn't know how long they stayed there, but when she opened her eyes, Joe, Lili, and Fernando were standing there. Fernando's suit was torn, as was Lili's dress, and Joe's jacket was covered in dust, but miraculously they were all unscathed.

"Let's go home," Joe said, offering his hand.

Maya took it and never looked back.

CHAPTER 41

The spray of the shower stung Mickey's cheek, surprising him, for he hadn't noticed any wounds on his face. He'd seen some blood on his hands from a few cuts and thought he'd gotten off easy from the raid. Perhaps he should have stayed longer at the scene of the bombing and continued to help, but his legs were just too heavy to move. The events of the whole day and night had drained every last drop of energy from his body. And Maya was now gone for good. He had held her so tightly in the mummy room that her heartbeat felt like it was pounding inside his own chest. It was as if he had been staying alive for the two of them, but that had passed and she had vanished, leaving him empty, with an overwhelming sense of loss.

He lowered his head and let the water droplets strike his neck and then his upper back, hoping it would dissolve the solid knot of tension that had collected there. His ears still rang from the screech of the falling bombs and the deafening roar of the explosions. He closed his eyes and saw black dots swimming across his field of vision. He raised his head and faced the cascading water, his mouth half open, leaving it up to the water to cleanse him or drown him.

He heard a faint knock on the door. At 2:30 in the morning? He stepped away from the water and listened. Yes, someone was at the door. Was his shower disturbing a neighbor? He quickly dried himself and donned his robe as he went to see. Looking through the peephole, he saw Hosni, his bawab.

"A visitor, sir," Hosni said.

Suspicious, he looked again through the peephole. The bawab seemed alone. He was smiling. He trusted Hosni, and there was something in the way he pronounced the word "visitor" that signaled mischief rather than danger. He opened the door and Hosni stepped aside, revealing her.

"Maya!" he said, shocked.

She stared at him, the harsh light of the hallway exaggerating the redness of her eyes. Her lips quivered as she tried to stretch them into the semblance of a smile.

"What are you doing here?" he asked, his throat constricting.

She didn't answer, her eyes fixed on him, her pupils fully dilated.

"Are you hurt?" he asked, scanning her up and down. She was no longer wearing the stylish white satin blouse he'd found so fetching. Instead she was dressed in a simple beige shirt over a black pleated skirt. Her high heels had been replaced by flats, and she wore no stockings. An ugly red wound was swelling on her ankle, but otherwise she seemed okay. He looked past her, down the hall. Had she come alone?

"Can I return to my post?" Hosni asked tentatively, looking from Mickey to Maya, not sure he'd done the right thing by breaking the rules and allowing a guest after midnight.

"Yes, of course," Mickey said, shaking away his stupor and gesturing for Maya to come in. He fumbled for the living room light switch, but she had already stepped inside. The light from the bedroom cast shadows across her face.

"What's going on?" he asked, noticing that her hair was a bit wet and tangled.

She moved forward and put a finger across her lips.

"Is everything okay with your family?"

"Shh," she said as she drew closer. She slipped out of her shoes, her eyes fixed on him as she traced his lips with a finger. Then, on her tiptoes, she kissed him.

He stood paralyzed, unable to respond while she persisted, her tongue probing his mouth and her hands reaching around the back of his neck. He responded this time, gently exploring her tongue with his own.

"I'm so sorry. Please forgive me," she whispered between breaths.

He tilted her chin and made her look at him. The cool, cruel expression he had seen on her face when she told him she didn't want to see him anymore was nowhere to be found. She looked pained now.

"Please forgive me," she repeated, her eyes pleading for pardon. "I didn't mean a word of what I said. There isn't a second that goes by that I don't think about you. Not a second," she sighed.

Her words soaked into him like warm sunshine, and he knew that they were true—he had felt it in her touch and kiss, but his mind was still struggling to absorb the fact that she was really here. He felt her breath, breezy and sweet on his face. It was real. He pulled her toward him, wanting to obliterate all trace of physical distance between them, and kissed her. She looped her arms around his neck tightly, and he slid his hand down her back. She wasn't wearing a brassiere and the thought of her free breasts enflamed him. The kisses swiftly became more and more passionate. They didn't know what not to kiss—every inch of each other's face was fair game—two dams bursting.

"I thought I was never going to see you again," he said.

"I'm sorry," she repeated, before losing herself in a deep and luxurious kiss.

Her hand moved to the knotted belt of his robe and rested hesitantly there for an instant. She looked up, her eyes revealing modesty, yet they were full of promises.

He smiled at her and took her hand, kissing it gently, but she brought it back to his belt and undid it, as their eyes remained locked. Her expression was now more determined. He was naked underneath. She reached down, groping for him, but once she had his erect member in her hand she became tentative, squeezing it perhaps too lightly while she stroked it awkwardly. She blushed when he gazed down to look at her and lowered his head the short distance to meet her lips to reassure her that everything she did was perfect. He lifted her to carry her to the bedroom, but not wanting to rush things, he carefully seated her on the dining table.

She raised her skirt and pulled him close to her with her legs wrapped around him. She planted kisses all over his chest. "You have just the right amount of chest hair," she murmured, playfully trapping a few of them between her lips and pulling gently.

He started opening the buttons of her blouse, but there were too many of them and he was overeager. He slipped his hand underneath and reached for her breast. It was firm and warm. He squeezed it, gently fondling her nipple and drawing a sigh from her. She hurriedly opened the rest of the buttons. She looked pale and vulnerable as she invited him to look at her bare breasts. They were modest in size, but perfectly shaped. He smiled tenderly and cupped her face in his hands, smothering it with kisses and meeting her tongue again. When he came up for air, he felt her tugging him down toward her bosom. He bent down and found her nipple. He captured it with his mouth and squeezed the other one between his two fingers. She threw her head back and clasped her hands behind her neck, her body feverish.

"I'm so happy you're with me," he said, returning to her lips after messing her hair by running his fingers through it. "I've been going insane. She loves me, she loves me not. She loves me, she loves me not."

She answered him by circling her arms tightly around him and pressing her head against his chest. His robe was fully open and she slowly removed it, one arm at a time. When he stood fully naked in front of her, she ran her hands up and down his chest and back, then around his hips, and bravely dared to glance down at his genitals as she quickly passed her hands over them. She planted a kiss on his belly button and began to hike up her skirt. She would give herself to him right here on the table.

"Let's go to the bedroom," he suggested.

He lifted her in his arms again, and after carrying her to the bed, he turned off the light. The window was open and the full moon threw off just the right amount of brightness. He knelt on the floor next to the bed and started undressing her, taking delight in each new discovery. She tensed as he began to remove her underwear, so he left it on. He told her that he wanted to make love to every single inch of her, from her feet to the top of her head, slowly. Still on his knees, he began with her toes. Nervous, she sat up a few times, begging him to join her on the bed. She missed him too much, she said. But he wouldn't and asked her to relax. She finally closed her eyes and entrusted herself to her lover.

He lightly kissed the wound on her ankle. "Does it hurt?" he asked.

She sat up and shook her head. "How can anything hurt right now?" she said. Then she slid off the end of the bed and joined him on the floor. He reclined against the bed frame. She removed her underwear and climbed into his lap, straddling him. And here they were again . . . lost in their intimacy, breathless and intoxicated in the sheer joy of being together. They both knew where this was heading, and though they could have prolonged the foreplay indefinitely, it seemed that she was starting to feel other emotions, becoming curious and maybe scared. There could be more play later.

"Now," she said.

He didn't dare ask if he was her first lover, but he knew that he wanted to be gentle and careful. "Come, let's go to the bed," he whispered.

She shook her head, though a shy grin belied her bravado. She did not need a bed.

That's when he understood how much she wanted to give herself completely to him tonight, that she was ready to overcome her inhibitions and break down every barrier and taboo between them, wanting them to be connected skin to skin, soul to soul. There was so much he didn't know about this girl, but he knew that there was nothing in the innermost recesses of her heart that would not be given to him tonight. He felt humbled by the vastness of her gift.

"I love you," he whispered.

"Would you mind repeating that?"

"I love you," he shouted.

She threw her head back and shouted back, "*Moi aussi, je t'aime*."

She kissed him savagely and reached for his penis. She rubbed it against her mound, squeezing it harder this time.

"One track mind," he joked.

He positioned her on top of him, her buttocks in his hands. With their eyes glued to each other, he penetrated her. Just a little. She closed her eyes and sat down further, but she grimaced and bit her lip. Then a smile peeked through and she settled down deeper. They did not move their bodies but softly inhaled each other's breaths for a long moment. Finally, they were there.

"Maya," he whispered.

"It's you," she whispered back. "You're the man I've been waiting for." She flipped her hair back and pressed her forehead against his.

He rolled her over so that he could be on top of her, careful not to slip out of her. He grabbed her skirt from the floor and folded it under her head as a pillow. Their limbs were intertwined, fitting perfectly together. He was slow and careful, every thrust counting and bringing them closer until the boundaries between them began to blur and there was no telling where her body ended and his began. Nothing else existed but the two of them. She turned her head, and he saw tears rolling down her cheeks. He stopped moving.

"Maya?" he whispered.

Her hand flew to her face to hide them.

"There are no more secrets between us." He gently pulled her hand back down.

"It's you," she whispered back. "I never thought I would have this." She smiled through her tears and engaged him in a wet kiss, her body writhing under him. "Come to me," she said.

He rose on his elbow and began thrusting harder, deeper, faster. Making love with her brought him to such ecstatic heights of sexual and sensual pleasure that it was almost painful. He wanted this to last all night, and he slowed whenever he felt he was approaching the precipice. She was breathing hard and moaning with pleasure, her nails clinging to his back, her head rolling from side to side as if to grab some moments of privacy to regain her strength. Finally, after a long and steady climb, they knew they were at the peak. He held her hands above her head, and with their eyes boring deeply into each other, they released themselves into an endless rollercoaster of waves.

Utterly spent, physically as well as emotionally, but deeply satisfied, he rolled over. A sense of completion, like nothing he'd ever known, washed over him. He had been aroused beyond mercy, her hesitant ways having excited him more than he ever imagined possible. She was panting hard, too, and started to laugh.

"We did it!" she said triumphantly.

He rose up and pulled the bedcover down off the bed and onto the floor to cover them. "Yes we did, my love," he answered, surprised at how naturally that word fell from his lips. "But I can't even begin to describe what I just experienced."

She smiled and snuggled up to him, putting one leg over his as he extended his arm under her head, offering it as a pillow. "I'll never forget this night," she said, burying her face in his neck.

"The night is still young," he said, softly kissing the top of her head.

"I wish it were," she said, her tone turning sober. "I'm going to have to leave."

He pushed himself up so he could see her face.

"My family thinks that I went back to help the wounded," she explained. "I took a shower and started crying hysterically. I called my uncle and made him take me to the hospital. From there I took a cab. I had to see you. I told the taxi to pick me up at four."

He caressed her cheek. "That means that we have another hour."

"I was counting on that." She buried her face into his neck again. "I love your smell."

"And I love everything about you. Everything. Tell me, do you really have to leave in two days?"

"Less than that," she responded. "So this time is precious."

"When am I going to see you again?"

"I don't know."

"Maya, please let me help you," he said, pushing her away again so that she could read his eyes. "I have lots of friends. What do you need? Money? Papers? Shelter? Anything. Just ask. I'll move mountains for you."

"We are okay, thank you." She smiled.

"Things are very unstable in the Sudan right now. The Italians can easily invade from Ethiopia. Why don't you go to Port Said like most refugees are doing?"

She rose on her side, one elbow on the floor, the palm of her hand supporting her head. "I can't tell you any more right now. Please accept that."

He started to formulate a series of questions in his mind, but as soon as he did, he knew in his heart of hearts that he didn't need to ask them. She had already answered his most basic question—she loved him. The rest was just logistics, and he knew that no matter what, he would make it happen.

"I'll write to you as soon as I can," she said. "But I can't promise anything."

"I understand," he said. " I'll wait as long as it takes. The American ambassador will always know how to contact me."

She nodded and smiled happily.

"Hi, beautiful," he whispered, stroking her cheek and neck, his eyes memorizing every detail of her face.

"Hi, handsome," she purred back, lying down next to him again.

"Come," he said, as he patted the bed and rose to his feet.

"I thought you'd never ask."

She slipped inside the sheets, and lying on her stomach, she ran her hands over them, her head on the pillow. "Mmm," she sighed. "They feel good. I wish I could spend the whole night with you."

"If I knew you were coming I would have changed the sheets," he laughed, joining her under the cover.

"No, I like them. They smell of you," she said, pressing her body close to his, her hand stroking the back of his neck. "Do you like the way I touch you?" she asked timidly.

"Everything you do is perfect," he answered, reassuring her and caressing her back with slow, circular, strokes, making his way down to the curvy small of her spine.

She took it as a challenge, and after nibbling gently on his neck, she had him lie on his back while she leaned over him, running her mouth over his chest, circling his nipples with her tongue while her hand stroked his thigh. She slowly kissed his stomach before continuing south. By then he was mercilessly aroused and tried to take her in his arms. "Tsk, tsk." She was not finished. He didn't want her to be uncomfortable and do anything she didn't really want to, but Maya had a mind of her own and had a growing confidence in her instincts. She started placing kisses up and down his thighs until the excitement became too much for him, and he scooped her up and spread her on the bed. Holding her arms above her head, he carefully pushed himself inside her. She responded with a cry of pleasure, biting his chest and thrusting her hips toward him. No foreplay this time. Now the lovemaking was desperate and selfish. They alternated between giving and taking, rolling into ever changing positions. Then suddenly, she threw her head back and quivered as she gasped for air, her body soaked in perspiration. She was done. His pleasure was now his to take; he could be as selfish as he wanted. Elevating her hips with his hands, he drove at her until he came, with a long, steady moan.

They collapsed, exhausted, but they could not bear to be pulled apart and their sweaty, slippery limbs remained intertwined.

Maya looked at the clock on the night table. It was a quarter to four. Time had passed much too rapidly. She was thirsty, and the time it took for him to fetch her a glass of water seemed insufferably long. When he returned to the bedroom, she was sitting up, looking at the picture of the two of them at the ball. She was lamenting the fact that he had a photo of them, while she had none. He promised to make her a copy and send it to her.

Now, with only a few minutes left, he put his robe back on, while she slipped back into her skirt. They stole kisses in between, unable to let go of each other. He wasn't sure how it started, but before long they found themselves in a passionate embrace on the bed. They couldn't possibly make love one more time, but they did. This time it was out of greediness, their bodies demanded it, and somehow they managed to ascend to those same indescribable heights and dive off the cliff together one last time.

He was aching at the thought of separating from her, but she did not let him walk her to the taxi. "It's already hard enough," she said.

CHAPTER 42

Were his eyes playing tricks on him? Kesner squeezed them tightly before reopening them, but the same blurry image reappeared—a Jewish Star of David dancing in front of him. It was dangling from the neck of a woman in white, her smiling face hovering above him. An angel?

"I'm Nurse Julia," the woman spoke softly, aware of his confusion. "You were hurt last night during the air raid at the museum. I believe you suffered a concussion, but you will be fine."

Kesner tried to raise his head, but his neck was stiff as hell, and his head hurt. Where was he?

"There were no more beds at the Anglo-American Hospital so they transferred you here to the Israelite Hospital," the nurse explained, her face drifting in and out of focus. She took his hand and checked his pulse. "Good," she declared. "Do you remember what happened?"

Kesner blinked. It was slowly coming back to him. He had been at the *Gone with the Wind* soirée. Then he recalled the girl. "Marianna Blumenthal," he whispered.

"Marianna? Was she your date?" she asked, looking down at his hand and not finding a wedding band. "What is your name, officer?"

"Officer?" For a second Kesner was confused as to which costume he had worn, then remembered it was his Polish uniform. It was a good thing he'd kept his disguises at Café Riche, because . . . his boat. He closed his eyes and an inexplicable wave of grief billowed inside him as he felt a tear glide down his cheek. "All gone up in smoke," he said, thinking of his boat and his dream house on the Danube.

"Yes. The fire. A lot of people got caught in the fire outside the museum," the nurse said. "Where were you when the bombing started?"

Kesner combed his memory. "There was an air raid?" he asked. All he remembered was that the marine at the museum gate would not let him inside and that he was waiting for Marianna Blumenthal to leave at the end of the evening.

"You don't remember explosions? Or loud whistles from the falling bombs?"

"They bombed the museum?" Kesner sat upright, grimacing as he tried to turn his neck.

"One bomb fell in the museum courtyard. They were targeting the Kasr el-Nil British barracks."

"Of course," he said, buttoning his shirt, which they hadn't bothered removing, while the rest of his uniform lay neatly folded at the foot of the bed. He had sent Rommel the barracks' plans that Sadat had given him. It was too bad they attacked on the very night Kesner happened to be next door.

"I'm Dr. Franco," a physician cheerfully introduced himself as he sauntered in and sat down on the bed next to him. "So, what do we have here? He lifted his stethoscope and listened to Kesner's lungs. "Would you breathe deeply for me?"

"The patient seems confused, Doctor," the nurse said. "I'm not sure he recalls the air raid."

"I remember everything. Just some details escape me," Kesner protested. He now recalled seeing Blumenthal's sister shaking hands with Léon Guibli. How fortunate. The notorious lawyer could provide a link to the scientist now.

"How many fingers?" the doctor asked, planting his whole hand in front of him. "What's your name, officer?"

"Five fingers, and my name is Captain Stefan Hanczakowski, third Carpathian Polish Second Corps," Kesner stated confidently, eager to get going. "I need to leave, Doctor. I must report to my platoon. All I need is an aspirin for my headache and I'll be fine." Camouflaging his neck pain, he pushed the cover away and dangled one foot out, ready to go.

"Not so fast, Captain," the doctor gently pushed him back. "We can contact your superior and I'm sure there won't be a problem. And definitely no aspirin. We don't want to risk internal bleeding, especially after a concussion. You may have some damage to the brain."

Fat chance of that. Kesner made such a fuss that after his reflexes and balance were checked and his blood pressure taken, they let him go.

"You forgot your pistol." The nurse came running after him and handed him the gun just as he reached the hospital's revolving door entrance.

That was not like him, and he hoped that the concussion would not cause any more stupid forgetfulness. He placed the pistol in his belt holster and headed directly for the downtown tram to Guibli's office, which he was familiar with from having personally followed the American spy there. Kesner expected to find him in his office at this time. He intended to extract the information he needed at gunpoint.

To his dismay, a police car was stationed in front of Guibli's office building and two policemen were standing on the lawyer's second-floor balcony. He backed away, trying to make sense of the situation, when he saw a man exit the building.

"What's going on upstairs?" Kesner asked the well-dressed gentleman. "I had an appointment with the lawyer."

"Good luck!" the man snorted. "His office has been ransacked and someone saw him leave, escorted by two Arabs. His secretary says files were taken."

Kesner hurried away. Hassan al-Banna had just last week abducted a Jewish lawyer in Alexandria. He was out to destroy a network of prominent lawyers in Egypt who had been facilitating illegal Jewish immigration to the Holy Land, in order to curry favor with the Grand Mufti of Jerusalem, who encouraged the development of the Brotherhood's cells in Palestine. Though Kesner dreaded facing the sheik after the fiasco of yesterday's ambush and the arrest of so many of his close associates, he had to find him, for Léon Guibli could very likely be his prisoner. He flagged a taxi to take him to his new go-between with the Brotherhood, Dr. Massoud's assistant. With some luck he might get to see the sheik within twenty-four hours.

"24 Sharia Emad ed Din," Kesner told the cab driver as he got in.

"I'll be happy to take you there," the driver answered, "but we must take a detour. There's some kind of problem. The whole area is blocked off by British tanks." He made a wide circle with his finger to emphasize how wide the cordoned area was.

"Tanks?" Kesner repeated, bewildered. "In the heart of the city?"

In the passenger seat of an old Hudson, a blindfolded Kesner was being taken to Hassan al-Banna's secret hideout. He was smiling though he hadn't slept a wink the night before. It had been a busy eighteen hours since leaving the hospital. Yes, God was on his side. He was no longer alone, and he had the Brits to thank for this unexpected opportunity to get back into the game. He now had a card to play. Kesner swelled with optimism as he reviewed how best to introduce his companion in the backseat, who was also blindfolded.

The car came to a halt, and everyone got out. Taking his

blindfolded passengers by the arm, the driver led them to what must have been a wooden door from the sound of his knocking.

"*Nars*." Victory, the driver pronounced, before the door creaked open and Kesner and his companion were ushered inside.

His blindfold was removed and the sheik appeared in front of him, framed by two strong brethren carrying machine guns. Their skullcaps matched the peeling green paint of the walls. Outside the window the day was breaking.

"Who is this man you have brought with you?" Al-Banna asked in his stirring, resonant voice.

"Someone who wants to help," Kesner answered and removed the man's blindfold.

The sheik smiled. "Anwar Sadat! What a delightful surprise."

"British tanks surrounded the palace last night," Sadat said coldly. "Ambassador Lampson used military threat to force the king to comply with a list of demands."

"He demanded that Farouk issue a prohibition against a transportation strike and wants the French Embassy—" Kesner started to explain.

The sheik raised his palm to stop him—he knew all too well what had happened.

"They have trampled on our sovereignty and I'm going to avenge the insult," Sadat said. "We are ready to cooperate with you. We can lead your men to ammunition dumps and arms depots. We will make the revolution, together."

Al-Banna opened his arms wide. "Come in, come in, s'aalam alekoum. We have a lot to talk about." He turned to Kesner. "We are very grateful to you for having brought us such a righteous man. Is there something I can do for you in return?"

Kesner cleared his throat. "There is. I believe you have in your custody a Jew, Léon Guibli. I must talk to him."

CHAPTER 43

Mickey lay in bed, his eyes fixed on the ceiling fan. He'd been up since five. Maya had bored right into his core. He sniffed the sheets in search of a lingering trace of her scent, which had so intoxicated him twenty-four hours ago. He wanted to bury his nose in her neck and inhale her again. His head swirled with emotions, and he savored the memory of even the most innocent of her gestures, the way she smiled, or the way she tossed her hair or held her chin in the palm of her hand.

He was jolted back into the present when he heard loudspeakers from a van roaming the street below, blaring away in Arabic. The only words he could make out were *Inglisi out*, which meant "out with the English," and *idrub*, which meant "fight." The proponents of the transportation strike were now taking their message to the street in a big way, he thought.

He was fed up with Cairo and everyone in it. Already feeling bad enough about his disastrous blunder with the Nazi spy, he had been chewed out again yesterday for it by the field police and MI5, who'd questioned him ad nauseam about his relationship with Samina. But thanks to his testimony that had led to incriminating documents they found in her home, they'd allowed him three days to leave the country instead of the original twenty-four hours. He didn't give a damn. He was ready to go as soon as he heard from Maya.

Suddenly he heard the crackle of machine-gun fire. What the hell was going on?

He threw the covers aside and raced to the window, stubbing his toe against the trunk he'd bought to carry the clothes and junk he'd accumulated since his arrival. He howled in pain.

Except for smoke billowing far away on the horizon toward the pyramids, everything seemed normal, just a typical, lazy Sunday morning, until he looked down on Soliman Pasha square and saw a Whippet armored car with a machine gun poking out of its turret. Just then the phone rang.

"Have you heard?" Hugh asked breathlessly. "There was a coup at Abdeen Palace last night. Lampson showed up with tanks and guns and forced the king to comply with a number of demands or lose his crown. He presented him with an abdication statement."

"Jesus Christ!" Mickey exclaimed as the implications dawned on him. "There will be riots."

"I'm afraid they've already started. There's a mob down in Giza. A gang of arsonists have destroyed the Auberge des pyramids and the Club Royal de Chasse et Pêche. The Mena House was spared, heaven knows why," Hugh informed him. "My friend Ali is in jail, mate. Just hung up the phone with his parents. He was caught a little while ago stealing an ammunition truck. He could be executed for treason. I'll tell you all about it. Can we still try to have lunch? Might be our last chance."

"For sure," Mickey said, wanting to see him before Hugh left for the front on Tuesday. It was time to reveal that he had been moonlighting as a spy, without providing the key details. He needed to warn him that MI5 might question him about the night they saw Samina at the Kit Kat Club. "Can we meet downtown or do you think the riots will spread to the center of the city?"

"I doubt it. I'm sure we already have it filled with armored vehicles, but it's going to be ugly. What can I tell you, mate? Empires rise and empires fall." Hugh spoke with resignation in his voice. "It won't be long before Gandhi kicks us out of India as well. Anyhow, I'll meet you at twelve at the Turf Club. I've just become a member. It's next door to that Jewish temple . . . You know . . . "

"Temple Ismalia. See you then."

On his way out of the building, Hosni hurried to warn him about what was being said over the loudspeakers outside—exhortations aimed at Egyptians employed by foreigners to poison their food or to strike against them because of last night's explosive events. Hosni was not proud of this.

"It's going to be a mess," Mickey told him ruefully.

When he arrived at the Turf Club, two buttoned down British officers were banging on the door. The doorman, a pompous sort, allowed them in, but turned Mickey away for not wearing a tie, even though there surely must have been one available for him to borrow. Club policy, the doorman proclaimed, and shut the door.

As he paced the street waiting for Hugh, the doors of the synagogue opened and a humming crowd, dressed to the hilt, came out along with a wedding party. Mickey watched with interest as the bride and groom emerged and the guests celebrated by throwing almond candy at them until a chauffeured limousine pulled up and whisked them away.

A young man approached him while removing his yarmulke. "Aren't you the American writing about the Jews here? I'm Bernard Agami," he introduced himself. "We met outside my uncle's orphanage in Daher."

"I remember. You work at the UK General Electric," Mickey said, recalling the young man's forthrightness and his generosity with his time.

"My cousin just got married," Bernard said, explaining his presence here. "Did you ever find the man you were looking for?"

"Unfortunately, no," Mickey answered. "I'm afraid Mr. Nissel wasn't very cooperative."

"Did you know that he and his family are in prison?" Bernard said. "He vanished from his office last week, and the next thing we knew, the whole Nissel family was arrested on a train bound for Palestine for using falsified visas."

"Is that right?" Mickey was surprised, having been told by Nissel's son that they had given up on the idea of going to Palestine.

"The Egyptian police received an anonymous phone call tipping them off." Bernard shook his head, scandalized. "Who would do such a thing? You must be finished with your article by now?" he asked in the same breath.

"I'm about to file it," Mickey said absentmindedly, his mind racing to Nissel's inscription of gratitude in Léon Guibli's book of bridges. Gratitude for what? Mickey would not be surprised if the lawyer had helped them. Surely Guibli, a Zionist sympathizer with high-level connections in the Egyptian government, would be in an excellent position to help. It all began to make sense. The new state needed men of science and engineering to build its future. Men like Nissel and Blumenthal. Mickey had a very strong inkling that the lawyer had been helping not only Nissel but Blumenthal as well. He had to get to him as soon as possible. But it was Sunday.

Mickey politely disentangled himself from the young man and left a note for Hugh at the Turf Club saying that something had come up and that he would call later. He strode off toward the Jewish community center around the corner, intent on getting Guibli's home address from Jacques.

It turned out that the lawyer was not a registered member of the community, and there was no record of his home address, but Jacques knew that he lived in Heliopolis, and suggested he drop by the home of Guibli's sister, Allegra Levi, who lived in Heliopolis as well. Allegra was very active in Jewish affairs, and Jacques was sure she would be happy to let him know how to contact her brother. As he left the center, Mickey decided it would be wise to tell Kirk he was pursuing the case again. He tried calling him, but the ambassador could not be reached. He considered calling MI5 but hesitated. His information was not firm enough yet and he did not want to incur their wrath. He'd go it alone.

He sped down Sharia El Gheish toward Heliopolis, narrowly missing the mob that was forming around the railway station. He made sure to avoid Ataba Square, where Jacques had warned him that firefighters were putting out blazes at Barclays Bank and the Rex Cinema. There was no telling which foreign institution would be the next target for the gangs of arsonists that had sprung up throughout the city, or where the next riot would start. Mickey had gotten a small taste of this danger when he left the Jewish community center and found a group of angry students a mere fifty yards away from his Jeep rocking a British truck back and forth with its terrified occupants inside.

As he entered Heliopolis, however, he was surprised to find the residents of the elegant suburb lunching al fresco along its pretty tree-lined avenues, oblivious to the rampaging taking place practically next door. The Arabs he'd stopped to ask for directions were courteous. It was as if the news of the night before had not reached this enclave. When he finally arrived at the Levis' building, the bawab was away from his station. He checked the names on the long wooden mailboxes and found a J. Levi on the second floor. Must be it.

When he reached the apartment he rehearsed his story. He

would say that he was from the American Embassy and needed to get ahold of Allegra's brother concerning an acquaintance of his whom the embassy was looking for. He would keep it vague and casual.

Mickey was taken aback by the sobbing and weeping he heard inside the apartment when a portly servant opened the door. Behind her another maid was covering the foyer's mirror with a black cloth, and he could see another black cover on the wall in the living room. Someone had just died in this household, and he felt awkward about his bad timing. "I'd like to speak to Madame Levi," he said. "It's about her brother, Léon."

The servant shook her head. *"Pauvre monsieur Léon (*Poor Mr. Léon)," she said, looking disconsolate. "I don't know if Madame—"

"My mother can't talk to anybody," a female voice said from inside the house as she made her way to the door. "Who is it?"

Mickey froze.

Lili was standing right in front of him, her face a mess from crying but looking just as much aghast at seeing Mickey there.

Surrounded by Joseph Levi, his wife, and Lili, Mickey frantically dialed the number of the British MI5 agent he had dealt with after failing to reach Kirk. He was reeling from the double whammy that Léon Guibli had been murdered and that Maya was Erik Blumenthal's sister. Blumenthal had been under his very nose the entire time. But he couldn't care about anything right now except finding Maya. The Levis knew nothing about the Nissel family but had told Mickey about the Brotherhood's target list. The body of Léon Guibli had been found a few hours ago dumped in front of the Bassatine Jewish cemetery with a sign around his neck: *Palestine*

Forever Islamic. Mickey was alarmed that the Brotherhood, which had participated with the German spy in the aborted ambush, might have learned that the Blumenthals were on the train to Palestine and told the spy.

"Commander Toppington is on the other line," an aide apologized.

"Please tell him it's urgent. Urgent," Mickey repeated, tapping his feet on the floor. He could barely breathe. "I have important news regarding a man the American Embassy has been looking for. He will know what I'm talking about."

It took forever for the Englishman to finish his call, and when he did, he shouted into the phone, "I've already warned you, Connolly, lay off this case. You've created enough problems for us."

Mickey quickly brought the commander up to speed. "They're on the two o'clock train to Ismailiya. You've got to stop that train," Mickey cried.

"First off, mate, it's Sunday, and I'm the only one here. Second, just in case you haven't noticed, Cairo is in flames and all our men are needed now. And third, we don't need you Yanks to tell us what to do."

Mickey lost it. "No wonder you slimy limies are losing this war," Mickey yelled, incensed by the man's obtuseness. "We'll probably have to come in and rescue your sorry asses. I'll go it alone." He slammed down the phone. He checked his watch. With some luck he could overtake the train.

"I'll show you the fastest way out of town," Mr. Levi offered.

CHAPTER 44

Sitting across from each other, Erik and Maya looked out the window in silence as the train chugged north along the Nile. Water buffaloes turned waterwheels by the river's edge, while further downstream, boys herded flocks of sheep and goats in neat single files—a tableau that must have existed since ancient times, Maya thought. After passing only sand dunes since leaving Cairo, the land here was brilliantly green. Nourished by water from the river, farms were flourishing. Fields of cotton and rice stretched out before her. The vitality of the landscape contrasted sharply to the way she was feeling.

"No peace for the wicked," Erik said, without turning his head, his face pale as a ghost. These were the first words he'd spoken since they'd boarded the train to Palestine.

Maya shook her head. "When will it ever stop?" she said.

She'd expected long embraces and perhaps tears when saying their good-byes to the Levis, but not the agony and guilt that she, Erik, and Vati had felt after learning that Allegra's brother had vanished. The police couldn't say for sure that the lawyer had been kidnapped, but it was a distinct possibility. The family, of course, feared the worst. The Blumenthals had refused to leave Egypt under the circumstances but the Levis vehemently insisted, explaining that there was nothing Maya's family could do and that their presence would possibly pose an increased danger to them. As a precaution, they'd put them in a hotel close to the train station the night before. Maya and her family couldn't help feeling responsible for what had happened to Léon, even though the Levis had assured them that they had all lived anticipating this possibility for some time. Léon had been involved in all sorts of risky and clandestine Zionist activities and knew what the consequences might be.

Maya absentmindedly twirled the seashell bracelet Lili had given her as a parting gift. Lili had also packed a suitcase full of clothing she insisted would look better on Maya than on her. And at the door, Allegra had handed them a glass of water, insisting that Maya and her family drink from it, honoring the custom that a symbolic sip of water from the Nile would guarantee their return in good health.

It had been two hours since the train had left Cairo, and they had drifted away from the river. The landscape was now just a large expanse of rolling sand dunes. Most signs of life had disappeared, except for rusty petrol cans that lay alongside a road that ran parallel to the railroad tracks and the occasional figure of a solitary Arab, miles from anywhere. Doing what? Going where? Maya wondered.

"Joe told me the American reporter was at the premiere," Erik said, jolting her from her reverie and awakening the Egyptian couple who shared their compartment.

"So?" she responded, feeling defensive.

"Nothing," Erik said. He looked at her as if it were the first time he'd seen her for a long time. "You look . . . well. I mean good. Pretty. That's all," he added.

"Sambousseks, boyos, and pasteles," Vati announced as he opened the bag of food Allegra had given them the night before and pulled out some nicely wrapped containers. Sitting next to Erik, he placed each item on the seat between them. "Look! Dates! Of every color," he exclaimed as he continued pulling things out of the bag.

Maya smiled. It must have been Lili who'd put them there. She knew how much Maya liked them.

"Would you care for something to drink?" their Egyptian neighbor asked. "We're going to the dining car." He tugged his emaciated wife along, looking dour in her long black skirt.

Maya smiled and shook her head, but as she did, the train jerked to a stop, propelling everyone forward and sending the food to the floor.

"What's going on?" Erik asked, pulling himself back up in his seat.

Maya got up and looked out the window. "There is an army lorry next to the tracks," she said as she watched two soldiers jump out of it while a third stood by, rifle at the ready.

The Egyptian man went to the window to see for himself. "Egyptian soldiers."

The floor was a mess with food all over. Maya knelt down and was helping her father gather it when she heard a commotion in the corridor.

The door suddenly slammed open, and two soldiers stood in the doorway. They sized up the group and exchanged a few words in Arabic with the Egyptian couple.

Maya straightened up, her heart pounding. Somehow she knew they'd come for them.

"Herkowitz?" one of the soldiers barked.

"Not here," Vati answered from the floor.

But Maya and Erik exchanged concerned looks. This was their name on their new passports.

"What is it?" Erik asked.

"Papers," the soldier demanded. "For you and you," he pointed to Erik and Vati, whom he helped back to his seat, grabbing him by the arm.

Maya did not like the way he manhandled her father and

panic shot through her. "What is this about?" she asked as calmly as she could.

"Not you," the soldier barked back at her. "You and you," he repeated, poking Erik's and Vati's shoulders with the tip of his rifle.

Erik coolly pushed the soldier's rifle aside. "I don't know what it is you men want, but our papers are in order. Maya, please," he gestured to her to hand over their documents.

As she started to dig through her purse, her father stood up.

"I protest," he declared in German, his jaw quivering. "You have no right to judge me. I am not garbage."

As the soldier moved to push him back down, Erik grabbed his father's hand, pulling him down to his seat. "Father, this is only perfunctory. There is no problem, is there, officer?" he managed to say in a soothing voice.

The soldier did not respond and gestured for Maya to hurry. "Papers!"

She found them and timidly tendered all three passports to the commanding soldier, who gave them to his comrade to examine. The two soon started to argue, fixing their gazes on Erik and Vati. One of them tossed Maya her passport, which she caught in midair. They addressed the Egyptian man in the compartment.

"They want to know which one of you is Erik Blumenthal," the man relayed.

"I am," Vati said, beating his chest and standing up again. "And I'm proud to be a Jew."

"Father, don't say stupidities. Sit down," Maya demanded, before addressing the soldiers. "My father is not well in the head, I'm sorry." She twisted her index finger against her temple to indicate that he was crazy.

"You and you. Come," the commanding soldier ordered Erik and Vati, pointing to the corridor with his thumb.

"Is something wrong with our papers?" Erik asked.

"Come." The commanding officer stepped forward and gripped Erik and Vati by their arms, getting them on their feet.

"I protest," Vati shouted, trying to wriggle out of the soldier's grip, but his comrade stepped in and, taking a firm hold, dragged him out of the cabin, while the other followed, tightly holding on to Erik, who did not even try to resist.

"Leave them alone! Stop it," Maya cried, and with the protective instincts of a mother bear whose cub is in danger, she jumped on the soldier who was dragging Erik out. But with the palm of his hand spread across her face, the man pushed her back inside. She lunged at him again and struggled to free her brother, but this time, the soldier slapped her sharply, sending her reeling back into the cabin and knocking her head against the wall. She was so stunned by the blow that it took a couple of seconds for the pain to sink in. The Egyptian couple came to her aid, the man yelling in Arabic at the soldiers, who yelled back at him and slid the door closed behind them.

"Please stop them," Maya implored as she regained her footing. She heard her father shouting for his violin and she rushed into the corridor, only to be confronted by a third soldier who'd sprung up out of nowhere, blocking her way. "Them only," he said.

"Vati, no!" she screamed, catching a last glimpse of her father and brother being taken away. She fought the soldier who was holding her back, kicking, yelling, and biting, blind with fury. He was caught off guard and lost his footing for an instant, and Maya was able to slip by him. She raced down the hallway, but he caught her by her hair and overpowered her.

"You're not understanding, miss," he said in perfect English. "You're not needed."

"Please let me go with them," she begged as the soldier dragged her back into the cabin. "Please, they are both so frail. Take me with you." Her knees buckled and she would have fallen had the soldier not held her so firmly.

Their eyes briefly met. He soon looked away and let out an exasperated sigh. Holding her tight with one hand, he opened the window and yelled in Arabic to the other soldiers who were taking Erik and Vati toward the waiting lorry.

"Okay," the soldier let up. "You're coming along, miss. But no more biting or I'll lock you up here."

She just had time to grab her mother's violin as he pulled her, sobbing, out of the compartment.

CHAPTER 45

Kesner parted the flaps of the large Bedouin tent. "*Allo*?" he singsonged, poking his head inside. Beyond the small entry area, the interior was divided into sections by a woven curtain and several sheets.

"*Henna*," a voice filtered back, and in seconds a sheet on the left was pulled aside to reveal an Egyptian soldier, the jacket of his uniform unbuttoned, his rifle at his shoulder.

Kesner didn't bother to acknowledge him as he entered, erect as a king and as jubilant as a groom on his wedding day. He only had eyes for the three figures seated on floor cushions on brightly colored rugs, the light from the petrol lamp above dancing on their sad faces.

"Erik Blumenthal, I presume," he greeted the scientist in German, recognizing him immediately. He extended his hand, but the Jew just glared at him.

"You have no right to detain us. Where are we?" Erik demanded.

The soldier rushed in and started to lift him under the arm.

"No, no, let him be," the girl cried. "His legs are weak." She jumped to her feet, but Kesner stopped her with a hand stretched across her stomach and forced her back down. He leaned toward the girl and lifted her chin to get a better look at her face. She looked quite unglamorous now with her disorderly hair and manly trousers, but she still looked pretty.

"Marianna, no?" Kesner cocked his head. "You look prettier in person than in the photo."

The girl jerked her head away.

Kesner straightened up.

"Let him be," Kesner told the soldier, gesturing to Erik. "I want you to take good care of him." Then, addressing the scientist, he said, "You will need strength for the journey you face, Mr. Blumenthal. A lot of people in Berlin are looking forward to meeting you. And you have no rights, I'm sorry. This is war."

"Who are you?" Marianna asked. "We did not do anything wrong."

"Maybe you didn't, but your brother here must have done something right. The führer wants him."

The girl turned to her brother inquisitively, but his face remained impassive.

Kesner shrugged. "I frankly don't know why," he said, addressing Erik. "Apparently the last paper you wrote was a winner. It's bringing you lots of fans, even from across the Atlantic." He winked.

Another soldier walked in, interrupting them. "I am Sergeant Ibrahim," the man introduced himself. "I led the squad that captured these people. We took both men because we were not sure which one you needed, and the girl—"

"I know, I know. You did a splendid job," Kesner interrupted. Though not part of the plan, he was pleased by the mistake. The old man and the girl could be used as leverage in the event the scientist proved difficult. He turned to Erik. "We are glad to have you with us, *Herr* Blumenthal. And we very much appreciate your great efforts in the service of humanity."

"What is he talking about?" Marianna asked her brother.

"They want me to help them build a bomb," Erik said with loathing.

"Is that what it is?" Kesner smiled and leaned down to look him in the eye, but as he did, Erik drove his elbow into Kesner's solar plexus, making him double up and gasp for air.

Ibrahim rushed to restrain Erik, who tried to wriggle out of his grip.

Marianna jumped at him. "Get your hands off him," she cried. "He's crippled, for God's sake."

Kesner lunged at the girl and pulled her away. He slapped her sharply, sending her reeling back into the tent and knocking her head against a copper pot. She looked at Kesner, dazed for an instant, her hand on her cheek, while the sergeant held his rifle in front of Erik's face. Erik pushed it aside.

"Where is my violin?" Vati lamented as he started to get up, but he lost his equilibrium and fell back on his buttocks.

Kesner looked at each of the Blumenthals in disgust. He pointed a warning finger at Erik. "I'm sure you want your father and sister to be comfortable. *Nein*?" he threatened.

"I need access to a radio," Kesner told Ibrahim as he exited.

"We have one in our lorry outside," Ibrahim said, but when they got outside he whispered gravely, "I have terrible news. Our leader, Lieutenant Anwar Sadat, has been arrested by the British, along with a number of our men."

"But that's impossible! I was with him this morning," Kesner protested. He'd had breakfast with the lieutenant around ten o'clock and discussed the train ticket information they'd pieced together from Léon Guibli's files, unearthing the Blumenthals' imminent departure for Palestine. Good thing too, because they had been unable to squeeze anything out of the rat lawyer himself.

"What about the plane he promised me to take them to Rommel?" Kesner asked. "Will it still be coming?"

"Indeed. The pilot has the map coordinates for this camp and will have everything ready by dawn tomorrow," Ibrahim answered.

Kesner felt immensely relieved and patted him on the arm. "Have faith. It's only days now before the Afrika Korps arrives and Egypt will become an independent nation."

CHAPTER 46

After finding the train to Ismailiya stopped in the middle of nowhere with no sign of the Blumenthals, Mickey requisitioned the phone box in the first restaurant he spotted. Ignoring the impatient glares of a teenager waiting outside the booth, he was beside himself, and to make things worse, the connection was bad and he had to yell.

"I told you! That's what the witnesses said. It was the Egyptian army," Mickey shouted to Kirk on the other end. "An army truck with three soldiers stopped the train. They knew exactly which car Blumenthal was in. He was traveling with his father and sister, and they took all three." He bit his lower lip.

"This makes no sense," Kirk said. "The army is not involved with immigration and passport issues."

"I know," Mickey said, putting his index finger into his other ear, so as to shut out the noise around him. "And why would they stop the train in the middle of nowhere to make an arrest, with Ismailiya only fifteen minutes away? Something's up. You have to call your friend General Neguib. I can't help thinking that the hand of the Nazi spy is involved here."

"Neguib has resigned his commission," Kirk informed him. "He was humiliated by what happened at the palace yesterday. Good thing you weren't in the streets this afternoon. Foreigners were being beaten up by angry mobs. Stores were looted and burned. The Turf Club was torched, along with five or six cinemas, and so was the Kit Kat Club—"

"Ambassador, Ambassador," Mickey tried to cut him off. His most urgent concern right now was Maya and her family.

"We're lucky to have caught an arsonist before he set fire to the Shepheard's Hotel. He was posing as an exterminator," Kirk went on as if he hadn't heard Mickey. "And the worst part about this madness is that the Egyptian police just sat back and watched it happen without raising a pinkie. This country will never be the same after this. And to think that Churchill is arriving—"

"Ambassador!" Mickey yelled. "I think the Blumenthal family was kidnapped. We have to find them."

A heavy sigh came from the other end of the line. "I think you're right. It does look like a kidnapping to me, and I have suspicions about who might have been involved."

"Who?" Mickey asked breathlessly.

"Some renegades within the Egyptian army who call themselves the Revolutionary Committee. MI5 has known about them for some time; in fact, they just put one of their leaders and his clique under locks. His handwriting matched a document they found at Madame Samina's—a deal guaranteeing Egypt's independence in exchange for their collaboration with the Germans. We have to get MI5 on this right away. I'll call Commander Toppington immediately."

"Hold on, hold on," Mickey said as he pressed the receiver tightly against his ear. "Is there any way I can talk to these officers from the Revolutionary Committee before MI5 does? I seriously doubt that the Brits will get anything out of them."

"I'm obliged to alert MI5 right away."

"Of course. But Egyptian soldiers, especially if they're anti-British renegades, are more likely to cooperate with Americans. Just buy me a little time so I can talk to them first? I can be there in two hours."

"Mickey," Kirk's tone veered toward patronizing, "what you did—finding Erik—was a *coup de force*, but—"

"There is no 'but,'" Mickey almost yelled. "If I can't interrogate these people alone, then at least make sure I'm present when MI5 does. This is not only about catching the spy. It's still about finding our guy and delivering him to Roosevelt. We have our own agenda," he reminded Kirk.

There was a silence on the other end of line. Mickey realized that he must have sounded overzealous.

"Erik Blumenthal's sister is the girl with me in that photo taken at the ball," he said, letting out a sigh. "I had no idea. I just found out."

Kirk did not say anything for an instant. "Give me a few hours," he said.

There was something dreamlike about his drive back to Cairo, alone, through the vast darkness of the desert. A whistling draft entering between the Jeep's canvas top and the windows made it cold, but Mickey barely noticed. He was lost in his thoughts about Maya. He tried to remember everything she'd ever said and put it in the context of her actual situation: the demanding family she'd referred to, the vagueness of her plans, the secretive phone calls. It was all to hide their illegal immigration plans, which, in light of the growing threat of the Muslim Brotherhood, had become extremely dangerous. The poor girl. What difficulties and horrors she must have suffered since leaving Paris, and before that as a Jew living in Hitler's Germany. It was a miracle that she still had a heart to give, and he loved her even more for opening it to him.

As he entered the outskirts of Cairo he could smell the gunpowder and ashes lingering in the air. He had to pass a number of checkpoints before he could reach Hugh's apartment. He'd decided to spend the night there, fearing his own place might be under surveillance.

"Mi casa es tu casa," Hugh said with a twinkle in his eyes when Mickey appeared at his door. He gave Mickey a pair of pajamas and left him in the privacy of the living room to call Kirk, who said that he was still working on arranging for the two of them to visit the jailed Revolutionary Committee officers. He asked Mickey to wait by the phone for his call.

Mickey collapsed on the sofa; he needed badly to unwind. "Swell joint," he commented when he heard Hugh return to the living room.

"And the rent is only one love letter a month," Hugh smiled mischievously as he settled into the flowery print of an overstuffed armchair. "So . . . " he bent forward and clapped his hands. "This article you're writing about the Jews of Egypt?"

"Baloney," Mickey admitted straight out. "I promise I'll tell you the whole story when I can." He crossed his arms when suddenly a new thought struck him. "Tell me about your friend Ali, you said he stole an ammunition truck?"

Hugh nodded. "After the humiliation of King Farouk, he turned against us," Hugh sighed. "He's being held at GHQ. They're fighting over who has jurisdiction—the Egyptian authorities or High Command. Either way, he's facing a stiff sentence, possibly death. Why?"

"Is he part of the group of officers arrested for conspiring with the Nazis?"

"Sadly, yes. How did you know?"

"I need to see him. Can you help me?" Mickey asked, springing to his feet.

The first light of the morning sky had barely appeared when Mickey spotted a sign on the side of the road, *Suez 20 km*. He had no idea where he was being taken, but he realized that the rugged reddish-brown mountains in front of him must be running parallel to the Gulf of Suez. This meant he was probably about eighteen miles or so south of Ismailiya.

He was still in disbelief at the succession of events that had brought him here. It was all thanks to Hugh, who had put Mickey in touch with Ali's parents and the family's lawyer. Mickey had conveyed Kirk's assurance that if Ali cooperated, the Americans would use their considerable influence with the Brits to be lenient on the young captain. In less than an hour Mickey found himself with the family's lawyer in Ali's cell, which he shared with five fellow members of the Revolutionary Committee. Ali denied any knowledge of the kidnapping and insisted that the lawyer also represent his comrades, who had remained present during the talk, and whom he claimed had been arrested without evidence.

Mickey corrected him. There was in fact, evidence. The field police had discovered a document containing a German promise of independence to Egypt in exchange for help from the Revolutionary Committee. The document had been found in the home of the dancer Samina who was being paid by a Nazi spy. It was apparently waiting to be sent to Hitler for signature.

The officers had become visibly disturbed by this information. Realizing he had touched a nerve, Mickey felt emboldened and pressed them for information regarding the Blumenthal abduction, promising help from the American Embassy in exchange, but they still denied knowledge. Dispirited, he'd gone back to Hugh's empty-handed and desperate. Perhaps the Brits would get better results through force.

So it had come as a great surprise when Mickey was awakened in the middle of the night by Sami, Ali's little brother, telling him that a driver in a black Plymouth was waiting downstairs to take them to the Blumenthals. He had to leave at once and tell no one.

En route, Sami explained that his brother and his comrades were outraged at being lied to and betrayed by the Nazi spy, who had sworn that the document guaranteeing independence had reached Germany and that Hitler had signed it. One of the jailed officers had been involved in planning the kidnapping and had arranged a mail plane for the spy to take his captives to Rommel. Furious that so many of their comrades' lives had been put at risk because of the spy's false assurances, they now wanted to abort the plan.

The Plymouth sped toward the safe house where the Blumenthals were being held, with Sami and the driver urgently needing to inform the Egyptian officers there about the betrayal. They would overpower the Nazi and transfer custody of the foreigners to Mickey. If the spy resisted, he would get what he deserved. Mickey prayed the plan would work as intended.

When they arrived at the edge of a Bedouin encampment, which consisted of a half dozen black tents, the driver, whose name was Fuad and who spoke only Arabic, barked an order. "You stay here until we call you," Sami translated as they strode away. A handful of children in bare feet followed them.

Mickey wasn't happy about staying behind. He got out of the car and paced.

A woman was squatting in front of a nearby tent, wetting dough from a bowl of water and flattening it between her palms. She was veiled in black and only her eyes were visible. When she encountered Mickey's gaze, she rushed inside in modesty, yelling at the children to do the same. He felt bad that his presence had chased her away. Oh well. He checked his watch. Two whole minutes had already passed.

"Sami!" he called. "What's taking so long?" he yelled, but no response came back except a low, menacing hiss, and he saw a pair of vultures circling in the sky overhead, ascending and descending. Impatient, he opened the driver's door to the car and honked the horn continuously until Sami and Fuad emerged from one of the tents with another man who was clad in loose cotton trousers and an Egyptian army jacket. He was closing his jacket with one hand, while holding a gun in the other. They all ran toward the car.

"Get in," Sami shouted. "They are gone, but we may still have a chance to catch them."

Mickey climbed in the passenger seat as he fought a rising panic. "Where did they go?"

"One of the Bedouins drove them to the airfield," the soldier with the loose trousers responded as he settled into the driver's seat and started the car. Fuad and Sami jumped in back. The soldier took off like a bandit.

"I'm Sergeant Ibrahim," the soldier turned to Mickey. "So our document never left Cairo, huh?"

"It never left Cairo," Mickey confirmed.

"I want to kill that dog with my own two hands," Ibrahim said.

Fuad said something in Arabic and spat.

"One of the men you met in the cell with Ali was their leader," Sami said.

Mickey turned around. "So, what's the plan?"

"Their plane is to take off at 6:35 promptly, five minutes before the normal mail plane departure from Suez," Sami explained. "This way they can fly in plain sight and not arouse suspicion."

Mickey looked at his watch. "But it's already 6:40."

"There's a chance they may be delayed because of the strong winds last night," Ibrahim said. "They probably have to clear a lot of debris from the runway."

Wind rushed through the open windows as they raced down a grade that seemed never to end. Ibrahim never slowed for rocks, encouraged by the cries of Fuad in the back with Sami, who wanted him to go even faster.

"We want to get there, not get wrecked," Mickey yelled. His face lit up when he spotted what looked like a runway near the remains of a Roman temple at the bottom of the hill. He squinted, urgently scanning the valley, but there was no plane in sight. A feeling of utter despair began to settle over him. However, just as they approached the bottom of the hill he heard an unmistakable roar, and as they drove past the only standing wall of the temple he saw it.

"A plane!" Mickey exclaimed as he spotted a small trimotor aircraft. Two men were in the open cockpit, but he couldn't tell who was in the enclosed cabin.

The pilot was revving the engine to nearly full throttle before turning onto the makeshift runway, a smooth field barely three hundred yards long that crossed the road and ended in a ravine. On the other side of the gully was a rock wall, an impossibly short distance for the plane to take off from. Yet the pilot was obviously prepared to do just that as he gunned the engine up another notch.

"Turn around!" Mickey yelled at Ibrahim, but as he did, he heard gunshots. Were they being fired at?

Ibrahim slammed on the brakes, and as he skidded into a U-turn, the Plymouth almost hit a Jeep that was hidden between the dunes, its two front doors wide open.

"Turn around!" Mickey ordered, grabbing the wheel from Ibrahim, who had frozen rigid.

As they turned, a figure raced onto the runway, arms outstretched, trying to block the plane as it rolled into takeoff position. It was a woman. A Bedouin man with a limp was chasing her, a rope hanging from his hand.

"Maya!" Mickey shouted at top of his lungs, jumping up from his seat, shouting desperately though he knew she was too far away to hear him. "Maya! It's me, Mickey!"

"She's going to get killed!" Sami shouted when an arm with a pistol emerged from the cockpit and began firing.

The Bedouin stopped in his tracks and then turned tail, hobbling away as fast as he could.

"Get out of the way," Mickey yelled at Maya as the car raced toward the plane. "Get out of the way."

From the backseat Fuad started shooting at the aircraft, while Sami, eager to get in on the action, lurched forward and grabbed Ibrahim's pistol.

Mickey held his fire. "Are you crazy? Stop shooting. We're too far away," he screamed. "We need our ammunition."

The clicks from Fuad's gun told the story—he had already emptied his weapon. Maya had run right in front of the plane, her arms waving. She fell to the ground, but quickly stood up again as the trimotor slowed and veered to the right and then to the left as the pilot tried to avoid her, but she valiantly followed its every move.

"Don't, Maya. Get out of the way!" Mickey screamed again. "It's me, Mickey!"

Though she was still a good fifty yards away, this time Maya turned her head toward them, but at that moment a shot was fired from the cockpit, and she fell to the ground.

Mickey felt a cold sweat come over him. "No!" he screamed. He began firing at the plane wildly.

"Not yet!" Ibrahim screamed. "Ammunition. Ammunition!"

Mickey stopped and breathed a sigh of great relief when he saw Maya curl into herself and roll away from the airfield.

The gap was closing as the Plymouth raced forward, and Sami carefully fired several shots at the plane's front tires. The aircraft started to zigzag, provoking congratulatory cries from Ibrahim and Fuad. Mickey fired at the cockpit, but a stream of bullets answered back, shattering the car's windshield.

Ibrahim slumped forward, blood gushing from his neck, his foot still on the accelerator. The Plymouth swerved wildly. Mickey grabbed the wheel, but it was too late. A second later, it sideswiped the plane, knocking its wheels askew and causing it to skid on its belly until a wing dipped to the ground, stopping it for good. Mickey fought to get the car under control as it sped toward the ravine, pulling hard on the emergency brake, but to no avail. Fuad screamed and Sami prayed. Mickey braced himself as the car spun sideways, rolled over, and crashed, landing on its side.

He found himself under Ibrahim's dead body, groggy but alive. His head was pressed against the dead man's back. The Egyptian's body had cushioned the impact, probably saving his life. His head pounding, barely able to breathe, he tried to push the man away, but was unable to extricate his left arm. He finally rolled the body far enough away to sit up, but became alarmed when he found his own shirt soaked in blood. Had he been shot, too? No, it was Ibrahim's blood. He heard groaning behind him and the creaking sound of the door opening. He turned his head, gasping at the pain in his neck, and saw Sami climbing out. Fuad was pressed against the window. His eyes were open and blood dripped from his forehead and lips, but he was able to move his head. He grunted. He was alive.

"Maya!" Mickey shouted and tried to open the door, but it was stuck. "Help me get out," he called to Sami.

The youth staggered back toward the car and forced the door open. "I'm bleeding," he complained, ready to faint.

"I know, I know, but you have to get me out," Mickey cried.

With great effort, Sami freed Mickey's arm and pulled him out before falling backward onto the rocks. He was bleeding from his cheek and was woozy from the accident, but he was okay.

"The driver," Sami said, a tremor in his voice. "He is dead!" He began to cry. "Where is my pistol? I need my pistol." He sobbed.

Mickey had no time to attend to him and turned toward the plane. Flames leapt from the tail of the cabin. He scanned the side of the airfield for Maya and saw with relief that she was safely on the ground. He searched the car and found his gun. He rushed toward the plane, but stopped when he saw a man's legs dangling from the open cabin door before the rest of his body became visible. Someone was lowering him to the ground. He collapsed on the runway. There was no sign of life in the cockpit.

"Erik!" Maya screamed from the bowels of her gut.

"Stay where you are," Mickey yelled at her. As he ran toward the fallen man, someone jumped out of the cabin. The Nazi. Mickey could see his face clearly and immediately recognized him though he'd been dressed as an Arab when he'd escaped the ambush. Mickey raised his gun and aimed. He was only forty feet away, but the German dropped to the ground to avoid being hit. He grabbed Erik around the waist and pointed a gun to his head. "Toss me your gun or I kill him," he warned.

"How far do you think you can get?" Mickey asked, keeping his gun trained on the Nazi.

"Toss me your gun or I kill him," the Nazi repeated.

"Everyone is looking for you. Surrender. At least you'll live."

"Maybe. But they will never get him alive." The German cocked his revolver. "Give me your gun," he yelled before suddenly swinging his pistol to the left and firing at Sami, who had run to Mickey's aid, hitting him in the leg and shoulder.

Maya started to shout, demanding her brother's release, but Mickey kept his focus, his eyes not leaving the spy for a second.

"Throw me your gun," the German yelled again, his pistol pressing against Erik's temple. "If we can't have him, neither can you."

"Please, Mickey, throw him your gun," Maya pleaded.

Mickey searched desperately for a solution. He knew the Nazi would kill Erik if he had to. Black smoke billowed from the ravaged hull of the plane as flames licked the fuselage. The tail of the trimotor broke off, releasing a geyser of orange and black plumes of smoke. The acrid smell of fuel filled the air. The plane would go up any second. He had no choice but to try to buy time.

"Throw it to me," the Nazi threatened.

Mickey lowered his gun and hurled it at him, but so forcefully that it flew past the German and skidded into the grass.

The spy raised his gun and aimed at him. He smiled, but before he could pull the trigger, a body came crashing down on top of him, knocking him and Erik to the ground.

"Vati!" Maya shouted.

The enraged spy hoisted the old man up by the collar and whipped him with his pistol before training his gun back on Mickey, who had started toward him.

"Father, Father," Erik moaned as he knelt over his father, who lay on the ground, breathing heavily.

Suddenly the airplane's raised wing split in two and burning metal exploded everywhere. The Nazi bent over to grab Erik, but with his last gush of energy, Viktor Blumenthal rose up and sank his teeth into the German's hand. The gun fell to the ground, and before he could retrieve it, Erik was able to sweep it out of his reach.

The spy lunged for it, but Mickey was too fast. Animated by a hatred so pure he didn't know he could harbor such a thing, Mickey flew at him. An animal now, he rolled on the ground with the fiend, biting, kicking, punching, scratching, and choking. He went for his eyes, his hair, his balls, barely feeling the blows he received in return. He finally straddled the spy and picked up a rock and smashed him in the face again and again and again, until he felt someone grab him by the shoulder.

"Stop, Mickey, stop," Maya said, sobbing. "He's already dead."

The Nazi had stopped moving, his mouth frozen open in a silent cry.

CHAPTER 47

While Erik stood solemnly over their father's burial site, Maya looked for the heaviest and prettiest stone she could find and placed it on the grave, next to the flowers she'd brought. She had no idea what the tradition of placing a stone on a grave meant, but as she bid her final good-bye, she told Vati that her love for him would be as enduringly strong as this very rock. He would forever live inside her, along with Mutter. How sad it was that Mutter and Vati, so inseparable in life, ended up being buried on different continents. One never knows what turns life can take, but one thing is certain: We are born alone and we die alone. And in between there is that thing called life, a certain reality that exists on a certain plane and seems real to our mortal eyes, but who knows what lies beyond that?

Maya turned her head and saw Mickey waiting for them in front of the taxi that would take them to the station where they would catch the train to Cairo. He waved gently to her. He'd stayed behind, wanting to give Maya and her brother some privacy. Mickey had been a rock for her. He didn't say much; he just listened and from time to time found the right words to comfort her. Gradually they'd filled in the gaps about each other's true identities. Erik had come clean as well, telling her about his work—bomb and all, though he seemed truly surprised and disturbed to learn that he had been the subject of an international manhunt. The US government was now promising them safe passage to America and would be taking care of all their needs once they arrived. It didn't matter where they went. She was just glad she would be going there with Mickey.

"I'm ready to go whenever you are," she said quietly to Erik as she slid up next to him, still limping from the gunshot wound to her thigh.

Erik stared blankly in front of him and began softly reciting a short prayer in Hebrew. There were tears on his cheeks. She was so deeply moved that she started to cry herself. He turned to her when he was finished and embraced her.

"Thank you for praying in Hebrew, Erik," she whispered. "You know how much this would have meant to him."

They stood for a long moment, rocking in one another's arms. She'd never felt this close to her brother before.

"Let's go," he finally said.

Not knowing when, if ever, she would be back, she took a long last look at the cemetery. Erik had chosen Vati's plot well; it was situated on the outskirts of the city of Suez, on a green mount with olive trees, and it had a beautiful view of the canal. With a little imagination, one could see all the way across the Sinai to the Holy Land. Like Moses. So you could say that Vati had made it to the Promised Land after all.

She took her brother's arm and they walked back to the taxi, leaning on each other for support. Mickey hurried to them and first helped Erik settle into the back of the cab before circling around and seeing that Maya was comfortably seated next to her brother. He smiled at her sweetly as he caressed her cheek and carefully closed the door for her.

"Onwards and upwards," Mickey said as he slid into the passenger seat and the cab driver took off.

She gazed out the windows, riding in silence. There were dark clouds in the sky, and it started to rain. It always surprised her that it could rain in Egypt. She wondered if it was also raining in Cairo, which was inland, far from the coast. The American Embassy had offered to put them up at the Shepheard's Hotel, but she preferred to stay with the Levis, at least for a few days. They, too, were in mourning, and she longed to be in the warmth of the family and to cry with them. She wanted to visit Léon Guibli's grave as soon as possible and pay her respects. He also lay underground now, just wrapped in a sheet like a cocoon. No caskets were used in Egypt, which had shocked her.

But what's the difference, really? Dust to dust. She just found it so hard to accept that one could disappear from the face of the earth like that. One day we're here, one day we're gone. We're truly just a fleeting memory. The thought saddened her but at the same time she was glad to be acutely aware that life had to be seized. And hers was waiting for her. She turned her head and looked at Mickey's back, catching his profile and admiring it. Just then, Mickey turned and addressed her and Erik.

"I spoke to Ambassador Kirk earlier," he said. "It won't be long for your visas to arrive. He has already started the paperwork." He winked at Maya, which gave her a warm tingle all over, like a caress traveling down her spine. Their eyes met and they smiled at each other, but she noticed Erik looking at them, making her blush and avert her eyes from Mickey.

"I hear that the new general, Montgomery, is doing a fine job rousing up the troops," Mickey said as he turned farther to face Erik.

"Let's hope this one can lead the Allies to victory," Erik said before turning his gaze to the window.

Maya was barely listening, lost in her thoughts about her father again. Who would put flowers on his grave?

"I heard that over eight hundred artillery guns were firing at the German lines early this morning," Mickey continued. "Apparently the noise was so great that the ears of the gunners bled."

His comments drew no response. Neither she nor Erik wanted to talk. She wished Mickey would stop trying to make conversation.

"Are you okay back there, Erik?" he asked after a little while. "Your neck? Not too stiff?"

"Not at all," Erik answered, before turning to Maya and smiling at her. He covered her hand with his, gazing at her tenderly. He squeezed her hand gently. The gesture carried more meaning than a thousand spoken words. She squeezed back. She loved him too.

"Want to wave hello to your friend King Farouk, Maya?" Mickey said after a long silence. "We're passing one of his palaces." He pointed with his chin toward her window. "Erik, did she ever tell you that the king fancied her?"

"Oh, please!" Maya said, wishing he'd stop.

But she knew he couldn't. He was just too excited about going back to Cairo with both the scientist and his girl. A double victory.

"The train station is around the corner," the cab driver said.

As they reached the station, they found people in the street kissing and dancing, while cars were honking their horns in celebration.

"What's going on?" Mickey asked.

The cab driver shrugged and rolled down his window. "What's going on?" he shouted in Arabic to a man standing nearby.

The man shouted back in reply and made a shrugging gesture.

"Big victory for the Allies at El Alamein," the taxi driver said, turning to Mickey.

Mickey stared at the driver for a second and then let out a gigantic whoop of joy while Erik and Maya turned toward each other, too dumbfounded to say anything.

Aswan, Port Said, Luxor, Minya, Alexandria, Cairo. Loudspeakers were blasting train arrivals and departures in Arabic, French, and

English, as Maya, Mickey, and Erik entered the station. All around them sailors were throwing their hats into the air and people were buzzing with excitement about the victory at El Alamein. Big band music started playing over the loudspeakers.

"Wait here," Mickey said, dropping their luggage. "I'm going to buy the tickets."

"Only two," Erik said. "I won't be going to Cairo with you two."

"What do you mean?" Maya asked, taken aback. She glanced at Mickey.

Erik looked at his sister with a calm smile. "I've been thinking about it long and hard," he said. "I'm going to take the train by myself to Kantara and on to Tel Aviv."

"But everything has been arranged," Mickey said, exchanging nervous looks with Maya. "Ambassador Kirk himself will be meeting you at the train station."

"I can no longer be involved in research that can be used to kill people. I'm sorry," Erik said to them. He turned to Maya. "It started back in Paris when I calculated the destructive potential of an atomic bomb based on my work."

"But the Germans might win the war if they build the bomb first," Mickey protested.

"There must be death during war," Maya added. "Twenty million people died in the last war. Nothing matters except stopping Hitler."

"We can win without it. Killing on this scale would be like nothing we have ever seen," Erik replied, "tens of thousands of people, just like that." He snapped his fingers. "And not just soldiers, everybody. Young, old, women, men, animals. Everybody. And for years the radiation from it would remain deadly."

"But Einstein shares your humanitarian views, and he's helping us," Mickey continued to argue, an edge of panic in his voice. "And not only him, but your mentor, Niels Bohr, and many of your colleagues are joining the cause. I understand what you're saying, but please come to Cairo and speak to our people first. They'll explain the whole program to you much better than I can. Besides, even if we create such a bomb, we might never have to use it. It will be deterrent enough to stop Hitler. You must come to Cairo."

"I am sorry," Erik said. "But at this moment I want to create, not destroy. I want to devote my life to building a nation."

"You can go to Palestine later and still do great things there," Mickey insisted, his face starting to redden. "Maya, please talk some sense into your brother."

Maya was frozen. She couldn't believe that her brother was bringing this up at the eleventh hour—just as the train was about to leave. Her head was spinning, and her heart was pounding. A tempest of thoughts assailed her.

"The decisive moment was seeing the boy killed right in front of my eyes on that farm outside of Poitier," Erik explained. He leaned forward and took Maya's hands into his own. "I know it was never your dream to go to Palestine."

"Don't be ridiculous. Who will take care of you?" Maya cried.

"Maya, I don't need you to be my nursemaid. The university people are going to take very good care of me, and in case you haven't noticed, I'm doing pretty well on my own."

"Oh, Erik, please. That's not what I meant. You are my brother. I love you."

"And I love you, which is why I don't want you to come with me," he said. His eyes were watering.

She was at a loss for words. She looked at Mickey with a lump in her throat.

"I'm going to leave you two alone," Mickey said. "I'll be waiting by the ticket booth."

"You should stay with Mickey," Erik said after Mickey was gone. "I may be infirm, but I'm not blind. I see the way you look at each other . . . I hear the love in your voices."

"Shush," Maya said, starting to tear up herself.

"Maya, this man loves you. I watched him risk his life for you. Even Vater could see that."

"Stop it," she protested. "Mickey and I will figure things out."

"No," he said firmly. "It's time to start your own life. I will be fine." He stroked her arm, reaching awkwardly toward her.

"I cannot be at peace unless I know you are well."

"You can be at peace. Nothing will make me happier than seeing you happy. Maya, it's time for you to think about yourself. You love him, don't you?"

She lowered her eyes. "But I worry about you."

"There is no need for that. I can't wait to get there and start working. I have lots of ideas. Maybe I'll meet a girl."

"A girl?" Maya asked, surprised.

"Why not? I'm not so bad looking."

She allowed herself a smile.

"Here." He handed her the violin he'd been carrying. "Take this with you. Give it to Soussou Levi. I know Vater would have liked that."

She shook her head and bit her lip, her eyes overflowing now.

"I think it best to say good-bye now," Erik said. "I can make it alone from here." He waved Mickey over to them and picked up his suitcase.

"He's going to Palestine," Maya told Mickey when he arrived. "Alone." She covered her mouth with her hand to prevent herself from sobbing.

"Take care of her. She's the dearest thing to me," Erik said, offering Mickey his hand.

"And to me," Mickey said as he reached out and embraced him.

Erik turned to Maya and took a step forward.

Maya stopped him with a raised hand. "Go," she choked, unable to contain her tears any longer. "Go!"

After a moment of hesitation, Erik started limping away.

Maya turned her head, unable to watch him go while Mickey held her tight. Her heart was sinking. Suddenly she looked back. "Erik!" she shouted at him in desperation. "When will we see each other again?"

He turned around and raised his clenched fist in the air. "Next year in Jerusalem!"

THE END

AUTHOR'S NOTE

Born into the second generation of a comfortable community of European Jews living in Heliopolis, a suburb of Cairo, I found myself abruptly expelled from Egypt at the age of three during the Suez Crisis of 1956 because of my mother's French nationality. My family took refuge in Paris, where I grew up feeling perfectly French and readily assuming that the Gauls were my ancestors. When I was seventeen my family moved to California, and I embraced the American dream: I went to college, then to law school, and got married. I was reconciled with the fact that somehow I was French, American, and Jewish, all at the same time. But shortly after my daughter was born, my Egyptian roots started gnawing at me.

Who was I? Who were my parents, and what had they been doing in Egypt? Who were the Jews of Egypt? Thus began my ten-year journey into the past. I started voraciously reading about the modern history of the country. What I learned was so compelling that I started to write what would become this novel.

During my research, I grew especially intrigued by the Egypt that existed during the early years of World War II, when Cairo was considered the Paris on the Nile. This was a pivotal moment in history, yet curiously, generally not well understood in America. Not only did the Allied victory at El Alamein help determine the ultimate outcome of the war, but

Britain's iron grip on the country exacerbated the deteriorating relations between the Arabs and the West and laid the foundation for many of the constructs of today's Middle East. I discovered a host of fascinating historical characters that I incorporated into my novel: Sir Miles Lampson and Alexander Kirk, the British and American ambassadors; William Donovan, the head of the Office of the Coordinator of Information and later director of the Office of Strategic Services; Anwar Sadat, the army officer who collaborated with the Nazis and later went on to become president of Egypt and the author of the first Arab peace agreement with Israel; King Farouk, who was overthrown in 1952 by a military coup led by Sadat and Gamal Abdel Nasser; Hassan al-Banna, the founder and leader of the Muslim Brotherhood; and Johannes Eppler and Hekmet Fahmy, the Nazi spy in Cairo and his Egyptian belly dancer collaborator, who were the inspiration for the characters of Heinrich Kesler and Madame Samina in the novel. I was so very pleased at how well all these real-life people's experiences meshed with my fictional story.

For dramatic purposes I have compressed the timing of some of the historical events in the novel: Rommels Afrika Korps actually first crossed the Egyptian border on April 14, 1941; his troops took over Tobruk on June 21, 1942, but were defeated at the Battle of El Alamein on November 11, 1942. The Egyptian army was notified by the British to hand over their weapons on November 20,1940, and then again in April 1941. Sadat was arrested for collaborating with Johannes Eppler on October 8, 1942; three days after the German spy's arrest. Churchill and Roosevelt announced the Atlantic Charter on August 14, 1941. The British ambassador gave King Farouk an ultimatum to accede to British demands or be deposed on February 4, 1942; outrage and social boycotts ensued but it wasn't until January 26, 1952, that angry mobs burned down British institutions in Cairo, including the Shepheard's Hotel.

The research for this book was extensive and I conducted many interviews and read countless books and articles. But I was most fortunate to have had access to the vast diaries of the British Ambassador in Egypt, Sir Miles Lampson, who was at the epicenter of that world. Short of divulging state secrets, he wrote about everything and everyone in Cairo with extraordinary detail. Artemis Cooper's *Cairo in the War* as well as Anwar Sadat's *Revolt on the Nile,* William Stadiem's *Too Rich, the High life and Tragic Death of King Farouk,* and Gudrun Kramer's *The Jews in Modern Egypt,* 1914-1952 also proved to be invaluable.

Most gratifying on a personal level, my research shed light on Egypt's Jews and put into context the stories my parents had told me of their lives there. I was surprised to learn of the deep amity that had existed between the Jews and the Arabs, and that it dissolved largely for political reasons related to the creation of the state of Israel. While my quest to learn about the Jews of Egypt impelled me to write this novel, they did not emerge as the central subject. Nevertheless it is important to me that the world knows that this community of wanderers, rich in traditions, who combined the savoir faire of the Europeans with the soul and warmth of the Arabs, once existed and flourished in an Arab land. Of the 80,000 Jews that lived in Egypt in 1941, only about forty remain today.

Juliana Maio
Los Angeles,
California
2014

ACKNOWLEDGMENTS

If it takes a village to raise a child, it took an army of incredibly supportive and generous people to give birth to this novel, and I will be forever indebted to them for the gift of their time, support, trust, and knowledge. Sadly, a number of them have passed, but their light shines brightly in these pages. They are John Waller, one of the first OSS operatives recruited by William Donovan and sent to Egypt after America entered the war; psychologist Victor Sanua, who devoted his later years to retrieving the heritage of the Egyptian Jewish community; novelist Michael Crichton, who encouraged me in the meticulous research that it took to write this book; my father-in-law, Lawrence Phillips, a war hero who liberated the first concentration camp in Germany and advised me on military matters; my mother, Sheila Maio, the strongest and most giving woman I've ever known, who shared with me her tales of growing up in Egypt. This book is in their memory and in the memory of my father, Fernando Maio, whose joie de vivre surely emanated from the life he lived in Cairo.

I started this book with only one key phrase in mind—*The Jews of Egypt*—and I cannot express my gratitude enough to Hugh Miles, who was with me at the beginning of this journey and helped shape this unwieldy epic before he went on to become an award-winning journalist and author. I'm also very grateful to historian Afaf Lutfi al-Sayyid-Marsot, professor emeritus of history at UCLA, for her suggestions as to the story's framework within Egypt's political theater.

Many authors can boast a guardian angel behind their work, but I was blessed with three: my magical and amazing editors, Jane Cavolina and Maggie Crawford, and Phoebe Larmore, who lent me her keen ear for story development. I owe so much to each of these women for their friendship, dedication, nurturing, and respect, and most of all for their tenacious belief in this book.

I also would like to thank Agatha Dominik, for reading draft after draft and standing by me through the whole process; Nicholas Meyer, for his generous advice and support; Jamie deBlanc, for gently coaching me in the art of writing prose; Gunther Schiff, my mentor, for sharing with me his traumatic experience of growing up as a Jew in prewar Germany; my mother-in-law, Sherry Phillips, for loving every single sentence I've ever written; my sister, Joyce Maio, for providing invaluable introductions for my research and joining me on an unforgettable trip back to Egypt; my brother, Léo Maio, for his undiluted love, depth, and intellect. Also, I'd like to thank Lucinda Karter, Amy Williams, and Elaine Markson for loving the book and for all their efforts on my behalf.

And to my two greatest loves—my daughter, Natasha, and my husband, Michael—a special thanks for their infinite patience and love. Their gift of love was so large that rather than letting me take this journey alone, they both plunged in with me, with my daughter taking special interest in all things Arabic, and my husband completely immersing himself in the pages of this book as I wrote them and giving me notes every night with his dreaded red pencil. He's been my rock, my lighthouse, and my knight in shining armor. Thank you both for sharing the nostalgia of once upon a time in Cairo . . .

ABOUT THE AUTHOR

Juliana Maio was born in Egypt but expelled from the country with her family during the Suez Crisis. She was raised in France and completed her higher education in the United States, receiving a BA from the University of California, Berkeley, and her Juris Doctor degree from UC Hastings.

Juliana practices entertainment law in Los Angeles and has represented internationally renowned filmmakers. Prior to practicing law she served as vice president of worldwide corporate and business affairs for Triumph Films, a joint venture between Columbia Pictures and Gaumont Films.

Juliana is the cofounder of Lighthouse Productions, an independent film and television company. She speaks both domestically and abroad about the Arab Spring. She lives with her husband and daughter in Los Angeles.